A YEAR FROM NOW

RAY HOBBS

Wingspan Press

Published in the United States and the United Kingdom
by WingSpan Press, Livermore, CA

The WingSpan name, logo and colophon are the trademarks of WingSpan Publishing.

ISBN 978-1-59594-615-7 (pbk.)
ISBN 978-1-59594-932-5 (ebk.)

First edition 2017

Printed in the United States of America

www.wingspanpress.com

Library of Congress Control Number 2017954707

1 2 3 4 5 6 7 8 9 10

This book is dedicated to the generation that answered the call.

SOURCES AND ACKNOWLEDGEMENTS

Scott, P., *The Battle of the Narrow Seas* (London, Country Life, 1945)
Dickens, P., *Night Action* (London, Peter Davies, 1974)
North, A. J. D., *Royal Naval Coastal Forces 1939-1945* (London, Almark, 1972)
Armstrong, W., *HM Small Ships*, (London, Frederick Muller, 1958)
Fearnley-Whittingstall, J., *The Ministry of Food* (London, Hodder, 2010)
Escott, B. E., *The WAAF* (Oxford, Shire Publications, 2011)
Escott, B. E., *Our Wartime Days* (Stroud, Sutton Publishing, 1995)
Rowe, A. & Andrews, A., *Air-Sea Rescue in World War Two* (Stroud, Sutton, 1995)
Beevor, A., *D-Day* (London, Penguin, 2010)
Fry, Helen., *The M Room* (CreateSpace, 2012)
MacDonald, J., *Our Mornings May Never Be* (Burnstown, General Store Pub, 2002)
Beck. P., *Keeping Watch* (Manchester, Goodall, 1989)
Hewitt. N., *Coastal Convoys 1939-1945* (Barnsley, Pen & Sword Maritime, 2008)
Pitchfork, G., *Shot Down and in the Drink* (London, The National Archives, 2005)
Baker, E., *A City in Flames* (Beverley, Hutton Press, 1992)
Holliday, J., *It's a Bit Lively Outside* (Castleford, Yorkshire Art Circus, 1987)
MacDonald-Ross, P., & Roberts, I. D., *Bandaging the Blitz* (London, Sphere, 2015)
BBC, *WW2 People's War,* recollections published on the internet (2003-6), now archived.

* * *

Like the central character of this story, my late mother was occasionally called upon to exercise her midwifery skills when expectant mothers were overtaken by events, and I am indebted to her for the technical detail regarding childbirth under emergency conditions.

I wish to thank my wife Sheila for her patience when she saw little of me during the writing of this book, particularly in the research and early draft stages. She was still available, however, to answer questions on matters that baffle the humble male, and took a lively interest in character development.

Finally I should like to thank my brother Chris, who has continued to act both as soundboard and as a ready source of ideas from planning to final draft as well as helping to fuel my enthusiasm throughout.

RH

Rear cover: image of Hull Docks after an air raid during the Blitz: Imperial War Museum HU_036199

GLOSSARY FOR READERS OUTSIDE THE UK

Note: ⁿ denotes naval terminology or slang

C of E:	Church of England
NHS:	National Health Service
Blitz:	the concentrated bombing of Britain in 1940-41
(Neville) Chamberlain:	British Prime Minister in 1939
Chara (*char-à-banc*):	archaic name for a motor coach
RAF:	Royal Air Force
Sprogⁿ:	baby or youngster
Alcock and Brown:	first transatlantic aviators (1919)
Penny Farthing:	early bicycle with a large front and small rear wheel
Starboardⁿ:	right
Portⁿ:	left
Op(eration):	mission
Lorry:	truck
NCO:	non-commissioned officer
(auto) Cannon:	small-calibre automatic weapon firing explosive shells
Spud:	potato
Deckheadⁿ:	ceiling
Marrer:	pal, buddy (north-east English dialect)
WVS:	Women's Voluntary Service
WRNS:	Women's Royal Naval Service
Jam:	jelly
Blighty:	home, the UK
St John Ambulance:	voluntary first-aid organisation
Suspender (lingerie):	garter
Lobby Lud:	character in newspaper competition
Gaffer:	boss (in any workplace)
Knocking shop:	house of ill-repute
Wardroomⁿ:	naval officers' mess

Cox'n, coxswain[n]:	in coastal forces, the most senior rating and helmsman
Jimmy, Jimmy-the-One, Number One[n]:	first-lieutenant, executive officer in a small ship
Flak:	anti-aircraft fire
Chip:	fried potato
Biscuit:	cookie
ATS:	Auxiliary Territorial Service, women's army
Wren:	member of the WRNS
Bowler (hat):	derby
Petrol:	gasoline
Rugby:	English forerunner of American football
Braces (men's accessory):	suspenders
AFS:	Auxiliary Fire Service
Batwoman/man:	officers' valet
Char (Hindi):	tea
Jimmy riddle:	bathroom break (cockney rhyming slang – piddle)
Civvies:	civilian clothing
Jolly Jack or simply 'Jack'[n]:	any British sailor
Doodlebug:	V1 flying bomb

1

AN EAST RIDING TOWN

2015

He was young, at least in Kate's eyes. She thought he must be about forty, and he was dressed soberly in a grey lightweight suit and pale-blue shirt that made his clerical collar less obvious than it might have been. He stopped in the doorway to consult a sheet of paper and then peered through rimless glasses at the note on the door. His greeting was almost apologetic.

'Good afternoon.'

'Good afternoon,' said Kate. 'Can I help you?'

'Oh yes, I think so.' He looked relieved, like someone who has finally found a recognisable landmark. 'I'm one of the hospital chaplains. I see you're C of E.'

'Lapsed these many years,' she admitted, 'but you're still welcome to drop in for a chat. You'll just have to forgive me if I don't leap up and put the kettle on for tea.'

'Of course. Is it all right if I call you Katherine?'

'Feel free, but most people call me "Kate".'

'Right. I'm James.'

'I'm glad to meet you, James. Come in and take a seat.'

'Thank you.' He made a note on his sheet of paper before sitting beside her bed. 'Would you mind telling me about your accident, Kate?'

'There's not a lot I can tell you, it happened so quickly.' The poor man was making an effort to be friendly so she decided to oblige him as far as she could. 'I'm told it was the kind of accident elderly people have quite often, although I'm not thinking of having them too often, if you see what I mean.'

'Quite.'

'I was at a funeral.' She searched her memory but without success. 'You know, it's the most awful thing but I can't remember whose funeral it was. The bang on the head can't have helped, I suppose, but in any case I go to so many nowadays.' Almost to herself she added, 'And the deceased are nearly all younger than me.'

'Don't worry. I'm sure it'll come back to you.'

'I suppose so. Anyway, as far as I can remember it was just after the funeral. We were being ushered out and I was chatting with a friend when I realised that someone wanted to pass, so I took a step backward to let her through, quite forgetting the flight of steps behind me.' She shrugged and then winced at the pain the small effort caused her despite the pain-killers. 'The funeral director had a glint in his eye, you know. I think he scented new business.'

'Surely not.'

'No.' She smiled at his shocked expression. It was the first fun she'd had since the accident. 'At least, I don't think so. To be honest, I don't remember all that much about it, only the pain after the shock wore off, and being told that my pelvis was fractured. It's a simple fracture, the least troublesome kind, but it's no less painful for that.'

'It must be quite awful.'

'Don't worry, it won't last for ever.'

'Let's hope not.' Still looking concerned but changing the subject, he asked, 'Have you any family, Kate?'

'Lots. I'm a great-grandmother and if I can hang around a little longer there's a chance I could soon add another "great" to the title.'

'How marvellous.' He consulted his notes.

'I'm ninety-five,' she told him to save him the effort. 'At least, that's what my family keep telling me. It's easy to lose track of your age as you grow older.' Smiling wistfully, she added, 'It's easy to lose track of most things.'

He shook his head in wonder. 'I'd never have guessed you were as old as that.'

'You're very kind.' She wondered if he was one of the full-time chaplains she'd heard about. So many things had changed in the NHS.... She realised her thoughts had wandered, and then he spoke again.

'I was going to ask if you'd like a visitor, a volunteer.'

'Well, thank you for the offer, but my granddaughter and her husband are coming this evening; at least, I believe they are. I imagine the whole tribe will descend at various stages, and there must be patients who have no visitors at all. I'm sure they'd appreciate some company.'

James nodded, but without obvious agreement. 'Kate,' he said, 'I'll be honest with you. I'm asking you to do this as a favour. You see, we have a volunteer who really needs the experience, and I think chatting with you might help her.'

'Do you really? In that case I'll do what I can, although I must say I'm surprised. I wouldn't have thought hospital visiting called for much in the way of training.'

'Hm.' He nodded again unsurely; it seemed to be a habit. 'The thing is, this lady, Rachel, is doing it as a form of therapy. She has to get out and meet people, and this is one way of doing it.' He smiled apologetically. 'I'm afraid I can't tell you any more than that. You do understand, don't you?'

'Yes, and don't worry. I enjoy a mystery.'

He got up from his chair and said, 'Thank you. I must go now. We're having a special service to commemorate VE Day.' He added, 'The celebration of Victory in Europe, you know.'

His explanation made her smile. 'Yes, I remember it well, and you're quite right to commemorate it.'

'Quite, but I'll be here in the morning to celebrate Holy Communion. Would you like to be included?'

Kate hesitated only minutely before saying, 'You know, I think I should. It's high time I made my peace with the Almighty, especially as my next backward flip could be my last.'

'You don't need an excuse, Kate.'

'No, you're right. I'll see you in the morning.'

'I'll look forward to it.' He seemed about to go and then remembered something. 'May I tell Rachel you'd like to see her tomorrow afternoon?'

'Please do, and then she can keep me awake. I've an awful habit of nodding off after lunch. Most unsociable.'

'Very well. Goodbye, Kate.'

She dozed for a little while until a nurse came to check her temperature and pulse. Her badge identified her as Nurse Leanne Shawcott.

'The equipment must make the job easier nowadays,' observed Kate, looking at the thermometer.

'It's certainly more efficient than the prehistoric gadgets that were around at one time,' said the nurse, scanning the notes and asking the usual questions. With that out of the way, her eye fell on Kate's copy of *The Times*, which lay open at the Register page. 'What have you been reading?'

'Someone I once met has died. I was reading his obituary.'

'Oh, that's sad.' She picked it up to glance at it briefly and asked, 'Do you read this kind of thing all the time?'

'Not this page. I haven't known all that many famous people, but this man was a fireman during the war. He was decorated for bravery during the Hull Blitz.'

'Oh.' It seemed that the Hull Blitz meant nothing to Nurse Shawcott. 'It's a bit sad, though, reading people's obituaries, isn't it?'

'It must seem so but I find myself doing it more and more as my contemporaries fall by the wayside. It's like being a member of a club that's no longer fashionable.'

Nurse Shawcott glanced at the top of the page. '*The Times*,' she observed. 'Heavy going, isn't it? Couldn't they find you something more user-friendly?'

'Well, I do find some of the concepts challenging, but at least the sentence construction is less complex than it was.' She smiled disarmingly.

'You're making fun of me, Kate.'

'What do you expect? I may be an old ruin but I'm not a half-wit.' Looking at the thermometer again, she asked, 'What was my temperature?'

'It was normal.'

'What's normal? It was ninety-eight-point-four in my day, but I imagine you work in Celsius now.'

'Yes, it was thirty-seven degrees. What do you mean, *your* day?'

'I was doing your job more than seventy years ago. I was a midwife when I gave up nursing to start a family.'

'Of course. I remember now. Mind you, there's a lot more to nursing nowadays. It's much more technical than it used to be.'

'Isn't everything?' It seemed so to Kate and, as she reflected further, she realised that she needed to relieve herself. It was a comforting thought that the equipment provided for that function was no more technical than it had been before the war.

⊛⊷⫸⫷⊷⊛

After a night of little sleep and a morning punctuated by the usual hospital noises and distractions it was a relief when her visitor arrived.

Rachel looked very much as Kate had expected a hospital visitor to look. She knew she shouldn't deal in stereotypes but she'd never really got the hang of political correctness.

'Hello, I'm Rachel.' The visitor paused, possibly wondering if Kate had remembered the arrangement. 'The Reverend Popplewell said you'd like a visit. Do you mind if I call you by your first name?'

'Please do, and it's "Kate", by the way, not "Katherine". Do take a seat,' she said, trying to hide her amusement. It was delightful that the chaplain was called Popplewell. 'Reverend Popplewell' sounded like a character in a children's story.

'Thank you.' Rachel perched, rather than sat, on the edge of her chair. Her presence so far, like her appearance, was apologetic. Her light-brown hair was tidily cut and brushed, although her ends were split, and no attempt had been made at styling. She wore no make-up and her plain blouse and trousers looked very much like social camouflage. Kate thought she must be about forty.

'Are you all right? I mean, you had a nasty accident, didn't you?'

'Yes, thank you. It wasn't very nice but I'm in safe hands now.'

Kate allowed herself a sly smile. 'I'm told they have the latest technology.'

'Oh yes, they do.' There was an awkward pause and then Rachel asked, 'Is there anything you'd like me to bring in for you?' Her right cheek twitched as she spoke.

'No, thank you. I've got everything I need.'

'Good.' It was clear from her features that she was working hard at making conversation. They were rather nice features too, and her complexion was very clear, a quality that possibly owed something to the absence of make-up, if that really was her habit.... She was rambling again. She forced herself to concentrate. The poor girl needed help with her awkwardness. She must concentrate on that. She asked, 'What do you do when you're not visiting the sick, Rachel?'

The question evidently surprised her. 'I... I'm an accounting technician. I do people's accounts, tradesmen and so on.' Again, her cheek twitched. 'I'm not supposed to talk about myself,' she said.

'But if I ask you to, that's all right, isn't it?'

'I suppose so.'

'You'll probably find me asking you the same questions again and again. My memory's not what it was. I can recall my early life in embarrassing detail but recent matters are another thing entirely.'

'It's only natural.'

'At my age, yes, but you're young. Have you always been a book-keeper?' The title 'accounting technician' brought to mind a picture of a clerk with a screwdriver.

'Yes, I used to work in an office but I had to leave that job seventeen years ago to look after my invalid mother.'

'I'm sorry. Is she still with you?'

'No, she died earlier this year.'

'You poor girl, and I imagine you're finding life difficult to cope with now?'

'Yes.' It was almost a whisper. 'Do you mind if we talk about something else.' Her nervous twitch had returned but she managed to find a new subject. 'As I came on the ward,' she said, 'I noticed some of the patients watching the VE Day celebrations on television.'

'Yes, it's a big one this year, isn't it? They did say how many years but I forget.'

'It's the seventieth anniversary.'

'Good grief, so it is. I know everyone says it, but it really doesn't seem all that long ago.'

'You remember it, then?'

'Oh yes, the war's quite difficult to forget when you're my age.'

'The media are calling you "The Greatest Generation".' The twitch had receded and Rachel's eyes were bright with interest.

Kate laughed good-naturedly. 'I don't know that we were all that great. We just happened to be there and we got on with our lives and our jobs because we had to.' It seemed odd to be talking about the war with a young woman trying to make sense of present-day life, but if that was what she wanted to talk about Kate was happy to oblige her. It was an easy distraction. 'There was a lovely song that was very popular that summer,' she said. 'It was called "South of the Border" and Al Bowlly sang it. I don't suppose his name will mean anything to you. He was killed in the Blitz, you know.'

'No, I'm afraid I've never heard of him. Was he really famous?'

'He was one of the great crooners of the age. It was such a tragedy.' She thought for a moment. 'I'm sorry. I was telling you something, wasn't I?'

'Yes, you were telling me about the outbreak of war.'

'Oh yes, that's right. I was at work when Chamberlain made his famous broadcast, so I didn't have the experience that day that everyone talks about. My earliest recollection of the war came about a week later at an extraordinary general meeting of Cullington Cycling Club.' She broke off to explain, 'I'm originally from the West Riding, you see. The circumstances that brought me here were largely beyond my control, not that I would have changed things even if I'd been able.'

'What did the meeting have to do with the war?'

'Ah well, someone had put down a motion to suspend the activities of the club for the duration of hostilities. It was a ridiculous motion and it was defeated by a huge majority. You should have heard some of the older end. I remember one of them saying that they'd never let the Kaiser dictate club policy and they certainly weren't going to accord that privilege to a figure of fun with a silly moustache. There was a lot of defiance at the time.' She stopped to recall the events of that evening in the function room of the Bay Horse Inn. She could almost smell the cigarette smoke and hear the raised voices. 'The meeting was a complete nonsense,' she said, 'but a few of us younger members got together afterwards in the lounge bar. There were three boys, another girl and me. As I recall, I was one of the youngest at eighteen – no, I tell a lie, I was nineteen, but still quite naïve. Some of us knew each other from school but we were all friends, despite the occasional disagreement.' She paused for a moment in recollection. Some memories were still quite painful. Eventually she said soberly, 'It was the last time all five of us met as a group.'

2

CULLINGTON

1939

Kate saw Jack Farthing at the bar and his smile told her he remembered her.

'Jack,' she said, 'I haven't seen you for ages. Where have you been?'

'Hello Kate. I'm just getting the drinks in. What'll you have?'

'Just a glass of lemonade, please.' She added self-consciously, 'I'm not a big drinker.'

'And to think I had you down as a regular gin-soak.'

'No, you didn't, and you haven't answered my question.'

'Give me a chance.' He added Kate's lemonade to his order. 'I've been at the Hull office for the past two years. I felt like the Prodigal Son when I arrived here.' He laughed shortly. 'That was until the meeting began and then I felt more like Alice in Wonderland.'

'Your hair's not quite as long as hers.'

'I know I'm due for a haircut,' he admitted, sweeping back a dark-brown lock from his forehead, 'but it's not as long as all that.'

'Not quite.' She dismissed the subject and asked, 'What have you been doing in Hull? I thought you worked for Farrar's Tours.'

'I still do.' He handed a ten-shilling note to the barmaid. 'I've had a sort of promotion since we last met.'

'Sort of?'

'Yes, I'm still a booking clerk but I'm sometimes allowed to go on guided tours. It's part of my training.'

'Oh, where have you been?' She added apologetically, 'People must ask you that all the time.'

He took his change from the barmaid. 'If you don't mind taking your drink and Dorothy's I'll bring Alan's and mine, and you're right about people asking me that. I've only been to Germany and France so far. Oh, and I went to Belgium once.'

'It sounds exciting to me.'

He handed her two glasses. 'What are you doing nowadays?'

'Nursing. I'm at Bradford Royal Infirmary.'

'Do you enjoy it?'

She wrinkled her nose. 'On the whole, yes. They always give the dirtiest duties to the most junior nurses but now I'm a second year it's much better. It's what I want to do, anyway.'

'I'm glad. Let's go and join the others.' He led the way to a corner table, where Dorothy and Alan were waiting.

'And about time too,' said Alan. 'We were wondering if you'd gone home.'

'Alan was wondering,' said Dorothy. 'I never said a word. Thank you, Kate.'

'So,' said Alan, 'you're still at "Farrar's Charas" then, Jack? Have you got your bus drivers' licence yet?'

'It's framed and on my bedroom wall along with my swimming certificates. Are you still punting on the Isis and carousing in the cloisters, or whatever you students get up to?'

'I came down three months ago, and I was at Cambridge, not Oxford.'

'It's an easy mistake to make.'

'As a matter of fact I got a double-first in classics and ancient history.'

'Oh, *bene factum*.' Jack delivered his felicitation with mock ceremony.

'What will you do,' asked Kate, 'with a degree in classics and ancient history?'

'When you're not boasting about it,' added Dorothy.

'Employers will always be on the lookout for someone with an enquiring and analytical mind,' he assured them. 'I should be all right when this war's over, and I can't see it lasting all that long.'

'Well,' said Dorothy, 'I can't ever recall our firm advertising for an expert on the Roman Empire.'

Alan looked peeved, and Kate watched him discreetly, feeling almost sorry for him. She sometimes thought of him and Dorothy as a matching pair. They might almost have been related, they were physically so similar, both tall and slim with dark, good looks. Unfortunately for Alan, however, the match was purely one of appearance, because Dorothy had never shown any sign of reciprocal attraction.

'I'm not so sure, Dorothy,' said Jack, as if he'd given the matter some thought. 'Alan may have a point.'

'Do you really think so?' Dorothy could usually match Jack for dryness.

'Yes, I do. Only last year my firm was looking into the winter holiday market, and I remember there were those who had serious doubts about the logistics involved, but the managing director put them straight. He said that if Hannibal could cross the Alps with a herd of elephants he was sure a Crossley motor coach was equal to the task.'

'Oh hang it all. You people never take anything seriously.' Alan stood up. 'I'm going to get some cigarettes.'

As Dorothy watched him go she said, 'I'm afraid Alan's in for a life of disappointment.'

Kate asked, 'Why do you say that?'

'Because no one will ever take him as seriously as he takes himself.'

'I suppose not.' She wasn't really interested. It all seemed unimportant, and she'd been wondering about something entirely different. 'Jack,' she asked, 'what's Germany like?'

'I should think Alan could tell you more than I can. He's spent much more time over there. I've only done a few trips.'

'But you must have formed an impression.' She preferred to hear it from Jack anyway.

'I certainly have. There are some beautiful places in the Rhine valley. There are castles, vineyards and forests. It's like something from a book of fairy tales. It's just a shame about the regime, as our people have only just realised. Believe it or not, there were signs everywhere in the towns, saying, *"Jüden Verboten"* and doors and windows were daubed with the Star of David just to let everybody know there were Jews living there.'

'How hateful,' said Dorothy, 'I mean literally. Suddenly I'm very conscious of my Jewish ancestry.'

'I didn't know you were Jewish,' said Kate.

'I'm only a quarter Jewish. It was my grandmother on my mother's side, a lovely old girl.'

Kate wondered if Dorothy got her lovely features from her grandmother. It was possible, and she was pondering that when a familiar and welcome figure entered the room.

'Hello, Maurice,' she said.

'Hello folks.' The newcomer wore the uniform of the Air Defence Cadet Corps. His fair hair was cut very short and he carried his side-cap in his hand. ' He clapped one hand on Jack's shoulder as a greeting. 'Hello again, Jack. How did the vote go tonight? I had a test so I couldn't come.'

'Hello Maurice.' Jack stood up to shake his hand. 'It's good to see you again. The motion was defeated, by the way. I couldn't believe it had been put forward in the first place.'

'Yes,' said Dorothy, 'reason prevailed, but the result was never in doubt, so we didn't need your vote. Alan's at the bar. If you catch him he'll buy you a drink.'

'Okay.' Maurice set off to find him.

Kate watched him go and said, 'He's really keen on the cadets.'

'He is, but he's struggling with navigation,' said Dorothy, 'and it's a source of potential embarrassment, so it might be a good idea to leave it out of the conversation when Alan's around.'

'If it's to do with maths,' said Kate, 'Maurice has my sympathy.'

'He's keen, though. That must help.'

'Let's hope so, Jack.' Dorothy glanced in the direction of the bar. 'Here they come.'

Alan resumed his seat, and Maurice took a stool from a neighbouring table.

'Some of the lads in the cadets have got their call-up papers,' he

12

told them. 'I should get mine soon. It's been more than a week now since war was declared.'

'Don't be in such a hurry,' Kate told him. 'Nothing's happened yet.'

'It's bound to start happening soon.'

Alan had been eyeing Maurice's uniform. 'I suppose I should have joined the Volunteer Reserve when I was at Cambridge, to make sure of getting into the Air Force,' he said. 'I'd have been sure of a commission as well, but when I failed the aircrew eyesight test I decided to concentrate on my studies. I chose the RAF as my first preference, though, so they must take that into account.' He looked across at Jack. 'Have you any idea what you're going to do, Jack?'

'The Navy.'

'Don't bank on it. They say it's the hardest to get into.'

'Not for me. I joined the RNVR two years ago when I first moved to Hull.'

'Two years ago?' Alan was evidently impressed.

'Yes, and I'm now trained in boat-handling, bends, hitches, ropes and cordage, and the operation and maintenance of the Mark Five Lewis Gun, among other things.' He added with mock pride, 'The Lewis is my speciality.'

'How special can a machine-gun from the last war be?'

'More useful in wartime, I'd say, than a degree in classics and ancient history.'

'Oh, very funny, I must say.'

Smiling involuntarily at the exchange, Kate asked, 'What's the RNVR?'

'The Royal Naval Volunteer Reserve,' Jack told her. 'It's known as "The Wavy Navy" because officers have wavy rings on their sleeves to tell them apart from regular officers.'

'Will you be an officer, do you think?'

'I shouldn't think so for a moment, Kate.'

'When I get into the RAF,' said Alan, 'it's the first thing I'll look into.'

No one seemed surprised, and even Dorothy made no comment, being preoccupied with her own plans.

'I haven't decided yet what I want to do,' she said. 'I feel I should do something if this war looks like lasting for some time, but for all we know there may be a peace agreement before long.'

'I can't see them settling it now,' said Jack. 'It's taken a long time, but even that naïve fool Chamberlain must have realised that Hitler's not to be trusted.'

'No, Jack, you're wrong,' said Alan confidently. 'Mark my words, a year from now it will all have blown over and we'll be sitting in this pub without a care in the world.'

3

'Dorothy was a beautiful girl.' Kate hadn't thought about her for a long time, but now, in her hospital bed, she had time to remember the friends of her youth. 'I was in awe of her at one time.'

'I imagine you were pretty in those days as well,' said Rachel.

'I'd never have called myself that, but what woman would?'

'It would be interesting to see a photo of you then.'

'Well, if you want to come again I'll ask my daughter to bring some in for you to look at.'

'Thanks, I'd really like that.' The familiar twitch had returned to her cheek, and she said, 'You know, this is the first real conversation I've had with anyone for... I can't remember how long.'

Kate reached out and took her hand. 'Would you like to tell me about it?'

'Not just yet. I will, but not yet.'

'All right, I shan't pry.'

Apparently keen to return to the original subject, Rachel asked, 'What was Dorothy really like, I mean as a person.'

'Oh, I liked her, and she was a good friend. She was always popular with the boys, as you'd imagine, but she was very careful with them.'

'What do you mean?'

'I think the best way I can put it is that she was wary of the way they thought of her. It irritated her that they seemed to see her as, well, nowadays we'd say a "sex object", but the term hadn't been coined then. You see, she was a bright and ambitious girl and she wanted more out of life than to be wanted for her looks. Unfortunately, society still had a long way to go.'

'It's difficult to imagine, just thinking about the way things are now. I mean society's far from perfect, but attitudes towards women must have been very primitive in those days.'

'They were.' Kate hadn't given it much thought recently but what Rachel had said was certainly true. 'Mind you, we'd never known anything else.'

Rachel nodded. 'Tell me about the others,' she asked. 'That's if you're not too tired.'

Kate patted her hand. 'I'll let you know when I'm tired.' Her thoughts returned to her friends. 'I'll tell you about Maurice,' she said. 'Dorothy had a soft spot for him in those days, partly because Alan used to tease him quite unfairly, and because he was such a lovely, genuine boy, full of enthusiasm and good humour.'

'So Alan was unkind to him?'

'Yes. You see, Maurice went to the council school and left at fourteen to work in the pickling factory, and Alan could be superior at the best of times. I used to stick up for Maurice, and Jack did when he was there, but it was usually Dorothy who delivered Alan's come-uppance. He was vulnerable where she was concerned.'

'Was he sweet on her?'

' "Sweet"? That's a lovely, old-fashioned word.'

'I've kept old-fashioned company for a good few years.'

'I was forgetting. Yes, he was keen on her, so when she gave him a verbal slap on the wrist it really hurt. But he asked for it.'

'Was he really so awful?'

'He could be awful sometimes, at least until he grew out of it, but I'll tell you more about him later. Let's stay with Maurice for now.'

'Yes, he sounds lovely.'

'He was. You know, Dorothy once told me there's the kind of man you're happy to have as a friend, the kind you might want as a husband or possibly a lover, and the kind you want to protect. That was Maurice. He was only a year younger than Dorothy but she still looked out for him. I did as well, but my interest in him was of a different kind.' She let her memory dwell on him a while longer. Eventually she said, 'He was desperate to get into the RAF. A great many young men were. It was still quite new, you see, and seen by many as glorious and exciting. They were known as the "glamour boys" because they were the media's darlings, but they soon discovered that war was anything but glamorous.' As she said that she was conscious of Rachel's hand beside hers on the bed. 'Rachel,' she asked, 'tell me something.'

'What?'

'I said I wouldn't pry, but after caring for your mother for so many years, why do you want to sit at another old woman's bedside?'

Rachel was silent for a moment, and then she said, 'It's not the same, not the same thing at all. I will tell you, but give me time.'

'All right.'

Returning to the war, Rachel asked, 'Did you experience any bombing?'

'Not at first. Apart from some sporadic raids and one particularly awful night there was hardly any to speak of in the area where we lived, and that was surprising when you consider we had the biggest aircraft factory in Europe, as well as steelworks and chemical factories.'

The door of the side ward opened and a nurse entered the room. When she came closer, Kate could see from her name badge that she was Nurse Loretta Stevenson, and her accent and appearance were unmistakably Caribbean.

'I hope your friend ain't wearin' you out, Kate,' she said.

'No, she's very welcome.'

'That's good. She's ninety-five, you know,' she told Rachel.

'I know.'

'How do you do it, Kate?'

It wasn't the first time Kate had been asked that question and she gave her usual answer. 'Exercise, red wine, gin with just a hint of tonic, sea air....' She lowered her voice. 'And things I wouldn't dream of telling you about.'

The nurse grinned and her eyes grew wide. 'Well, they seem to have done the trick,' she said. Still smiling, she left the room and closed the door.

'Nurses didn't have first names in the old days,' said Kate. 'We even addressed one another by surname. It was a tradition that felt strange at first but we soon got used to it.'

'It sounds very strange to me,' said Rachel.

'We didn't wear trousers either, although I suppose they're more practical than a dress. Much more practical, in fact, but most unflattering with those short tunics, especially for anyone with a big....' She closed her eyes in exasperation. 'I'm sorry. What were we talking about?'

'About the war. Were the boys called up straight away?'

'Yes, Jack was first, then Maurice and Alan.'

4

J ack's introduction to full-time service was an eight-week-long course at *HMS Excellent*, the Royal Navy's gunnery school on Whale Island in Portsmouth Harbour. He was familiar with the Navy's practice of naming shore establishments, or 'stone frigates', as if they were ships, and he'd been to a few, but *Excellent* was different from any he had known. Training was intensive, discipline was harsh and inflexible and ratings went everywhere at the rush, but Jack survived the course and emerged fully-trained in the operation of small-calibre anti-aircraft guns, which included his 'speciality', the Mark Five Lewis machine-gun.

His first draft was to *HMS Wrathful*, a destroyer recently taken from the reserve fleet and returned to service. Her meagre anti-aircraft armament had been augmented by two twin-mounted cannon of the kind known familiarly as 'pom-poms', and twin Lewis guns mounted on each wing of the bridge. The ship, like the Lewis gun, was a veteran of the previous war but that made her no less venerable in Jack's eyes. He felt respect mingled with affection for his first ship, with her rakish lines, her battle honours and her magnificent crest: a snarling beast mounted above the motto, *CAVETE FURORE MEO*, which Jack translated proudly as 'Beware my Wrath.'

The ship was in Portsmouth harbour prior to her working-up exercises, and Jack and several others were cleaning the messdeck when the Bosun's Mate peered down the hatch with an unusual enquiry.

'Are any of you lot keen on art?'

Three hands went up, including Jack's, although he wondered what art had to do with modern naval warfare.

'Right, you three, follow me.' The 'Buffer' led them to the paint store, where he equipped them with brushes, paint kettles and tins of grey paint. 'Your first masterpiece,' he told them, 'will be the funnels. You're to paint out the old flotilla-leader's marking and make 'em both as good as new.' He looked from one to another, taking in the baffled stares. 'The old one's from a long way back,' he explained, 'but *Wrathful* is going to war again and you sprogs are going to be heroes.'

One of the hands seemed resentful at having fallen for the Buffer's subterfuge, but Jack was inclined to be philosophical. Cleaning, painting, scraping and polishing were all part of a seaman's lot, and painting was marginally preferable to cleaning ship. It wasn't a bad life at all and as he opened a tin of paint and began stirring he found himself wondering how the others from the cycling club were faring.

⊛⊷⋵⊱⋇⊰⋵⊶⊛

In spite of his stated preference for the RAF, Alan was ordered to report to Deepcut Army Camp in Hampshire for basic training, which brought with it a series of shocks and surprises. He learned in his first week that no one would be considered for officer training before they had completed basic training. He also learned that his best boots, on which he'd lavished much wax polish, water and hours of effort, were a disgrace, and when he appeared on parade with one top pocket unbuttoned, the sergeant asked him at stentorian volume if he were breast-feeding. His most trying problem, however, was his relationship with others of his platoon. It seemed that trouble was never far away.

On one occasion he sat on his bed to dab ointment on his blistered feet. 'No one should be treated like this,' he said to anyone who might be listening. 'It's too demeaning for words.'

The man on his right regarded him with his habitual scowl and asked, 'What's that mean, then?'

'What does what mean?'

'What you just said.'

'It means that they're treating us like animals rather than human beings.'

The man, whose name was Moss, scowled more deeply and said, 'Why don't you say so, then, 'stead of usin' words none of us 'as ever 'eard of?'

Alan shrugged. 'I was speaking English, which happens to be my first language.'

'I'll tell you what you are, Lofthouse,' said Moss. 'You're a clever Dick. You use big words 'cause you reckon it sounds clever. Well, it don't work in this hut.'

'Whether it works or not, what's wrong with being clever?'

At this point the man whose bed was opposite Alan's joined the conversation. 'You'll find out what's wrong with being clever,' he said, 'if you go on talkin' to us lot as if we ain't got a brain to share between us.'

It was a situation that Alan could neither understand nor remedy and after an unpleasant incident in the cookhouse he put in a request to speak to the platoon officer, confident that something would be done.

❧·⁂·❧

Once Maurice had been kitted out at the depot at Warrington, he reported with several others to RAF Westfleet in Cheshire for basic training.

His accommodation was in a corrugated steel Nissen hut, where he and his fellow recruits answered to Sergeant Handyman, a man of weather-beaten features, a loud voice and, it seemed, no more than a rudimentary sense of humour.

'Right, you lot,' he said, using the form of address that seemed to be universal, 'let's find out who you are.' Pointing to the man on Maurice's left, he asked, 'What's your name, lad?'

'Brown, oh eight two, Sarge.' They had been issued with their service numbers that morning with the instruction that in answering or giving their name they were required to give the last three digits.

The sergeant looked around the hut with an air of theatrical disbelief. Finally he said, ' "Sarge," he calls me, as if we've known each other for years.' Rounding on the unfortunate airman, he said, 'You, my lad, are a new recruit, an aircraftman second-class, the lowest form of human life, and I will trouble you to address me by my full rank. I didn't spend half my life earning it to have it cut short by the likes of you. Got it?'

'Yes, Sergeant. Sorry, Sergeant.'

'Good, and save your service number for the officers. It makes them feel important.' He moved on to Maurice. 'Name, lad?'

'Alcock, Sergeant.'

Sergeant Handyman closed his eyes in disbelief. 'Do not jest with your sergeant,' he advised. 'That's if you want a long life. Now, I'll ask you again and this time you'd better give me a sensible answer. What is your name?'

'Alcock, Sergeant. It really is.' Maurice took out his pay book to show him.

'Blimey,' said the sergeant, 'and your name's Brown, is it?' He challenged Maurice's neighbour again.

'Yes, Sergeant.' Brown showed him his pay book.

'Well, all I can say is you two had better be on your mettle, because with names like Alcock and Brown, the RAF is going to expect a lot from you.'

They learned more about the RAF's expectations later in the course, when they were interviewed individually by an elderly wing commander.

He looked first at Maurice's test paper and then at the report from the Air Defence Cadet squadron. Finally he said, 'I see you've been on the Navigator/Bomb Aimer course, Alcock.'

'Yes, sir.'

'Hm. Navigation seems to have been a sticking point.'

For the first time Maurice felt uneasy. 'I should be all right, sir.'

'I'm afraid "should be" isn't good enough, Alcock. A navigator has to get his aircraft to the target and then safely home. The success of the operation and the lives of the crew, not to mention the safety of a valuable aircraft, depend on him.'

'Yes, sir.' Suddenly Maurice felt a hollow deep in his stomach.

All the time he'd battled with the mathematics of navigation he'd been convinced he would win through. Failure was too awful to contemplate, and now it seemed that his dream was about to evaporate. Miserably he said, 'I'm desperate to get into aircrew, sir. It's all I've ever wanted.'

'Oh, I don't doubt your keenness.' The wing commander consulted Maurice's report again. 'You got full marks for enthusiasm and commitment, and they're both very important qualities, but on the basis of this report I can't recommend you for training either as a pilot or as a navigator/bomb aimer.'

It was as if the door that had been closed on him was now locked and barred. He grasped desperately at the remaining possibility. 'What about gunnery, sir? I could do that.'

'You'd have to do some elementary navigation on that course as well.' The wing commander considered that for a moment. 'Mind you,' he said, 'it's hardly what you were doing with the ADCC. Also,' he said, referring again to Maurice's record, 'Sergeant Handyman says you did particularly well on the ranges, both with the rifle and the Bren light machine-gun.'

'I've had some experience, sir, with the Cadets.'

'I see.' The wing commander picked up his pen. 'Well, I'll tell you what I'm going to do, Alcock. I'm going to post you to Number Fifteen Personnel Transit Centre until the next Air Gunners' course becomes available. When that happens, you'll be posted to RAF Penrhos in Wales. How does that sound?'

It was a moment of euphoria for Maurice. In the space of a minute he'd gone from utter dejection to blessed relief. He was quick to react. 'Thank you, sir! I mean thank you very much, sir! I know it's not what I had in mind to begin with but I'll put everything I've got into it. I won't let you down, sir.'

The wing commander smiled for the first time and said, 'I know, Alcock. I'm sure you won't.'

Alan came to attention in Second Lieutenant Pearson's office.

'Stand easy. What have you come to see me about, Lofthouse?'

Mr Pearson was a fair-haired young man with boyish features, but Alan was confident he would get a mature and sensitive hearing.

'It's to request a transfer to a different platoon, sir.'

'Really? But you've only a short time here before you're posted for signals training. Why do you want a transfer at this stage?'

'I'm being... victimised, sir.' He'd been about to say 'bullied' but he thought that might sound juvenile.

Mr Pearson's expression darkened. 'Victimised by whom?'

'Oh, not by the NCOs, sir. No, it's the others in my hut.'

'What, all of them?' His tone betrayed his disbelief.

'Pretty well, sir. They seem to resent the fact that I've had a better education than they have and they never tire of reminding me of it.'

The officer closed his eyes. It was clear that he thought very little of Alan's complaint. 'And what form do these reminders take?'

'Usually verbal, sir, but yesterday at breakfast I was just carrying mine to the table when one of them barged into me and knocked it out of my hand. I know it was deliberate, sir, because he was grinning when he said, "Look where you're going, Lofthouse." All the others were laughing too. And it's not just that, sir. Their language is permanently foul and their conversation is limited to, well, the usual level. They discuss it in the most basic terms.'

Mr Pearson smiled. 'No one's going to change the language of the barrack room, Lofthouse. It's a fact of life, and men of all platoons, companies and regiments will always talk about sex. Such is the nature of mankind. But tell me, does the fact that it's you against the rest tell you anything, I mean beyond the fact that you find it unpleasant?'

It seemed to Alan an odd question to ask. 'I'm not sure I understand what you mean, sir.'

'I'm asking you if it's completely one-sided or if you've maybe given offence at some time. You see, you're asking me to accept that you're in the right and the others are all totally at fault.'

'Well, I'd say they are, sir.'

'Hm.' The officer examined the document on his desk and said, 'I see your education was at Cullington Grammar School.'

'And Corpus Christi College, Cambridge, sir.'

24

'Oh yes. What did you read there?'

'Classics and ancient history, sir.'

He looked again at the document. 'So you did. It says so here.'

'I intend to apply for officer training as soon as I'm allowed, sir.'

'Do you, by Jove?' He finished thumbing through Alan's service documents and leaned against the back of his chair. 'In that case,' he said, 'you have to realise that there's rather more to being an officer than simply having a good education. For one thing, you have to be able to get the best out of people, and you won't do that by looking down on them. You do look down on the others in the platoon, don't you, Lofthouse?'

'It's not exactly how I would put it, sir.'

'No, I imagine it's difficult for you to admit, but you've as good as said it. Listen, Lofthouse, there are men in this platoon who struggled to pass the army's intelligence test, never mind Oxbridge entrance.'

'Surely not, sir.'

'I have the results in writing. I know also that one of those men is the best marksman in the company, and another man with absolutely no knowledge of the Peloponnesian War or Latin cases and declensions impressed his instructor yesterday by completing the assault course in record time and with the added weight of the injured man he was carrying over the last obstacle. Qualities come in different forms.' As a gesture of finality he closed Alan's file. 'As for the rest, you'll have to make allowances and try to see their qualities. Accept their rough, untutored ways and maybe they'll be more accommodating too. No army unit is of any use at all unless it can operate as a team, and being a team member is something at which you need to work very hard, Lofthouse. Do you follow me?'

'Yes, sir.'

It wasn't the solution Alan had been seeking; in fact it seemed to be no solution at all, but he decided to take the advice because it was his only option and, as Mr Pearson had pointed out, he would soon be leaving Deepcut for training with the Royal Corps of Signals.

5

'I had this photo taken shortly after I started nursing,' said Kate. 'Look at the 'butterfly' cap. That was to show I was a probationer.' She added casually, 'It was a bugger to fold into shape.'

'You were pretty,' said Rachel, visibly surprised by Kate's choice of language but trying not to show it. 'I thought you would be. What colour was your hair?'

'It was medium brown, I suppose, with reddish lights, someone told me.'

'You were very slim in those days,' said Rachel, adding hastily, 'not that you haven't a good figure now.'

'It would be a miracle if I were a size ten at my age. Either that or I'd be starving to death.'

'Is that what you were, size ten?'

'That's right.' She laughed lightly. 'An American airman once told me I'd be size eight where he came from. He'd worked in a clothing factory before enlisting and he said that American sizes are always one less than ours. It sounded terribly flattering.' She turned a page of the album and found the picture she was looking for. 'Dorothy was size ten,' she said, 'and tall, as you can see.'

'She really was lovely, wasn't she? She wore nice clothes as well, if this photo's anything to go by.'

'Ah well, she worked in ladies' fashions and got staff discount.' Suddenly an odd memory came to her. 'I remember saving up for a new frock. In those days a student nurse's pay was abysmal and I'd been saving for some time. Anyway, I remembered seeing a frock I really liked. I suppose it was quite an ordinary cotton frock but I thought it looked rather special. It was in the end-of-season sale where Dorothy worked, but I still couldn't afford it, so she said she'd keep an eye on it because there might be further reductions. Well, I wasn't too hopeful, but about a week later she turned up at the nurses' home with a parcel for me. She'd rescued the dress in the nick of time. She'd seen someone point it out to a friend and, as they looked quite interested, she snatched it up when they weren't looking, and told the assistant she wanted it. She was taking an awful risk. Even as an assistant buyer, which made her very senior, she could have been in trouble if those women had known she was staff.'

'So she was kind as well as pretty.'

'Yes, not everyone knew her as I did. Some, especially men, found her distant, but I never did.' She leafed again through the album and found the group picture she'd been looking for. 'This was at one of our club rallies,' she said. 'You can see Dorothy here, and me next to her, and behind us there's Alan, Maurice in the middle and Jack at the end there.'

'Alan was rather good-looking, wasn't he?'

'I suppose he was, although he never appealed to me. I grew to like him rather more but I never fancied him.'

'The other two boys look very happy.'

'Yes, they were both sunny characters and they were good friends too, just as Dorothy and I were.'

Rachel's attention strayed for a moment to a picture of a young man in Air Force uniform. 'This is Maurice, isn't it? Was his hair actually blonde? It's difficult to tell with black-and-white photos.'

'Yes, and it had a natural wave as well. Alan used to call him "Goldilocks".' She turned the page to change the subject.

6

Maurice's first leave came at the beginning of April, marking the end of the air-gunners' course.

His mother held him in an ecstatic hug and asked, 'When do you have to go back?'

'Steady on, Mum. I've only just arrived home. I've got forty-eight hours, so I have to be at Benton by Sunday night.'

'Where on earth is that?'

'It's in Leicestershire.'

She released him and stood back to enjoy the spectacle of her son in uniform. 'A sergeant already,' she said, taking in the stripes on his greatcoat. 'You've done well.'

'It's only because I'm aircrew,' he said. 'They promote us to sergeant when we pass the course. Everybody else has to do it the hard way.'

'You must have done well,' she insisted, 'or they wouldn't have promoted you.'

'All right, I passed the course. Now, will you let me take my coat off before I melt? It's roasting in here.'

'We're lucky to have a fire. There've been times the coal wagon couldn't get through to us because of the snow.'

Maurice nodded. Everyone said it had been the coldest winter they could remember.

'Give us your coat. I'll hang it up for you and then I'll put the kettle on. Come and talk to me while I do it.'

'Okay. By the way, you'll need these,' he said handing her the food ration coupons for his leave.

'Good lad. I hope they're feeding you all right.'

'Yes, they are, and I'll get even better rations when I start flying.'

'I should hope so.'

It was good to be at home with all the familiar things around him: the black iron range, the tab rug in front of the fire and the old mantelpiece clock ticking noisily, as if it resented being excluded from the conversation. They chatted for a while and as well as asking questions about life in the RAF his mother acquainted him with the latest news. Alan had been home on leave and was expecting to go overseas soon. It seemed he wasn't all that keen on the army, whereas Jack, who hadn't been home yet, was enjoying life at sea. His sister Mary was eight months gone with her first baby, so Jack might be an uncle by the time he saw her.

It seemed to Maurice that the Cullington mothers always knew what everyone else's offspring were doing and he listened in mild amusement until his mother said, 'Oh, and Katherine Whitehead's at home this weekend. She's been on nights at a first-aid post and it's her first bit of time off in ages.'

'Kate?' That was a bit of luck, depending on what she was doing with her time off.

'Yes, I know you're quite keen on her. I thought you'd like to know.'

'We're friends, Mum, that's all.'

'Well, you could do a lot worse. She's a nice lass.'

Maurice looked at his wristwatch, a recent purchase on the strength of his promotion. It wasn't quite twenty-past eight. 'I'm just going down to the phone kiosk, Mum,' he said. 'I won't be long.'

'All right, love. Remember to close the black-out curtain before you open the door. Mrs Jenkins down the road got fined last month for showing a light.'

'Okay.' He drew the curtain firmly before slipping out into the blacked-out street, almost stumbling into a man crouched over a cigarette, which he held cupped in his hand. They exchanged a brief greeting, as strangers did, and Maurice walked carefully on. He'd no idea how that silly story had started about glowing cigarette ends being visible from five thousand feet. It was nonsense, but some people would believe anything.

He almost collided with the telephone kiosk, having come upon it so suddenly. Thankfully it was empty, so he stepped inside and picked up the receiver.

'Number, please?' It was one of the operators he remembered from before the war. He recognised the rise and fall of her voice.

'Cullington one-four-eight, please.' He knew Kate's number by heart, although not from frequent use. There were some numbers you just remembered; at least that was what he told himself.

The phone rang a few times and Mr Whitehead came on the line. Maurice pressed the button and heard the clatter as his two pennies were released. 'Hello, Mr Whitehead. It's Maurice Alcock.'

'Hello Maurice, are you on leave?'

'Yes, I hope you're all okay. I wondered if Kate was at home.' Calling time was limited and pleasantries had to be brief.

'Yes, she is. I'll bring her to the phone. It's good to hear from you, Maurice.' The phone went down with a gentle bump, and a few moments later he heard Kate's voice.

'Maurice, where are you?'

'I'm in the kiosk at the end of Sevastopol Terrace. I haven't been back long and my mum told me you were at home.' He felt terribly nervous but summoned the courage to ask, 'Are you doing anything tomorrow?'

'What have you in mind?'

Somehow he managed to say, 'I wondered if you'd like to go to the pictures.'

'Well, I told my mum and dad I'd spend the evening with them. They haven't seen much of me lately.'

'Fair enough.' It was a lot to expect.

'There's tomorrow afternoon.'

'Tomorrow... yes.' He wasn't getting the brush-off after all. He thought quickly. 'If we go to the Picture Palace we can go to the café there as well.'

'What a lovely idea. I haven't seen a film for months. What's on? Never mind, it'll be a surprise.'

'I'll call for you at two o'clock, then.' The pips sounded, telling him his two minutes were up. He'd no more pennies.

'Right, I'll look forward to it. 'Bye.'

The line closed before he could say more, but he was happy. Unlike Alan, he'd long since given up on Dorothy and he'd found over a period of time that the more he saw of Kate the more she appealed to him. Although she was a year older, he'd known her in the juniors at school. She'd passed the scholarship and gone to the grammar school, of course, but it hadn't changed her. She was just as friendly as she'd always been. And now he was jubilant because he'd just made a date with her.

❦❖❖❖❦

On the following morning Alan's signals class at Swalebridge in Yorkshire was called to a lecture by Captain McGregor, one of the medical officers. A screen and projector had been set up and whilst the occasion was clearly important enough to involve the MO no one had any idea what his subject would be. The class waited to be enlightened, until, at exactly 0900, Captain McGregor entered the room with the orderly who was to operate the projector.

'At ease,' he told the class in a throaty accent that betrayed his roots in Dundee. 'Smoke if you wish, and relax while you may, because what I have to show you will make you squirm.' He rolled the 'r' with malicious vigour.

'You are approaching the end of your course,' he reminded them, 'after which you will be posted to your units prior to deployment, very likely overseas.' He paused with an enigmatic smile. 'Once there,' he continued, 'I have not the slightest doubt that you will lose no time at all before putting your private parts into places where, frankly, I would not care to insert a chimney brush.' He stopped again, no doubt to enjoy the effect he was creating. Some class members stared at him open-mouthed, although Alan suspected mystification rather than horror. The MO was a gifted performer, but his accent and extravagant language would be a challenge for most of them.

'France is full of fair maidens,' he went on, 'and, of course, some who are not so fair but who are no less accommodating, and that is before we consider those whose profession it is to offer their services in return for remuneration.' After another of his dramatic

31

pauses he raised his voice to say, 'But, make no mistake, the one thing those sirens all have in common is the capacity to infect any man foolish enough to partake of the delights on offer.' Turning to the orderly, he said, 'Lights out, and let's have the first slide.'

The orderly carried out the order, and there were expressions of disgust from the class.

'That, my boys, is a penis infected with gonorrhoea. Look on in horror.' He went on to describe the disease, which seemed terrifying enough, and its treatment, which sounded even worse.

'Slide number two.'

Gasps became groans.

'If this makes your hair curl then my task is almost done.' The slides that followed and his description of syphilis excited fear and nausea in equal proportions, at least in Alan, who feared that some of the class were still finding the lecture hard to follow.

'But help is at hand.' Deftly, the MO produced a packet of condom sheaths and held them up for his audience to see. 'I must warn you that they are not fool-proof. Short of complete abstention, however, they are your most effective safeguard.'

At the end of the lecture he invited questions and showed no surprise when there were none. The reaction came later in the hut.

'What was he goin' on about?' Bramhall, a serious man with thick, dark eyebrows, had sat expressionless, like several others, throughout the lecture.

Someone said, 'It was all about diseases and spoggies, but most of it went over me 'ead.' Then, after a moment's thought, he inclined his head in Alan's direction and said, 'I bet "Prof" knows all about it.'

There were sniggers, and Bramhall asked, 'Is that right, Prof? Did you manage to follow it?'

'Yes.' Alan had also been thinking about the MO's lecture and the memory was far from pleasant, although that had little to do with the subject matter. There had been times when he too had used unnecessarily elaborate language, and no doubt for the same reason. It was a pathetic reason, and he was painfully reminded of his conversation with Second-Lieutenant Pearson. He'd resented his platoon officer's advice at the time but now it seemed harshly relevant when his classmates' ignorance was making them pitifully vulnerable. He put down the boots he'd been about to polish and said, 'I'll explain it to you if you like.'

Bramhall asked, 'Do you reckon you can?'

'Let's give it a try, shall we?' No one disagreed, so, feeling rather like a schoolmaster, he said, 'The MO was trying to say that if you have it off with a woman you've only just met, and particularly with a prostitute, you could get one of the diseases he showed us. Gonorrhoea is bad enough, as you saw, but syphilis is a damned sight worse. It's harder to treat and it will very likely kill you. Your best bet is to use a condom... a spoggy. It's not perfect but it'll give you some protection.' Then, adding his own contribution, he said, 'Mind you, I'd be inclined to give the prostitutes a miss altogether.'

'Yeah, there's no sense in paying for it.' Bramhall seemed to be acting as spokesman for the others.

'Not when it can do horrible things to you,' agreed Alan.

One of the others asked, 'Is that really all he had to say?'

'That's right,' said Alan, 'but it's pretty important, don't you think?'

'Yeah.' The man was thoughtful. 'So, how is it you can understand a windbag like the MO and the rest of us can't?'

Alan hesitated. From his arrival at Swalebridge it was the longest conversation he'd had with the others. He might just be making some progress.

'It's all to do with what you're used to,' he explained. 'What did you do before you were called up, Bramhall?'

'I was a painter and decorator.'

'Ah, well, I haven't a clue about hanging wallpaper, and I expect most of you have knowledge and skills that are beyond me. I was at university until last year.' He saw heads nod as suspicions were confirmed. 'And being at university is all about listening to windbags and making sense of what they tell you.'

They looked at one another, exchanging nods and smiles. 'You know, Prof,' said Bramhall, 'we had you down as a right stuck-up bastard but maybe you're not so bad after all.'

'Well, I'm glad about that.' He was curious about Bramhall's accent. 'Where are you from, Bramhall?'

'Sheffield. What about you?'

'I'm from Cullington, near Bradford.'

Bramhall looked surprised. 'You don't sound Yorkshire,' he said.

'Well, that's something else university does to you. You learn a lot of new things but it's easy to forget about your roots and other things that matter.'

'What did you learn?'

'Oh, it was mainly about the ancient Greek and Roman civilisations and their languages.'

Bramhall seemed disappointed. 'What use is that?'

Alan recalled a similar conversation with Jack and the others. 'As far as this war's concerned,' he said, 'absolutely no use at all.'

———※※※———

The film was 'The Stars Look Down,' apparently based on a book that Kate had enjoyed, so that was good. For Maurice, it turned out to be an excellent film with the additional benefit of having Margaret Lockwood in it. The real bonus, however, was that Kate was there, although they were well into the film before he found the courage to take her hand in his. When he did, she simply glanced at him and smiled. Around them, couples were getting up to all kinds of antics but he didn't think she'd appreciate any of that.

At the end they walked through the foyer, talking about the film they'd just seen, and entered the familiar Art Deco café, where they found a table quite easily. A soldier and his girlfriend brushed past them in a hurry to get to theirs. The soldier said, 'Sorry, Sarge. Sorry, miss.'

'That's all right,' Maurice told him.

As they sat down, Kate said, 'Wasn't that nice? He called you "Sarge".'

'Yes, and I'm not a real sergeant. It's not as if I've had to put years of service in to get it.'

'Of course you're a real sergeant. You've got three stripes to prove it and you've also got a wing.' She peered more closely at his observer's brevet and asked, 'What does "AG" stand for?'

'It means "Air-Gunner". They wouldn't let me do anything with navigation because I'm hopeless at maths, but I'm happy enough. At least I'll be flying.'

'Don't be hard on yourself, Maurice. You've done well.'

The waitress arrived before she could say more, and Maurice ordered the set afternoon tea, which, because of rationing, consisted of a selection of finger sandwiches, a piece of unspecified cake and a pot of tea for two.

'Are you sure about this, Maurice? I'd help if I could, but a nurse's pay goes nowhere.'

'Don't worry.' Shyly, he said, 'I like your frock. You look really nice in it.' It was dark blue and quite a simple design but his compliment was genuine. He was noticing lots of things for the first time, like the tiny mole beneath her right ear, which also pleased him in an odd sort of way.

'Thank you. It took some getting but it was worth the effort.'

'What do you mean?'

'Someone else nearly bought it instead, but I was lucky enough to have an influential friend there at the time.'

'Dorothy?'

'Who else?'

'What's she doing nowadays?'

'She's still in the same job. I don't think she'll do anything about war work or anything like that until something major happens.' She added, '*If* something major happens.'

They waited while the waitress set down the tea things, and then Maurice said, 'I don't think this so-called "phoney war" will be phoney for much longer, and it hasn't been all that quiet for some. There was the sinking of the *Graf Spee* and the boarding of the *Altmark*, when they rescued all those merchant seamen, and there was *HMS Courageous* being torpedoed.'

'Yes, I was going to accuse the Navy of keeping it all to themselves until you reminded me about the last one. That was terrible.'

Maurice had something on his mind that had nothing to do with the war at sea but which was no less important to him. 'Kate,' he said, 'will you write to me?'

'Of course I will. I'd have written to you before but you didn't leave an address.' She fumbled in her bag and found her diary. 'Give it to me now, before we forget.'

'Okay, it's "Sergeant M.J. Alcock, 9762174, RAF Benton, Leicestershire." '

'Consider it done,' she assured him, putting her diary and pencil away.

After the sandwiches and cake had arrived, Kate gave the tea a stir and asked, 'Shall I be "mother"?'

'Yes, please.' He would be happier for her to be his girlfriend but in his shyness he kept that to himself.

She poured out the tea. 'You'll never guess,' she said, suddenly remembering. 'Jack's going to be an officer. It was the last thing he'd planned but he says he'll do anything to stop the other sailors calling him "Penny", although I don't know what else he expects with the surname Farthing. It was always the same at school.'

'I'm not really surprised. I mean about going for a commission. I always thought of Jack as the kind of bloke who should be in charge, but in a quiet way, not like Alan.'

'I know what you mean. It seems his "action station", whatever that is, is firing a gun on the bridge.' She broke off to ask, 'Isn't that the thing the captain stands on to give his orders?'

'Yes.'

'Well, one of the officers on the bridge asked him what he did before the war, and when Jack told him, he said that someone who can take holidaymakers abroad and use his initiative to sort out their problems must be capable of something more demanding than a seaman's duties. He has to do three months at sea and then he can do the training.'

'Well, good for Jack. To be honest, I thought Alan would be the first to do that.'

Kate transferred a ham sandwich to her plate and said, 'Alan's been having a difficult time. Dorothy had a letter from him last month and it was one long moan about the army and the idiots in his hut. She sent him a soothing reply but her view is that he causes most of his problems. I must say, though, I hope he settles down soon. It must be awful for him.'

'Yes, it must.' It was difficult for Maurice to sympathise with

Alan, but if that was how Kate felt he was content to agree with her. There was, however, one member of the group who'd so far not been mentioned. He asked, 'What about you, Kate? What have you been doing?'

'Nothing, absolutely nothing worth mentioning.'

'My mum said something about a first-aid post.'

'That's right. The government are moving nursing and medical personnel to places where they'll be most needed, and my place of need is a first-aid post in St Martin's Church Hall. I have to assess which cases can be treated and which have to go to Casualty. I think they were expecting widespread bombing, but so far it hasn't happened. I've been there three months and so far I've attended to four black-out victims, and by that I mean people who've walked into lamp posts or parked cars.'

'I walked into the telephone kiosk last night when I went to phone you.'

'Oh,' she laughed, 'how awful.' She stroked the back of his hand, a gesture that gave him more pleasure than perhaps she realised.

He asked, 'What would you rather be doing?'

'Any proper nursing would be better than being bored to tears every night. I was on obstetrics before all this and I enjoyed it. I'd like to do some more.'

'What's that?'

'Obstetrics? It's midwifery, delivering babies.'

'Ugh.'

'It's lovely,' she insisted. 'It's the most natural thing in the world, and there's no thrill like holding a newly-born baby and hearing it cry for the first time.'

'If you say so.'

'Each to her own, I suppose.'

Maurice eyed his piece of cake. It resembled Madeira cake with the addition of a few lonely sultanas. He said, 'I've only got four in mine.'

'You're lucky. I've only got two.'

'You can have one of mine.'

'Are you sure, Maurice? I mean this is generosity on a grand scale.'

'I want you to have it.' He lifted the sultana gently with his cake knife and deposited it on Kate's plate.

'Oh, Maurice, what can I say?'

A woman at the next table told her companion in a stage whisper, 'Them two are in love. I knew it as soon as I set eyes on 'em.'

Maurice and Kate each remained serious. Eventually Kate asked, 'Is your mum going to the station with you?'

'No, she has to work.' His mother was a canteen supervisor at the police station, and hungry police officers had to be fed.

'I'll come and see you off. What time's your train?'

'Will you really? It's nine-twenty in the morning.'

'Right, I'll see you down there.'

It was a development that couldn't have pleased Maurice more. When they left the café he insisted on taking her home and seeing her to her door, where they stood awkwardly inside the large stone porch.

'Are you going to come in for a while?

'No, I'd better not.' In his current state of mind he didn't think he could cope with Kate's parents.

'Well, thank you for a lovely afternoon.'

'You're welcome. Thanks for coming.'

'I'll see you tomorrow, then.'

'All right.' He wanted very badly to kiss her but he'd had no experience with girls as sophisticated as Kate. He was letting the initiative slip away and he felt powerless to do anything about it.

She asked, 'Is nine o'clock all right?'

'I should think so.' It was too awful. 'Kate, I....'

'What?' Her voice was gentle, as if she'd known all along how he felt.

Lamely, he said, 'It's really good of you to come tomorrow.'

'It's no trouble.' Smiling, she inclined her head, and he bent self-consciously to kiss her cheek. Then, because he feared his chance was about to disappear for ever and because he could restrain himself no longer, he seized her waist and pulled her toward him. Her lips were slightly parted and he bent to kiss them.

7

'You know, I've been in this hospital almost two weeks now. I imagine they'll be sending me home as soon as I can walk. I hope you'll still visit me then.'

'Of course I will.' Rachel was impatient for Kate to carry on with the story. She asked, 'Did you see Maurice off at the station?'

'I certainly did. It was the kind of moment you never forget.'

'It happened very quickly, didn't it? I mean your feelings for each other.'

'Not all that quickly. We'd known each other a long time.'

'But things moved on that afternoon at the cinema, didn't they?'

'I can't deny that.' Kate smiled, wondering a little about Rachel's interest in her former life. She asked, 'Have you got someone tucked away, Rachel?'

'No.' Rachel looked down at her hands and her facial twitch returned.

'You must have had at some time.'

She looked up again in surprise and said, 'You're very direct.'

'I have to be. At ninety-five I can't afford to waste time, and if I don't ask you about things when they occur to me I'll forget all about them and never be any the wiser.'

After an awkward pause Rachel said, 'There was someone years ago, but it was never going to work out.'

'Why not?'

There was a shrug in her voice as she said, 'I had to look after my mother.'

Kate took her hand and held it.

'I had to sacrifice so many things.'

'You poor girl.'

'I'm thirty-eight,' she protested weakly.

'A mere child.'

'No, I'm not.'

'Compared with me you are. The best part of your life lies ahead of you.'

Rachel was silent, seemingly content to leave her hand in Kate's. Eventually she said, 'It's my turn to ask you a personal question now. Did you love your mother?'

'That's a good question, better than you think. You can live with someone so that however much they irritate you, you feel the loss when they die, and you can do that without actually loving them.' She thought about that for a while and said, 'My father and I had a special relationship but I can't say the same about my mother.' She saw tears forming in Rachel's eyelids and squeezed her hand. 'Help yourself to tissues,' she said, offering the box with her free hand.

Rachel dabbed at her eyes and then surprised Kate by returning to the story. She asked, 'Can we come back to Maurice later? You've still not told me very much about Jack.'

'No, I haven't, and if my memory serves me true it was at about the time Maurice went off to Benton that Jack's part in the war really began.

8

After working-up exercises in the Atlantic, *Wrathful* was ordered to Norway, where units of the fleet were providing air defence during military operations. There, with other destroyers, she shared the task of protecting the anti-aircraft cruiser *Curlew* from U-boat attack.

The main threat, however, came from the air in the shape of the Heinkel 111 medium bomber and the Junkers 87 dive-bomber, known as the Stuka. The latter had a particularly daunting reputation, even among those who had not yet seen it first-hand, largely from newsreel footage from Spain and, more recently, Poland. Its appearance alone had a malevolent quality, with its inverted gull wings, its claw-like fixed undercarriage and 'Jericho Trumpet' sirens, which emitted a deafening scream when diving, a sensation as unnerving as their designer had intended.

As French troops were landing at Namsos, *Curlew*'s radar detected a wave of aircraft approaching from the south and the information was communicated immediately to the destroyer screen.

At his action station on the starboard wing of the bridge Jack kept a lookout and waited. The breath-taking beauty of the fjord and the novelty of being on active service were now temporarily forgotten. Inside his duffel coat, steel helmet, anti-flash hood and gloves he perspired copiously despite the freezing weather. By contrast, his mouth was completely dry and his tongue felt like charcoal.

In one of those rare moments when his father had spoken

about the last war he had described the scene before an offensive, and Jack had been able to form a vivid and disturbing picture from his description of preoccupied faces, terse fragments of conversation, nervous and compulsive fidgeting, the mixed stench of rum and vomit and the inescapable presence of fear. For those who survived their first offensive, the fear returned each time, sometimes worse than before, but most men saw it as their personal challenge and learned to cope with it. Coping was all they could do, and the secret was to concentrate on *doing* something, so each man checked repeatedly that his bayonet was correctly fixed, that his magazine was pushed fully home into his rifle and that his gas mask was stowed ready for immediate use. Such checks were practically unnecessary but the distraction they afforded was invaluable. Jack knew that just as he knew his guns and their mounting were in perfect order but he elevated, depressed and trained them. In that way he prevented his hands from shaking.

He hadn't long to wait before one of the lookouts reported aircraft approaching from starboard. Tiny specks at first, they quickly became identifiable as Stukas.

With her superior range *Curlew* was first to open fire and, as they came within range of the small-calibre guns, the voice of *Wrathful*'s First Lieutenant came over the loudspeaker.

'Barrage, commence, commence, commence!'

Breathing slowly and deliberately, Jack took aim and squeezed the triggers, adding his tracer bullets to those of the other gunners. Together with the exploding shells from the pom-poms and the more sophisticated weapons of the newer destroyers, they created a frenzied kaleidoscope of fire. There was a bigger explosion, too, as a Stuka received a direct hit from *Curlew*'s secondary armament, and Jack was transfixed for a moment by the sight of an aircraft and two men blown to fragments. Hurriedly he collected himself and trained his guns on a new target. The meticulous and repetitive training at Whale Island served him well as time and again he aimed and fired. The hammering of the twin Lewises against his shoulders and hands felt reassuring and empowering, and when it became necessary to change magazines his loading number did

42

so in the same smooth and practised manner so that Jack could resume fire.

It was a wonder the attacking aircraft hadn't yet hit the troopship. Instead they seemed to be concentrating on the shore installations and the now disembarked and scattered troops. That was until the last three switched their attention to *Curlew* and the destroyers, and the hideous screams reached a new level as *Wrathful* came under attack.

With heightened urgency Jack lined up his sights on the leading aircraft and fired, only to see his tracers go wide. The Captain had taken evasive action by turning hard-a-starboard, a manoeuvre that doubtless saved the ship but which, for the moment, Jack found particularly frustrating. He applied himself again and was training his guns on the next Stuka when he heard a loud cheer above the gunfire. The aircraft that had just attacked *Wrathful* had stalled in mid-climb and, masked by the smoke that poured from its fuselage, was plunging into the water. *Wrathful* made another violent turn, this time to port, and the bombs of the remaining Stukas followed the stricken aircraft into the waters of the fjord.

The order to cease firing seemed unnecessary as the last of the aircraft disappeared, but it was no less welcome and as Jack unfastened the strap that attached him to the mounting he began to breathe naturally again, grateful to have survived and strangely elated by the experience.

After a moment the Tannoy system crackled.

'D' you hear there? D' you hear there? This is the Captain speaking. Well done everyone, and particularly the port pom-pom crew, who have just shot down our first aircraft. This is a milestone for the ship, and we shall celebrate it in the time-honoured way at our first opportunity. That is all.'

There was a loud cheer from the ship's company at the promise of a double tot of rum, but for Jack there was an infinitely greater reward in the knowledge that he'd faced his personal challenge and emerged with his honour intact.

Maurice was happy too. Far from regarding his specialisation as second-best after the initial disappointment, he was putting the whole of his effort into training as an air-gunner. So far, he and the rest of the crew had taken part in gunnery exercises and then gone on cross-country flights to get the feel of being airborne. Soon they would practise night flying. He was looking forward to that.

He also had another reason for being happy, and that was his new relationship with Kate. For a long time he'd imagined her interest in him was no more than platonic, and now he could barely believe his good fortune. He lay on his bed re-reading her latest letter.

Dear Maurice,

I'm glad you're enjoying whatever it is you're doing, and it doesn't matter that you can't tell me about it. It's enough for me to know you're happy.

We had great excitement last night, when a man fell off his bike outside the post. Yes, that's as exciting as it ever gets (excuse me while I yawn). The man was blind drunk, so I'm afraid I hadn't much sympathy for him. I just cleaned him up, dressed his wounds and sent him on his way. I ask you, have I been training all this time just to give first-aid to drunken cyclists?

I saw Alan again last week, but only briefly because he was on embarkation leave. Like you, though, he couldn't say where he was going. To be honest, I don't think he knew. However, one thing that surprised both Dorothy and me was that he wasn't the Alan we've all known. He was really quite modest, at least by his standards, and he even asked after you and said how well you'd done to pass out as a sergeant-observer. I wasn't going to comment on the change, but Dorothy came straight out with it and asked him if he'd had a visit from three spirits or maybe suffered a blinding light on the road to Damascus – you know what she's like – and Alan just said that the army was teaching him a lot about things that matter. Even Dorothy was impressed.

By the way, you should get a letter from her soon. She said she'd write to you and Alan and Jack as well, but take note – we have to call her 'Dot' now. She thinks 'Dorothy' sounds too formal. Also, 'Dot' uses less paper and ink. It's her latest contribution to the war effort.

I have to go now and get my beauty sleep before the night-shift. I can hardly wait to see you again, so take special care!

Hugs, kisses and lots of love,

Kate XXXXX

When he thought of her, which he did frequently, he also could barely wait. He just had to see her again before he was posted to somewhere perhaps at the other end of the country. Surely they would be granted forty-eighters at the end of the course. He certainly hoped so.

Situated on the outskirts of Béthune in Northern France, with a three-ton lorry, various items of wireless equipment and so far no letters from home, Alan was less happy.

He and Harry Bramhall had been posted to the same unit and they now shared the lorry with a corporal named Robertson. Alan and Harry had formed a much easier relationship since the medical officer's lecture, and they were able to work together without difficulty. The problem was Corporal Robertson, who seemed incapable of civility except of a grudging kind toward senior NCOs and officers. He treated his inferiors with loutish disdain.

He was currently at his bench, having just received a signal from 12th Infantry Brigade HQ. His sleeves were rolled up to expose arms covered almost entirely with tattoos; in fact most of his body had been tattooed at some time, reminding Alan of a fairground attraction he'd once seen.

'Got a fag, Lofthouse?' The corporal held out his hand without taking his eyes off the signal pad in front of him.

'You know I've stopped smoking.'

'Yeah, I forgot. You don't do nothing naughty, do you? What about you, Bramhall?'

'That's ten of mine you've had, Corporal.' Harry took out a cigarette and passed it to him.

'If you've learned to count you're not completely useless.' He lit the cigarette and held out a three-page signal, saying, 'Get that decoded, you two, and take it to His Nibs.' The reference was to 2ⁿᵈ Lieutenant Bourne, the officer in charge of the unit.

Alan took out the code book and he and Harry began decoding the signal under Robertson's disapproving eye.

'Get a move on, you two. You haven't got all day.'

'It's not easy with your handwriting, Corporal,' said Alan. He saw Harry close his eyes, no doubt at the thought of what must surely follow. For his part, Alan couldn't have cared less.

'What's wrong with my writing?' Clearly Robertson was preparing for a major confrontation, the kind he enjoyed most.

'Let's just say there's room for improvement.'

The corporal left his seat so violently that for a moment the vehicle rocked from side to side. 'Listen to me, Mister Clever Signaller Lofthouse,' he said, leaning forward so that he could jab at Alan's chest with his fist. 'I suppose you think that's funny.'

'Oh, I can be a lot funnier than that.'

'So you think you're clever as well, do you?'

Irritated by the invasive fist, Alan left his seat and took a step backward to answer him. 'Compared with you, Corporal, I'm a bloody genius.'

'What did you say?' There was fury in Robertson's eyes.

'You heard me. I said—'

'I heard what you said,' shouted the corporal, 'and you are going on a charge!'

Alan shrugged. 'Okay, let's have some fun.'

Harry groaned.

❦

There were repeated encounters with the *Luftwaffe*. Because of commitments in France and at home the number of fighters in Norway was hopelessly inadequate, so that the Navy's anti-aircraft role remained as important as ever. In a very short time enemy bombing had rendered Namsos Harbour unusable, and the flotilla was ordered to Aandalesnes to cover a withdrawal. The experience at Namsos had been a valuable one, because *Wrathful*'s gun crews among the rest had learned two very important facts about the Stuka dive-bomber. The first was that once it was committed to its dive it was incapable of changing course, and this meant that where there was room to manoeuvre a ship could take avoiding action. The second was that the Stuka was extremely difficult to hit when diving, but once it had pulled out and was climbing again it was slow and vulnerable, as Jack soon discovered for himself.

During an attack off Aandalesnes *Wrathful* had just made a timely turn to port, and Jack quickly retrained his guns on the attacking aircraft, which was starting its creeping ascent. For several glorious seconds he had a steady target in his sights. He aimed carefully ahead of it, squeezed the triggers and saw his tracers hit the fuselage and one wing. There was a thick stream of smoke before the aircraft stalled and fell crippled into the sea.

This time the cheers were for Jack and when rum was issued the call went up for 'sippers', a sip from each man's tot. The practice was strictly illegal and was only possible when the issuing officer and any senior ratings were absent from the messdeck. Each tot consisted of two-and-a-half fluid ounces of over-proof rum. Even when it was diluted with water it was a hefty measure and it wasn't surprising that Jack was in a talkative mood after being honoured in this way.

'It was one of those defining moments,' he told 'Tug' Wilson, his opposite number on the bridge Lewis guns.

'What's that mean, Penny?' Some of the others were wondering too.

'It was the kind of moment that's so important you remember it for the rest of your life.'

'I'm surprised you can remember anything,' said Tug, 'after what you just put away.'

'Everyone has these moments,' Jack went on happily. 'They're very important.'

Someone asked, 'Was that your first?'

'No, I've had a few.'

'Go on then, tell us about one,' asked Tug.

'All right. There was the time I saw full female nudity for the first time.' Suddenly he had everyone's attention. 'I was fourteen and I was on holiday with my family in Scarborough. There was a girl in the hotel. I think she must have been eighteen or maybe nineteen.'

'What did she look like?' The enquiry came from the leading hand of the mess.

'Is it important?'

''Course it is. We want to see the full picture, don't we?'

'Okay, she had fair hair, almost blonde, and blue eyes. She was quite tall and very slim. Is that enough?'

'Slim all over?' The leading hand was still hungry for detail.

'She had bumps in the usual places. Anyway,' he went on, 'she was a keen knitter. She was at it all the time and she'd even knitted herself a swimsuit.'

'What was it like, Penny?'

'It was dark-blue, one-piece with shoulder straps.' He eyed the leading hand and said, 'I don't think it had pockets, although it might have—'

'Get on with it, Penny.'

'I was just giving you the details. Anyway, the next time we were on the beach we saw her. She was changing into her new swimsuit.' There were several intakes of breath. 'No, that wasn't when it happened. She was changing under a towel. I didn't see anything.'

'After keeping us in suspense like this it'd better be good, Penny,' the leading hand advised him.

'All right, I'm coming to it. She went into the sea and swam for a while, and then she came inshore and stood up in the shallows. That's when it happened.'

'Go on,' they chorused.

'The wool was hopelessly weighed down with sea-water and the straps had slipped over her shoulders.'

'Yeah?' The chorus waited.

'And the whole thing plunged down to her knees.'

'Well, go on,' urged Tug.

'She was lovely, and everything was in its right place, at least as far as I knew. You have to remember it was a new experience for me. Mind you, I must say I felt just a shade let down.'

'Why?' Clearly the others weren't at all disappointed.

'Because I could see she wasn't blonde at all. It was a dead give-away.'

'What happened then, Penny?' The leading hand was keen to see the story through to its end.

'Oh, she covered herself up as best she could. My mum tried to distract me by offering to buy me an ice cream, my dad offered to take me for it and my sister couldn't do anything for laughing. She was the only member of the family who wasn't embarrassed.'

Tug was looking suspicious. He asked, 'Was that story true, Penny?'

Jack could hide his amusement no longer. 'No,' he admitted, 'but you enjoyed it, didn't you?' He held up his arms to ward off the boots and other projectiles that came flying his way.

⊕⊶ᴈ⊶ᴋ⊱ᴇ⊷⊛

In a commandeered farm building near Béthune Alan stood to attention before 2nd Lt Bourne. The officer was seated behind a wooden packing case, which he used for a desk. Corporal Robertson stood by the window.

'At ease, Lofthouse. Stand easy. Now, Corporal Robertson has reported you for insolence to a non-commissioned officer. He says you called him stupid. Is that right?'

'Not exactly, sir. I said that compared with him I was a genius, sir.'

'It amounts to the same thing.' The officer sighed, no doubt at the waste of his time. 'What have you to say for yourself, Lofthouse?'

'I'd like to make a complaint, sir.'

'What?'

'Corporal Robertson assaulted me, sir.'

'Is this true, Corporal?' The officer turned in his seat to address Robertson, who was struggling to contain his anger.

'No, sir. I hardly touched him.'

'But he did touch me, sir,' said Alan, 'and that constitutes an assault. May I demonstrate, sir?'

'If you must.'

49

Alan placed his fist against the apoplectic corporal's chest and pushed him backwards.

'Someone, tell me I'm dreaming,' said the officer. 'We're supposed to be conducting a war here and I have a charge of minor insolence and a complaint about an equally insignificant assault. Can neither of you find a sense of proportion?'

Alan was the first to speak. 'I agree that this whole thing is ludicrous, sir, and I shall be happy to withdraw the complaint if Corporal Robertson will drop the charge of insolence.'

'Well, Corporal?'

Robertson gave Alan a look of pure hatred before saying, 'I agree to that, sir.'

'Thank goodness for that. Leave us for a moment, will you, Corporal?' He waited until Robertson had left, and then said, 'You're an intelligent man, Lofthouse, perhaps a little too clever for your own good. You got away with it this time but it won't always be so easy.'

'I can see that, sir.'

'Good, and for goodness' sake remember we're supposed to be fighting a war.'

'Yes, sir.' In the rural peace and quiet of northern France it was easy to forget that.

9

Kate returned the photo album to the top of her locker.
'They're sending me home soon,' she told Rachel. 'They send younger people home much earlier than this. It's only because I'm an old crock that they've kept me in so long. It's harder for tired old bones to knit, although I must say the x-ray looked encouraging this morning.'

'But how will you cope? You'll be on crutches, surely.'

'Ah well, when I say "home" I don't mean "home, sweet home." I'm going to a nursing home, just until I'm active again and then I can return to my bungalow.' She added with a good-natured grimace, 'I don't think I could stand being cooped up with old people for longer than that.'

Rachel's eyes still showed her concern. 'Will you still let me visit you?'

'Of course I will. I don't know what I'd do without our afternoon sessions.'

'Really? I thought they were for my benefit.'

'Perish the thought. I'd have gone potty in here without your visits.' She looked over her glasses at Rachel and said, 'Even so, I'm glad if it's helped you.'

'You'd be surprised.' Rachel laid her hand on Kate's and squeezed it gently.

'You know,' said Kate, 'you can tell me anything. After ninety-five years I'm unshockable.'

'I know.' As she looked down the familiar facial twitch returned.

'It was your mother, wasn't it? I mean having to care for her all

51

that time and having no life of your own. I expect you've resented that over the years, and now you feel guilty.'

Tears formed in Rachel's eyelids. 'How did you know?'

'It's been written all over your face since you first arrived, but you really confirmed my suspicions when you told me about your lost romance.'

'That was just one instance.'

'I'm sure there were others, but I'm going to respect your wishes and leave you to tell me about it as and when you feel able.' It would be better that way, at a time when she could give Rachel's problem her full concentration. For now, Kate was beset by memories. Looking through her photo album had taken her back to the summer of 1940, a time that was so awful for Jack, for Alan and for most people, when the so-called 'Phoney War' gave way to the brutal reality of Hitler's *Blitzkrieg*.

10

After a rocking, lurching journey of about an hour the lorry stopped outside a small roadside café.

'Ha,' said Harry Bramhall, 'grub at last.' Food was ever his priority.

When on the move 2nd Lt Bourne and Corporal Robertson occupied the cab while Alan and Harry made themselves as comfortable as they could in the back, although it was a questionable kind of comfort, and it was a relief for them to climb down, if only for a spell.

'We'll eat our rations here,' the officer told them. 'I'll see if I can get us all some coffee. If I can it's on me.' He was about to go inside, when a man, hairless apart from a drooping moustache, appeared. Alan imagined he must be the proprietor.

'*Monsieur,*' said the officer, mustering his school French, '*nous voudrions quatre cafés au lait, sil vous plaît.*'

'*Mais oui, monsieur.*' The proprietor re-entered the café and emerged a couple of minutes later with a tray bearing four cups of coffee and a jug of milk, but when Mr Bourne offered to pay, he protested. '*Non, monsieur, il n'y a rien à payer.*'

'*Merci bien, monsieur. Vous êtes très généreux.*'

Harry looked on in bewilderment. 'What was all that about?'

'The coffee's on the house,' Alan told him. 'He won't take anything for it.'

'He probably thinks we're all goin' to our deaths,' said Robertson.

'That's right, Corporal,' Mr Bourne told him, 'keep everyone's spirits up.'

'It's impossible to make sense of any of this,' said Alan. 'What's happened, sir? I mean one minute we're twiddling our thumbs and the next we're in full retreat.'

'There's no mystery, Lofthouse. We are the victims of two decades of disarmament, of politicians burying their heads in the sand, and a superbly-equipped and highly professional German army doing what it's been practising for far too long. To put it bluntly, the British Expeditionary Force is up the creek without a paddle. We're ordered to make for Dunkirk, to await orders there and to hope against hope that the Navy, unlike the people who dropped us in this mess, knows its arse from its elbow.'

When they'd eaten, they continued to the next junction to join the main road about five miles distant. However, the lorry came to a halt after only a couple of miles. In the back of the vehicle Alan and Harry had no idea what was happening until they peered around the canvas sides and realised the nature of the problem. As far as they could see, the road was packed with refugees, some with handcarts, others weighed down with bags, old peasant women in dark-brown shawls, younger women with children, men pushing and carrying, some leading heavily-laden donkeys, one young woman even pushing an old man in an ancient wicker invalid chair, and all moving slowly and doggedly toward the coast.

2nd Lt Bourne left his seat in the cab to speak to them. 'This is hopeless,' he said. 'We're going to drive straight over the crossroads – we'll just have to push our way through the crowd – and we'll take a minor road that should take us almost parallel to the main road, give or take the odd winding detour.' He said with a rueful smile, 'I suppose things could be worse.'

They set off again and reached the crossroads, where they nosed gently through the line of refugees. If any of them resented the intrusion they made no show of it but continued on their way, almost oblivious to the lorry now lurching on to a road that was little more than a track.

In fact they had only just joined the road when they heard the snarling roar of aircraft engines. The vehicle stopped abruptly and the officer shouted to them to get out and take cover. Alan and

Harry grabbed their rifles and vaulted over the back to crouch in the ditch at the side of the road.

'Get away from the lorry,' shouted Robertson. 'If it's hit we'll go up with it.'

As they spread out along the ditch, the twin-engined aircraft flew over them so low that Alan could see the pilot's face quite plainly. He was grinning at them and, as a grin was usually a friendly sign, it seemed they were safe for the present. That was until the aircraft completed the circle and swooped on them, firing as it came.

Suddenly the cacophony of the cannon and machine guns was joined by the screams of the refugees. Alan raised his head to see what was happening on the road, and was deafened by a huge explosion as the lorry's fuel tank was hit. From the safety of the ditch He could feel the heat on his face from the fiercely burning vehicle.

⊷⊱⊰⊱⊰⊶

Norway was now a memory, but for some reason leave had not been granted. Instead, *Wrathful* had been refuelled and re-ammunitioned at Chatham and was leaving harbour once again. Jack had seen a number of destroyers slip their moorings and he imagined that more than one convoy was forming up. It seemed the only explanation until they reached open water and the Captain broadcast to the ship's company.

'Whilst we've been occupied with the campaign in Norway,' he told them, 'things have been going badly in France. The British Expeditionary Force has been obliged to fall back on the port of Dunkirk, and a large-scale evacuation is now in progress.

'The port itself has been rendered useless, and it is impossible for destroyers to get close enough inshore to pick up the evacuees, so the Admiralty has commandeered civilian craft of more than thirty feet overall length to act as ferries between the beach and the destroyers. In addition, a large number of private individuals have lent or taken their boats to assist with the evacuation.

'I'm not going to minimise the danger over there. Dunkirk is only within the range of a few fighter squadrons on the south coast, and the army and the rescue fleet are coming under heavy air attack. That is where we come in. It seems that *Wrathful* gained something of a reputation off Namsos and Aandalesnes, because we've been given the task of drawing the *Luftwaffe*'s attention away from the rescuers so that they can get on with their job.

'Things are going to be hectic over there but I know that each of you will make the greatest possible effort to make this vital operation a success. Our ETA is sixteen-thirty today. Good luck everyone. That is all.'

Jack stood at his action station on the bridge, trying to digest the news. It seemed inconceivable that Britain was on the brink of defeat, and yet it was official. The BEF had been pushed back to the coast. Before he could ponder the matter further he was surprised to receive a visit from the Captain. Hurriedly he came to attention and saluted.

'Hello, Farthing.' The Captain returned his salute. 'Are you ready for this? I'm expecting you to bag another Stuka at least.'

'I'll do my best, sir.'

'I know you will.'

'I just don't understand it, sir, the army caving in so soon. It's unbelievable.'

'They were caught with their pants down, Farthing. It all happened at a speed that took them completely by surprise. The enemy call it *Blitzkrieg*. It means "lightning war".'

Jack nodded.

'Of course, you speak German, don't you? Have you spent much time over there?'

'A little, sir. Most of my trips were to France. I was in Dunkirk last year, as it happens.'

'Were you, by Jove? Well, I doubt if you'll recognise it this afternoon. I gather it's rather flatter than it was.' He seemed about to leave, but then he said, 'Your three months' sea time should be up soon, shouldn't it?'

'That was last week, sir,' said Jack, surprised that the Captain had remembered it, and at such a time.

'Well, let me wish you well on the course. I think you'll make an excellent officer.'

'Thank you very much, sir.'

As the captain left him, Jack tried hard to come to terms with the knowledge that he might soon become an officer. Like his experiences over the past several weeks, it seemed the stuff of adventure stories, but before it could become reality he had to survive the current operation.

❂┄❊⊱┃⊰❊┄❂

Alan lay in the ditch until the sound of the aircraft was no more and the only noise came from the road, where a number of refugees had fallen victim to the attack. The wailing of the survivors was distressing enough, but his main concern was for Harry and the others.

'Harry, are you there?' As he spoke, he realised it was a silly question. It was an opinion that his friend seemed to share.

'Aye, I'm still here.' His voice sounded strained. 'I'd thought about going to a football match but I couldn't drag myself away from all this excitement.'

Alan stood up and looked around him. Almost immediately he spotted Robertson and 2nd Lieutenant Bourne. Robertson was only recognisable by the stripes on his tunic. He was unmistakably dead and, on close inspection, Mr Bourne appeared to have taken a single bullet through the head. For a moment Alan felt queasy, but then he saw Harry a short distance away, huddled over something. He couldn't see what it was until he got closer, and then he realised that his friend was holding his right thigh.

'I've been hit, Prof, a splinter or something.' He jerked his head towards the burning lorry and asked, 'Are them two all right?'

'No, they're both dead.'

'That's a bugger. Mr Bourne was all right.' He added, 'For an officer.'

'Agreed.' Alan crouched beside him and unslung his haversack. 'Let's get a field dressing on it,' he said, taking out his first-aid kit. 'Where's the wound?'

'It's here.' He pointed to a place above his knee. 'A few inches

57

higher and I'd have been singing soprano.' He winced at the pain. 'As it is I'll have to settle for playing the harp.'

'Nonsense. The first thing is to stop the bleeding.' Using his penknife, he cut an area of the rough cloth away to reveal a jagged wound that was bleeding heavily.

'Careful with that knife, Prof,' Harry protested. 'I want to be all in one piece when I report to Saint Peter.'

'You're not going to meet him yet.' He took out a large field dressing and clamped it to the wound with one hand while he wound the bandage with some difficulty around Harry's leg with the other. 'I'll have to make it tight enough to put pressure on the wound,' he said. 'Then I can move you.'

'How? I can't go far like this.'

'You can't walk with it like this, it's true, but I'll find a way.' He'd wondered about asking one of the refugees to give his friend a lift on a cart, but the thought died at birth. The sobbing and wailing reminded him, if any reminder were needed, that the refugees had enough problems of their own.

'What would the Romans have done, Prof? I reckon they'd have left me here, like you'll have to if you're going to get away.'

'I'm not leaving you here, and I don't know what the Romans would have done, but I think I've found you a chariot.' At the side of the road lay the invalid chair that had carried the old man. It was evidently of no interest to the surviving refugees, who were occupied in tending the wounds of others.

'Wait here,' said Alan.

'Funnily enough, I wasn't thinking of going anywhere.'

The old man lay where he'd fallen from the chair. His throat was a bloodied mess, and Alan guessed that the bullet had struck him from behind. The young woman lay head-first in the ditch, where the torn remains of her dress left her largely uncovered. He searched around and found a woollen shawl, which he draped over her lifeless body. It was a foolish, quixotic gesture, but restoring a little of her dignity seemed to compensate her in a strange kind of way for taking her property.

The back of the chair was damaged, presumably by the bullet

that had killed the old man, but he pulled it upright and pushed it forward on its wheels. It ran easily enough so he continued to where Harry lay on the ground, staring in disbelief.

'What are you going to do with that thing?'

'I'm taking you to the seaside, Grandpa.' As he spoke, he was surprised by the relief in his voice.

'But even with that I'll slow you down.'

'Wait a minute.' Alan nerved himself to return to the bodies of 2nd Lt Bourne and Robertson. He held his breath to keep himself from retching as he detached their webbing belts and the corporal's water bottle and haversack and brought them back to the wheelchair. 'Take your belt off, Harry.'

Harry looked at him in alarm. 'What for?'

'Relax. I need it to control the steering.'

'I can steer it all right.' Harry pointed to the long lever.

'You could lose consciousness.'

'Go on, cheer me up.'

'Later. I'm a bit busy just now.' He helped Harry into the chair and placed the haversack in his lap. 'You take care of that. There'll be a spare dressing in it at the very least. You may even find some cigarettes to replace those he sponged off you.'

'You know, Prof, every now and again that university education surprises us all and you come up with a good idea.'

With the three webbing belts Alan made a strap that served as a harness, keeping Harry firmly in his seat, as well as a means of operating the steering lever from behind.

They began the next stage of their journey, hoping fervently that Mr Bourne's map reading had been sound. The map had gone with the lorry.

All Jack could see of Dunkirk was a seemingly endless pall of thick, black smoke, and he feared that the town had been completely destroyed. It was his first impression at fifteen miles and it remained with him until the burning, toppled and scarred remains became visible, at which point his attention strayed, because suddenly he was aware of other things. A destroyer stood at the eastern mole hurriedly embarking troops whilst others made for home at high speed, their decks packed with soldiers from the crowded beaches. Coasters, tramp steamers, colliers and assorted merchant ships waited gamely in deeper waters until they also could take their turn at the mole, whilst the most wonderfully bizarre collection of vessels worked close inshore. There were Thames barges under sail, drifters, lobster boats, pleasure boats, paddle-steamers from seaside resorts, tugboats, sailing yachts and dinghies, cabin cruisers and boats of every description, not all of the minimum length prescribed by the government but no less welcome. Such had been the response to the government's appeal.

There was wreckage in the sea as well, exposed mastheads that served as a stark warning of a similar fate, and buoys marking wrecks in the approaches. It was impossible to see at first how many vessels had been sunk, and it was probably not such a good idea to dwell on it.

His thoughts were interrupted by a shout from Tug Wilson.

'Aircraft fine on the port bow!'

Jack could make out eight-plus Stukas, possibly ten, and he was lining up his sights when the First Lieutenant gave the order to open fire.

It was almost like Norway again. Only the scenery and the temperature were different. The clammy perspiration and the dry mouth were the same. So too were the screams of the diving Stukas, and Jack watched, horrified, as they attacked the defenceless men waiting on the beach. As each aircraft began its slow, lumbering climb, he fired and saw his tracer curve away. If the range was too great for the Lewises to have any real effect he hoped at least that his efforts would unnerve the enemy pilots and spoil their aim, although, if he were honest, he knew that wherever the bombs fell they would inflict harm. The sad truth was that the Lewis gun was obsolete and that a pair of the modern Vickers guns, a pom-pom, or an Oerlikon or Bofors would have inflicted infinitely more damage.

He saw one Stuka fall victim to gunfire from another destroyer.

It was the only one to be shot down in that raid, but he told himself there would be ample opportunities in the days ahead. The vast number of men on the beach pointed to a lengthy operation and one which the *Luftwaffe* was naturally keen to curtail.

⊶┈╂⊹╎⊱╎⊱⊷

Harry, who had slept on and off for the better part of three hours, suddenly roused himself, moaning in a guarded way that convinced Alan he was in more pain than he admitted.

'Where are we, Prof?' He looked around at the flat, grassy landscape.

'About ten miles north of where you started snoring.'

'I can't help it, I'm in pain.'

Alan wondered how he could feel pain when he was asleep, but he left the question unasked and said, 'There's nothing I can do. If you like, I'll put you an extra dressing on but I don't think it'll do much good.'

'No, Prof, leave it alone. It's the jolting on this bloody road that does it. Can't we get back on to the main road? It's not up to much but it's better than this cart track.'

'All right, but we'll have to share it with refugees. I can see some of them from here.' He peered ahead. 'I think there's a junction about half a mile up the road.' He'd seen other remnants of the BEF taking a cross-country route, but there was no point in trying to join them as the wheelchair would never have coped with the rough terrain.

'Prof?'

'Yes?'

'Now I've woke up, I need to water me donkey.'

'What?'

'You know – strain the spuds, empty the kettle, put the fire out, point Percy at the plumbing....'

'Do you mean you need to pee?' Some of the toughest characters Alan had met in the army were surprisingly coy about their natural functions.

'That's right.'

'All right, I'll help you up.'

61

Harry was quiet for a moment, and then he said, 'I think I'll need you to prop me up an' all.'

'Hey ho.' Alan lifted him to his feet and helped him to the side of the road. Even though the area was deserted it seemed only proper to use the ditch rather than the road.

'Stand behind me and steady me.'

'All right.' Alan held him securely under his armpits and they stood together like acrobats in an unlikely circus act, the one steadying his partner in readiness for their trademark finale.

'Prof?'

'Yes?'

'Can you lower your hands a bit? I'm all hunched up and I can't reach me fly.'

'All right.' Alan adjusted his grip.

About fifteen seconds passed, and then Harry said shyly, 'Prof?'

'Yes?'

'I can't do it.'

'You were desperate a minute ago.'

'I still am. I just can't do it when there's anybody close by.'

'But if I walk away you'll fall over.'

'I know.'

Alan gave the problem some urgent consideration and said, 'You need to relax.'

'I know.'

'A good laugh might help. What's the funniest thing you can remember?'

'I can't think. Just a minute, yes, I can. It was George Formby in "Off the Dole". I nearly died laughing at that.'

'Do you mean you actually find George Formby funny?'

'Yeah, and I'm not the only one.' Pressing though his current problem was, his tone was quite defensive.

'All right, wait a minute.' With a deep sense of sacrifice Alan cleared his throat to sing, and he'd just reached the third line of 'When I'm Cleaning Windows,' when Harry convulsed.

'Stop it, Prof,' he begged as soon as he could speak. 'It hurts like hell when I laugh.'

Offended but nevertheless mindful of his role, Alan asked, 'Would you rather I whistled? They say it works with children.'

'No, it's all right now.' Sure enough, Alan heard the long-awaited cascade hit the bottom of the ditch.

'It wasn't the song that made me laugh,' Harry explained later, still with tears in his eyes, 'it was your singing. It was horrible, not a bit like George Formby.'

'I'm relieved to hear it.'

Once more on the road, Harry unfastened the straps of Robertson's haversack. 'I don't know what he's got in here,' he said, 'but it's bloody heavy.' He opened the flap and gaped in surprise. 'Well, well, well. Our corporal was a hoarder as well as a selfish bastard.' He took out a bottle of *vin ordinaire* and a tin of bully beef. 'The bugger was keeping these for himself.'

'Now, Harry, you shouldn't speak ill of the dead, even though he was a selfish bastard.'

'I know, but have you got something to open this bottle?'

Alan took out his penknife and handed it to him. 'It's got a corkscrew on it,' he said.

'Who's a good boy scout, then?' Harry opened the knife and plied the corkscrew. 'You can have first swig,' he said, 'as you're doing the pushing.'

'Thanks.' Alan took a drink from the bottle and screwed up his face. 'It tastes like communion wine,' he said.

'Does it? I'm a Methodist and we use blackcurrant cordial. What are you?'

'C of E.'

Harry took in the information and said, 'You know what they say, don't you?'

'What do they say?'

' "Church for ale and chapel for tail." But you don't drink a lot, do you?'

'No, but I bet you've kept the chapel tradition going.'

'No, I haven't. The lasses where I live are all well brought up. They want a wedding ring on their finger before they'll allow liberties. Mind you, if a willing woman walked up to me now I'd turn her down in favour of some of this bully beef. Me stomach thinks me mouth's on strike.'

It seemed that not even pain could inhibit Harry's appetite. 'You're the one with both hands free,' Alan told him.

'Fair enough. It's just as well these cans come with a key to open 'em. I bet you haven't got one of them on your penknife.'

'It has everything else you need.'

'So it has. You're a good scout. That's what posh folk say in the pictures, isn't it?'

'Yes, but I don't think it has anything to do with the boy scouts. It's more likely to be a reference to the college servants at Oxford. They're called "scouts" and they're always doing favours for undergraduates.'

Harry offered him a chunk of bully beef on the end of his knife. 'Didn't you have them at Cambridge?'

'Thanks. Yes, but we called them "bedders" because they made the beds, among other.... Oh good, I can see the junction ahead. I'll get you on to that main road.'

'As I said, Prof, you're a good bedder.' He yelped as the invalid chair negotiated another pothole.

'Chin up, Harry. We'll soon be there.'

'What I don't understand is why you're doing this.'

'Why I'm doing what?'

'You know, pushing me in this bloody contraption.'

'I'm doing it because if you try to walk it'll open up that wound and you'll bleed all over France.'

Harry groaned again, partly in impatience. 'You know what I mean. Why are you dragging me along when you could get there a hell of a lot quicker on your own?'

'I like to have company on a journey.'

Harry craned his head round and saw that Alan was serious. 'You're not going to give me an honest answer, are you?'

'No.'

As they came to the crossroads a woman in the now-familiar dark-brown peasant clothing approached them.

'*Monsieur*,' she said to Alan, '*avez-vous, peut être, d'eau, sil vous plaît?*'

'*Mais oui, madame.*' He offered her his water bottle and she drank from it gratefully. '*Merci beaucoup, monsieur,*' she said, handing it back to him. '*Vous êtes trés gentil.*'

She told him she was going to live with her sister just outside Dunkirk, and he felt sorry for her because she believed she would be safe there from the Germans. It seemed that the old blimps at the War Office weren't the only people who believed in fairies.

Alan hung her bags from the invalid chair and they walked along chatting, with Alan translating for Harry's benefit. After a while Harry commented on the column of black smoke on the horizon and the old woman enlightened him sadly.

'*Voilà Dunkerque, monsieur.*' She sounded terribly disillusioned. Alan, however, was in two minds. The smoke and the noise of shelling or bombing were far from encouraging, but at least they were travelling in the right direction.

At the next junction the Frenchwoman announced that she must leave them as her sister lived only a short distance away. Almost tearfully she thanked them for the water and their company. '*Bonne chance, messieurs,*' she said.

'*Et vous, madame. Bonne chance.*'

Harry asked, 'How many languages do you know, Prof?'

'French, German and Italian.'

'What about all that Roman stuff you told me about?'

'Latin and Greek don't count.'

'I'm not so sure, mate. It seems to me you never know who we're going to meet on this trip.'

'You're right there,' said Alan, looking in the direction the old woman had taken. 'I don't know who these blokes are, but they're in good shape.' After some of the weary examples they'd seen on the retreat, the newcomers who joined them at the crossroads looked as if they were about to go on parade.

Alan spoke to their corporal. 'What outfit are you, Corporal?'

'We're the Lifeguards, mate, and we're on our way to Dunkirk. We must be among the last. They say they've been evacuating for a week now and we don't want to miss the boat.' He laughed self-consciously and added, 'And I mean that literally.'

'Just follow the smoke, Corporal.'

'That's what I thought.' He gave them an apologetic look and said, 'I'd invite you to join us but I think you'd struggle to keep up.'

'I'm sure we would, Corporal. Good luck.'

'Good luck, mate.' The Lifeguards moved off along the side of the road, and the refugees, who had so far ignored all fellow travellers, made room for them.

'You've got to admire their spirit,' said Harry, wincing again as the chair jolted over a hole in the road. 'Even the Frogs respect them.'

'What a balls-up, though. Whether it was the politicians, the General Staff or whoever was responsible for this shambles, they really know how to betray the most loyal and trusting of men.'

As they approached the town, the foul, acrid stench of smoke became stronger and it was evident that the oil refinery was ablaze. Dunkirk was a scene of devastation.

Refugees were gradually drifting away to their various destinations and before long Alan and Harry encountered more army personnel, both British and French. They were weary and dishevelled and they all shared the same haunted look.

They also passed motor transport now stationary at the roadside. A sergeant of the Royal Army Service Corps was directing drivers to immobilise their transport.

'Just let the oil out and leave the engine running,' he told them. 'Don't leave anything for Jerry.' Then his eye fell on Alan and Harry. 'What's your unit, lads?'

'Royal Signals, Sergeant, attached to the Second Infantry Division. Our lorry was strafed and our officer and corporal were killed.'

'Oh? How far have you come?'

'About twelve miles, Sergeant.'

The sergeant was impressed. 'Good man. Well done. There's only this road open into the town. You'll find naval beach parties there and they'll direct you to the beaches at La Panne.' Looking at Harry's bloodstained bandage, he added, 'You'll find a dressing station on the sea-front. It's marked with big red crosses so you can't miss it.' He grimaced as a shell screamed overhead, and said, 'You just have to hope the Germans do.'

They continued down the road in company with the silent procession of men through the smoking remains of the ancient port, and followed the directions of a junior naval officer. They found the party of armed ratings reassuring. It was evidence that a kind of order still existed.

Eventually they reached the sea front with its baffling kaleidoscope of ships and boats, and the sprawl of khaki-clad humanity that had been the BEF.

❦

Jack was surprised to learn that the evacuation had been going on for six days when *Wrathful* arrived at Dunkirk. It was on the following day, however, that success came in the shape of two Stukas destroyed. The port pom-pom crew claimed the first but had to share the second with Tug Wilson. Jack was pleased for him but he was still eager to claim another. He'd never considered himself at all aggressive until that first raid, when he'd seen men helpless on the beach and at the mercy of the attacking aircraft. Now he was as keen as anyone to bring one down.

There were more opportunities as fresh waves of Stukas attacked the ships waiting off-shore. Again and again the Captain turned *Wrathful* this way and that to avoid the falling bombs, and Jack tried repeatedly to train his guns on the climbing aircraft. Eventually he managed to line up his sights on a promising target and had opened fire when he felt a savage blow against his right shoulder. A second or so later he was hurled forward against the gun mounting, and at that point he lost consciousness.

❦

A tired and harassed-looking Lieutenant looked down at Harry's bandaged leg and said, 'Leave him here. I'll get someone to clean his wound and dress it. The rest will be up to the Germans when they arrive.'

It wasn't what Alan wanted to hear. 'With respect, sir—'

'I really haven't time to argue.'

'I can't leave him, sir. I have to get him home.'

67

'I'm sorry. They're only taking walking wounded. The Germans will be obliged to look after him.'

Desperation prompted boldness. 'As long as I can hold him upright, sir,' he insisted, 'he's walking wounded.'

The surgeon wiped his brow with his hand. 'In that case, my friend, on your head be it. Come back for him in....' He glanced wearily at the patients waiting for treatment. 'Come back in a couple of hours.'

Now thoroughly tired and footsore, Alan walked down to the sand dunes with the intention of simply lying down and resting. There he found men sleeping, talking in groups or just sitting in silence, seemingly too tired even to talk. Incredibly, though, four men were putting the others to shame by playing a game of 3-card brag, which they did with intense concentration until someone shouted, 'Take cover! The bastards are back!'

Alan flung himself into the nearest hollow and flattened himself against the ground, gouging the sand with his fingers in a pitiful effort to dig himself further into the hollow. All he could hear was the screaming sirens of the Stukas, the rattle of machine-gunfire and the deafening crash as each bomb exploded.

Some of them fell terrifyingly close, so that with each blast he felt a rush of air over the dunes that served as the only protection. Grimly he held on, praying for the bombardment to cease.

Eventually the Stukas departed, leaving behind them the cries and moans of the wounded punctuated by urgent calls for stretcher bearers.

Alan brushed the sand from his face and opened his eyes, surprised to find a man beside him.

'Hello marrer,' said the man, also dusting himself off. 'I'm Wilkie, Second Durham Light Infantry. Who are you?'

'Alan Lofthouse, Royal Signals.' It seemed ridiculous in the circumstances, and relief must have had a lot to do with it, but he offered his hand, which was still shaking. 'My friends call me "Prof".'

'You must be a clever man,' said Wilkie, shaking his hand. 'How long have you been here, Prof?'

'We just arrived today. My mate's in the dressing station.'

'We've only just arrived an' all. What a bloody welcome that was.'

Alan nodded his heartfelt agreement. Where d' you come from?'

'We were part of the rear-guard on the River Dyle over in Belgium. We held Jerry there for two days before they ordered us to withdraw. What a bloody shambles.' He shook his head at the memory of it.

'I meant where in England.'

'Oh, I see. I'm from Sunderland. Maybe you've heard of it.'

'Where?' It sounded like 'Soondlnd,' but then he recognised the name in spite of the Wearside accent. 'Oh, Sunderland. They build ships there, don't they?'

'Well, they're maybe buildin' some now, and not before time, I'd say. I was a fitter in the shipyards but I spent more time out of work than I did bringin' a wage into the house. What about you?'

'I'm from Cullington in Yorkshire. I was at university before the war.' He was almost ashamed to admit it to a man who'd been unemployed, and he was surprised when Wilkie received the information philosophically.

'I don't blame you, marrer. I don't know the first thing about it except that it beats bein' on the dole.'

Alan was studying the lines of men that stretched down to the beach, and the makeshift jetties formed by half-submerged motor vehicles. 'There must be a system of some kind down there,' he said, 'but it's hard to see how it works.'

'On the beach, d' you mean? Why aye, there's a system all right. As the boats pick 'em up we move down there an' take our turn. It won't take all that long because we're the tail-end now. They've evacuated most of the BEF.' He waved his hand vaguely over the dunes and the beach and said, 'Most of these lads have been pulled out of the rear-guard, same as my unit was.' He indicated a group of men in a neighbouring dune. 'That lot are Green Howards. They were holding part of the Dunkirk perimeter until the Welsh Guards relieved them. That's how tail-end we are.'

'Do you think we stand a chance?'

'Of bein' picked up, you mean? Well, I can't see the Navy lettin' us down.'

'Can't you?' Being let down had become so distressingly familiar that Alan couldn't help but be sceptical.

'Looking at the way the army's buggered things up, I reckon the

Navy's got to pull the irons out of the fire, and they've not done a bad job so far.' He looked up at the sky and added, 'I don't know if we've still got an air force. If we have an' they've been over, it must have been when I was havin' a pee or somethin', 'cause I seem to have missed it.'

Alan was disinclined to argue. Unlike Wilkie, he wasn't at all confident they would be evacuated before the Germans arrived, and the reason for the apparent absence of fighters was a mystery to him too. He looked at his watch and said, 'I'd better go to the dressing station and see if they've finished with Harry.'

'All right, marrer. I'll keep your place.'

Alan walked back over the dunes and up the bank to the dressing station, where he found a number of men on the grass outside. They were all bandaged or splinted, and he was surprised to see one of them in an invalid chair that looked very similar to Harry's. When he looked more closely he realised it was the same chair. He was about to demand an explanation, but checked himself when he realised that its new occupant had bandaged stumps for legs.

'Prof!' The shout came from near the entrance to the dressing station, where Harry sat on the grass, now re-bandaged and holding a pair of crutches. 'I let 'em take the wheelchair,' he said. 'The poor bugger who's in it now is waiting for Jerry to come and take him prisoner, God help him.'

'He should be all right,' said Alan. 'There are rules about the treatment of prisoners.'

'There are rules about bombing and strafing poor, defenceless buggers like us but I haven't noticed Jerry bein' all that law-abidin'.'

'There's a chap saving a place for us in the dunes,' Alan told him. 'It's just a matter of taking our turn. We should be picked up by a ship at the mole or by one of the small boats.' He hoped he sounded more confident than he felt.

'Like Mr Bourne said, let's hope the Navy knows its arse from its elbow.'

Gently, Alan helped him to his feet and half-carried him down to the hollow, where he introduced him to Wilkie. Their arrival was timely, because they'd only just settled in when they heard someone shout, 'Take cover!' The Stukas were back.

Jack could see very little beyond the deckhead light. His head hurt abominably and his right shoulder felt as if someone were twisting a knife inside it. As he was lying in a bunk, he could only deduce he was in the sick bay, a suspicion that was confirmed when a sick berth attendant leaned over him to ask, 'Are you all right, mate?'

'I think so. What happened?'

'There was a near miss. The bomb exploded on our port side and you must have been thrown against a bulkhead or something. That's a hell of a black eye you're brewing. You look as if you've been five rounds with Joe Louis.' More professionally he added, 'The Surgeon Lieutenant's seen you and he'll be back when he can. He's got his hands full just now.'

'My shoulder hurts like hell.'

'I'm not surprised. You also stopped a bullet from one of the Stukas.'

'So that's what it was.'

The SBA, who was particular about details, corrected himself. 'Well, you didn't exactly stop it. It went straight through you. I've dressed the wound as well as I can but you'll have to go to hospital.' Then, like a parent promising a treat by way of consolation, he said, 'You're bound to get leave.'

It made no sense to Jack. 'How am I going to hospital,' he asked, 'when we're less than a mile off the French coast?'

'Ah, that's where we were when the bomb went off, but a lot happened while you were having your zizz. That near miss did a lot of damage. The Engine Room Branch shored things up and they've been able to keep us afloat, but *Wrathful*'s been ordered back to Dover.' He broke off to acknowledge an impassioned request from another patient and said to Jack, 'I'll see you later, mate. That bloke needs attention.' He added, 'Not everyone got off as lightly as you.'

Alan had only catnapped through the night, partly because of the cold and discomfort but mainly because of his concern for Harry. Blood had continued to seep through the dressing and his friend screwed up his eyes and bit his lip frequently to prevent himself crying out with pain.

The evacuation had continued through the night and there had been a regular procession of men along the mole, where the larger vessels were embarking them with commendable swiftness. Accordingly, Alan, Harry, Wilkie and some of the Green Howards moved down to the water's edge. Men were picking their way along the lines of vehicles that the naval parties had run into the sea, but it was out of the question for Harry. Instead, they waited for a boat to come inshore, thankful in their exposed position that for once the *Luftwaffe* was sleeping late.

Before long, two cabin cruisers slipped into position about twenty-five feet from the water's edge and their owners issued the long-awaited invitation.

'I can take a dozen.' The gentlemanly offer came from a grey-haired man in the nearer of the boats.

'Come on, Harry. Put your arm round my shoulder.' Being a tall man, Alan stooped to make it possible, but for the diminutive Wilkie there was no need. Instead he said, 'Lean on me, marrer, an' just leave everythin' to Prof an' me.'

Together they trawled him through the unhelpful shallows until eventually they reached the boat.

'We have a wounded man here,' Alan told the owner. 'If we come on board first we can pull him up.'

The grey-haired man offered a hand to each of them and they climbed gratefully aboard while Harry clung fiercely to one of the deck cleats.

With some difficulty they hoisted him aboard. The Green Howards followed and soon the boat was full. Its owner revved up the engine and took over the wheel from a boy who couldn't have been more than fifteen.

'I'm Henry Barrett,' the owner told them. He wore sea-boots, corduroy trousers and a seaman's jersey but his accent told of a gentler existence. 'My young friend William insisted on coming along to crew for me. It makes a change from delivering groceries, doesn't it, William?'

The boy's exhausted grin confirmed that it did.

'I'll see if I can get you aboard one of the ships. If I can't we'll just have to join the convoy.'

Alan asked, 'How long have you been here, Mr Barrett?'

'Three days, maybe four. We've lost track of time, but we came as soon as we heard the appeal. We're a little under the thirty-foot minimum but we didn't see why a technicality should prevent us from lending a hand.' He glanced over his shoulder towards the emptying beach and said, 'I think the job's nearly done, don't you?'

'Incredibly, yes, I do.'

Harry had fallen asleep, but Wilkie was groaning. 'I'm goin' to be sick,' he told them. 'I'm always seasick.'

'Be thankful you're at sea,' Alan told him, 'because, against all the odds, we're finally on our way home.'

11

'This is very nice,' said Rachel, sizing up the bedroom like a
parent relieved that her newly-independent offspring has
found somewhere suitable to live.

'My son and my daughter were both keen to have me stay with
them but I preferred to come to this place as it's only for a few
weeks. My family sometimes make me feel like an invalid and I'm
really quite robust.'

'What a lovely word, Kate. I suppose you are quite robust. I
hadn't really thought about it.'

'I only gave up cycling when I was seventy-six, and that was
because I'd no one to keep me company.'

Rachel scanned the photographs on the chest of drawers and
her eye came to rest on one of a very young naval officer. She
touched it and said, 'That's Jack, isn't it?'

'Yes, that one was taken by a photographer in Hove shortly after
he got his commission.'

'When was that?'

Kate studied for a moment and said, 'It would be about three
or four months after he returned from Dunkirk. He was wounded,
you know, and he had to get fit again before he could begin his
officer training. He was very frustrated, and I'm afraid he wasn't
the only one. It was an unsettling and uncertain time for most of us,
that period after Dunkirk.' She closed her eyes to revisit the events
of that summer. They seemed so fresh in her mind that she was
reluctant to break the spell.

After a while Rachel asked her, 'Do you want to rest?'

'No, no, I'm fine. I get carried away with memories. You know how one leads to a whole string of them.'

'It must have been awful.'

'It was for some. You have to remember that not all the soldiers returned from France. A great many were killed and many more were taken prisoner. Most of them spent the next five years in captivity.'

'Five years.' It wasn't surprising that it challenged Rachel's imagination.

'And for the rest of us there was the threat of invasion. The first thing that happened was that the ringing of church bells was stopped.'

'I heard about that.'

'Yes, they were to be rung only as a warning of invasion.' Memories were coming quickly now. 'Children had already been evacuated from London and other cities, and sent, for good or ill, to live with families in the country. The rest of us prepared for the worst. We all had gasmasks, you know. We'd been carrying them since the outbreak of war.'

'Really?'

'Yes. If an air-raid warden or a policeman saw you without your gasmask you could expect trouble. Poison gas had been used so freely in the Great War that everyone expected the Germans to drop gas bombs. They never did, but the explosive ones and the incendiaries were bad enough.' She paused again, remembering. 'My father and Jack's father had both served in the First World War and they joined the Local Defence Volunteers. I imagine you'll have seen "Dad's Army".'

'Yes, it's very funny.'

'It is, but apparently it wasn't quite like that. They took their training very seriously and men who were really too old for that kind of thing had to spend nights on patrol after a full day's work, sometimes in awful weather. It was often anything but funny.'

'You said Jack was frustrated. Why was that?'

'Oh, he just felt that he'd been unable to make his contribution to the Dunkirk evacuation. To be wounded and hospitalised after just two days was galling for him, and he couldn't wait to go back into action. He was always impulsive.' She smiled, remembering some of his more precipitate moments, before collecting her thoughts again. 'Mind you, I think it was worse for Alan, as it must have been for a lot of Dunkirk veterans.'

12

Jack attempted to rearrange the soft cushion his mother had given him, but without success.

'Anything I can do?' Alan left his seat to help him.

'Oh yes, please. Would you mind moving this cushion up so that's behind my shoulder? The blasted thing keeps slipping down.'

'Of course.' He lifted the cushion and held it in place while Jack leaned against it.

'That's better. Thanks, Alan.'

'What's better?' Jack's mother came into the room with a tray of tea things. In honour of Jack's homecoming and Alan's visit she'd taken out the best china service, an honour usually reserved for guests, Christmas, Easter, Whitsuntide and Harvest Festival.

'I was just making Jack comfortable, Mrs Farthing,' said Alan, returning to his chair.

'Oh, that's nice, and it was good of you to come. You must have had a rotten time over there as well. I remember how worried your mum was 'til she got the postcard from Dover. Mind you,' she confided, 'I was no better.'

'It wasn't too bad, Mrs Farthing. We came home in one piece, and that's the main thing.'

'Well, I'm glad to see you back. I'll leave you lads to talk. Let the tea stand for a minute or so before you pour it.'

'I'll do that. Thank you, Mrs Farthing.'

Alone again, the two men looked at each other in silence for maybe half a minute, during which the telephone rang in the hall. They both ignored it, and then eventually Alan spoke.

'They say they brought back more than a third of a million of us, counting the French.'

'It was unbelievable.'

'When they got us on board the destroyer the deck was crammed full of us. I remember one of the French chaps next to me had tears in his eyes as we left. He'd no idea when he was going to see his homeland again.' He paused, recalling the scene. 'I can't tell you how ashamed we felt when we landed at Dover, Jack. The British army had just suffered the worst defeat in its history, and suddenly the Salvation Army and WVS were giving us sandwiches and mugs of tea as if we'd just won a battle, and people came to the station as well and gave us things out of their rations that must have left them with nothing.'

'Maybe they realised it wasn't the army's fault. My skipper told me the Germans had perfected a new kind of high-speed warfare. No one was ready for that or for anything else, I imagine, after years of disarmament.'

Alan nodded his agreement. 'During all that time only Churchill had the right idea, and they called him a warmonger. What do you think, Jack? Do you reckon he's the man for the job?' He lifted the teapot lid and satisfied himself that the tea was brewed.

'Yes, I do.' It seemed strange that Alan should ask for his opinion. It was as if he didn't trust his own judgement, which was most unlike him.

'I'm inclined to think he's the only man for the job.'

'He's made mistakes, it's true, but he has one thing Chamberlain and Lord Halifax lack, and that's fighting spirit.' He tried to lean forward, but Alan stopped him.

'Stay where you are, Jack, I'll bring it to you.' He added milk to Jack's tea and handed it to him. 'Apparently, in his maiden speech as Prime Minister he spoke about victory.' He shook his head in disbelief. 'But at least he's being positive.'

'My dad says that if he's convinced himself of something he's got the ability to make everyone believe it.'

'Maybe things really will change now.'

'And maybe we'll stop trying to shoot down Stukas with weapons from the last war.'

Jack's mother interrupted their conjecturing by opening the door and saying, 'That was Katherine Whitehead on the telephone, Jack. She's got some time off and she's coming to visit you later on. I told her how you were getting on and how you have to see the Admiralty surgeon to have your stitches out, and she said something I didn't quite understand about soaking your bandages off before you go. I've no doubt she'll tell you what she meant.' Still puzzled, she asked, 'Where are you going to find an Admiralty surgeon round here? We're miles from the sea.'

'There's one in Bradford, Mum. He has a surgery near the Royal Infirmary. He's just an ordinary family doctor, but the Admiralty pay him a retainer to look after blokes on leave.'

'Oh, I see. Well, you can talk about that with Katherine when she comes.'

'One thing I've kept wondering,' said Alan when Mrs Farthing had left the room, 'is why the RAF was so conspicuous by its absence over Dunkirk. Some of the chaps there got quite bloodthirsty about it but I'm inclined to think there must have been a good reason for it.'

'Our skipper mentioned that on the way across. He said the RAF had only a few airfields that could operate fighters at that range. It makes sense, doesn't it? And then someone else I met in hospital told me he'd seen Hurricanes attacking German bombers over Ostend, no doubt trying to stop them before they got to Dunkirk. At all events they must have been spread pretty thinly.'

Veterans of the evacuation said that only those who'd been there had any idea of what it was like. Alan and Jack had both experienced it and it was good for them to talk. What they most needed now, though, was a distraction, and for Jack that began just a few hours later when Kate arrived.

⚓

Just the sight of her, pretty, smiling and full of good humour was the pick-me-up he needed. She leaned forward to avoid touching his fragile torso and gave him a friendly kiss on the cheek.

'Welcome home, sailor.'

'Thanks, Kate. Let me take your hat and coat.'

'Don't worry about that. I don't want you stretching and hurting yourself.'

'I'll be all right.'

Jack's mother forestalled further argument by hanging them up for her.

'Thank you, Mrs Farthing. Do you mind if I use your bathroom?'

'Of course not. You know where it is, don't you?'

'It's not that. I just want to change Jack's dressing and we're probably better doing it in there where we've got access to hot water.'

'Oh, I see. Well, help yourself. Is there anything you need?'

'No thanks, I've got everything here.' She held a haversack marked with a red cross. 'Oh, by the way, Mrs Farthing, Dorothy Needham's coming later but we'll most likely be finished by the time she arrives.'

'Oh, that'll be nice.' Jack's mother was wary of Dorothy, particularly where her son was concerned, but on this occasion she no doubt welcomed her visit for his sake.

'Come on, Jack.' Kate led the way up to the bathroom.

Jack followed uncertainly. He asked, 'Why are we doing this, Kate?'

'There'll be congealed blood under that dressing,' she told him, 'and most doctors haven't time to do what I'm going to do, which is to soak it off. That way it won't hurt.'

'I see.' He sat obediently on the cork-lidded box and allowed her to unbutton and remove his shirt. He'd received similar treatment from nurses in hospital, but it felt strange to be undressed, albeit down to the waist, by someone he remembered as a little girl at school. He'd had a number of new experiences recently and this was the latest, but it was by no means unpleasant. Bossy she might be, but she was very gentle, easing his shirt away from his right arm, and then replacing the sling.

'This must be where the bullet came out.' She touched the scarred flesh behind his shoulder.

'That's right.'

'It made an awful mess, worse than where it went in.' She ran water into the hand basin and soaked a cotton-wool pad in it before applying it to the dressing.

'It's very good of you to do this, Kate,' he said, wincing only a little.

'Not at all, I'm just keeping my hand in.' She rinsed the pad and applied it again. 'Your mum said something on the telephone about being mentioned in dispatches. What does that mean?'

'Oh, the Captain mentioned me in his official report after Norway. It'll go down on my service documents as a pat on the back.'

'Come on, spill the beans. What did you do?'

'I shot down an enemy dive-bomber but it was more by luck than skill.'

'Oh, I like a modest hero.'

'I'm not a hero, Kate, just a bloke doing his duty.'

'But you're modest, and that's good.' She tweaked at the dressing and gave it another application of warm water.

'A little bird told me something about you,' he said with a sly note in his voice.

'Oh, what was that?'

'It was about you and Maurice, actually.'

'That's right,' she laughed. 'That came as a surprise to most people.'

'Not to me.'

'Didn't it?' She peeled the dressing away so that he hardly felt it. 'You hadn't been around long enough to notice anything.'

'I saw the way you two looked at each other after the meeting at the Bay Horse. Romance was definitely abroad.'

'And now I suppose you're going to tease me about it.'

'No, I'm not. You're right for each other.'

'Thank you, Jack.'

'You're welcome.' He felt a small tweak. 'What was that?'

'That was the last of your stitches. I've just taken them out. The wound has healed beautifully so I'm just going to put some padding over it to protect it. Are you okay with sticking plaster? Not allergic or sensitive to it?'

'I use it all the time.'

'*All* the time?'

'Yes, I'm accident prone.'

'In that case,' she said, peeling off a length of sticking plaster, 'you'd better go very carefully when you show your scars to the doctor. Look both ways before you cross the road and keep a sharp look out for street lamps, especially in the black-out.' She laughed. 'Maurice collided with the telephone kiosk when he went out to phone me on his last leave.'

'It must have been the excitement. When's he likely to be home again?'

'At the end of this month, we hope. After that he'll join an operational squadron, so it'll be anybody's guess when his next leave will be.'

'I hope I'm still here when he comes home, just for a quick word between lovers' trysts.'

'I get precious little time off, so I'm afraid trysts will be rare and fleeting.' She finished dabbing him with a towel and picked up his shirt. 'Right, it's time to get dressed.'

'Thanks again, Kate.'

'It's no trouble. Give me your right arm first. That's right.'

Dressing felt easier without the bandages, and before long they were downstairs.

'The Surgeon-Commander said I was very lucky,' he told her as they sat down, 'but it was bad enough.'

'Maybe he meant that the bullet could have done a lot more damage. An inch lower and it would have pierced your lung. That wouldn't have been funny.'

'It just nicked the top of the lung, apparently.'

'In that case you should be thankful for small mercies.' She added with a smile, 'I suppose I qualify as a small mercy.'

'You're an angel of mercy.'

'And you're a smooth-talking scoundrel. Wait 'til Dot gets here. You'll be all over her and you'll forget I exist.'

'I'll never do that, Kate.'

'Famous last words.'

As if to test his resolve, the doorbell rang. 'That'll be Dot,' said Kate getting up, but Mrs Farthing was there before her.

'You have another visitor, Jack,' she announced a minute later, showing Dorothy into the sitting room.

'Jack,' said Dorothy, inclining her cheek but avoiding his sling-bound arm, 'what on earth have you been up to?'

'It wasn't my fault, Dot. Come and sit down.'

'I expected you to be swathed in bandages, with maybe a hole to breathe through.'

'My chest was thoroughly bandaged but Kate very kindly changed all that. She even took my stitches out.'

Dorothy pulled a face. 'I'm glad I wasn't here, but it's good that you did that for him, Kate.'

She was as appealing as ever in a navy-blue polka dot dress, although Jack couldn't help visualising her in the uniform of one of the women's services, preferably the WRNS. The black stockings were very persuasive.

If she were aware of his scrutiny she gave no sign of it, but chatted in her usual way.

'I've just come from a Women's Institute meeting at the Temperance Hall,' she told them.

Kate's eyes opened wide in amusement. 'I don't believe it.'

'Oh Kate, can you really see me baking cakes and making jam?'

'No.'

'Neither can I. I went with my mother because they had no one to play "Jerusalem" on the piano. Apparently it's their anthem and they sing it at every meeting. I did it for them but I don't fancy it as a regular job.'

'Maybe you should join the forces,' suggested Jack, still clinging to his mental picture. 'That would get you away from their clutches.'

'I may do that, but first I want to hear what you've been up to. We haven't seen you since September, and everyone but you has been home on leave. Where've you been hiding?'

It was one of those moments that, had he been able, Jack would have preserved for all time. After the grim reality of the past three months here he was with Kate, so caring and capable, and Dorothy, who'd never taken anything seriously in her life. Together they provided the ideal tonic.

'I've been to Portsmouth and all over the Atlantic, then to

Norway and France.' Relaxed though he felt, he was reluctant to say much more.

'Pretty much like your civilian job, then?'

'Almost the same,' he agreed.

'I nearly forgot,' said Kate conveniently. 'Have you seen Mary since you came home? She must have had the baby by now.'

'She brought him to see us yesterday. He's six weeks old.' It had been good to see Mary, but the baby had cried the whole time he was there. It wasn't a restful experience for a brand-new uncle in convalescence.

'Lovely.' Mary had been a staff nurse at the infirmary when Kate was in the first year of her training. 'What's he called?'

'George.'

'Is that all?'

'George Albert Edward, but I can't see him owning up to all those names when he's older.'

'I'm sure the King would feel flattered,' said Dorothy. 'I wonder how many Winstons will be born this year or next. I can't imagine there'll be many Nevilles. Can you?'

Kate was still enjoying Mary's firstborn. She asked, 'Who does he look like?'

'I don't know, Kate. They all look the same to me.'

'Isn't that just like a man? They have no soul where babies are concerned.'

'I take some enthusing as well,' admitted Dorothy. 'Maybe it will creep up on me one day and I'll be vitally interested in names, birth weights and baby clothes, but for now I'll leave all that to you, Kate.'

'I had another visitor this afternoon,' Jack told them. 'Alan was here.'

'What was he like?' The question came from Dorothy. 'He'd undergone a sort of sea-change the last time we saw him, hadn't he, Kate?'

'He was certainly different.'

'I was very surprised,' said Jack. 'It was good to sit and talk with him. Did you know he'd pushed a wounded man twelve miles to Dunkirk in an ancient wheelchair?'

'Did he?' Clearly, Dorothy was astonished.

'He wasn't boasting. He told me about it very matter-of-factly, although it was obviously important to him. He told me the man was his first and only friend in the army. He felt he had to get him back to Blighty.'

'He did say the army had taught him a lot,' said Kate thoughtfully.

'Well I never,' said Dorothy, equally thoughtful. 'Good for him.'

It was something to think about, although they discussed other topics as well, and by the time the girls got up to leave Jack felt quite revived.

As they prepared to go, Dorothy said in her mischievous way, 'Are you ready, Kate? You take the right cheek and I'll take the left.' They kissed him together, and that felt good too.

⊕┈3┈╬┈3┈╠⊛

The experience of Dunkirk had done more for Alan than he had at first realised. Most importantly it had given him a growing sense of self-belief far removed from the old veneer of superiority that still embarrassed him whenever he was reminded of it. Getting Harry from the scene of the burned-out lorry to Mr Barrett's cabin cruiser and finally on board *HMS Sabre* had given him more satisfaction than anything else he could remember, and that included his double-first at Cambridge. He and Harry had naturally exchanged home addresses before parting.

Life was better for another reason too, but that had begun before Dunkirk, when he was on embarkation leave. It was the last time he and Dorothy had met, and the hopelessness of his cause had finally come home to him. He had no idea how it happened. He only knew that it had been surprisingly painless. More than that, it was as if he'd been relieved of a great worry, and he'd boarded the troopship in a more contented state of mind than he'd known for some time.

At around the time Kate and Dorothy were taking their leave of Jack, Alan emerged from the Regal Cinema in Cullington. He'd sat through a crass, upbeat newsreel item about Dunkirk that he'd found irritating, but the main film was *Over the Moon*, starring Rex Harrison and Merle Oberon, and its carefree, pre-war innocence had more than made up for the newsreel.

As others stepped gingerly into the blacked-out street, a girl beside him stumbled over the kerb and was about to fall into the road. He grasped her arm to support her and asked if she was all right.

'Yes, thanks,' she gasped, regaining her balance. 'If you hadn't caught me I'd have measured my length.' She was smiling, and the girl who was with her smiled more broadly and said, 'You're Alan Lofthouse, aren't you?'

'That's right.' He failed completely to recognise her.

'I'm Iris Rush and this is my friend Muriel. We both work at the Town Hall.' She studied his blank face and said, 'You still can't place me, can you? You helped me once with my Latin translation.' Turning to Muriel she said, 'It was the best grade I ever got.'

Recognition dawned. 'Iris, of course. I'm sorry.'

'Well, I expect you've had more things to think about lately than who you were at school with. Anyway, it was nice to see you again.'

'Wait a minute. Are you going to catch a bus?'

'No, we're walking.'

'But you can't walk home alone in the black-out.'

'It's only five minutes up the road, and there are two of us. Muriel lives not far from me.'

'All the same, let me see you home.'

Iris looked at Muriel and the decision was made. 'Well, only if it's not too far out of your way. It's very kind of you.'

'Not at all.'

As they walked, they talked about the film and other films they'd seen. Apparently Iris and Muriel went to the pictures almost every week, and Muriel went sometimes with her boyfriend, who also worked for the council and was waiting to be called up. She gave him that information in case he thought her boyfriend was a shirker, which he certainly wasn't, she assured him.

Iris asked, 'Where are you based, Alan?'

'They haven't let me in on the secret yet.'

'What do you mean?'

'I've just got back from Dunkirk,' he explained. 'I have to report to Swalebridge on Monday. After that it's anyone's guess what they've got in store for me.'

'Dunkirk?' Iris sounded shocked. 'It must have been awful.'

'It wasn't too bad,' he told her, 'but it wasn't quite as jolly as they made out in that newsreel.'

'I never pay any attention to them,' she said. 'Most of 'em are daft anyway.'

They stopped at the end of the next street. It was where Muriel lived and she thanked Alan again.

'See you in the morning,' said Iris.

She and Alan walked on. 'I live in Holdsworth Street, just round the corner,' she said. 'Would you like to come in? Everyone'll be in bed by now but I can offer you a cup of tea. It's the least I can do.'

'I'd like that. Yes, please.'

When they reached the house, Iris opened the door with her latch key and put a finger to her lips, a warning that turned out to be in vain, because a woman's voice came from the upstairs landing, where she could be seen dimly.

'Is that you, Iris?'

'Yes, Mum. I've brought a soldier home. I'm going to run away with him as soon as I've packed my bags.'

'All right, love. Good night.'

'Good night.' Iris shook her head. 'She's quite deaf. I was shushing you because of my little brother. Mind you, the cat's out of the bag now. He'll want to know all about you in the morning.' She switched on the light and said, 'Come through to the kitchen and I'll put the kettle on.'

Alan followed her and took a seat at the deal table while she made tea.

'What did you do,' she asked, 'before you were called up?'

It seemed to follow him around like a shadow. 'I was at university,' he said. He'd long since stopped referring to it by name.

'It was a silly question, wasn't it? You always came over at school as a lad with a bright future.'

'I may have given that impression, Iris, but I sometimes wonder if I'm all that clever.'

'You got me an A-plus for Latin translation.'

He couldn't argue with that. 'Okay,' he said, 'now it's my turn. What do you do at the Town Hall?'

'I'm in the typing pool. I take shorthand and type letters for bossy, self-important civil servants, but the job isn't without its laughs. We get the low-down on everybody. We know who's working a fiddle, who's having an affair, who's got his eye on the Borough Treasurer's job, and just about everything. You can't beat it for gossip.' She laughed. 'I bet you think I'm awful.'

'No, I don't.' As she put the teapot on the table, he saw her under the kitchen light. She was far from awful; in fact she was rather attractive. She had long, brown hair with what looked like a natural wave, and small, regular features, but most pleasing of all from Alan's point of view was her smile, which was warm, genuine and, it seemed, seldom absent for long.

'It must be irritating,' she said, pouring out the tea, 'when you've come back from something like Dunkirk and you see one of those silly newsreels that get it all wrong.'

'It is,' he agreed. 'It's blatant propaganda and it's dishonest. Did you see those men giving the thumbs-up and winking at the camera?'

'Yes, I did. It looked false to me.'

'It was orchestrated. I saw the newsreel people arranging it as if they were shooting a comedy. Most of those blokes were hungry, thirsty and exhausted, and they deserved better than to be treated as performing monkeys.'

She passed the milk. 'Would you like to put your own in? You know how much you like.'

'Thanks. I shouldn't moan. I feel as if I'm abusing your hospitality.'

She shrugged good-naturedly. 'I asked you a question and you answered it. Anyway, when men like you go to war for us, it's only right for people like me to listen to you.' She cocked her head in thought and said, 'That wasn't quite right, was it? I usually mix up "I" and "me" and that kind of thing.'

'You got it right this time. Anyway, I know what you mean, and that's what really matters.' He stirred his tea, thinking about what he was going to ask her next. Eventually he said, 'Iris, have you got someone you, you know... a....' He was making an awful mess of it.

'A boyfriend?' She smiled. 'No such luck. There's a dearth of interesting men at the Town Hall.'

'I see. I wondered if you'd like to go to a dance on Saturday. I saw it advertised in the local paper.'

'The dance at the Town Hall?' She was laughing.

'Oh heck, I'd forgotten about that.'

'It's all right. At least I know my way there, and it's not like working, so don't worry. Yes, I'd like that very much.'

13

'Iris was a nice girl. She was just what Alan needed at the time.' Kate gave a reflective sigh. 'It was such an eventful summer. "A Nightingale Sang in Berkeley Square" was very popular just then. It had nothing to do with what was happening but it was a lovely song and it captured everyone's imagination. My generation have never forgotten it.'

'I'll find it and download it.'

'Make sure it's Anne Shelton and not one of the others.'

'Why?'

'Everyone recorded it, including all the usual suspects, but no one sang it quite like Anne Shelton.'

Rachel made a note in her diary and returned to the main topic. 'When did you know there wasn't going to be an invasion?'

'It was looking less likely by nineteen-forty-one, I suppose, but it wasn't until that summer that we began to relax.'

'I'm amazed you can remember these things in such detail.' Rachel was turning absently through one of Kate's photo albums.

'I told you before,' said Kate, 'Nineteen-forty is nothing like the problem for me that half-an-hour ago can be.' She watched Rachel as she turned the pages without apparently looking at the pictures, and said, 'You're not at your best today.'

'I'm sorry.' Rachel put the album back on the bedside table. 'It's my mother's birthday tomorrow.'

'How do you feel about that?'

'Confused, I suppose.'

'I've been meaning to ask you what your mother's condition

was that made her an invalid.'

'Oh, osteoarthritis, high blood pressure, diabetes.... She had a heart condition as well.'

'Do you know what the heart condition was?'

'No.' The familiar twitch returned. 'She always insisted on seeing the doctor alone.'

'I see. Osteoarthritis can be disabling but there is treatment to ease it, thank goodness, and I speak from experience. As for high blood pressure and diabetes, they can usually be managed with medication and diet. It's the heart condition that's the mystery. Tell me, what was the cause of her death?'

'It was a blood clot in the lungs.' The twitch became more pronounced. 'Prolonged inactivity was mentioned as the likely cause.'

Kate nodded. 'A pulmonary embolism. That's why they get hospital patients up and about as soon as they can nowadays.'

'My father spoiled her, you know. He was forever at her beck and call, pandering to her needs, and then when he died....'

'She expected you to take his place?'

'Yes.'

Kate took her hand and squeezed it. 'And all this time you've been feeling guilty for something that wasn't your fault.'

'I suppose I have.'

'You poor girl.' She looked towards the window and saw bright, blue sky. 'What are we doing,' she asked, 'sitting indoors on a day like this? Let's have a walk in the garden. Do you mind?'

'Not at all.' She offered a hand.

'Thank you, Rachel, but I need to do this for myself.' She levered herself upright and seized her crutches.

For some reason Rachel began to talk more easily in the garden.

'She was very manipulative. You'll have gathered that from what I've told you, but it was much easier to give in than to object. I always had that lurking worry that if I didn't take her seriously something might go terribly wrong. Do you know what I mean?'

Kate nodded.

'The guilt is so hard to shake off.'

'But you're not guilty of anything.' She stopped beside a flower bed and pointed with one of her crutches. 'Just look at these peonies. Aren't they lovely?' She continued to admire them for a while before saying, 'It's not for me to tell you how to live your life, Rachel, but don't you think you should decide what you're going to do with the rest of it?'

'I suppose so.' Then, in a way that had become familiar, she changed the subject completely and asked, 'What was so eventful about that summer?'

'Which summer, dear?'

'Nineteen-forty. You said it was such an eventful summer. You'd just told me about Iris and Alan.'

'Oh yes. Let's sit down for a while.' She eased herself on to the nearest bench. 'It's best not to sit for too long,' she confided. 'These benches leave ridges on your bottom that you can feel for hours.' After a moment to gather her thoughts she said, 'Yes, that summer Jack was told to report to a place in the south of England for officer training, and Maurice was granted forty-eight hours before joining his squadron near York. It could hardly have been more convenient for us.'

'How lovely.'

'It was.' She was thoughtful for a moment. 'But it was still an uncertain time. To begin with there was the Battle of Britain. From July to September the *Luftwaffe* tried its hardest to annihilate the RAF, which it had to before an invasion could take place. We saw nothing of it because it happened mainly over south-east England, but we read about it and heard reports on the wireless. It was very touch-and-go until well into September, as I recall, and then there was the air raid.' She lapsed into thoughtfulness again, each memory leading to another.

'Which air raid?'

'What?' She made an effort to marshal her wits.

'You mentioned an air raid during the summer of nineteen-forty.'

'Oh yes, that's right, the night they bombed Bradford.'

14

It was after eleven o'clock when the sirens sounded. There had been a couple of minor incidents within the past few weeks so no one took very much notice at first. It wasn't until the repeated *crump* of anti-aircraft guns could be heard coming from the east, followed by the steady, droning beat of multiple aircraft engines that it became obvious that a raid was imminent.

Kate reached for her steel helmet and checked that her gasmask was close at hand. Outside the hall an air-raid warden bellowed a warning to someone to take cover. A minute later he stood in the entrance to the hall, shouting urgently, 'Get ready! There's 'undreds of 'em!'

Kate's colleague Jessie Underwood, a woman in her thirties and one of the Civil Nursing Reserve, asked, 'How many?'

'I don't know for sure.'

'Well, go out an' count 'em and then you can come back and tell us.'

In spite of her natural anxiety, Kate smiled.

The warden gave them both a furious look before taking his warning somewhere where it might be taken more seriously.

' "Get ready," indeed. Did you hear that, Whitehead? Who does he think he is?'

'Maybe his wife's the boss at home and it's the only chance he gets to lay the law down.' It was a mental picture that had appealed to Kate ever since her father had used it to describe someone in the LDV, only it didn't sound quite so funny now.

'You could be right at that.' The engine noise was much louder, and Underwood seemed about to say something else but stopped suddenly, because from nowhere there came an unearthly whistling noise, a note falling in pitch that lasted several seconds before cutting out completely. A few moments later there was a deafening explosion and the hall shook like the victim of an earthquake. Kate felt her heart pounding, and when she tried to speak she was unable to because her mouth was completely dry. Underwood's face was the colour of tallow, but she managed a smile and winked at Kate. It was the stimulus Kate needed, and her sense of duty reasserted itself.

The bell of a fire engine sounded, and then several more bombs fell, but they appeared to be moving further away and it seemed for a few seconds at least that the danger had passed. But then the explosions returned, distant at first and then approaching with menacing certainty, like monstrous footsteps, each preceded by the ghastly whistling noise. Again, the church hall shook and somewhere in the dressing area a window shattered.

Kate pulled aside a corner of the dividing curtain to ask in a voice that sounded deceptively normal, 'Is everyone all right?'

A white-faced St John Ambulance girl said shakily, 'Yes, we're okay.'

'You'd better sweep the glass up before somebody falls on it,' she suggested. It would get them occupied. They were all very young and inexperienced, although it seemed to Kate that no one had experienced what was happening now.

The outer door opened and a warden ushered a woman and two men into the hall.

'Come under the light,' Kate told the woman, whose head wound was bleeding copiously. 'Is this your only injury?'

'I hope so. It's bad enough.'

'It needs stitching but you'll be all right.' She put a thick dressing over the wound and said, 'Warden, will you take this patient to Casualty, please.' She saw Underwood attending to one of the men, so she beckoned to the other. As she did so, another bomb landed and the man winced. Kate tried not to.

'I got 'it on the 'ead,' he explained.

'Let me see.' Kate examined the wound, which seemed

superficial enough. 'Look straight at me,' she said. 'I want to see your eyes. Follow my finger.'

'It's been a while since I got man'andled by a young lass like you.'

'Behave yourself. Do you feel dizzy?'

'No, but me 'ead 'urts.'

'Do you feel nauseous?'

'What's that when it's at 'ome?'

'Do you feel sick?'

'I'm sick of all this bangin' an' crashin'. It were just t' same in t' last lot, 'cept we were over there instead of over 'ere.' He considered his comparison and evidently found it incomplete. 'We 'ad mud an' rats an' lice to put up with in t' trenches an' all,' he concluded.

'Well, I think we can manage nicely without those things. Come through here and I'll get someone to dress your wound.' She led him behind the curtain. As she left him another bomb exploded and two more windows shattered. The task of criss-crossing window panes with sticky tape had been an awful nuisance all those months ago but it had been worthwhile. Things were bad enough without having to contend with flying glass as well.

Underwood held the dustpan while Kate swept up the broken glass. A gust of wind blew one of the blackout curtains into the room and Kate called to one of the St John girls, 'Get some sticking plaster and stick these curtains to the window frames.'

'Underwood grinned and said, 'Who's a bossy-boots, then?'

'You know me better than that, Underwood. I just feel braver when I'm telling people what to do.'

'You and me both.'

'As things are, I don't think we'll be reported for showing a light.'

'No, I think we can safely say the Germans know where we are.'

They braced themselves as another explosion shook the hall violently. Incredibly, the electricity supply remained intact and the lights stayed on, which was fortunate, because more casualties were arriving.

The two nurses carried out the necessary triage, six patients being treated on the premises and just one requiring the services of the Casualty Department. When the last was safely in the treatment area, Underwood said, 'It's suddenly quiet out there. Do you think they've got bored and gone home?'

As another bomb fell, Kate said, 'I don't think so.'

More followed, and the tiny church hall shuddered repeatedly under the onslaught. Casualties arrived, and with them the wardens brought news of the carnage outside. One said, 'The Odeon picture house has copped it.' Another told them that Rawson Fruit Market was no more. As each unofficial report came in they wondered if any of central Bradford remained standing, but the greatest shock for Kate came when she heard of the damage to Kirkgate and Westgate.

'My friend works there,' she protested.

'Not now she doesn't.' The warden looked and sounded exhausted, a reminder that worse things were happening.

After a while things became quiet again, and Underwood said, 'I'm saying nothing this time. It's too much like tempting providence.'

'Let's keep our fingers crossed.' Kate inclined her head towards the treatment area. 'Those girls still have their hands full. I'll put the kettle on.'

'You're a trouper, Whitehead.'

As she stood alone in the kitchen, Kate felt her legs wobble, and she grasped the rim of the earthenware sink to steady herself. The 'All Clear' hadn't yet sounded and there could be more bombers on the way. She had to keep calm because there was work to be done.

The kettle eventually boiled and she was able to brew a pot of tea, which she poured for everyone.

Two of the St John Ambulance girls reached for their cups with shaking hands, causing Kate to be thankful they hadn't seen her a few minutes earlier. She touched them both on the shoulder and said, 'Bear up. You're doing a grand job.' Looking around the room at the others, she added, 'You all are.'

Back at the triage station she handed Underwood her tea. 'I got the shakes out there, in the kitchen,' she confided.

'I don't think there's anybody in this hall who could thread a needle just now, so don't worry about it.'

The 'All Clear' sounded at two-forty, and then it was time to tidy up the hall so that they could leave it as they'd found it.

At the end of the shift they locked the hall, left the sandbagged entrance and stepped on to a pavement covered in broken glass, so that every footstep made a crunching noise. They were also aware of the reek of smoke from a multitude of fires, some of which firemen were still damping down. Hoses lay in the road in profusion like exhausted snakes.

Saddened and weary, Kate took her leave of Underwood and made her way past toiling firemen, wardens and ambulance crews to the nurses' home, where she sank into bed and fell promptly asleep.

⊕◅⫸◦|◦⫷▻⊕

A week passed and, with no further appearance by the *Luftwaffe*, Kate was allowed a night off. She spent the evening with Dorothy at her home in Cullington.

'I was so angry,' Dorothy told her, pouring her a gin and tonic in honour of her recent adventure. 'We'd heard bangs and crashes in the distance, and in the news that morning they reported that a northern town had been bombed, and I thought it was probably somewhere on Tyneside, where they build ships and things, and then I found they'd bombed my place of work. It was too much.' She glanced at Kate irritably and asked, 'What's so funny?'

'You are.' Kate stopped laughing and wiped her eyes. 'It was all right for them to obliterate Newcastle or Sunderland but bombing your office was a step too far.'

'You know I didn't mean it like that.'

'I know. It was just the way it came out.' They'd known each other so long that they were adept at reading between each other's lines.

'I think it was magnificent, though, the way you stayed at your post and tended the wounded. I don't think I could have done that.'

Kate made a dismissive gesture. 'I was just doing my job, and I wasn't the only one. There was Underwood, who came back into nursing to lend a hand because of the war, and there were volunteer first-aiders there, people who train in their spare time. There were lots of us and we worked together as a team.'

'I'm still impressed.'

97

'All right. As my best friend you're allowed to be impressed.'

'But wouldn't you rather be back in the hospital?'

'Of course I would. I should be training on Women's Surgical, but I was told to man the First-Aid Post and that's where I have to stay until they send me somewhere else.'

'I believe this is where they say in the films, "*C'est la guerre*".' Then, more seriously, she asked, 'Have you heard from Maurice recently?'

'Oh yes, I had a letter from him yesterday, and it might have been quite informative, but whoever censored it was somewhat enthusiastic with the blue pencil.'

'What did he say?'

'He said he's fed up with the *blue pencil*. It's not *blue pencil*, and he can't wait for the *blue pencil* to arrive, because they'll be a big improvement on the *blue pencil*.'

'Oh my goodness,' laughed Dorothy. 'He could have given away so many secrets. I think a little power may have gone to someone's head. There must be lots like that.'

'I imagine so, but tell me, what are you going to do now that Hitler's put you out of work?'

'I've given that a lot of thought,' said Dorothy, looking like someone with important news, 'and two days ago I called at the RAF recruiting office. I've signed up to join the Women's Auxiliary Air Force.'

15

'How did the physio go this morning?'

'Very well, thank you.' Kate raised her walking stick in celebration. 'No more crutches; in fact, if you'll pardon the metaphor, I'm on the final leg now. I could be home by the end of the month, and that will be a welcome development.'

Rachel took her usual seat. 'That's good news indeed. I'm sorry I haven't been in for a few days. I've had a lot of work to get through.'

'There's no need to apologise. I hope you haven't neglected your work to come today.'

'No, I'm up to date now. Is there anything I can do while I'm here?'

'I don't think so, but I'd like to show you some more photos I've found.' She picked up an album from the occasional table by her side. It was made of coarse, grey pasteboard held together with parcel string. 'This was recycling *à la* World War Two,' she explained. 'I keep it for old times' sake. I was lucky to find a photo album of any description in those days.' She found the page she wanted. 'There I am,' she said. 'That was shortly after the air raid, I think.'

'Did you still wear that uniform at the first-aid post?'

'Oh yes.' She smiled at the memory. 'We had steel helmets as well.'

'Like the soldiers wore?'

'There was only one kind.'

'I can't imagine you in a steel helmet.'

'Oh well, I didn't wear it for long. When they were satisfied that Bradford wasn't going to be subjected to a nightly blitz they let me go back to the Royal Infirmary.' She turned another page and said, 'That's Dorothy wearing an officers' shirt. It caused quite a stir.'

'Were they allowed to do that?'

'Yes, although it has to be said that Dorothy always regarded uniform regulations at best as rough but amusing guidelines.'

Rachel regarded the picture wistfully. 'She looks terribly *chic* in this photo.'

'She would have looked *chic* in hessian tied up with string, believe me.'

Rachel's twitch made a half-hearted appearance. 'She had a head start on most women, didn't she?'

'Oh, she had her looks and her figure, but she also had a sense of style, and no one's born with that.'

'Don't you think so?'

'I'm sure of it.' She gave Rachel a searching look and said, 'You're in need of an emotional pick-me-up, aren't you?'

'How did you know?'

'I notice these things, and I've been in similar situations myself, so I'm quite sympathetic.'

'What sort of pick-me-up do you have in mind?'

Kate hesitated. 'It's not for me to tell you how to live your life.'

'No, but I'm struggling with it. What do you suggest?'

'I'm not saying it's bound to work for you.'

'Now I'm intrigued. Tell me.'

'All right, I will. I have a personal morale restorer who does wonders for me.'

'Have you really?' It was as if Kate had suddenly owned up to growing cannabis in a window box.

'You know how some people have a personal trainer? Some, I'm told, even have a lifestyle guru, which sounds too laughable for words. Mine is much more down-to-earth. My hairdresser is my morale restorer. I've gone to her sometimes feeling quite despondent, I've had a cut and blow-dry or, *in extremis*, what my late husband used to call "a complete overhaul", and I've left the salon feeling that the world was a much better place.'

'You are being serious, aren't you?'

'We're discussing your state of mind, Rachel. Of course I'm being serious.' But not as serious, she imagined, as Rachel, who clearly needed time to consider advice of such a novel kind. 'Think about it. You've nothing to lose.'

'I suppose not.'

'And in the meantime let me find some pictures I want to show you.' Kate turned the pages of the album, a difficult task with arthritic fingers, but she found a photograph of her mother, her father and herself taken in the autumn of nineteen-forty. She remembered wearing the dark-blue frock that Dorothy had rescued for her. It was the only decent one she had at the time so it had become the dress for important occasions, and the family photograph was one of those occasions. She remembered it particularly because it was taken shortly before her big row with her mother.

16

It was a rare night off for Kate and she had decided to spend it at home. Her father was at the rifle club, now headquarters of Cullington Home Guard, as the Local Defence Volunteers were now called. Most people had only the vaguest idea what the Home Guard was supposed to do, but her father, a veteran of the last war, took it very seriously, as the others did. There was even talk of him being given his old army rank of captain, and he liked that idea.

Kate was knitting a scarf for Maurice. Her mother was making a cardigan for herself and listening to a musical play on the wireless. It was called *Hide and Seek*, and Kate hadn't been giving it her full attention as it didn't really appeal to her. She liked musical theatre but her taste was more for Irving Berlin and Jerome Kern.

After a while her mother reached across and switched it off, muttering something about preferring a sensible play. 'I'll switch it on again later for the news,' she said.

Mention of the news prompted Kate to say, 'I don't understand why Italy has invaded Egypt. What has Egypt done wrong?'

'I don't know. You'll have to ask your dad about that.' She glanced at the clock. 'That's if he bothers to come home. He's out 'til all hours with that Home Guard.'

Kate couldn't blame him but she kept her opinion to herself.

'It's nice to have a night off, isn't it?'

'Yes, it is. I'm going to request forty-eight hours when Maurice gets leave. I can't see them refusing me.'

Her mother considered that information. Clearly, something

about it disturbed her, although the warning signs had been there for some time. Eventually she said, 'You mustn't get too carried away, you know.'

'What do you mean?'

'I mean I don't want you getting too involved with him.'

'Why ever not?' Kate could sense where this was leading and she was already angry.

'I've nothing against him. He seems an honest enough lad, but I'm sure you can do a lot better.'

Kate put down her knitting. 'In what way?'

'You could find someone with prospects. I mean to say....' She left the sentence unfinished, as if the rest were obvious to anyone with a scrap of sense.

'What do you mean to say?' Kate struggled to control her anger. 'What's wrong with his prospects?'

'He's a maintenance mechanic at Needham's, for goodness' sake. What kind of future has he there?'

'He's actually an air-gunner in the RAF and he'll soon be fighting for his country. I think that's more important than who's going to be the boss's next blue-eyed boy.'

'Don't you take that line with me, my girl. We'll have some respect in this house.' She gave her daughter a long, stern look before starting another row of knitting.

'It's a pity *he's* not entitled to any respect in this house.'

'Of course he is. I'm just saying there are lads in your dad's work with a future ahead of them. You know them all from school.'

'And none of them is half the man Maurice is.'

Her mother thrust her needles into the ball of wool. 'It's a waste of time talking to you. You won't listen to sense. It's ever since you went to live in that nurses' home. I shudder to think what goes on in that place.'

'Well, maybe that's where I belong.' Kate snatched up her knitting and took it upstairs before her mother had time to object. Once in her room she sat on her bed furiously deciding her next move, not that she had any real choice. She had to be where Maurice could reach her, and that meant a posting to York or Harrogate if such a thing could be wangled, or staying put, at least for the time being. She would simply have to fend off her mother's objection to Maurice until the time came when her future was hers to decide.

Eventually, with her mind made up, she repacked her overnight bag. She'd exchanged angry words with her mother on a number of occasions, but never openly defied her until now. This was different. She had no intention of letting herself be browbeaten where Maurice was concerned. There was still time to catch the eight-thirty bus, and an early return to the nurses' home was certainly preferable to staying at home.

When she appeared downstairs with her bag she found her mother ready with her familiar well-rehearsed temper.

'And just where do you think you're going, young lady?'

'Back to where I belong.'

'Here is where you belong.' Her forefinger pointed downward in the kind of imperious gesture Kate resented so much.

'Well, it doesn't feel like it. I'm going back to the nurses' home.'

'Oh no, you're not, my girl. Until you're twenty-one you'll do as I say. Maybe you'll have learned some sense by then.'

Kate continued resolutely to the door. 'My twenty-first birthday is only four months away,' she said firmly. 'Maybe I should start practising now.' She let herself out, slamming the front door behind her.

At RAF Mapleton in Shropshire Dorothy was also aware of the hand of authority. She and nineteen other recruits had suffered the indignity of the process known as FFI, or 'Free from Infection' and now, naked down to the waist, they awaited the main part of the medical examination.

For Dorothy nudity was little more than a reminder of the school changing room and, whilst she'd found the FFI inspection intrusive, she accepted it as unavoidable. Others less-composed and now thoroughly mortified by the intimate nature of the process had emerged scarlet-faced from the doctor's room, attempting to preserve with awkwardly-folded arms what remained of their modesty. They stood together at one end of the room taking what comfort they could from the knowledge that they were not alone.

A diminutive redhead with a strong north-eastern accent said to Dorothy, 'I'm not as shy as that lot but I still wasn't keen on droppin' me pants so he could look at me twinkle.'

'Is that what you call it?'

The girl shrugged. 'It's what me mam always called it when we was little, an' I've never called it anythin' else.' She eyed Dorothy curiously and asked, 'What do you call yours, then?'

A little taken aback, Dorothy hesitated before saying, 'I've never really called it anything.' When she thought about it she realised that she'd never needed a name for it; in fact, looking back on her childhood, she was sure that any reference to that part of her anatomy would have earned at least a maternal raised eyebrow. 'I suppose "twinkle" is as good a name as any,' she said, not wishing to sound disapproving. 'You don't mind if I use it as well, do you?'

'Haddaway.' The girl looked scornfully amused. 'You don't need my permission.'

'I was just being polite. By the way, what does "haddaway" mean?'

'It means "bugger off," but not really, if you see what I mean. I'm not tellin' you actually to bugger off. I'm just tellin' you not to be so daft, like.'

'Quite right too. What's your name? I'm Dot.'

'Connie. Constance, really, but I don't like to be called that. It's too posh for me.'

'Glad to meet you, Connie.'

'Me an' all, Dot.'

They shook hands matter-of-factly, as if introductions in the semi-nude were a daily occurrence. Dorothy was glad of it. Recalling Alan's early letters from Deepcut barracks, she knew she was about to meet girls from diverse backgrounds and that her best option was to embrace the experience. Besides, she liked Connie already for her directness and her cheeky smile.

Connie peered at the head of the queue and said, 'They've started lookin' for nits.'

Dorothy followed her gaze. 'Just thinking about it makes me itch.'

Connie nodded. 'At least it doesn't happen every day.' The

thought seemed to lift her spirits, because she smiled and asked, 'What did you do before all this, Dot?'

'I worked in a department store.'

Connie's eyes grew wide. 'One of them posh places like Binns in Newcastle, where rich folks gets their clothes?'

'That's right. I worked in Ladies' Fashions.'

'What, behind the counter, like?'

'Well no, I was assistant to the buyer, the person in charge of the department.'

'Ye gods an' little fishes! Me mam'll never believe us when I tell her I've made friends with a posh lass who worked in one of them places.'

Dorothy smiled at her description. 'I'm not posh, Connie. I was lucky to get the job.'

'Believe me, bonny lass, where I come from anybody who still has knees in her stockings is posh.'

'Where do you come from?'

'Jarrow.'

'Where the hung…? Oh dear me, I'm sorry.'

'Aye, where the hunger marchers came from. Me dad an' me Uncle Stan was with 'em.'

'I'm sorry, Connie. It just slipped out. I wasn't thinking.'

'Don't worry about it. I'm proud of what they did. It was that Stanley Baldwin and Neville Chamberlain who should have been sorry. Three hundred miles they walked an' the miserable buggers wouldn't even meet 'em.'

'Yes, they were disasters in more ways than one.'

'Aye well, it's history now.'

'What did you do before you joined?' She hoped Connie wouldn't say she was unemployed too.

'I was a parlour maid in a big house in Morpeth. It was better than no job at all but it's not what I want to do for the rest of me days. I mean there has to be more to life than, "Connie, Master Edward is coming home from school today. Make up his bed and be sure to put a hot water bottle in it before eight o'clock. See to it that it's nice and hot." I'm not kiddin', Dot, it's more than flesh and blood can stand sometimes.'

'I'm sure it is, but you did that accent brilliantly. Have you ever thought about acting?'

Connie shook her head dismissively. 'It's easy enough when the only way you can get over your frustration is by pokin' fun at 'em behind their backs.'

A corporal medical orderly said, 'Stop talking, you two, and come and stand at the table.'

They did as they were told while another orderly inspected their hair.

'Okay Ginger.' The corporal nodded to Connie as a girl emerged from one of the doctors' rooms. 'It's your turn to see the Medical Officer in Room Two. Off you go.'

Connie gave Dorothy a cringing look and went for her medical.

Soon it was Dorothy's turn. 'Room One for you, Snow White,' said the corporal, who seemed to treat everyone with equal disrespect.

Dorothy entered the doctor's room, where a Squadron Leader of venerable age asked her name.

'Needham, sir.' They had not yet been given their service number. She assumed that her surname would suffice.

'Ah yes.' He ticked her name off a list and said, 'Come over here and let me listen to your heart.'

He went on to test her physique, her upper and lower limbs, her hearing and her eyesight, before asking a number of questions that seemed irrelevant but harmless.

In retrospect, it amused her that, like the doctor who performed the FFI, he'd asked her to lower her 'drawers'. It seemed that in Air Force parlance her Paris-designed silk and merino mixture French knickers were no more than 'drawers'. Well, the recruiting sergeant had assured her that the joining process would be a great leveller.

⸙

Now promoted to lance-corporal, Alan marched one of the classes under instruction to the room where, six months earlier, he and his classmates had mustered for the MO's lecture. This time, however, the subject was to be Security, and the lecture would be delivered by an officer of the Intelligence Corps.

The Company Commander and his visitor arrived on time and Alan called the class to attention.

'At ease.' Captain Wanstall waved his swagger stick in a vague 'at ease' gesture and introduced the visitor, a tall, elegant officer with a pencil moustache. 'This is Lieutenant Phipps of the Intelligence Corps,' he told them. 'I want you to listen very carefully to everything he tells you. I cannot stress too strongly the importance of security in signalling.' Turning to the visitor, he said, 'Carry on, please, Lieutenant Phipps.'

'Very good, sir.'

Alan was particularly interested to hear what the visiting officer had to say, because he knew him very well, and it was evident from the officer's surprised smile that recognition had been mutual.

The lecture was quite good, beginning with physical security, which basically meant keeping things under lock and key and avoiding idle talk. From that he went on to talk about safe practice in signalling. He told them how the enemy could build up a complete picture from fragments of carelessly donated information, and cited instances from the previous war when things had gone awry through careless practice. In all, it was routine stuff but no less necessary.

At the end, when Captain Wanstall dismissed the class, Lieut. Phipps spoke to him and it was clear that he was talking about Alan.

'Corporal Lofthouse,' said the Captain, 'Mr Phipps tells me that you and he are old acquaintances from Cambridge. He'd like a word with you. When you're finished, perhaps you'd show him to the officers' mess.'

'Very good, sir.'

'Well, well, well,' said Phipps when they were alone, '"Lofty" Lofthouse unless I much mistake. What on earth are you doing languishing in the ranks?'

'I've been kept pretty busy, sir. Too busy, really, to do anything about it.'

'For goodness' sake, old man, drop the "sir", at least when we're alone. We haven't seen each other since I don't know when. Didn't you get a double-first? More than I did, I have to say.'

'That's right. Actually, I've been trying to live that down. It's not greatly appreciated in the barrack room.'

'I don't suppose it is.' He took out his cigarette case and offered it to Alan.

'No thank you, sir... Greg. I don't smoke nowadays.'

'Very sensible, old man. What have you been up to?'

'Oh, the same as everyone else, really. I went to France, returned via Dunkirk and I've been here ever since.'

'Mm.' Greg nodded as if in thought. 'What are your modern languages?'

'French, German and a bit of Italian.'

'What standard?'

'Higher School Certificate in French and German but my Italian's only School Certificate, I'm afraid. I did get a distinction.' Sensing that Greg had something in mind, he added, 'Actually I spent quite a lot of time in Germany before the war, so I'm fairly fluent in German.'

'Good.' Greg continued to nod. 'We're a new outfit, you see. We were only formed a couple of months ago and we're looking for chaps like you who can think beyond the glaringly obvious. It's rather like the stuff I was telling your chaps about just now, about piecing together scraps of information and making sense of them. It really is a brain game. Would you be interested in a commission in the Intelligence Corps?'

'You know, I think I should.'

'All right, I'll wangle you an interview. If that goes well your commission should go through on the nod.'

❄❀❁❀❄

Dorothy looked in dismay at the heavy lisle stockings, elasticated bloomers and roll-on girdles as the storekeeper placed them before her. 'Who on earth is going to wear these things?' Her question was rhetorical but the storekeeper responded all the same.

'You are, chook, same as everyone else in this outfit. If you can't take a joke you shouldn't have joined.'

She pondered the problem as she and the others were issued with bedding and directed to their accommodation, a long, corrugated Nissen hut heated by a single stove. There they each took possession of three square sections of mattress, known mysteriously as 'biscuits', and the corporal showed them how to make and stow their bedding as well as how to lay out their kit for inspection. Apparently they had to include one pair of the navy-blue elasticated knickers known as 'blackouts', which meant that Dorothy would be free to alter the others into French knickers and keep them out of sight of authority. Unfortunately there was nothing to be done about the lisle stockings.

'I stocked up on grey silk stockings,' she told Connie, 'and now I find we're not allowed to wear them on duty.'

'You'll just have to keep 'em for off-duty, then.' Connie gave her a cheeky look and asked, 'Any chance of a loan sometimes, do you think? Stockings, I mean.'

'Of course.'

The corporal interrupted their conversation to say, 'You'll be given brown paper and string tomorrow. It's to parcel up your civilian clothes and send them home. That's the last you'll see of them 'til you go on leave.'

'Don't you believe it,' whispered Dorothy. She had plans for some of her clothes.

However, uniform worries gave way later to frustration as recruits struggled to arrange their bedding over the hard biscuits. It had looked easy when the corporal gave her demonstration but now the business of arranging sheets and blankets so as to keep out the cold draughts seemed a task for experts. Dorothy solved the problem for the time being by wrapping herself in a cocoon-like arrangement and relying on sheer dog-tiredness to ensure sleep. Even so, she was disturbed during the night by the sobbing of some of the girls, and was not surprised when, in the morning, a number of them exercised their right to leave the WAAF after one day.

After an unappealing breakfast of unsweetened oatmeal porridge the remainder paraded again, this time for inoculation against diseases that most of them never knew existed, after which they were assessed individually for ability and aptitude.

The interviewing officer was Squadron Officer Crosby, a veteran of the Women's Royal Air Force formed towards the end of the previous war. She had greying hair caught back in a bun and dark-rimmed glasses and, according to the corporal who was acting as usher, had spent the inter-war years teaching mathematics in a school for girls.

When Dorothy's turn came, Miss Crosby examined her record and said, 'I see you have a School Certificate.'

'Yes, ma'am.'

'In fact you did frightfully well, matriculating with, let me see, five distinctions and one credit. That's right, isn't it?'

'Yes, ma'am.' Dorothy failed to see how an above-average School Certificate could be described as 'frightful', but she kept that thought to herself.

'Such a shame your credit had to be in mathematics.'

For Dorothy it was more of a minor miracle. The credit was the result of hard work rather than any aptitude or ability. However, she said simply, 'It was my weakest subject, ma'am.'

'Ah well, at least it was better than a mere pass.' She read further, pushing back her spectacles as they threatened to make an excursion to the end of her nose. 'You left school at sixteen. Why was that?'

'I had the offer of a traineeship, ma'am, and as things stood at the time I opted for the bird in the hand, so to speak.'

'Quite.' The Squadron Officer seated her spectacles firmly on the bridge of her nose and looked again at the document before her. 'Your father is no longer with you, I see. I imagine that might also have come into the equation.'

'No, ma'am, he was killed in nineteen-seventeen, just three months before I was born, but he left us financially secure. The decision to leave school and start work was a purely common-sense one based on the employment situation at the time.'

'Did you actually need to work?'

'No, ma'am, not for any financial reason. I just wanted to do something useful.'

'Very laudable, I must say. What were your duties as an assistant buyer?'

'Purchasing was an important part of the job, ma'am, but there was considerably more to it than that. The buyer was in over-all charge of the department and, as her assistant, I shouldered some of the responsibility for planning and day-to-day management.'

'So you were in authority over how many staff?'

'When I was left in charge, seven, all told.'

'As many as that?' Miss Crosby looked up sharply and, like snow off a roof, her spectacles skidded over the end of her nose. 'Confound these things,' she said, retrieving them from her inkstand. 'I really must have them tightened.' Then, returning to the matter of Dorothy's service document, she said, 'That's a great deal of responsibility for a girl of your age.'

'I was trained up to it, ma'am. It didn't seem a lot at the time.'

'Well, it seems to me that you could be an ideal candidate for a commission.'

'Really, ma'am? It hadn't crossed my mind.'

'Well, you should think about it. In the meantime, what do you see yourself doing?'

'I wondered about signals, ma'am. I want to do something that's directly to do with the war if at all possible. I took quite naturally to learning Morse code and semaphore in the Girl Guides.' She omitted to say that she had been dismissed from the Guides after six months for persistent disobedience.

'Very well. I'll add a note to your document to that effect.' She wrote something at the foot of the second page before removing her glasses. 'One more thing....'

'Yes, ma'am?'

'You're a most attractive girl.'

'Thank you, ma'am.' Compliments were pleasant enough, but this one was completely unexpected.

'And you're likely to attract the attention of men on any RAF station on which you're likely to serve. I would advise you to be extremely careful in your dealings with them.' She added darkly, 'Not all of them are men of integrity.'

'So I understand, ma'am.'

She left the office and walked back to the hut, trying to make sense of the conversation she'd just had. She was a likely candidate for a commission because she had a School Certificate and because she'd wielded authority over a handful of people. That made no sense at all. Surely it took more than a qualification in largely-irrelevant subjects and, for all Squadron Officer Crosby knew, she might have been very ordinary at her civilian job. In any case she wasn't really interested in becoming an officer. It wasn't as if the Air Force was to be her career. Life in the ranks would be fun and sometimes challenging but she felt she could survive most things.

As for the other thing, she'd been aware for some time of the carnal aspirations of the male sex but she couldn't help wondering how desperate a man would have to be to have designs on a girl who wore grey lisle stockings and, for the time being at least, elastic-legged blackouts. Some men welcomed a challenge, it was true, but there were limits.

She saluted a passing officer of some description, as she'd been taught, and was surprised by the friendly smile he gave her when he returned her salute. After pondering the matter for a minute or so she decided that maybe the WAAF uniform wasn't so challenging after all.

≈≕≓∗⊁∗≓≔≈

Self-conscious in his new uniform with the single gold, wavy ring on each sleeve, Jack sat before the interviewing officer, an elderly captain with medal ribbons from the last war.

'Congratulations on completing your officer training, my boy.'

'Thank you very much, sir.'

'I imagine you've given some thought to what you'd like to do next?'

'Well sir, I rather see myself on convoy escort duty. I've served in a destroyer and, I mean, that's where it's all happening, isn't it, sir?'

'Not all of it, Farthing, not by a long chalk. You seem to me to be a man who likes to be in the thick of the action. You did well in the Norway Campaign and you certainly did your share at Dunkirk. How is the shoulder, by the way?'

'Completely healed, thank you, sir.'

'Good, good.' The captain peered at Jack's documents again and said, 'No, I should forget destroyers if I were you.'

Jack was intrigued. 'May I ask why, sir?'

'Yes, you may. It's coastal forces for you, my lad. You'll enjoy that. Lots of action.' He closed Jack's folder with a gesture of finality.

113

'You'll join *HMS St Christopher* next week. That's the coastal forces training base at Fort William in Inverness-shire.' He stood up to shake Jack's hand. 'I wish you the best of luck,' he said. His sincerity had an ominous overtone.

17

'Turn around and let me see the back.'

Rachel half-turned self-consciously.

'Lovely. I'm glad you went for the bob. It's just right for your face.'

'The hairdresser advised me. She was very helpful.'

'I told you she would be, and she's done a good job as well. Do sit down, by the way.'

'This is a lovely house.' Rachel took the other armchair. 'I imagine this is a nice town to live in as well.'

'Yes, it's a friendly town. I'm glad you found me without any difficulty. My directions can't have been too chaotic.'

'They were clarity itself.' She looked around the room with its array of family photographs. 'It must feel good to be in your own home again,' she said.

'It certainly is. When I opened the door it was like being greeted by an old friend.' She stood up carefully. 'Would you like some tea?'

'I'll make it.'

'Now, Rachel, you know I like to keep active. Let's go into the kitchen and make it together.'

'All right.' She waited for Kate to lead the way and said, 'You were right about morale.'

'About what, dear?'

'About a new hair-do being a morale booster. It takes some getting used to but it's made me feel an awful lot better about myself.'

'Well, I'm glad it works for you as well as me.'

'Where's your kettle?'

'It's behind you. If you'll see to that I'll do the rest.'

'Fine.' Rachel filled the kettle and switched it on. 'Do tell me about the aftermath of the row between you and your mother.'

'The only aftermath was that I went home only when I absolutely had to. It was a shame, because I missed seeing my father. I kept in touch with him, of course.'

'How did he take things?'

'About the parting of the ways? He understood my point of view, he sighed and shook his head a lot, but that was all. He'd spent his married life accommodating my mother and I suppose he found it impossible to change.'

'Rather like my father.'

'I suppose so. Meanwhile, whenever Maurice had leave we went to his house. That was if I had some time off. Otherwise, he used to call for me at the Nurses' Home and we'd go for a bike ride together. It wasn't very satisfactory but, as people were fond of reminding one another at the time, there was a war on.' She smiled at a recent memory. 'An odd thing happened to me yesterday,' she said. 'I needed some oil for the hinges on the front door, so I went to the bicycle shop for it. I was fascinated by the bikes they had for sale. You wouldn't believe the gears they have nowadays. I can't see why they need so many.'

'Well, it's been a while since you bought one.'

'About fifty years,' she confirmed. 'A young man came and spoke to me. I think he was amused that an old woman was interested in the latest technology.'

'I imagine he would be. Did you tell him you used to be a keen cyclist?'

'Yes, he was quite surprised. I was surprised, too, when I saw what people have to pay for a bike nowadays. Much of it's to do with lightness, apparently. Even I could lift one of them quite easily, but I still think it's a lot of money to spend on a bike. The young man was surprised when I told him how Maurice used to make a return journey of seventy miles or so on one that cost him five pounds.'

18

By March 1941 Maurice's squadron had completed its conversion to the Halifax heavy bomber and was operational, which meant that his trips home occurred far less frequently.

'It's in the lap of the gods now,' he said on one of those occasions. 'They always close the station twenty-four hours before an op.' They were at Maurice's house, his mother was at work, and they'd just emerged from an ardent and somewhat lengthy clinch for a snatch of overdue conversation.

'I'm glad you remembered to tell me.'

'Oh, I'd have remembered some time.'

'I suppose you would,' agreed Kate. There were lots of things she wanted to discuss but they had too little time together for much talk.

'Is the Blue Pencil bomber as good as you thought it would be, or shouldn't I ask?'

'Yes, but it's best not to talk about it.'

'So it's all very Blue Pencil, then?'

'Yes.'

They kissed again, security having been observed, until Kate found it necessary to retrieve his hand from beneath her skirt. 'No, Maurice,' she said firmly.

'I'm just curious. I want to know how those suspender-things work.'

'You know very well how they work.'

'I'm just getting to know you a little bit at a time.'

'Well, let's leave the naughty bits and concentrate on the good bits.'

'That's what I thought I was doing.'

'Poor old Maurice.' She stroked his hair. 'We've had this conversation before, remember? We'd be mad to let things get out of hand.'

'It'll be as safe as houses. You can't get pregnant if I wear a thingy on my you-know-what.'

'I could, even with a thingy on your you-know-what. Those things are far from fool proof.'

After some urgent thought Maurice tried a new approach. 'Why don't we get married now? I mean instead of waiting. I can't see why we have to wait, anyway. You're twenty-one now and you can do as you please, and we could manage on my sergeant's pay.'

Kate heard him open-mouthed, and tried not to show her amusement. 'Just so that you can have your wicked way with me? What kind of reason is that for rushing into marriage? In any case, with invasion likely and every other upset war can bring, it's the worst possible time to get married. I love you, Maurice, and I said I'd marry you, but not until things are more settled.'

'Oh well, that's something anyway.'

Now she couldn't help laughing. 'You're like a little boy who's missed a special treat.'

'I'm a grown man who's missing the best treat of all.'

'Oh, Maurice, I'm sorry.' She laid her head on his chest. 'I just daren't do anything at this stage. It would be catastrophic if I got pregnant now, so please think about something else.'

'It's hard to think of anything else when I'm with you. That's the effect you have on me.'

'You silver-tongued rascal. Tell me another.'

'All right.' He sat back and ran his hands through his ruffled hair. After a moment he said, 'Guess who I saw last week.'

'Lobby Lud?'

'No.'

'Father Christmas?'

'Stop mucking about, Kate.'

'All right, I give in.'

'I saw Alan.'

'Where?'

'The "Punch Bowl" in York. I was waiting to meet a mate, and then Alan walked in with two other brown-jobs. He's an officer now.'

'Yes, I know. What was he like?'

'Well, that's the funny thing. I'd decided I wasn't going to take any old buck from him, even with the difference in rank, but in the end I didn't have to. He was fine. We had a good old natter and a drink together as if we'd always been proper mates.'

'What was he doing there? I thought he left Swalebridge when he was promoted.'

'Ah well, he's in intelligence now, and he'd been back there for a briefing of some kind. It's all very hush-hush but, anyway, good for him. Do you think Dorothy might change her mind about him now?'

Kate shook her head firmly. 'She's been surprised by things she's heard about him, but an awful lot of water's passed under that bridge.' She gave him a quaint, sideways look and said, 'You were one of her devoted admirers at one time, weren't you?'

'I think we all were, but I knew that as long as I worked at Needhams I was a non-starter. There was no future for me with the gaffer's niece.'

'So,' she pouted, 'you had to settle for me.'

'It wasn't like that, Kate,' he protested.

'I know, I was only joking.' Serious again, she said, 'Dorothy's my best friend but I have to say she's a free spirit, and the man who gets her for keeps will have to be an accommodating soul.' A memory came to mind that made her smile. 'Do you remember the time she went away to that boarding school and came back after a year?'

'Yes, I never did hear what happened.'

'They just couldn't get her to toe the line so they waived the usual term's notice and asked her mother to take her away. They must have been in a hurry to see the back of her. It was quite funny at the time, and she was completely unrepentant throughout the whole thing. I remember wishing I could be as rebellious and get away with it as she did.'

'Do you think it's because her mother spoiled her?'

'No, it was quite the opposite. She tells me her mother was always afraid she would grow up to be like her father, who was apparently a man of spirit, meaning, I suppose, that he didn't always do what Mrs Needham wanted. At all events, she brought Dorothy up very strictly. Unfortunately twenty-three years later she still hasn't learned that the heavy hand isn't the answer.'

'Dorothy will have to knuckle under now she's in the WAAF. Even they have to do as they're told.'

'I can't see Dorothy conforming easily.'

'We'll see.'

Returning to the previous subject, she said, 'It's good that Alan's seen the light. I take it you parted the best of friends?'

'Yes, and I'm glad we did. I prefer it when I'm all right with everybody. There's no future in playing daft games and being at loggerheads all the time.'

'No, there isn't.' She stroked his arm, feeling the coarse fabric of his shirt and remembering why Dorothy found them so awful. 'You're too nice to be at loggerheads with anyone,' she told him.

In fact he was too nice for words, even if she had to keep the lid firmly closed on his manly ardour.

⸻ ❋ ⸻

Three hundred miles to the north Jack waited to learn about his draft.

Prepared as usual to make the best of a *fait accompli*, he'd shrugged off his disappointment and gone about his coastal forces training in such a positive way that he quickly became enthused. He and the others practised ship-handling, high-speed manoeuvring and depth charge, gun and torpedo attacks until they could carry out those tasks with practised ease. They learned about their arch-enemy, the torpedo boat known to the British Navy as the E-boat; they handled motor torpedo boats, motor gunboats, motor anti-submarine boats, and the less-glamorous but highly practical motor launches. Of all those types Jack's preference was undoubtedly the motor torpedo boat, in which he saw himself speeding across the foam at forty knots

120

to carry out hit-and-run attacks on enemy convoys. It appealed more than anything else to his impetuous nature.

When his turn came to enter the inner *sanctum* he found the interviewing officer in a sunny mood.

'Take a seat, Farthing, and let me offer my congratulations on successfully completing the course.'

'Thank you, sir.'

The captain glanced at the report in front of him and said, 'You've done rather well, and I'm delighted about that. You know, it's quite heartening for an old professional to see you temporary chaps rising to the occasion.'

'Thank you, sir.' There was little else Jack could say.

'Enjoy the course, did you?'

'Yes, thank you, sir. It was an excellent course.'

'Good, good. Now, how do you see your future in the service?'

'Oh, in an MTB, sir. That's what I'd like more than anything else.' He'd imagined his performance on the course would put him in a strong position.

'Really, Farthing? Have you given any thought to the life-expectancy of a first-lieutenant in an MTB? It's not what I'd call enticing.'

'Well, sir, we've all got to take a risk some time, surely.' He tried to sound positive but he could guess where the conversation was leading. Suddenly he had an awful sensation of *déjà vu*.

'Also the MTB and the MGB are very limited, you know.'

'In what respect, sir?'

'Damn it, Farthing, they're the prima donnas of coastal forces. They're perfectly all right when the sea state's like plate glass, but just see what happens when there's a force eight blowing and there's a job of work to be done. They're as much use as a novice in a knocking shop. Take it from me, Farthing, when the MTBs and MGBs are tied up in the lee of a harbour wall it's the MLs that are out there doing the job.'

Jack imagined that the kind of speech he reserved for officers lucky enough to be drafted to MTBs and MGBs was somewhat different. With a heavy heart he said, 'I take it my appointment is to an ML flotilla, sir.'

'Yes, Farthing, but not just any ML flotilla. You're joining an experienced, seasoned outfit that's earned itself an excellent reputation on the east coast. I almost envy you.'

Jack refrained from offering to swap jobs with him. Instead, he said, 'Thank you, sir. I'll do my best.'

'I know you will.' He offered his hand. 'Good luck, Farthing, and enjoy your leave.'

⚜

Dorothy completed her course at No. 1 Signals School at Cranwell, gaining high marks in all disciplines. She'd also arrived at a welcome compromise with regard to her lingerie, and one which had so far evaded the eye of authority, unlike her shirts, which attracted the notice of several NCOs and officers. True to form, the first to challenge her was an assistant section officer, the lowliest of her calling.

'I say, where did you get that shirt?'

'I bought it from stores, ma'am.'

'But they're for officers.'

'Yes, ma'am. That's why I had to buy it.'

Clearly the officer was trying vainly to recall some King's Regulation or Air Ministry Instruction that forbade the wearing of officers' clothing by other ranks. In the absence of such a ruling she asked, 'Why are you wearing a shirt intended for an officer?'

'Because it's so much better than the scratchy things I was given, ma'am.'

'Oh, so you're used to quality, are you?' It was evident from the heavy sardonic tone that the officer suspected she was never going to come off best.

'Yes, ma'am. I worked in women's fashions before the war, and clothes are important to me on a personal level too.' She was conscious by this time that everyone in the W/T room was listening to the conversation, and it was evident from the deepening colour of the assistant section officer's cheeks that she was also aware of it.

'Where did you work before you joined the WAAF?'

'In a department store in Bradford, ma'am. You won't have heard of it.'

'I should think not.'

'No, it is rather exclusive.'

The officer hesitated and, seemingly unable to find a suitable response at short notice, said, 'Oh well, carry on.'

'Yes, ma'am.'

It was a modest victory, the best kind because they were soon forgotten. Dorothy welcomed a little fun but had no wish to cause ill-feeling, which was as well, because Cranwell wasn't yet finished with her. She and two of her classmates had been selected to remain there as instructors, an appointment that carried with it the welcome privilege of accelerated promotion to corporal, with its attendant increase in pay. The job just continued to improve.

After a welcome and enjoyable leave, during which he'd spent as much time as possible with Iris, Alan had been posted again, this time to a mysterious-sounding department in London. So, with absolutely no idea of what to expect or with whom to make contact, he arrived as instructed at the headquarters of something called MI9A in Room 424 of the Metropole Hotel in Northumberland Avenue.

His knock was answered by a young man whose shoulders bore the two pips of a full lieutenant.

'Second Lieutenant Alan Lofthouse, sir, Intelligence Corps,' said Alan, sounding more confident than he felt, 'told to report to this address.'

'Step inside a moment.' The young man opened the door wide enough for Alan to enter. 'A word to the wise, old man. It's best to keep your name, rank and outfit *sotto voce*. You're on War Office territory, fair enough, but you don't want everyone to know your business.' He closed the door firmly and said, 'By the way, I'm Theo Fulbright. Just call me Theo. No point in standing on ceremony. Major Whiteley is expecting you. Follow me.' He led the way past a row of desks manned by officers who paid the two men only brief attention, and stopped at the end of the row to address a major whose middle-aged features included a chevron moustache and the doleful appearance of a disillusioned walrus.

'This is Lofthouse, sir.'

'Thank you, Fulbright. How do you do, Lofthouse?' He indicated a chair beside his desk. 'Take a pew and tell me how much you know about our little setup.'

'I know nothing at all, sir. I was simply told to report to MI Nine A.'

'Good. Security is vital.' Major Whiteley gave him a quick smile before resuming his habitual air of solemnity. 'What's happened, Lofthouse, is that you've been poached from general duties to work with us.' With a small gesture he indicated the other occupants of the room, saying, 'Most of these people represent the Directorate of Intelligence, Section Nine, otherwise known as MI Nine. Their primary purpose is to assist in the escape of our chaps who are currently prisoners-of-war, and to help those still at large to evade capture. On the other hand our function as MI Nine A is to gather intelligence by interrogating German and Italian prisoners held in Britain. Pretty straightforward, eh?'

'Crystal clear, sir.'

'Good. We have certain premises where we question the more senior officers in civilised surroundings, and you may soon become involved in that, but your clientele, at least for the time being, will be of a lowlier kind, and you'll have the task of interviewing those characters in their transit camps once they've been medically screened.'

'Medically screened, sir?'

'Yes, the Italians arrive here coughing and gasping, some of them crawling with vermin, and they have to be screened. Those with infectious diseases are promptly isolated. Don't worry, Lofthouse, you won't catch anything. That's what the screening process is about.' He stopped briefly and asked, 'Any questions so far?'

'No questions as such, sir, but I have to point out that my Italian is somewhat basic. I only took it up to School Certificate.'

The major shook his head dismissively. 'Most of 'em speak English. In any case, your Italian's bound to improve with use. You'll be trained in interrogation techniques, of course.'

'I see, sir.' At least he didn't have to pick that up as he went along. He made a mental note to buy a new Italian dictionary.

❖❖❖❖❖❖

Jack's leave went by all too quickly before he had to report to HM Motor Launch 84.

He knew only a little about her, that she was almost twice the length of the MTB on which he'd trained and that she was capable of only twenty knots. However, she carried an impressive arsenal of depth charges as well as a 3-pounder quick-firing gun and twin machine guns.

He boarded the ship from the dockside and found the captain on the upper deck.

'Sub lieutenant Farthing, sir,' he reported, 'come aboard to join as First-Lieutenant.' He felt pompous just saying it. He and the captain would be the only lieutenants in the ship's company, but that was nevertheless his title and he had to report as such.

The Captain, a dark-haired and bearded RNVR lieutenant greeted him without ceremony. 'Welcome aboard. I'm Owen Thomas,' he said with a handshake and more than a hint of a Welsh accent. 'I expect you'd like a drink. Come down to the wardroom.' He led the way below via a vertical ladder to a tiny room furnished with bunks, a table and a bar. 'What'll you have, gin?'

'If you don't mind, sir, I'd rather have beer.' Air raids and redirected rail traffic had made his journey a long one and he was ready for a long drink.

'Me too.' His host opened a bottle of Bass and poured it neatly into a tumbler. 'I'm afraid you won't have much time to familiarise yourself with the ship, Number One. We're going out tonight to rendezvous with a south-bound convoy. It's the usual kind of thing – mainly colliers – and we'll be taking the time-honoured route through "E-boat Alley" to the Thames Estuary.' He handed Jack his beer and poured one for himself, raising his glass to his new First Lieutenant. '*Iechyd da.*'

'Your very good health, sir.'

Lieutenant Thomas took a hefty swig at his beer and asked,

'What do you know about E-boat Alley, Number One?'

'Not very much, I'm afraid, sir, except that it's anywhere in the North Sea that's in range of the E-boats.'

'That's a rough geographical description, but it's much more than that.' He opened two more bottles of Bass and handed one to Jack in readiness. 'Sit down,' he said, 'and prepare to be demoralised.' When Jack was seated he continued. 'E-boats are fast and well-armed and they're a perpetual nuisance to our convoys. Sometimes it's like the Battle of Britain out there, only wetter and colder. Occasionally, as escorts, we have a destroyer as well as a converted trawler or two, and sometimes our dashing colleagues show up with their MTBs and MGBs. At other times we have to cope with the buggers alone.' It was evident from his patter that it wasn't the first time he'd given the briefing, and he stopped casually to drain his glass.

'The Hotchkiss Quick-Firing Three-Pounder,' he went on, 'is only as quick as it can be reloaded, aimed and fired, and the machine guns are only useful for raking the E-boats' decks and possibly relieving them of a gun-crew or two, or maybe the captain if we're lucky. Our best weapon is the depth charge. On a shallow setting it can break an E-boat's back, but it's risky. We do have to get out of the way pretty smartly. Are you with me so far?'

'Yes, sir.'

'You don't look scared, Number One. I must be losing my touch. Anyway, suffice it to say, things can get a trifle hairy out there, as you'll soon discover.'

'I'll prepare the charts, then, and look over the ship, sir.'

'After lunch will do, Number One. You're a typical Englishman, you are. All matter-of-fact and let's-get-started. That's why I joined, you know. The job can't be left to the English and the Scots. It calls for flair and imagination, and the Welsh have the monopoly of those two qualities.'

'Is that the only reason you joined, sir?'

'Well not exactly. I mean there's self-preservation, I suppose. It's bad enough having to live next door to the bloody English without having the Nazis move in as well.' He smiled mischievously and asked, 'Have I offended you, Number One?'

'Not in the least, sir. I'm a Yorkshireman, and that makes me as cross-grained and rebellious as any Welshman.'

'Oh yes? Play rugby, do you?'

'I played at school, sir, but I'm more of a cricket man, really.'

'So that's the state of things, is it? Oh well, we have to be thankful for what we can get, I suppose. Cricket's all right in its way, I'll admit, and it goes down well in Glamorgan, but rugby's the game for men of passion.'

'I do have hidden depths, sir. It's a Pennine characteristic.'

Thomas eyed him speculatively. 'You know,' he said, 'it's hard to tell when you're joking or when you're serious.'

'I've been told that before, sir.'

'Hm.' It seemed to give him an idea. 'Do you play poker?'

'I'm afraid not, sir.' Jack had no interest in card games.

'There's a few of us in the flotilla who get together sometimes for a game. You wouldn't think I was brought up strict Methodist, would you? Anyway, you'd be welcome to join us. Nothing reckless, you understand. We play for modest stakes and that way no one goes back to his ship fit to drown himself. What do you say?'

'Thank you, sir. I'll give it a try.'

The Lieutenant looked relieved. 'Good. You're all right, you know. I wondered at first what we were getting. "Trained at Whale Island and mentioned in dispatches," they told me. I said, "The last thing we need around here is a bloody hero," but they ignored me as usual.'

'I'm not a hero, sir. I was lucky, that's all.'

'Now I know you're all right.' He seemed about to expand on that compliment but before he could say more there were footsteps on the ladder and a tall petty officer with a weather-beaten countenance arrived outside the doorway.

'Oh, Cox'n,' said the Captain, this is Mr Farthing, our new First Lieutenant. Meet Petty Officer Simmons, Number One.'

The two men greeted each other and shook hands.

'Simmons is the only professional seaman on board. If he left us, the only course would be to abandon ship.'

'Oh, think you'd manage without me, sir,' said the Cox'n. 'By the way, sir, the ammunition and rum issue have arrived. Everything's correct.' He handed him a list on a clipboard. Thomas glanced at it and signed at the bottom.

'Permission to carry on unloading, sir?'

'Carry on by all means, Cox'n.'

'Aye aye, sir.' He saluted and left.

'Lunch beckons, Number One.' As he led the way, he said, 'Now you're officially accepted I think we can relax the protocol. When we're on the job I'm "Sir" and you're "Number One", but at other times I'm "Owen" and you're.... What *is* your first name, Number One?'

'Jack, sir.'

'How appropriate. A sailor by baptism as well as inclination. Come along, Jack.'

After lunch Jack went over the ship, inspecting the guns and depth charge projectors, all of which were his responsibility, and by eighteen-hundred he felt as confident as he could be at such notice.

❧❦❧

With the engines running smoothly and all hands closed up to their stations for leaving harbour, Thomas turned casually to Jack and said, 'Take her out, Number One.'

'Me, sir?'

'You've got to start some time.'

'Aye aye, sir.' Jack took a deep breath. 'Let go for'ard.'

The response came, 'All gone for'ard, sir.'

'Let go aft.' Mentally, he went through the drill, anxious not to make some elementary blunder such as trying to leave the berth with one spring still secured. 'Let go after spring.' Then, into the wheelhouse voice pipe he ordered, 'Slow ahead port, slow astern starboard.' He heard the Cox'n repeat his order. Thomas seemed happy enough for the time being, so he called, 'Let go for'ard spring.' Then, into the voice pipe again, 'Stop starboard, stop port. 'Midships.'

'Stop starboard, stop port. 'Midships,' repeated the Cox'n. 'Starboard and port engines stopped, sir. Wheel's amidships.'

'Slow ahead together.' Gradually the ship nosed her way out of the dock and into the outer harbour, where Jack began to breathe normally again.

'Nicely done, Number One,' said Thomas. 'I think you'll be all right.'

19

Rachel waited for Kate to gather her coat in and then closed the car door. As she got into the driving seat she asked, 'Can you manage the seat belt?'

'I could if I could find the hole to put it in.'

'Let me do it.' Rachel pushed the latch plate home, fastened her own belt and started the engine. 'Are you sure there's nothing else you need while we're here?'

'No, thank you, dear. It was just the bank.' Kate examined the unfamiliar interior and said, 'This is a very nice car.'

'Thank you. You told me that when I picked you up.'

'I'm sorry.' She shook her head in fatalistic acceptance. 'That's old age for you.' After a while she said conversationally, 'You know, Rachel, you've been hiding your light under a bushel.'

'In what way?'

'This is the first time I've seen you in a skirt and, you know, you have absolutely nothing to hide.'

'I haven't been hiding anything, Kate. I just wear trousers for convenience, that's all.'

'What's changed?'

'To make me wear a skirt? It was having my hair bobbed. It sort of led to other things.' She pulled into Kate's driveway.

'A manicure, for one thing, I see.'

'You don't miss much, do you?' She switched off the engine and got out.

'Everyone notices hands,' said Kate, opening her door. 'Like shoes, they say a lot about you.' Looking down at her comfortable

130

and somewhat worn footwear, she added, 'When you get to my age you can afford to relax.'

'You're a treasury of information, Kate.' Rachel helped her out of the car. 'And the surprising thing is you guide my footsteps without ever seeming to give advice.'

'That's because it's not for me to dictate how you should live.' Kate fumbled in her bag for her house key. 'Oh damn this arthritis. Anyway,' she continued, 'at ninety-five, what could I tell you about fashion? I just leave you to explore things for yourself, and in your own time you'll find what appeals to you.' She found the key and unlocked the door. 'Now, let's have a cup of tea before we do anything else. Shall we have it in the garden?'

Rachel prepared tea and they sat with it on the lawn.

'I've had it in mind to get some new garden furniture,' said Kate, 'but I don't know if it's worth the trouble at my age.'

'Of course it is. You've more time to enjoy it now than you've ever had.'

'I suppose so.' She was distracted as a twin-engined aircraft of some kind flew over the house.

'You only really see them with propellers at this time of the year,' commented Rachel. 'Apart from the little private ones, I mean. It's the season for air shows, apparently.' She added self-consciously, 'I only know that because one of my clients is keen on that sort of thing.' She asked, 'Are you all right, Kate?'

'Mm?' Kate realised she'd been staring into the distance after the aeroplane. 'I'm sorry. I was remembering something, and you know how the memory keeps branching off and making its own journeys. At least mine does.'

'Do you want to share it?'

'I don't know, although maybe I should. I was remembering that horrible spring of 'forty-one.'

20

Maurice's seat was as hard and uncomfortable as any in the Halifax but he would have to endure it for seven hours, so he wriggled occasionally to rearrange the creases in his behind. He wriggled his toes inside his fur-lined boots as well in an effort to keep them from turning numb. Even in April night-time temperatures at high altitudes were bitterly cold. He watched the Yorkshire coast recede in the failing light and shivered until distraction intervened in the form of an exchange of banter between the mid-upper gunner and the bomb-aimer. Eric, the latter, appeared to be questioning his colleague's taste.

'Do you really fancy that WAAF from the pay office, Phil? Tell me you're only kidding.'

'Why not? What's wrong with her?'

'She's a man-eater with a lot of miles on the clock, mate.'

'No problem, Eric. I'll have her melting in my arms.'

'She'll wear you out.'

'I don't care as long as she smiles afterwards.'

'Smile? She'll die laughing at your efforts.'

Bested in the joust, Phil looked for conversation elsewhere. 'What about you, Maurice? When are going to walk your Kate up the aisle?'

'Not yet. She wants to wait until things are more settled.'

'Ah, she's got the bird in her hand but maybe she's wondering if there might be something better in the bush.'

'Or under it,' suggested Eric.

Maurice was quick to disabuse them. 'You blokes haven't a clue.

Kate knows quality when she sees it. She's quite happy with what she's got in her hand.'

There was a burst of immoderate laughter from several quarters.

'I didn't mean it that way,' Maurice protested, but he was saved further embarrassment when a fourth voice came on the intercom.

'Pilot to crew: cut it out, everybody. It's time to test the guns.'

They each fired a short burst in turn. Maurice's occupied about two seconds.

'That was short and sweet, Rear Gunner,' commented the pilot.

'Only testing them, Skipper. I'm saving my nine yards for a night-fighter.'

'Good man. Now, everyone keep a sharp lookout.'

Maurice meant what he'd said about his nine-yard belt of ammunition, although he knew that a night-fighter had the advantages of surprise, speed, manoeuvrability and superior armament whereas the Halifax's guns were purely defensive.

Through the alloy-framed panes of the rear turret he searched continuously for enemy aircraft and, as he did so, he couldn't help thinking about Kate. It wasn't unusual, because he thought about her most of the time, flying or on the ground, and his most recent visit came readily to mind. It was wrong of him, he knew, to keep pestering her for the other thing. She'd made it clear how she felt, and the last thing he wanted was to upset her. He could still scarcely believe his luck at having her as his girlfriend, so maybe sex could wait its turn. He would just have to hold on until then.

It was pitch dark now; because of Double Summer Time sunset was about ten o'clock, which still felt strange. He wriggled his toes again, and then his whole body. It was freezing cold in the rear turret. He was cramped as well, so that, each time they came home after an op, he found himself bent at ninety degrees as he stumbled out of the aircraft, but he wouldn't want to be anywhere else. The RAF had been his guiding star from childhood, and the rear turret of a Halifax bomber was the ultimate place to be, particularly when the bomber was G for George. He liked the skipper and the other crew members, and they'd accepted him. He peered through the gunsight of his four Brownings, reminded of his good fortune.

They flew on into the night unconscious of time until eventually the Navigator said, 'Landfall in thirty minutes, Skipper.' Now everyone was fully alert. They were within easy range of night-fighters from bases in Holland as well as Germany. Maurice elevated and traversed his guns in anticipation.

Eventually he heard, 'Front-Gunner to Pilot: enemy coast ahead, Skipper.'

'I see it.' They were making landfall over Norderney, one of the East Friesian Islands, where they would alter course for Bremen.

The Navigator passed the new course to the pilot, and presently Maurice watched Norderney fade into the distance. A feature of being a rear-gunner was that he was the last member of the crew to see most things. The enemy coast was now behind them. Before long they would cross another, and Maurice would see that disappear too.

'Wireless Operator to Pilot: I'm picking up a lot of German *Telefunken*, Skipper.'

'Yes, everyone keep your eyes open for night-fighters.' The order was hardly necessary but no one was taking any chances.

As they flew on, the flak increased and the rear turret was illuminated repeatedly by star shell and exploding flak. Sometimes it was even possible to hear the clatter of shrapnel against the fuselage.

It seemed an age before the Bomb Aimer drew the pilot's attention to the target, which was already well ablaze.

'Two minutes, Skipper,' said the Navigator.

'Right, we'll stick to this angle of approach. It's possible to be too clever at this stage.'

'Bomb-Aimer to Pilot: bomb doors open, Skipper.' The flak increased until they were almost over the target, and then the Bomb Aimer spoke again.

'Left, Skipper, left, left....'

For Maurice and the rest of the crew those thirty seconds felt like an age.

'Left again, Skip, hold it, hold it... bombs gone.'

Freed of its bomb load, G George lurched upward. It was always an anxious time in a crowded sky, with aircraft above them as well as below, but all was well and the Navigator gave the course for the first leg of the journey home.

Flak became intense again, bursting around the attacking bombers, and Maurice watched in horror as a Halifax astern of them fell from the sky, shrouded in flames. He was unable to read its identification letters.

Then he was jerked out of his horror by a shadow, a black shape that was somehow blacker than the sky around it, and he yelled into the intercom, 'Corkscrew starboard, Skipper! Night-fighter starboard quarter down!' He braced himself as the pilot flung the Halifax violently to starboard, and then he searched hurriedly for the fighter. He found it, now to port and almost level with G George.

'Port quarter, Skipper! He lined up the Brownings and squeezed the triggers in a long burst until he saw one of the night fighter's engines burst into flames. Then, as he was about to report his success to the pilot, suddenly and with absolutely no warning, his world was enveloped in blinding light.

⊙┅┇⊹┋⊹┇┅⊙

The patient who beckoned Kate was the one she'd brought round from anaesthesia twenty-four hours earlier.

'What can I do for you, Mrs Slingsby?'

'Just a quick word, love.' The patient waited until Kate was beside her and said in a cautious whisper, 'Now that I've had this....' She pointed vaguely to her lower-middle region.

'Hysterectomy.'

'Now I've had it all taken away, can you tell me how long it'll be before it's all right to, you know...?'

'Before it's all right to what, Mrs Slingsby?'

'You know,' she insisted, almost mouthing the words silently. 'I mean before I can... *be friendly* with my husband. He's coming in tonight and he's bound to ask.'

'Do you mean you want to know when you'll be able to have sexual intercourse again?'

'Hush! Keep your voice down. I don't want the whole ward to know my business.'

'I'm sorry, I really don't know. You could ask Sister Davy, or you could speak to one of the doctors.'

Mrs Slingsby looked horrified. 'I can't talk to a doctor about a thing like that.'

'Why ever not? It's what they're there for.'

'But they're all fellas.'

'Well, surely you talk to your husband about those things.'

'Me? No.'

'What, never?'

'Not in twenty years of married life.' She motioned to Kate to come closer and said, 'When I put t' light out and get into bed, he waits for me to settle an' then he just sort of coughs, like this. "A-huh, a-huh," and then I say, "All right but be quick," and he, you know, does it.' Now with the subject finally broached, she became a little more expansive. 'I can't think what he sees in it, meself, but it helps keep the peace.'

Kate nodded understandingly. 'I can see now why you want to know.'

'You're not married, are you, love? I can tell.'

'No, I'm not.'

'Just you wait.' She added ominously, 'You'll find out.'

Kate hoped innocently that it would turn out rather better than Mrs Slingsby had described it. Her experience sounded too awful for words. 'I'll ask Sister to have a word with you,' she said. 'She'll be able to tell you more than I can.' She took the patient's thermometer from its receptacle, shook it well and placed it under her tongue before checking her pulse. As she did so, she thought about Mr Slingsby and wondered if he had even an inkling of how serious his wife's operation had been. Someone should certainly tell him, and she would mention it to Sister when she asked about the other thing.

Mrs Slingsby's temperature was ninety-eight and her pulse was sixty-eight. Kate was recording them on the chart when one of the probationer nurses approached her.

'Nurse Whitehead,' she said, 'Sister wants to see you in her office.'

'Thank you, Nurse.' She wondered what Sister Davy wanted. She couldn't think of anything she might have forgotten or done wrong, and that was usually her reason for summoning a member of the nursing staff to her office.

She walked the length of the ward and knocked on the office door.

'Come in.'

When Kate opened the door she noticed with some relief that Sister Davy didn't look particularly cross.

'Come in and take a seat, Nurse Whitehead.' She pointed to a wooden chair beside the desk and waited for Kate to sit down. 'I shan't beat about the bush,' she said. 'You're engaged to be married, I believe.'

'Not officially, Sister.' It was true; they hadn't yet bought the ring and placed a notice in *The Yorkshire Post*. Even so, she imagined Sister was going to point out what Kate already knew, that a married woman had no place in nursing. She was ready for that. She was not ready, however, for what Sister Davy was about to tell her.

'We've had a telephone call from Mrs Alcock.'

'Mrs Alcock?' She couldn't imagine why she should phone the hospital, unless.... The possibility came to her like a blast of cold air. Something awful must have happened to Maurice.

'I'm terribly sorry, Nurse Whitehead. 'There's no easier way I can tell you. I'm afraid your fiancée has been killed in action.'

21

'I was stunned. Somehow I couldn't take it in. It was like being on the edge of something awful but at the same time not being a part of it. Do you know what I mean?'

'Yes, I think so.' Rachel moved her chair to be closer to Kate and, because there was nothing more helpful she could do, she held her hand.

'I spent most of that night with Mrs Alcock. We just sat in front of the fire and she wept and wept. She had to, I suppose, because she was doing my share as well as hers.' She spent a moment in recollection and said, 'I was never a cry-baby. With my upbringing it would have been impossible anyway, but I just couldn't understand why I was dry-eyed when the man I loved had been killed. It was a mystery at the time.'

'I suppose we never know how we're going to react.' She squeezed Kate's hand supportively. 'How long were you like that?'

'It's hard to say. I was tearful at odd times, and particularly after the memorial service, but I didn't really give way until weeks later.' She made a visible effort to move on and said, 'The worst thing was that there was no part of him to go back to, if you see what I mean. There was no grave, of course; the plane just exploded and fell to the ground in flames. The crew of another bomber saw it happen. Maurice's plane was attacked by a fighter and they saw that hit by gunfire. It went down in flames as well, but then another fighter attacked and Maurice's plane blew up, as I told you.'

After a pause Rachel asked, 'Shall I make some fresh tea, Kate?'

'Not for me, dear, but thank you for offering.'

'All right, and I know what you mean. Even after a cremation it's possible to go back to where the ashes have been scattered or buried.'

'Yes, there was nothing at all until the fifties, when they built the memorial at Runnymede. That's for airmen who have no known grave.'

'I see. It was a long time to wait, wasn't it? You mentioned a memorial service, though.'

'That's right. That must have been the bleakest time of my life. I was trying to come to terms with everything, and that's when a girl really needs her best friend. I needed Dorothy as I never had before, but they wouldn't let her come. They only ever granted compassionate leave for close relatives.'

'What about your parents?'

Kate shook her head sadly. 'Relations between my mother and me were at rock-bottom and my father was in Bedford on business.'

'I suppose Jack and Alan couldn't be there either.'

'You're right. They were both refused leave. Until the day of the service I thought none of my friends would be there.'

22

After breakfast Jack made his way back to the ship. The day was sunny, they wouldn't be on patrol for another twelve hours, and he might have been in a much happier mood had his request for compassionate leave been granted, but it hadn't, and he found that exasperating. He'd been shattered by the news of Maurice's death and quite naturally he'd wanted to be at his old friend's memorial service. He felt dreadful when he phoned Kate to tell her; in fact he still ached for the poor girl each time he thought about it.

As he entered the dock he was surprised to see wooden packing cases alongside the ship. It seemed that something major was about to happen, and he hurried on board to find out what it could be. Owen was waiting for him.

'Good morning, Number One.'

'Good morning, sir.'

'Do you believe in Santa Claus?'

'Devoutly, sir.'

'Quite right. He made an early delivery last night.' He inclined his head towards the merchandise on the dockside. 'They've sent us the new depth charge throwers and they're getting rid of the museum piece aft and replacing it with twin Oerlikons. We'll be a proper warship at last.'

'So we will, sir. The thought occurred to me the moment you uttered those spell-binding words "depth-charge throwers" and "Oerlikons." A proper warship, I thought, armed with modern weapons and, if last night was an example, Druids' curses.'

'There's nothing Druidic about my curses, Number One. They're just plain, honest foul language. Swearing in Welsh makes me feel better.'

'It does as much for me, sir.'

'I'm gratified to hear it, Number One, but listen. The dockyard people will be here to start work soon, so we're stood down for forty-eight hours. Now, one of us has to be here around the clock, so I've spoken to the Base Commander and he's happy for me to cover for you. I'd get off now if I were you and you might be home in time for the service.'

⊷⊷⧖⫶⧖⊶⊷

Kate and Mrs Alcock were the first to arrive at Bradford Road Methodist Church, largely because Mrs Alcock was strict about punctuality. She said it came of working at the police station.

Once inside the church Kate looked around her with casual interest. She'd been brought up in the Church of England and this was different from the church interior she knew. As well as ground floor seating it had a balcony along three sides, and the pulpit was between the two levels. Behind that there were pews, presumably for the choir, and then, like a huge altar in itself, the organ. Music was evidently important in Methodist worship, and rightly so.

Beside her Mrs Alcock sat quietly in control of herself. Kate recalled the night they'd spent after hearing the news. She'd never known anyone cry as much as Mrs Alcock had. She'd quickly run out of hankies, and Kate was obliged to get towels from the airing cupboard. It had been an awful night, but now it was time to put on a brave face. Mrs Alcock was bearing up well.

There was as yet no sign of the Reverend Haigh, and Kate wasn't too unhappy about that. He was young, actually not much older than Kate, and relatively inexperienced, but that was no excuse for his lack of tact and understanding when he visited Mrs Alcock. Even in her confused state Kate had been unimpressed.

His first question was, 'How would you describe your son, Mrs Alcock?'

141

Kate had wanted to remind him that he was dealing with a grieving mother and that her son had a name.

'I remember him as a sober lad,' he prompted. 'I think it's fair to say that, isn't it?'

Mrs Alcock had merely nodded.

'A young man of sober habits,' said Mr Haigh, making a note, sobriety being presumably high on his list of virtues. 'So many young men go off the rails at his age.'

'Maurice never left the rails,' Kate assured him, absently assembling a list. 'He didn't drink to excess, at least not very often, he didn't waste his substance on riotous living, he didn't consort with the wrong kind of girl – I can vouch personally for that – and he certainly didn't write things on walls.' She realised she was talking about Maurice in the past tense when all the time she expected him to walk into the house and ask what the fuss was about.

'That was my impression of him,' said Mr Haigh unsurely.

'But there was much more to him than that, and it would be unforgivable if we didn't do him justice.'

'Of course. What can you tell me?'

That was better. She struggled again to organise the thoughts that floated around inside her head. 'Maurice was loyal to his friends, he was honest, he had a generous nature, there wasn't an ounce of guile in him and he was the most genuine man I've ever known. Also, it was his lifelong ambition to fly with the RAF and what happened was the most awful tragedy.' She hadn't used the dreaded word and she wasn't going to either. As long as she could avoid using it there was a chance the whole thing would turn out to be the awful nightmare she suspected it to be. She would wake up and everything would be fine.

Forcing herself to concentrate again, she glanced over at the minister's notebook and asked, 'Have you got all that?'

'Yes, thank you.' Mr Haigh rested his pen on his book, perhaps wondering where he'd gone wrong.

But that was in the past. Kate was satisfied that the minister had a true picture of Maurice and that neither he nor Mrs Alcock would be short-changed. She was too confused to care much about herself.

The organist was playing something soft and obscure, at least to Kate's ear, and people were arriving. She noticed two off-duty policemen, no doubt from the station where Mrs Alcock worked, but she didn't recognise any of the dozen or so other people who'd turned up.

The service began as they'd planned it, with a prayer followed by the first hymn 'The King of Love My Shepherd is.' Kate had helped Mrs Alcock choose the hymns when the poor woman was struggling to make sense of everything. She hoped they were still acceptable.

The hymn ended and Kate sat down, suddenly helpless. Maybe it was the stuff the doctor had given her. She had no idea, but she remained seated for the rest of the service, only vaguely aware of the proceedings, and even then seeing them through something akin to frosted glass.

At the end Mrs Alcock introduced her sister, who'd travelled up from Derbyshire, and together they greeted everyone and thanked them for coming. They were mainly family, and one of them, an aunt of Mrs Alcock, insisted on telling Kate repeatedly how sorry she was for her. It was during this exchange that she noticed Mrs Alcock shaking hands with someone in a dark-blue raincoat and a peaked cap. Then she saw the single, wavy ring on an epaulette and recognised its owner.

'Jack, I thought you weren't coming.' Tears momentarily blurred her vision and she let him gather her up in the hug she'd been missing ever since Sister Davy had given her the news.

'So did I, but they let make a flying visit. Kate, I'm desperately sorry. I've lost a good friend, I know, but it's a thousand times worse for you.'

'I know. At least, I think I do. I'm not sure any more what I know. I'm not even making sense.'

'I'm not surprised. Do you want me to see you home?'

She shook her head wearily. 'No, thank you. Home isn't the happy place it should be. I haven't been there for ages.'

'Oh yes, I remember now, but what about your dad? He'll be worried about you.'

'He doesn't know. He's away on business, anyway.'

'When do you have to be back on duty?'

'I'm officially on sick leave.' She screwed up her eyes, thinking for a moment it might help her think more clearly. 'I'm taking a prescription that makes me stupid,' she explained helplessly.

'All right, come home with me. You can have my bed tonight. I have to get back to the ship.'

'Oh Jack, I don't want to be a nuisance.' She buried her face helplessly in the gabardine folds of his coat.

'You won't be, and I'll never hear the last of it from my mum if I don't bring you home. Come along, Kate, the fireside and the teapot beckon.'

'All right.' She still felt unsure but when they'd taken their leave of Mrs Alcock and her sister she took Jack's arm and they made the short journey to his home.

'My mum said she might be out with the WVS,' he said, unlocking the door, 'but I'll put the kettle on and we'll have a wet.'

'A what?'

'A wet. That's what we sons of the sea call it. Owen, my skipper, calls it something else, but he's Welsh so he has strange names for everything.'

She let him take her hat and coat. 'I don't want to use up your mum's tea ration,' she protested.

'You won't. I've brought her a pound of tea, a two-pound tin of plum jam and a pretty hefty tin of corned beef, so I can assure you of a warm welcome as well as a diet of tea, jam and corned beef. I can assure you it's what sustains us at sea and we all swear by it.'

For the first time in days she smiled faintly. 'Do you ever stop talking nonsense, Jack?'

'I have my lucid moments.' He took her into the sitting room, where a coal fire glowed enticingly. 'Now, make yourself comfortable while I attend to things.'

She sat on the sofa and stared into the fire, trying to recall the series of events that had brought her to Jack's house. Those powders were really clouding her concentration, and she could remember only vaguely what had taken place back at the church. Her main recollection was that Jack had arrived unexpectedly, that she'd been relieved beyond words to see him, and that for the first time since the whole dreadful business began she'd had someone to lean on.

She was still gazing at the fire when Jack returned with the tea things.

'We'll have to let it mash for a minute or so,' he said, putting the tray on the low table.

' "Mash" is a funny word.'

'What word would you use?'

'I'd say "brew".'

'All right, we'll let it brew instead. I expect it'll taste much the same.'

Kate wasn't very interested in tea. 'I don't understand, Jack,' she said. 'I never saw you in the church – you just sort of appeared outside it.'

'I arrived late, actually during "The King of Love" and I sat at the back so as not to cause a disturbance.' He piled more coal on to the fire and sat down beside her.

'Oh well, I'm glad you came.'

'So am I. It's an awful shame Dorothy and Alan couldn't come, I know they would have if they'd been able to get leave.' He lifted the teapot and said, 'I imagine it's both mashed and brewed by this time. Don't you think so?'

'I imagine so. No sugar for me, thank you.'

'Yes, I remember.' He stood up when he heard the kitchen door being closed. 'That'll be my mum,' he said. 'I'll get her a cup and saucer.'

He left the sitting room door open and, after the usual greeting, Kate heard him tell his mother about their visitor. Then Mrs Farthing came into the room.

'Kate,' she said, holding out her arms to her, 'I'm so sorry, love. What a rotten thing to happen.' She paused in mid-hug to ask, 'Won't your mum and dad be worried about you?'

'Kate's dad's away on business,' Jack told her, 'and the bricks have been up between her and her mother for some time. I told her she could stay here for now.'

'Well, of course she can. Let's sit down and have a cup of tea.' She sat on the sofa with Kate, so Jack moved to one of the armchairs.

'As for you, young man,' said Mrs Farthing, 'where did all that stuff come from, the tins and things on the kitchen table?'

'Oh, I didn't want to see it go to waste so I brought it home.'

'I didn't bring you up to go around pinching things. Won't anybody miss it?'

'No, and even if they did I'd just say it was destroyed by enemy... by accident. We always say that when they question the rum requisition and they always accept it.'

'Oh well, I hope you're right. At all events it'll eke out the rations nicely.' Then, patting Kate's knee, she said, 'I'll make up the bed in Mary's old room and put a hot-water bottle in it for you.'

'Kate can have my room, Mum,' Jack told her. 'It'll save you having to make up a bed.'

'Where will you sleep then?'

'I have to go back tonight.' He consulted his wristwatch. 'There's a train I can get at six o'clock so I'll have to make a move before long.'

Her face registered her disappointment. 'Why do you have to go so soon? We've hardly seen anything of you.'

'It's not a normal leave, Mum. Owen's standing in for me but I don't want to impose on him more than I have to.'

'It seems such a shame.'

'I suppose it must, but I wouldn't normally have been granted leave. I just wanted to pay my last respects to Maurice and see Kate as well. I was lucky they let me come.'

'I'm glad you came.' The words seemed to come with no conscious effort, rather like a reflex action, but Kate was nevertheless glad she'd spoken them.

'I wish I could stay longer.' Jack perched on the arm of the sofa to reassure her. 'But I'm leaving you in safe hands.'

'That's right, Jack,' said his mother. 'We'll look after her.'

Looking at his watch again, Jack stood up. 'You can both see me to the door,' he suggested. 'That would be nice.'

'Hark at him,' said his mother, 'bestowing favours.' Nevertheless she took Kate's hand and they accompanied him to the door.

He took his coat from its hook and kissed his mother. 'Tell Dad I'm sorry I missed him. Hopefully I'll have longer next time.' He gave

Kate a final hug. 'Take it easy,' he said, 'and let my mum spoil you. She never spoiled me, of course. It was the rod of iron for me, but she has a soft spot for you.'

'Thanks for coming, Jack.' Her eyes filled with tears again.

He kissed her cheek. 'It was the least I could do. I only wish I could be more useful.'

'Take care, Jack,' said his mother.

'Yes,' said Kate fearfully, 'take care.'

'I'll wrap myself in cotton wool.'

23

'I was in denial, although we didn't call it that in those days. They just called it "shock" and treated it with those awful powders I was taking.'

Rachel looked mystified. 'Powders?'

'Yes, it was common in those days to dispense solids in powdered form so that they could be dispersed in water. In my case it was phenobarbitone, a sedative that was in regular use in those days. I'm afraid all it did for me was to make me so yonderly I didn't even know what day it was. It was like floating in space, and nothing felt real. I stopped taking it – I think it may have been the night Jack left, or around that time.'

'But what a good thing Jack was able to come.'

'Yes, I missed him terribly when he went back to his ship. His parents couldn't have been kinder, and I've never forgotten that, but there was something special about Jack. I don't think he realised it at the time, but he helped just by being there. It's impossible to explain.' She shivered involuntarily. 'Is it just me, or has it turned colder?'

'I think it has.' Rachel got to her feet. 'Let's go inside. I'll bring the tea things in.'

They retreated into the house and when they were settled Rachel asked, 'Were you ever reconciled with your mother?'

'I don't think that's quite how I would describe it. My father came when he heard the news and found out where I was – I imagine Mrs Alcock would have told him – and he took me home. Whether through sympathy or conscience, my mother was on her best behaviour and we were soon back on speaking terms, which, in a way, was a kind of relief, but it was still an awful time.'

'It must have been horrible. Were you off work for long?'

Kate smiled at the thought. 'No, no one was off work for long in those days. I had to go back after a day or so, but I knew I couldn't stay there. I wanted to go where I was really needed. There was nothing I could do to those responsible for all the horror but I could do plenty for those they were hurting. That's why I requested a posting.

24

If Kate wanted to be at the centre of things, her posting to Hull Royal Infirmary provided the answer. The Yorkshire sea port was being bombed nightly and with previously unimagined ferocity. Her introduction to the Blitz came when the sirens sounded shortly after she stepped off the train and followed her fellow passengers to the nearest public shelter. It was an above-ground facility that provided protection against bomb-blast but which would still be vulnerable to a direct hit. This information she gathered from fragments of conversation around her, which included the usual tired but ever-popular expressions: 'Direct hits on shelters are few and far between,' and 'If it's got your name on it....' Such clichés were nothing more than morale-sustaining crutches, or so it seemed to Kate.

The shelter was about twenty yards long and with a narrow aisle down the middle and chairs and bunk beds along the sides. Across the aisle from where Kate sat a young woman was putting a boy and a girl to bed head-to-tail in a single bunk. For no particular reason she asked the woman, 'Are they twins?'

'Yes.' Smiling, she cast her eyes to the ceiling and said, 'They say trouble always comes in twos and threes. Thank goodness I was spared a third.'

'How old are they?'

'Just seven. They went to live with a family down in Dorset when t' war started, but they were miserable there and there were nowt happening up here, so I brought them home.' She glanced upward again. 'More fool me.'

'You weren't to know.'

'I suppose not.' Looking at Kate's suitcase, she asked, 'What about you? You're not from Hull, are you?'

'No, I'm from Cullington.'

'What are you doing over here with all this lot goin' on?'

'I'm a nurse. I was trying to get to the Royal Infirmary when the sirens sounded.'

'Well, you nearly made it. It's only two streets away, only they're not lettin' anybody through tonight.'

A man's voice said, 'Just keep your fingers crossed it's still standing in t' morning.'

'Go on, smiler,' said the woman, 'cheer us all up.' Turning again to Kate, she said, 'I'm Joan Hardacre, by the way, an' these two are Michael and Jennifer. Their dad got taken prisoner in France, the careless blighter.' She dusted her hands. 'Right, you know all about me. What about you?'

'I'm Kate Whitehead.' It was difficult to think of anything else. Married people with children were far more interesting than single girls.

'Well? Have you got a fella?'

'No.' She was disinclined to say more than that.

'Somebody'll put that right before very long. You're a nice-lookin' lass.'

'Thank you.' She was grateful for the distraction when Jennifer sat up and said, 'Mummy?' Then, receiving no immediate response, she tried again. 'Mummy?'

'Go to sleep.'

'I can't sleep without a story.'

'And me,' said Michael. 'I can't neither.'

Joan pulled up the blanket and tucked them in. 'You know I'm not good at stories.'

'We don't mind,' said Jennifer, sounding like someone who was used to making allowances.

'I know one,' said Kate. 'Do you want to hear it?'

'All right.'

She crossed the aisle and sat beside their bunk.

Jennifer asked, 'Why haven't you got a boyfriend?'

'I had one but I lost him.' She added, 'I'm careless too.' That seemed to satisfy Jennifer, so she began. 'Once upon a time there were three billy-goats and their family was called Gruff. They lived in a field beside a river and they had no mummy or daddy.'

'Our daddy's in prison,' announced Michael in a loud voice.

'No, he isn't,' his mother told him. 'He's a prisoner-of-war. The Germans have got him.'

'It's the same thing.'

'No, it isn't.'

'If you want a story,' said Kate, 'you'll have to listen and not interrupt.'

'All right.'

She continued. 'One of the billy-goats was quite small and he was called Little Billy-Goat Gruff. The next one was big and he was called Big Billy-Goat Gruff, but the third one was so big and had such huge, hard horns he was called Great Big Billy-Goat Gruff.'

Someone further along the shelter said, 'They're coming. I can hear their engines.'

So could Kate. It was the same rhythmic beat, the *thrum-thrum-thrum* she remembered from that night in Bradford. She concentrated on the story.

'The billy-goats were fairly happy living on their side of the river, but one day....'

The engine noise was growing louder. As it did so, a battery of anti-aircraft guns opened fire.

'One day, Little Billy-Goat Gruff said, "This grass is too short. There's not enough to eat." '

Inevitably Kate heard the first shrill whistle of a falling bomb, the moment's silence and then the explosion that shook the ground beneath the shelter. She leaned closer to the children and continued.

'And then Big Billy-Goat Gruff said, "Yes, I'm starving too," and Great Big Billy-Goat Gruff said, "So am I." '

The children's faces were pallid. Joan leaned over them, stroking their hair. Kate said, 'It's all right, children. Just listen to the story.' More bombs fell and soon they heard an urgent ringing as fire engines raced to their destinations.

'Little Billy-Goat Gruff said, "They say the grass on the other side of the river is sweet and tasty. I think I'll cross over and find out if it's true." But Great Big Billy-Goat Gruff said, "You mustn't do that, Little Billy-Goat Gruff. There's a troll living under the bridge, and they say he eats billy-goats."

In spite of her fear Jennifer asked, 'What's a troll?'

'A troll is a nasty person who's unkind to everyone.'

'Like Hitler?'

'Yes, just like Hitler.'

A whole stick of bombs fell close by and the explosions were deafening. The shelter rocked and then someone said, 'That were t' railway station, you can bet.'

Determined, Kate carried on.'But Little Billy-Goat Gruff was very brave. One morning he got up early while his brothers were still sleeping, and he began to walk over the bridge. He got almost to the middle, when suddenly from underneath the bridge a huge troll with a terrible voice and eyes the size of saucers leapt up, snarling, "I eat billy-goats who dare to cross my bridge." Little Billy-Goat Gruff thought about making a dash for it across the bridge, but he changed his mind and ran all the way home.'

The whistling of the bombs was hideously loud. 'It's all right,' Kate told the children. 'This shelter and this bunk bed are very strong. Nothing's going to hurt you.' It was as if bombs were falling all around them, threatening and creeping ever closer. Kate held Jennifer close while Joan did the same for Michael.

'Little Billy-Goat Gruff kept very quiet about his adventure, and the next morning Big Billy-Goat Gruff got up early and set off for the bridge.'

A bomb burst nearby and everyone flinched when shrapnel hammered the exterior of the shelter, causing fragments of cork to fall from the anti-condensation layer on the ceiling.

'He got to the bridge and he'd just reached the middle, when suddenly the troll leapt up and snarled....' She broke off and said, 'Say it with me.'

Fearfully but obediently the children joined in. ' "I eat billy-goats who dare to cross my bridge!" '

'Big Billy-Goat Gruff thought about making a dash for it to the other side, but the troll was so huge and terrible that he turned and ran for home.'

Bombs were falling in quick succession so that the whistles and explosions had become inseparable and were now part of the general, hellish pandemonium.

'What was the troll's name? Jennifer clung to the story as if it were a lifeline.

'His name....' Kate thought quickly. 'His name, believe it or not, was Adolf.'

'So he really was like Hitler.'

'You couldn't tell them apart. They had the same ridiculous haircut and the same silly moustache. '

Amid the noise Joan caught her eye and grinned. 'They must 'ave learned their manners in t' same place an' all,' she said.

'Now, Great Big Billy-Goat Gruff had the feeling that something was going on, and he said to his brothers, "Have you two tried to cross the bridge?" Well, they had to tell the truth to their big brother, so they told him they had, and he told them how silly they'd been. All the same, the next morning he got up very early while his brothers were sleeping and he set off for the bridge.'

The cacophony outside was seemingly unending. Joan still clung to Michael and Kate held Jennifer as tightly.

'Great Big Billy-Goat Gruff reached the bridge and began to cross it. When he reached the middle, Adolf leapt out of the water and snarled....' She paused and said, 'Ready, you two?'

Together they recited, ' "I eat billy-goats who dare to cross my bridge!" '

'But Great Big Billy-Goat Gruff didn't care. He took ten steps backward and snorted angrily, scraping the ground first with his right hoof and then with his left. Then he leapt forward and charged at Adolf, hitting him with his big, hard horns. Adolf fell into the river and was never seen again, so the three billy-goats crossed the river and found that the grass was as sweet and as tasty as they'd been told, and they lived there happily ever after.'

Kate and Joan held the children close until the explosions became fewer and further away. Then they tucked them up and settled them for the night.

Joan took a thermos flask from her shopping bag. 'I'll use t' cap,' she said, 'an' you can 'ave t' cup.'

'Lovely.' She took the tea that Joan poured for her and although it was sweeter than she liked it she felt it strengthen her.

From further along the aisle an elderly man leaned towards Kate to say confidentially, 'I'll tell thee what, lass. I don't know what that story did for them bairns but it did plenty for me an' my missis.'

⊶⊰⊱⊷

Jack, Owen and Petty Officer Simmons stood on the bridge drinking tea. Jack had just emerged from an early training session with four seamen on the twin Oerlikons. Only two would be required to operate them at any one time but reliefs had to be trained, although one of them, Ordinary Seaman Kirby, had reservations about his instructor's credentials. He also seemed to be under the mistaken impression that authority was safely out of earshot.

He asked, 'How does the "Jimmy" come to be training us? What does he know about it? He hasn't been an officer more than two minutes.'

Next the group on the bridge recognised Leading Seaman Allen's voice. 'I'll tell you what the Jimmy knows, Kirby,' he said. 'He was training on small-calibre weapons at Whale Island when you were still at school, and you may be surprised to know he's a regular Mexico Pete with the Lewis gun. The Cox'n told me he shot down two Stukas over Norway.'

'Go on.'

'He did. He was mentioned in dispatches for it. Make no mistake, the Jimmy's a good hand.'

'Well, I never.'

'So instead of dripping about him you'd do better to listen to him an' learn what you can.'

Jack, who'd been smiling broadly throughout the conversation, said, 'I think I owe you a Stuka, Cox'n. I can only recall getting one.'

'Well sir, I always think it's as well to get a new officer's reputation off to a solid start.' Smiling, he inclined his head toward the group on the after deck and said, 'Young Kirby's only a sprog and already he thinks he's Fletcher Christian, but I reckon Leading Seaman Allen's got things well in hand.' He finished his tea and said, 'Good day, gentlemen.'

Owen watched him go. 'Do you see what I mean about Simmons, Number One? The linchpin of any small ship's company is its cox'n, and Simmons is one of the best.'

'We're lucky to have him, sir.'

'Well done, Number One. You're progressing well.'

Jack smiled. 'You know, sir, there are times when you sound just like a schoolmaster.'

'It's not surprising, because that's what I was before the war. I was the village schoolmaster, a respected figure, believe it or not.'

'So when did you join the RNVR?'

'Oh, three years before the war. I should be due for another half-ring soon, you know.'

'I'll drink to that, sir.'

'Good, and I'm glad you mentioned drink, because you've reminded me of something that's very important. You're invited to a little diversion tonight as we're stood down, and I think you're in need of it. Some of the others are going to join us in a game of cards. It'll do you good.'

It was true that Jack needed a diversion. He'd returned from Cullington feeling quite helpless, and he hurt inside when he thought about what Kate was going through. He'd had no experience of bereavement and, although he'd tried to hide his concern, her state of mind worried him.

⊶⊰⊱⊱⊰⊷

The All Clear sounded half-an-hour before dawn, which, because of Double Summer Time, came at seven-forty-five, so Kate hurried through rubble-filled streets where pedestrians were allowed and around them where they were not. Firemen were still damping down and wardens and Heavy Rescue teams searched the wreckage for survivors and casualties.

Kate approached a fireman who was closing a valve on a trailer pump. Having tightened the wheel he accepted a mug of tea from a girl in Salvation Army uniform and said wearily, 'Thank you, love.' Finding Kate beside him, he said quite conversationally, 'Good old Sally Army. They don't have to be here but they are, every single night without fail, looking after the inner man.' He sipped his tea gratefully and asked, 'What can I do for you, love?'

'I'm looking for the Royal Infirmary,' she told him.

'It'll be easier to find than it was yesterday.' He pointed straight along the street to a huge, dark building. 'It's one of them that's still standing. You can see it from here, look.'

'Thank you.'

'That's all right, love.' He grinned. 'It's as well we managed to save it for you. Let's hope we can keep it up.'

'Yes, I must go.' She hesitated, not knowing quite what to say in the circumstances, and settled for, 'Good luck.'

'Good luck to you an' all, love. Do a good job at the hospital.'

'I'll try.'

It was well after eight o' clock when she arrived at the nurses' home and reported to the sister in charge.

'I'm sorry I'm late, Sister,' she said. 'I was caught in the raid and I was told they weren't letting anyone through.'

'Quite right, Nurse, and you can relax. You'll report to Sister Cooper tonight and join the staff on the children's ward. Your shift begins at seven but you'd better report at six-thirty. Sister Cooper is keener than most on punctuality.'

Kate was as pleased as she could be in her current state of mind. She'd never worked on a children's ward and it was important for her to make good any gaps in her training before she took her final exams. One thing puzzled her however.

'Are there many children left in Hull, Sister? I thought most of them would have been evacuated at the beginning of the war.'

'You'll be surprised how many mothers brought their children home when things were quiet.' She left the rest unspoken, and it seemed to Kate that children and adults were equally vulnerable when bombs were falling.

⇒⊷⊹⊱⊰⊹⊶⇐

Henry Cartwright, skipper of ML 87, sat back on his borrowed bunk and said good-naturedly, 'I vote we quit while we're behind and let young Jack stand us all a drink out of his winnings.'

'Agreed.' George Ferris of ML 85 still looked a trifle incredulous. 'Are you sure you've never played poker, Jack?'

'Positive, sir. I don't usually play card games at all. It's been a new experience for me.'

'Shame on you, Owen,' said George, 'I thought you'd brought up your *protégé* better than that. Doesn't he know he's forbidden to use the "s" word when the boys come out to play?'

'It's his first,' pleaded Owen. We mustn't expect too much of the boy.'

'Especially when he's flying the gin pennant,' agreed Henry. The two sub-lieutenants nodded in respectful agreement.

'Give the gin a fair wind, Jack,' urged Owen.

'And the Scotch,' added Henry.

Jack plied both bottles liberally and entered the tally on his mess chit.

'The same rule applies to runs ashore,' George told him, and my reckoning is we're well overdue for one. What say you all?'

There was a chorus of general accord, which quickly gave way to a mood of nostalgia, in which the captains related stories to their junior colleagues of riotous nights on the town, which seemed usually to begin in a local hostelry called The Boy and Barrel.

The proceedings continued in the same spirit and Jack plied the gin bottle, so that long before the end of the evening he was convinced he was in the best possible company. Owen's prescription had been the right one.

⊷⊱⊰⊱⊰⊷

Kate had the briefest of meetings with Sister Cooper, who was Night Sister, and learned that her superior on the ward was Staff-Nurse Atherton, a pleasant young woman with an air of kindly efficiency.

'I gather you've had an awful time lately,' she said. 'We had to know about it so we could keep an eye on you.'

'I see.' It seemed everyone knew her business. 'I'm quite capable of doing my job, Staff.'

'I'm sure you are, Nurse, but you're going to be caring for vulnerable patients, and we have to be careful.' Her tone softened for a moment and she said, 'For what it's worth, you have all my sympathy.' She became business-like again. 'Now,' she said, 'it's time to settle the patients for the night, or as much of it as Goering will allow. When the sirens sound we take them down to the big shelter below. They're all ambulant so there's no problem there.'

'Very good, Staff. I'll get them to make their final visits and put them to bed.'

'You've got the idea, Nurse. If any of them says he doesn't need to do it now, tell him he has to. Whistle if necessary.'

'Is it always the boys?'

'Nearly always, as you can imagine.'

Kate went about her duties, and it wasn't long before settling the patients for the night became her favourite task. It was a time for sensitivity, when little children were homesick and missing their mothers. At such a time a cuddle and a few words of comfort from a nurse were the best medicine available, and Kate was convinced that no job on earth could be more rewarding.

When the air-raid sirens sounded it was necessary to take sleepy children from their beds, to guide their awkward limbs into slippers and dressing-gown sleeves and to shepherd them to the underground shelter, where Kate's repertoire of bedtime stories was in regular demand.

Almost two weeks after she joined the hospital the ward gained a new patient, a girl of nine called Olivia, who required eye surgery.

'She's a sensitive case,' Staff-Nurse Atherton told Kate. 'She's not very bright and she doesn't say much; in fact the poor little waif hasn't an awful lot in her favour.'

Such a description alone was sufficient to arouse Kate's sympathy. She kept a close eye on her and explained as well as she could that the operation would enable her to see better and why she mustn't eat anything for six hours beforehand. The operation was scheduled for the following morning.

When Kate went on duty the following night, however, she learned that Olivia had only just come round from the anaesthetic.

'The surgeon was delayed,' explained Staff-Nurse Atherton. 'The railways to the west have been badly disrupted by bombing, and he wasn't able to operate until three o'clock this afternoon. The trouble is, she has to keep still for twelve hours after the op. She's wedged in with pillows to make it easier for her but it's still a lot to ask. I'm dreading another air raid tonight, because she simply mustn't be moved.' Half-apologetically she came to the point. 'Will you special her?'

'Of course, Staff.' To 'special' a recovering patient meant staying at her bedside and attending to every need, a monotonous but necessary duty.

'If she complains of dryness she can have a little water, enough to wet her mouth but no more than that. After what she's been through we don't want the poor child to choke to death, and she is rather prone to fluids going down the wrong way.'

'No, Staff.' Kate took her seat beside the child's bed. Her patient was framed, as Staff-Nurse Atherton had said, with pillows that immobilised her as far as possible, and one eye was covered by a dressing, so that she looked even more helpless than before. It was easy to feel sorry for her.

After a while one of the probationers brought Kate a cup of tea, which was welcome in itself as well as affording a break from the monotony.

'It's a pity you've no knitting or anything like that,' said the nurse.

Kate was aware that she hadn't knitted anything since losing Maurice. 'I could do some mending,' she said. On a children's ward there was always mending to be done. Some of the poorer children had no nightwear of their own and calls for hospital pyjamas and nightdresses were frequent, so that buttons came off and seams parted company as a matter of routine.

'I'll fetch you some if you like.'

'Yes, please. It beats reading the laundry marks on the linen.'

The nurse returned with a pile of pyjama jackets and the sewing box, and Kate worked contentedly until the same nurse tapped her on the shoulder an hour later,

'Can I relieve you?'

'Oh yes, please.' She put her work down and stood up. It was good to straighten her legs for a few minutes.

When she returned she found Olivia still asleep. She thanked her relief and took her seat again until at about eleven-thirty the sirens sounded their nightly warning.

Available staff began the grimly familiar evacuation and Staff-Nurse Atherton stopped by Olivia's bed to say, 'Are you all right, Nurse Whitehead?'

'I'm fine, thanks, Staff. I'll stay with her.'

The staff-nurse gave her arm a supportive squeeze and said, 'Good luck.'

'Good luck, Staff.'

The last of the patients and staff left the ward and, with nothing else to do, Kate folded the pyjama jackets she'd mended, beginning with the largest and laying the others on top in order of size until she'd created a pyjama pyramid. It was pointless but better than simply waiting. The process was inevitable, like the beginning of a recurring bad dream, and it wasn't long before the familiar sequence began with the *crump, crump, crump* of the guns south of the river, and then the monotonous engine beat, like the opening bars of a satanic symphony featuring the whistle and blast of falling bombs, the bells of the fire engines and ambulances and the cries of the injured.

Olivia opened her undressed eye when the first bomb fell close by, but Kate was quick to reassure her.

'It's all right, Olivia. You've had your operation. Just lie still and everything will be all right.' If she sounded confident, the pandemonium outside contradicted her but she didn't care as long as Olivia believed her. She glanced at her fob watch. It was barely midnight.

The whistling became ever shriller as bombs fell nearer, and Kate crouched close to her patient, still whispering reassurance that she no longer felt. She heard again the giant footsteps that signalled a stick of approaching bombs, and flinched when one came screaming down horribly close, so that four of the ward's outside windows were blown in. Mercifully the bomb left Olivia's end of the ward untouched but she still left her seat and leaned across the bed to shield the child with her body for as long as the area around the hospital, and possibly the hospital itself, was singled out for destruction.

Looking at the terrified white face beneath her, she could do no more than repeat her desperate words of reassurance.

'It's all right, Olivia. Everything's going to be all right.'

There were hurried footsteps on the corridor outside the ward and before Kate had time to wonder who might still be in the building, a fireman burst through the swing doors and, seeing Kate there, asked urgently, 'Are you all right, love?'

'Yes, thank you. I can't leave my patient.'

'No, I can see that.' Looking at the smashed-in windows, he asked, 'Can I pull the bed into the middle of the ward for you, to get it away from the window?'

'No, please don't do that. She mustn't be moved.'

'That window could come in at any time.' He seized the nearest bed and began dragging it across the polished floor.

'The brakes are on,' Kate told him.

'I haven't time to worry about that.' He pulled it until it was beneath the window and then dragged the big table from the middle of the ward until he could hoist it on to the bed and across the window. As he did so the drawers fell out, tipping files and X-rays on to the floor, not that Kate cared much in the circumstances.

'Thank you,' she said with a great deal of feeling. 'What's your name?'

'Ted Lawrence. Why do you ask?'

'I just wanted to know the name of the man who was kind enough to do that for us.'

He laughed. 'It was nothing.'

A voice came from along the passage, calling out something Kate didn't catch, and the fireman answered, 'Just a nurse and a patient, Dave. The patient can't be moved.'

The invisible colleague asked, 'What's the nurse like?'

'What's she like? I'll put it this way, Dave. It's a good thing for her I'm a respectable married man.' He smiled at Kate and said, 'Take care, love, and good luck.'

'Good luck. Thank you again.'

The fireman went on his way, and she said to Olivia, 'There, we're safe from broken glass. Wasn't that kind of him?' She braced herself when another load of bombs fell nearby. She'd felt somehow braver when the fireman was there.

By four-forty the raid had dwindled to nothing, and the All Clear sounded at a little after five, leaving Kate limp and exhausted. At six o'clock she handed the responsibility for Olivia to the day staff.

⁂

She slept for most of the day and went on shift at seven o'clock feeling brighter than of late. She reasoned that if there were to be another raid, which was likely, it couldn't possibly be as bad as the previous night's. At the very least she wouldn't be alone.

She walked on to the ward, intending to check on Olivia, and was surprised to find her bed empty. She saw the day-shift sister leave her office, but decided against approaching her. Instead, she tapped on the office door and pushed it open. Staff-Nurse Atherton sat at Sister's desk looking strangely solemn.

'Come in, Nurse Whitehead,' she said.

'Staff, where's Olivia?'

'Sit down for a minute, Nurse. You did an excellent job last night, and Night Sister's going to speak to you about it.'

'But Olivia's bed's empty.'

'I know. Olivia did magnificently as well, keeping still all that time. The danger should have been past.'

Now Kate knew. She asked quietly, 'How did she die?'

'It was the cruellest thing. She had a violent bout of coughing that led to a cerebral haemorrhage. She died before anything could be done. They found a feeder on her bed. The most likely cause of the coughing seems to be that she tried to give herself a drink and choked on it.'

Kate closed her eyes, trying to hold back her tears. She felt Staff-Nurse Atherton's hand on her shoulder.

'This is where I'm supposed to tell you that you should never become emotionally involved with a patient, but you know that as well as any of us. You've had a rotten time lately and after last night no one can blame you for caving in.' She patted her shoulder. 'Stay here until you're more settled. I'll speak to Night Sister.'

Kate heard the office door close. Her shoulders heaved, and the tears nature had denied her flowed unchecked for the first time in weeks. She wept for Olivia, for Maurice and for the defiant, embattled people of Hull because at that moment it seemed that they were all part of one seamless tragedy.

25

'Sympathy for junior nurses was a rare phenomenon in those days, so I was lucky to be on Jane Atherton's shift. I must have stayed in that office for at least fifteen minutes before going on duty, and that was unheard of.'

'But you needed it.'

'I certainly did, Rachel. I can think of a number of possible reasons why I behaved as I did after Maurice's death but I can't put my finger on any one of them and say for certain it was that one. It's still a mystery to this day.'

'I'm full of admiration for the way you carried on in spite of everything. I don't know how you did it.'

For Kate there was no mystery. 'There's nothing like having to care for people to take your mind off your own problems,' she explained. 'As for the Blitz, it was a fact of life and we had to cope with it.' She was silent for a moment, remembering. 'It was wonderful how the people of Hull coped. The *Luftwaffe* came back that night and hit the docks and city centre again. In that week alone, I think, more than four hundred people were killed and the number of injured was overwhelming.' She stopped and corrected herself. 'No, that's the wrong word, because we weren't overwhelmed; we *dealt* with the situation. It was horrendous, but we carried on and, you know, the people didn't waste time feeling sorry for themselves. Defiant as ever, they just got on with their lives.' Suddenly she smiled at a long-forgotten memory. 'There was a fish-and-shop close to the hospital, and its owner used to keep customers informed about the availability of her stock by a series of bulletins chalked on a blackboard in the window. One day it read, "Owing to Hitler your fish will be littler." Another time it said, "Owing to Hess your chips will be less," and then the shop was wrecked in a terrible air raid, and she chalked up her final bulletin and stood it outside the flattened building. It said simply, "Owing to Göring I've had to go whoring." '

'Wonderful. But how did the emergency services cope with something on that scale?' It was a fair question, given that there had been no emergency of that enormity since the war.

'They had to bring in reinforcements from outside the city that week, but Hull's fire and ambulance crews and the air-raid wardens were unbelievable through the Blitz and the four years of bombing that followed. It wasn't always as bad as that week in May, thank goodness, but they never left us alone for long. We'd no way of knowing this at the time but, after London, Hull was the most heavily bombed city in Britain.'

Rachel blinked. 'I didn't know that and I've lived all my life in the East Riding.'

'It's not widely known.' Kate could think of many long-forgotten incidents and some that were justly remembered. 'Did I tell you about the fireman who came on the ward when I was looking after Olivia?'

'The one who blocked the window with a bed and a table? Yes, you did.'

Kate shook her head. 'My memory.... I can't remember what I've told you now.'

'You're doing well. I'm just afraid of over-tiring you.'

She patted Rachel's knee. 'I'm fine. What was I saying?'

'It was about the fireman blocking up the window,' she prompted.

'Yes, that's right. Ted Lawrence was his name. I heard later that he'd been awarded the George Medal for bravery during that week. On one occasion he came close to losing his life when he went into a burning building to save a family that was trapped. I remember reading his obituary when I was in hospital, about the time you and I met, and I was surprised to learn that he was six months younger than me. He seemed so capable and grown-up then.'

'I imagine you were too, although maybe you didn't realise it at the time.'

'It's possible. I don't suppose we ever grow up in our own eyes, even in such times.'

'Did you spend the rest of the war in Hull?'

'Quite a lot of it, but not at the Royal Infirmary. It was so badly damaged the night after Olivia died that they had to evacuate the patients and staff to other hospitals. They sent me to an isolation hospital to the west of the city.'

Rachel looked puzzled. 'What's an isolation hospital?'

'They're long since gone. They were hospitals in their own grounds, where they treated people with contagious diseases in the bad old days.'

'Like TB?'

'Yes, they moved those patients into the country to make room for us.'

'Were things much the same for you?'

'Life was less hectic there than at the HRI, in spite of the bombing, and I had time to keep in touch with my friends. It was also during that time that my life began to return to normal.'

26

Now at Trent Park, a requisitioned mansion in Middlesex, Alan read through the letter quickly before inserting it into the envelope. He had a meeting with Major Whiteley in five minutes' time and he didn't want to be late.

Dear Kate,

What a terrible time you've had lately. I've purposely not written to you since my note telling you that I couldn't be with you for the memorial service. I was sure you wouldn't want to be bombarded with letters at such a time. I'm heartened, however, to hear that life is becoming more bearable for you. Long may it continue.

On a somewhat selfish note I confess I'm eternally thankful that I was able to put things right between Maurice and me when I did. It was such a shame it couldn't have happened sooner. He had qualities I could never claim.

I'd like to be able to tell you fascinating stories about what I'm doing but for obvious reasons I can't. However, I'm more than happy to hear your news, so let's keep writing.

I'm due in a meeting now, so I must close. Take care.

Love and best wishes,

Alan.

He straightened his tunic and walked along the ornate landing to Major Whiteley's office, where he knocked on the door.

'Come in.'

Alan walked in, closing the door behind him.

'Ah, Lofthouse. Coffee?' There was a tray on Whiteley's desk. 'Help yourself.' His manner was urbane but direct and he seldom wasted words. The ribbon of the military cross on his tunic indicated service in the previous war, but no one knew how he had spent the inter-war years. His life was as veiled as his work with MI19, as the department was now known.

He waited for Alan to pour a cup of coffee, and then said, 'I've got a special job for you. It's somewhat different from what you've been doing.'

'I'm intrigued already, sir.'

'And so you should be. This matter is more sensitive than any you've handled so far. I want you to visit Number Three Pioneer Corps Training Camp in Richborough.'

'Where's that, sir?'

'It's near Sandwich in Kent, although the camp won't be there much longer. They're moving the whole bag of tricks later this month to Westward Ho!' He made a gesture of distaste and said, 'What a damned silly name that is. Who came up with the exclamation mark, I'd like to know?'

'I believe it takes its name from the title of Charles Kingsley's novel, sir. It was set close by, in Bideford.'

'I never came across it. Not at all the kind of thing I like to read. Anyway,' he said, returning the subject of the meeting, 'you may be wondering what's so sensitive about pioneers under training, so I'll tell you.' He stopped to refill his coffee cup. 'Help yourself when you're ready, Lofthouse.'

'Thank you, sir.'

'You see, the Corps has among its ranks a number of aliens released from internment camps in the past few months. They're mainly Italians, Austrians and German-Jews, and the reason they're in the Pioneer Corps is that no one is sure just how loyal they are to this country, so they haven't yet been trusted with anything more warlike than a pickaxe and a shovel.' He stirred his coffee noisily. 'I don't suppose locking them up at the outbreak of war did much for our popularity, and I can quite understand that, but now we need some of them to work with us.'

'As listeners, sir?' Alan was aware that personnel were

being recruited to monitor via a system of bugging devices the conversations of German officer prisoners held at Trent Park.

'Yes, but we also need men who can gather intelligence by mingling with the prisoners, to put it bluntly, to act as stool pigeons.' He passed a folder across his desk to Alan. 'Your job is to talk to this chap Josef Arnswald and gauge his loyalty to his adoptive country or, maybe more to the point, his hatred of the Nazi regime. He reached our shores only a short time before war was declared, so his story could be interesting. Spend some time with him, report back to me on Friday and then you can begin your leave.'

⚜

Dorothy's letter was less formal than Alan's.

Dear Kate,

I'm still devastated that I couldn't be with you at the memorial service. It must have been hell for you. I thought about you all the time and I'm glad for your sake it's out of the way. I tried every argument I could think of to get leave but I got nowhere. If the flight officer had been a flight lieutenant, i.e. male rather than female, I might have stood a chance, but no such luck. Nature is squarely to blame. On the other hand, though, I'm glad Jack made it. He could only have been good for you.

Now, on the subject of this extraordinary power you claim to have, let me tell you there is no such thing, person or influence as a jinx. It's sheer superstition. Maurice was killed in action; the little girl died because of a tragic accident and neither of those deaths was your fault. Take that fanciful idea and drop it in the nearest dustbin, where it belongs. There, I have spoken!

Dotty ideas apart, I'm glad you're feeling more in charge of yourself. They say it's a long road but it gets you there in the end, and remember, you can pour out your feelings to me anytime. I'll come and see you when I get leave, and then we'll be able to talk properly.

Now I've said it, I can't wait – civvy clothes, decent stockings, shoes worthy of the name, no collars and studs, and a drink with my best friend. That's something I can look forward to, and I suspect I'm not the only one. What say you?

Meanwhile – and you'll love this – a pilot officer asked me if I'd like to meet him off the station for a drink. He tried to make it sound like the kind of treat that would turn a girl's head, but I turned him down. I didn't fancy him at all but I just said I'd rather not if he didn't mind. Well, you should have seen the incredulity on his face, and then he asked me if I was involved with someone else, as if that could be the only reason why I'd turn him down. The arrogance of the man! I told him I was spoken for, which is true – by the first man who appeals to me as much as I appeal to him, even though he doesn't know it yet.

But that's all in the future, whereas right now I hear the call of duty. I'll write again. Keep smiling.

Lots of love,
Dot.

⚜

Jack's letter was also a tonic.

Dear Kate,

Thanks for your letter, which is greatly appreciated and more than ever welcome because I've been very concerned about you. I'm glad you're feeling more together and that the bricks are down again between you and your mother. It's not an ideal situation, I know, but surely one war is enough.

Do you like cod, haddock, plaice, sole, turbot, halibut, mullet, mackerel, snell and whiting? I did until recently, when an unscheduled explosion stunned everything in sight, thereby creating an abundance reminiscent of the day the disciples struck it rich on the Sea of Galilee. We cast our nets over the side and pulled in enough to keep us and the base galley going for at least a week. Can you imagine fish at breakfast, lunch, dinner, snacks, midnight feasts, and at every available opportunity, until you'd give all your chances here and to come for roast beef and Yorkshire pudding? I may never ask for a fish and two penn'orth again. Or maybe I will; some memories are mercifully quick to fade.

There's just one member of the ship's company who's not bored with fish, and I don't suppose he ever will be. He has no imagination to speak of, and it's my belief that everything tastes much the same as far as he's concerned. His name's Geordie because he joined us at Newcastle and, as you may have guessed, he's the ship's cat.

But what about you? You've got a new hospital and possibly new colleagues and patients. Tell me all about them and what's going on. I won't understand most of it. How could I? I know more about visas than seizures, but I'll know you're picking up the steps again, and that's the main thing.

Take care and keep in touch.

Love and reinforcement,

Jack.

Josef Arnswald looked initially promising. Obvious Jewish features would have ruled him out for what Whiteley had in mind, as he would never have been able to win the confidence of any German officer, but his appearance was encouragingly commonplace and therefore unlikely to arouse suspicion.

'You can relax, Arnswald,' said Alan offering him a cigarette. Although he no longer smoked, he always took them into an interrogation. It was remarkable how a cigarette could sometimes pave the way to a useful indiscretion. 'You're not in trouble,' he assured him. 'I'd just like you to tell me how you came to leave Germany and come to Britain.'

'But I have told this already, sir, to the officer at Immigration and then to another officer from the army.' He accepted the cigarette and let Alan light it for him.

'I know you have. I want to go over it with you again. There may be something you forgot earlier, something that could be important.' He looked at the document in front of him. 'I see you worked at the University of Hamburg until May nineteen-thirty-six.'

'That's correct, sir. I taught mathematics and philosophy there until Jews were excluded from posts in schools and universities.'

He delivered the information in a matter-of-fact way, and Alan suspected that his dismissal had not been his worst experience.

'How did you make a living after that?' He consulted the dossier again. 'You didn't arrive in Dover until July nineteen-thirty-nine. That's a period of more than two years.'

'Two years and two months,' confirmed Arnswald. 'I made a living of a kind by teaching mathematics and English to the children of anyone who was prepared to take the risk of doing business with a Jew.'

'Your English is excellent,' Alan told him.

Arnswald smiled patiently. 'If you consult your notes again, sir, you'll find that I attended Cambridge University from nineteen-twenty-eight until nineteen-thirty-one.'

'Yes, I see it now, but it doesn't say which college.'

'I'm surprised to hear that. I was at Corpus Christi College.'

'So you were. Who was Master at the time?'

The question seemed to amuse Arnswald. 'William Spens,' he said. 'As far as I know he still holds the office today, but I don't think you'll find that in your notes, sir.'

'I don't need to. I was at Corpus too.' He watched Arnswald for his reaction and saw only mild amusement. 'You were interned when war was declared. Do you resent that?'

'I wouldn't say I resent it. I feel impatient sometimes. I realise that security is highly important, but I think it can be taken too far.'

'Do you feel that this interview is a case of security being taken too far?'

'I really shouldn't say, sir.'

'Feel free to air your views. It's not a disciplinary offence.'

Arnswald hesitated. 'So far, sir, you have asked only one question that has not been asked before.'

'The question about Spens?'

'Yes, sir.'

'All right. How do you feel about being conscripted into the Pioneer Corps?'

'I feel privileged, sir.'

Alan suspected more than an element of irony in Arnswald's reply. 'Why do you feel privileged?'

'Because British conscripts are required to demonstrate low achievement in order to enter the Pioneer Corps; we aliens, who include university professors, performing musicians, scientists and men of letters are taken simply on trust.'

Alan had to smile. 'Yes,' he said, 'I'm aware of the paradox, but let's tackle another question. How do you account for Hitler's attitude towards the Jewish race?'

'Surely it is for Hitler himself to account for his attitude, sir. I'm merely one of his victims.'

'Of course. Let me put it another way. 'What do you think is the reason for his attitude?'

'I believe it began, if I may use an English expression, with a bee in the bonnet, a preoccupation that led to a fixation and eventually became an obsession. The British, the French and the Americans claim to have defeated Germany in nineteen-eighteen by force of arms, whereas Hitler believes that Germany was betrayed by Jews and communists. The Jewish race has always provided a convenient scapegoat. For the communists it is a new experience but they will learn quickly enough.'

'You seem to accept the situation.'

'What can I do about it?'

'Quite, but I might have expected anger or at least burning resentment.'

'You think I feel neither of those emotions?' For the first time he seemed ruffled. 'The Nazis took my wife, my job and my freedom, they conducted a campaign of hatred, they burned the synagogues and even now they're taking Jews from their homes.' He was now visibly angry. 'And you think I don't care!'

'I'm sorry to hear about your wife. It just says here simply that she died in nineteen thirty-seven.'

'That is as much as I was prepared to say when I was interrogated. I shall tell you now that she intervened when she saw members of the *Sturmabteilung* tormenting a Jewish child. They beat her so savagely that she died of internal injuries.' His voice shook as he said, 'Please do not accuse me, sir, of feeling no emotion.'

'I'm sorry, Arnswald, both for the loss of your wife and because

I obviously misread your feelings. I had no wish to insult you or her memory. Please forgive me.'

For a moment Arnswald said nothing, but simply made a repeated palms-down gesture, possibly calming himself. Eventually he said in a voice that still trembled, 'It's very rare for me to become so excited, sir. I, too, apologise.'

'There's really no need.'

'I am a philosopher. Logic tells me that anger against a remote enemy is impotent, and so I try to control my feelings, only sometimes it's not so easy when I am frustrated. I wanted to join the British army to fight against the Nazis but instead they put me in this labour corps.' He spread his hands in a hopeless gesture.

Alan closed the file. 'Arnswald, how would you feel about helping us? I mean as a German speaker.'

'What kind of work are you talking about?'

'I can't tell you yet, but it's about gathering intelligence here in England. We're not talking about sending you to Germany or anything like that. I'm afraid that's all I can say at this stage, except that you'd be hitting the Nazis much harder than you ever could with a rifle in your hands.'

Arnswald gave a bland smile and said, 'If the Nazis come there will be no need to send me to Germany.'

'It's not likely, Arnswald.'

'How do you know? Everyone is talking about locking up bicycles, hiding road maps and fighting the Nazis on the beaches. Only you are confident Britain will not be invaded.'

'I can't tell you how I know. I can only say again that an invasion is now most unlikely.' He took out his cigarette case and offered it to Arnswald. 'Will you join us?'

'Very well. Whatever you want me to do cannot be worse than mending roads.'

'Good man.' Alan offered his hand. 'We'll be in touch.'

27

'I don't know how anyone can walk in heels like stilts.' Kate turned away from the shoe she'd been examining and returned her attention to Rachel, who sat within a circle of shoes that had somehow failed to inspire her. The assistant attending to her was suggesting a further possibility but after fifteen minutes' deliberation and trying-on Rachel made her decision.

'I like the courts best,' she said, pointing to the pair she'd first tried.

'A good choice,' said the assistant. 'It's the courts, then?'

'Yes, I've decided.'

'How are you for shoe cream?'

'Will you put some in the box, please?'

'Certainly, madam. Would you like shoe trees?'

'So I can grow my own?'

The assistant's expression remained unchanged. 'To preserve their shape, madam.'

'Yes, I'm sorry. I didn't think it was all that funny either. Yes, I'd better have shoe trees as well.'

The assistant took the shoes and their box to the counter. Kate said, 'You know, Rachel, I believe you're regaining your sense of humour.'

'How do you know I had one in the first place?'

'It's not the kind of thing you acquire in your thirties.'

Rachel paid for her purchases and they made for the door. 'If you've got everything you came for, I thought we might find somewhere for lunch.' She added, 'My treat, of course.'

'How very kind.'

'Do you like Italian food? There's a restaurant just down the street from here.'

'I think I know the one you mean. My grandchildren took my daughter and me there for Mothers' Day. It was lovely.'

'Okay, we'll go there.'

As they walked the short distance to the restaurant, Kate asked, 'Do you eat out often?'

'I haven't for ever such a long time but a client brought me to this one quite recently.'

'Oh?'

'Yes.' Rachel caught the teasing look in Kate's eye and smiled in turn. 'It was supposed to be a business meeting, but what is there to discuss? He hands over his invoices and receipts and I turn them into trading and profit-and-loss accounts. I think he was just unsure of himself.'

'How did you feel about it?'

'Flattered, surprised and... all right, I didn't feel terribly sure of myself either.'

'You're more confident that you were when we met.'

'I should say so. I was a nervous wreck, but thanks to you I'm seeing light at the end of a very long tunnel.'

'I don't know that I had much to do with it, Rachel. You've made your own way.'

'Oh well, let's not argue.' She held the door for Kate.

'So are you going to see him again?'

'I see him regularly. He's a client.'

'You know what I mean.'

'Kate, you're impossible. Let's just say there's a possibility we may do it again.' She asked a waitress for a table for two and they followed her to a far corner.

'Honestly, Rachel,' said Kate peering at the menu, 'I don't eat very much nowadays. Just a main course would be nice.'

'And then I'll talk you into a *dolce* later.'

'Maybe you will. You know, Rachel, I think it's good for you to go on dates.'

'Kate, you're being naughty again.'

'All right. What is *pesce*?'

'Fish.'

'Of course.' Kate had been thinking about fish lately. It had something to do with Jack. She tried to remember when the thought had come to her but it was tantalisingly elusive. And then she remembered. It was one of his letters after Maurice was killed. Talking about the Blitz and the HRI had reminded her of it.

'Jack once told me a strange story about fish,' she said.

'What on earth did he tell you?'

'It was in one of his letters, actually, but then he told me the full story later. He had to be careful what he put into a letter, you see.'

'I imagine so. What would you like to drink, Kate?'

'Oh, a glass of dry white, please.'

'Okay, tell me about Jack and his fish.'

It was a relief to be able to remember the story. 'He was escorting a convoy or something, and they found a floating mine, so they shot at it with rifles. He said the idea was to make holes in it to let the sea in, but one of them hit one of the bits that stick out – I think they're called horns – and detonated it. There was a huge black cloud, and then when it dissipated, they looked around and found the sea full of dead fish, all floating on the surface.'

'How awful.'

'Well, apparently not, because this happened quite often, and they lowered nets into the sea and pulled them out. He complained about having fish at every meal, and that was astonishing because in those days we were thankful for anything that was off the ration.'

'In that case why did he complain?'

'Knowing Jack, I think it was just a silly story to make me feel better. He was good at that. So was Dorothy.'

'I've been meaning to ask you about Dorothy. Did she ever find a man she liked?'

Even after seventy-four years Kate smiled at the memory. 'She certainly did. It was around Christmas, as I recall. She'd been posted to a station just across the river from where I was.'

'It was good that something nice happened as well as the trauma.'

'I suppose it was traumatic. People used to emerge from the

178

air raid shelters and see the carnage the bombers had left behind; more often than not they had to clear up damage to their own homes, but later they'd hear Churchill broadcast to the nation, and he put new heart into them.' She paused while the waitress put down two glasses of wine, and then went on. 'Yes, there was no shortage of bad news in those days, but there were two events that changed the course of the war. There was Hitler's invasion of Russia, which meant that we were no longer alone and that the threat of invasion was past. The other came at the end of the year with the Japanese attack on the American fleet. It was a tragedy for them but it brought them into the war. With them on our side we could begin to look ahead from mere survival and start thinking in more positive terms.'

'I can see that, but when I mentioned something nice I was thinking more of personal things.'

Kate had to think about that. Eventually she said, 'After all this time I really can't recall what the boys were doing but good things happened that Christmas for both Dorothy and me; in fact it happened rather earlier for me, shortly after I'd passed my exams and become a staff-nurse.'

28

Returning from leave, Kate was obliged for the second time that year to step off the train and head for the nearest public shelter. Air raids had been happening less frequently since July; in fact there had been only two in September and one in October, so she was as surprised as the other passengers when the sirens sounded. It seemed that November's turn had arrived.

She took one of the seats near the door of the shelter, a spot that was unpopular with some because of its proximity to the outside world, but Kate was less worried, experience having taught her that a direct hit anywhere was likely to be fatal. It was better simply not to dwell on the possibility.

As usual, conversations began between neighbours, most of whom were strangers, although no one cared about that. An elderly man seated beside Kate had assumed the task of reassuring her, believing her to be a visitor to the city.

'As soon as you opened your mouth I knew you weren't local,' he said.

'No, I'm from Cullington.'

He smiled when his suspicion was confirmed. 'I thought you were a Wezzie.'

Kate was used to the locals' pet name for inhabitants of the West Riding. It was good-natured and harmless. 'I work here,' she told him. 'I'm a nurse.'

'I thought you looked like a nice lass. There's nowt wrong wi' nurses.'

Kate had known a few who might easily have caused him

to change his mind but she kept that to herself. 'I'm used to the bombing,' she told him. 'I was at the HRI until they had to move us out.'

He shook his head at the calamity. 'It's the biggest wonder any of you got out of there alive.' He continued to shake his head. 'That Hitler's got a fair bit to answer for.'

Someone said, 'It sounds like he's coming back to do a bit more.'

The familiar gunfire from south of the river gave way to the throb of aircraft engines. Kate knew that the anti-aircraft batteries never fired at aircraft when they were over the city for fear of adding to the carnage below, and now they had fallen silent. Before long the first explosions could be heard and they weren't far away.

Some of the occupants were playing the familiar but grim game of guessing which parts of the city were being hit. There was always someone who knew better than the rest, but they all stopped talking when the door burst open and a small boy half-tumbled into the shelter. His face was white and his eyes were wide with terror.

'Come inside, lad,' the old man told him. 'I'll shut t' door behind thee.'

'It's me mum,' the child gasped. 'Baby's on the way an' the midwife hasn't come.'

He looked to be no more than about eight or nine, and his face was smeared with tears. Kate asked, 'Where do you live?'

'Just round the corner.'

'What's your name?'

'Stanley Jenkins, miss.'

'All right, Stanley, show me the way.' She ushered him out of the shelter and felt the door being closed hurriedly behind her.

'This way, miss.' Stanley broke into a run and she followed, for once wishing she were wearing her flat, uniform shoes. It was no occasion for heels, but finding the way was made relatively easy by the light from the fires that had already broken out. The air, however, was thick with acrid smoke and the stench was overpowering.

A bomb burst uncomfortably close, showering the street with shrapnel, and she grabbed Stanley and held him close against the nearest doorway until the shards of steel had stopped falling.

A warden crossed the road, trying to head them off and shouting, 'Get under cover!'

'I'm a nurse going to an emergency,' she told him. 'Let us through.'

His tone changed abruptly. 'All right, love. Good luck.'

'Round here, miss.' Stanley led her into a narrow side street and finally to the door of his house.

Kate followed him inside and closed the black-out curtain. Some habits were too ingrained to be ignored. 'Mrs Jenkins,' she called, 'where are you?'

'I'm in here.' Through the sounds of destruction outside, the voice came from the under-stairs cupboard, a favourite place for a family without a shelter.

'Wait here, Stanley.' She opened the cupboard door and found her patient on the floor beside an assortment of brushes and other cleaning paraphernalia. The cupboard was illuminated by a single battery lamp.

'I was terrified about Stanley,' said Mrs Jenkins, who clearly had enough to worry about. 'He just ran off before I could stop him.' She was short of breath and perspiration covered her forehead, although those symptoms were more likely to stem from her immediate condition than from anxiety.

'He did well,' Kate told her. 'He came to the shelter and found me.'

'Hang on,' said Mrs Jenkins, moaning with a contraction, 'you're not the midwife I saw this morning.'

'No, I'm a nurse, and until the midwife arrives I'm your best option. How long have you been in labour?'

'I'm not sure.' Anxiety and the air raid had robbed her of clear thinking.

'Try to remember when your contractions became harder and more frequent.'

'It would be about six o'clock. I was just starting to cook.'

'Have your waters broken?'

Mrs Jenkins paused as a bomb whistled down. It exploded, shaking the house. 'Yes,' she said, collecting herself, 'it happened then, when I was in the kitchen.'

So she'd been in labour about five hours. 'Let's have a look.'

She lifted the woman's skirt and realised that she was still fully clothed. 'We'd better get these off,' she said, pulling down a pair of voluminous drawers. 'You can't give birth down your knicker leg, you know.' She made an examination and found that the baby's head was well down. She asked, 'When did the midwife last see you?'

'This morning when she gave me the enema. Is it ready to come?' She braced herself, either with a contraction or in response to another bomb that rattled the doors and windows of the house.

'It won't be long, Mrs Jenkins. Everything's fine.' She crawled out of the cupboard and called for Stanley.

A terrified voice said, 'I'm in the kitchen, miss.'

She found him under the kitchen table just as another bomb came whistling down. It was a sensible place to shelter in an air raid. 'Stanley,' she said, 'I need you to help me. Will you find me some towels, as many as you can, and a pair of scissors and a clothes peg? Can you do that?'

'Yes, miss.'

'Good boy. Bring them here, to the kitchen, and then go back under the table and stay there.'

'Right, miss.' He seemed steadier now he had something to do, and he ran upstairs, presumably to find towels. Meanwhile, Kate searched the drawers, where she discovered a pair of kitchen scissors. She was looking for string in the absence of a peg when Stanley came down with an armful of towels.

'Good boy, Stanley. I just need a peg now.'

'I know where they are, miss.' He leapt into the scullery and returned with one.

'Right, Stanley, I want you to hide under the table again. You're going to hear your mum cry out and make a lot of noise. Mums always do when they have babies, but you mustn't be frightened. She's going to be all right.' She really hoped so. Childbirth was troublesome enough without an air raid thrown in as well.

She left Stanley under the table and re-joined Mrs Jenkins, who was still worried about her son.

'Where's Stanley?'

'He's under the kitchen table, Mrs Jenkins. He'll be fine.'

'He's a good lad.'

She made another examination. 'He certainly is.'

'I've tried to keep quiet for his sake,' she said, 'but the pains are getting worse.'

'Don't worry, I've warned him. If you need to shout, holler away.'

Mrs Jenkins obliged with a deafening howl.

'That's right. With the next one, push!'

She yelled again. 'I could kill him for this!'

'Who?'

'My husband. Like as not he's sittin' in the sun, taking it easy while I'm going through purgatory, and it's all his fault. "Don't bother with a hot water bottle," he said. "I'll warm you." Men!'

'Where is he?'

She cried out again. 'In the desert.'

'Don't forget to push.'

'How can I forget?' She let out a full-blooded roar just as Kate was conjecturing about the relative calm outside.

'You know,' she said, 'I believe they've finally gone home.' It was a huge relief for Kate, but Mrs Jenkins was understandably too preoccupied to notice. Instead, she tried to roll over.

'Do you feel more comfortable on your side, Mrs Jenkins?'

'Yes, I think so.'

'All right, I'll help you over. Now bring up your right leg.'

Her patient obliged, and the yell that accompanied the action was her best effort yet. Kate fancied she heard the doors and windows rattle in sympathy.

The crown was now visible and Kate steadied it, allowing it to emerge gently and gradually between contractions.

Soon the head was born, and immediately she saw that the umbilical cord was coiled around the baby's neck. 'All right, Mrs Jenkins, you can push it out now.'

Mrs Jenkins gave a holler that must have been heard around the block, and the baby slid into Kate's welcoming hands. Swiftly she unwound the cord and rubbed the baby's back. She was rewarded immediately by the sound that never failed to fill her with joy. She cleaned the crying infant's nose, eyes and mouth as well as she could and wrapped her in the softest towel she could find from Stanley's collection.

'What is it?'

'You've got a lovely baby girl, Mrs Jenkins. You can roll on to your back again now.' Kate pegged and cut the cord before placing the bundle in her mother's arms, breathless with relief at having delivered a live and seemingly healthy baby. All babies were special, but Blitz babies were a blessing. 'Here, you can get acquainted with her while I finish everything off.' The important thing now was for the placenta to emerge intact, and that could take a long time, maybe half-an-hour or so. She massaged the area over the womb and was eventually rewarded when Mrs Jenkins gave a final, involuntary convulsion and the placenta and its membrane fell on to the towel below. It seemed intact and she wrapped it in the towel for later inspection. 'I'd better see how Stanley is,' she said. It had been a long time for the poor little scrap to be alone.

The 'All Clear' sounded just as she found him still beneath the table, possibly oblivious to the air raid but hiding from a situation he barely understood and which filled him with terror. She crouched beside the table and said, 'You can come out now, Stanley. Your mum's had the baby and they're both fine. You'll be able to see your baby sister when they've both had a bath.'

Whether or not the news had registered, Kate had no idea because as he was staring at her there was a heavy knock on the door and he went out of habit to answer it. He returned shortly with a woman in a uniform hat and coat. She carried a medical bag and looked confused.

Kate asked, 'Are you the midwife?'

The woman nodded. 'Who are you?'

'I'm a nurse from the HRI. The mother and baby are in the stair cupboard. They're both well but in need of bathing.' She couldn't help adding, 'You must have come a long way.'

'No, not all that far, but I had other patients to see, and then the raid started, so there was nothing I could do.'

'It's just as well Stanley came and found me.' Kate stifled her impatience and looked at her watch. 'As far as I can tell, the placenta's intact. The baby was born at about ten-past four. You'll have to weigh her yourself, and I haven't had to time to clean them up yet.'

'Right, I'll go and see them now.'

Kate washed and dried her hands. The fire in the kitchen range was quite healthy so there would be ample hot water for bathing, although that was now the midwife's responsibility. She knelt down in front of Stanley and wrapped her arms around him. 'You've been a very brave boy,' she told him, 'and a great help to your mum and me. I know it was very frightening for you but it's all over now. Soon you'll see your mum and your baby sister and it'll all seem worthwhile.' She gave him an extra hug to confirm it. 'And now,' she said, 'I think your mum deserves a cup of tea after all her efforts. Let's put the kettle on.'

She would get no sleep before going on duty at seven but that was of no consequence. What really mattered was that after all the horrors of the past months something wonderful had happened. New life had emerged amid the carnage and hatefulness of the Blitz, and she knew she would enjoy the memory of it over Christmas, into the New Year and possibly for a long time after that.

❦

Dorothy's new posting was to Market Linfield in Lincolnshire, where she found lots happening, including preparations for a concert organised by the WVS to help finance extra comforts for people bombed out of their homes. When Dorothy heard about it she wanted to help but she couldn't think of anything she could do that would entertain an audience of townsfolk, airmen and WAAFs. Back at Cranwell she'd played the piano in the canteen occasionally for the others to sing along, but she couldn't see that going down any better than classical music, which was where her real strength lay. It seemed she had nothing to offer, and she'd almost given up when Flight-Officer Armstrong spoke to her one morning.

'Corporal Needham, one of the Polish chaps is outside wanting to speak to you. He says it's about the concert. Mind you, if he's trying to pull a fast one I hope you'll tell him to wait until you're off duty.'

'Yes, ma'am.' Puzzled for the moment, Dorothy left what she was doing. The amorous activities of some Polish servicemen had given their countrymen a reputation that wasn't universally deserved,

186

but there was always a chance that Miss Armstrong might be proved right in her suspicion.

She opened the door and looked into the beaming face of a sergeant navigator. Like most aircrew, he was young, maybe in his mid-twenties, and tall with dark-brown, swept-back hair and grey eyes.

'Good morning,' he said. 'Are you Corporal Need-ham?' His voice was tantalisingly deep and he rolled his 'r's in a way that Dorothy found beguiling.

'Needham, yes. What can I do for you?'

'I am Jakub Wasiliewski. You are, I believe, pianist.'

'Well, I play a little, yes.'

'I come straight to the point. I am singer and I need accompanist for concert for the bombed people. Flight Lieutenant Bennett was my accompanist but he unfortunately is no longer.' His smile faltered as he imparted the last piece of information.

Dorothy had no need to ask why. Flt/Lt Bennett's aircraft was one of those shot down over Essen the previous night. 'I know,' she said. 'I'm sorry. What are you going to sing?'

'It goes without saying that the ladies of the WVS understand that if we are on op. I don't be there, but I hope there will not be op. In that case I shall sing just two Christmas songs. They are "O Holy Night" by Adolphe Adam, and "Nazareth" by Charles Gounod. You know these songs?' As his accent placed a 'k' sound after words ending in 'ng', the subject was perhaps a little unfortunate, but the effect wasn't without charm.

'Yes, we used to sing them at school.'

'Good. It goes without saying that I shall bring the music for you. When will you rehearse with me?'

'I come off duty at eighteen-hundred and then I have to eat. I could meet you after that.'

'Good. Please come to the sergeants' mess and I shall take you to room where there is piano.' Something seemed to be fascinating him.

'Is something the matter?'

'No, not the matter. I am thinking only that I come to see pianist-girl and I find the fission of beauty.'

'Fission?' She tried not to laugh. 'That's a split in something, isn't it?

'No, I mean to say this thing that I see.'

'Oh, a *vision*. Well, thank you for the compliment, Sergeant, but you must keep your mind on the job.'

'My mind is on the job. By the way, have you a name for me to call you?'

'My name's Dorothy but you can call me "Dot".'

'That is very nice. I am Jakub, but the skipper and the other blokes call me "Jake". I believe they are making the fun but I am happy with this name.'

'All right, Jake, I'll come to the sergeants' mess at eighteen-thirty.' She reached for the door handle and hesitated. 'By the way,' she asked, 'what's your voice? I think I detect maybe bass-baritone.'

'No, I am *basso profundo*.' He sang a few gloriously deep notes to demonstrate, and Dorothy felt her legs weaken and her usual reserve begin to falter.

﹡﹡﹡

A round, bespectacled man seated opposite Alan folded his *Daily Express* with an air of satisfaction. 'It looks like Hitler's finally come unstuck,' he observed.

'Or stuck,' suggested Alan.

The man chuckled. 'That's a good one. Yes, they're stuck in the snow all right. It was bound to happen.'

'History repeating itself,' agreed Alan.

'What?'

'Russia's winter climate stopped Bonaparte in his tracks, didn't it?'

'Oh yes, that's right.' He looked pointedly at Alan's shoulder flashes and said, 'I see you're in the Intelligence Corps.'

'Yes, but no jokes about military intelligence, please. I've heard them all.'

'I wouldn't dream of it. I just thought, well, you must know a thing or two.' He looked around at the sleeping occupants of the compartment and winked at Alan.

'About what?'

'You know,' he insisted. 'You must have an idea of how the war's going.'

Alan shook his head solemnly. 'No, I know hardly anything. In any case, you'll find it all in there.' He pointed to the man's folded newspaper.

'But....'

'What?'

The man looked around the compartment again and, having satisfied himself that the other three occupants were still asleep, whispered, 'I bet you know if the powers-that-be have something up their sleeve.'

Alan peered through the window. The train was approaching Cullington Golf Club, which meant that he was only two minutes away from his station.

'You mustn't breathe a word to a living soul,' he warned.

'Not a word.' The man stared at him, anxious not to miss a detail.

'The latest thing,' Alan mouthed almost silently, 'is zoological warfare.'

The man blinked.

'In the shape of trained mice.'

'Mice?'

'Sh.' Alan put a forefinger to his lips. 'Yes, mice.' He leaned forward conspiratorially. 'As we speak, containers are being made that can be packed with mice and parachuted into the industrial heart of Germany. They're designed to break open on landing, and the mice will make for the nearest factory.'

'Then what?'

'It takes less than half a minute for a mouse to gnaw through an electricity cable. Think of what a thousand mice can do. Production in the Ruhr Valley will be halted in a matter of weeks.' He took his bag from the luggage rack and picked up his gas mask case. 'In no time at all Hitler will have no more tanks, aircraft, armoured cars, rifles, machine-guns, bombs or shells with which to prolong the war, and he'll be forced to throw Germany and himself on our mercy.' He stepped into the corridor, putting a forefinger to his lips again in caution. 'Keep it under your hat.'

It was hardly worthwhile taking a taxi for the short journey so it didn't matter that there wasn't one available, fuel rationing having spread them more thinly than ever. Instead Alan was happy to walk the familiar route to his home.

He walked past the public baths and swimming pool that he remembered from childhood and along the imposing front of Britannia Mills until he came to the road that took him past the public library and eventually to the large Edwardian house that was his home.

He wasn't surprised to find the door locked; he'd caught an earlier train than he'd originally planned, and his mother wouldn't be expecting him for another three hours, so he put his bag in his room and went down to the kitchen, where he found a note on the table. It read:

Welcome home, Alan. Dad left this afternoon for a meeting at head office tomorrow, back Tuesday. I'm at the WVS, back by half-past four. Careful with the tea. It's all we have 'til Monday.
Love, Mum. X

It wasn't the welcome he'd anticipated. He was pleased his mother was 'doing her bit,' to use the prevailing expression, with the WVS, but an all-day stint on the Sunday her son was due to arrive on two days' leave seemed a bit much. He decided to call on Iris. At a little after two in the afternoon she must surely be at home.

He buttoned up his greatcoat again and walked the short distance to Holdsworth Street. The temperature had fallen since his arrival and the vapour from his breath was clearly visible as he made his way down the street, so he was relieved when he reached the house.

The kitchen window was slightly open, and he could hear Iris inside, chatting with someone until she heard the knock on the door. He heard her say, 'Go and see who it is, Edward. I've got my hands in water.'

Alan wondered for a moment who Edward was, but then the door opened and revealed a young man in dark-rimmed glasses, a

Fair Isle jumper and grey flannel trousers. He seemed disturbed to find Alan on the doorstep.

Iris called, 'Who is it?'

'Tell her it's Alan.'

The young man, presumably Edward, paled visibly but he had no need to relay the information, because Iris had already recognised Alan's voice.

'Oh heck,' she said, appearing in the hallway. 'I wasn't expecting you 'til later.' She cast an apologetic look in Edward's direction and said to Alan, 'You'd better come in for a minute.'

'Are you sure you can spare a minute?'

'There's no need to be like that.' She stood aside to let him in. Edward hovered uncertainly in the background.

'I was going to write to you.'

'Well, I suppose the thought was there.'

'Alan, you're not making this easy for me.'

'I don't see why I should. Correct me if I've misread any of this, but it seems to me that Edward here, presumably a civilian and therefore readily at hand, is now keeping your home fire burning, which means that my services are no longer required. Is that a fair assessment of the situation?'

'It's not how I'd have put it.' Perhaps at a loss quite how to put it, she said, 'Listen, Alan, I was going to speak to you later and explain. The last thing I wanted was to hurt you.'

'I'm not hurt.'

'Aren't you?' She seemed genuinely surprised and relieved.

'No. Disappointed and disillusioned, maybe, but not hurt.'

It was true. Iris had been good company and he'd looked forward to seeing her again, but he'd never become involved with her to the extent that their parting could be painful for him. He was thankful for that.

⚜

Dorothy was relieved to find that the upright piano in Saint Mark's Church Hall was tuned and in good condition. As heavy rain and poor visibility had caused all flying to be cancelled for the next few days, Jake would perform as planned and she was looking forward to it.

They sat together in the tiny backstage area and listened to a corporal fitter who was billed as a comedian. So far his jokes had been on the *risqué* side for a village gathering, and his delivery was clumsy and ill-timed. He was getting only sporadic and half-hearted laughter from the villagers and considerable barracking from the RAF community. Even Jake, usually so tolerant and good-natured, felt inclined to comment, 'Let us say openly he is very bad.'

Dorothy smiled. Jake collected idiomatic expressions like souvenirs and displayed them at every opportunity. As well as 'It goes without saying' and 'Let us say openly,' he had recently acquired 'Just the two of us,' which Dorothy liked for personal reasons.

Eventually the comedian came off to polite applause from the locals and a variety of harsh comments from those in uniform, and Dorothy became quite apprehensive. Jake's style of singing was different from the kind his colleagues usually enjoyed and she didn't want him to suffer the same reception. Still, cold feet or not, it was time for him to go on stage and for her to go to the piano. The master of ceremonies announced them, and the two went to their places to be greeted with whistles and catcalls.

Jake waited for the noise to cease. When he was satisfied, he said to the audience, 'Because Christmas will be soon, I wish to sing "O Holy Night" by Adolphe Adam.' Remarkably the audience remained quiet, and Jake motioned to Dorothy to begin the soft, arpeggio introduction. At the sound of his deep, resonant voice the faction that had been so vocal and restive became transfixed and sat spellbound throughout the song, hesitating for a second after the last note had ended and then breaking into enthusiastic applause.

His second song 'Nazareth' was so popular that the master of ceremonies motioned excitedly to him to sing an encore. Jake held up his hands to the audience, who became silent again.

'Thank you,' he said, 'you are very kind. I give my excellent accompanist a moment to find the music.' He glanced at Dorothy for confirmation that she had, and went on. 'I wish to sing a Moravian Christmas song. I'm afraid I must sing in Polish. I don't know the English words.'

He went on to sing the carol that Dorothy knew as 'Infant Holy, Infant Lowly' and, if the words themselves meant nothing to most of the audience, their exotic unfamiliarity must have evoked thoughts for those obliged to celebrate Christmas in a foreign land, away from their families.

Together once more and secure in the semi-darkness, Jake said, 'You accompany me very well, darlink. May I kiss you now to celebrate our performance?'

'Oh, I think so, Jake.' She'd always known it would happen, just as she was sure of where it would eventually lead, but she raised her face to his all the same. She was momentarily aware of someone on stage reciting 'The Shooting of Dan McGrew' but then she became conscious only of Jake's lips touching hers.

They kissed slowly and deeply, and then after a minute or so she heard the flimsy backstage door open and close again, and she broke away from Jake, who seemed surprised.

'What is the matter, darlink?'

'Someone just came in,' she whispered, 'and I'd just as soon not do this in front of an audience.'

'No,' he agreed, 'not in front of the audience but just the two of us.'

They sat down together as awkwardly as couples do when their intimacy has been interrupted, and Dorothy asked, 'Do you know what would be really nice?'

'Yes, darlink.' He stroked her knee through the serge fabric of her skirt.

'Behave yourself, Jake.' She removed his hand but held it between hers, where it felt huge. 'I was going to say how nice it would be if we were to go to a restaurant together and eat in a civilised way, as a change from eating in the mess with everyone else.'

'Yes, but where we can do this thing?'

'We could go into Lincoln tomorrow. I've got a pass for forty-eight hours and flying is still cancelled.'

'Yes, out of the question that I can leave the station.'

'Why can't you?' It had seemed so straightforward. She couldn't imagine what the problem could be.

'No, I mean that of course it goes without saying I shall be able to leave the station.'

She tried not to look too relieved; he was confident enough already. 'You know,' she said, 'we should take a closer look at some of those English phrases of yours before there's a serious misunderstanding.'

❧⚜❧

Alan had enjoyed showing the new officer around Trent Park. She was a second subaltern, the ATS equivalent of a second lieutenant, but her commission was more recent than his, which made her his junior.

He knew a great deal about her, having been involved in her procurement for Trent Park. He knew that she was twenty-two years old and that, except for five years spent at an independent school in England, she had grown up from the age of three in Berlin, where her father had been at the British Embassy. From leaving school she had worked as a shorthand typist and trainee secretary with a freight forwarding company in Berlin.

It wasn't her secretarial skills, however, that had interested MI19, but her perfect knowledge of German. Alan had located her in a pay office in Aldershot, where she was bored, frustrated, under-employed and therefore delighted when told she would be working in intelligence.

Those were the basic facts about Second Subaltern Gwen Davidson, but Alan had noticed also that she had light-brown hair, blue eyes, a trim figure, an appealing smile and a friendly manner, all of which made her particularly attractive in his eyes.

'Things have developed here to an extraordinary extent over the past year,' he told her as they walked towards the officers' mess. 'I'll never forget my first interrogation. It was at a POW camp for Italians in Lancashire. I had to wring whatever intelligence I could out of an army captain and I was feeling very unsure of myself. I tried to remember everything I'd been told about interrogation techniques and waited nervously for him to be brought to me. Eventually the door opened and he came in with one of the guards, who introduced him. Then he sat down unceremoniously in front of me and said, "Okay, wadda ya wanna know?" '

'Oh,' she laughed, 'what a relief.'

'It was, but we've learned a lot since then, and we've achieved a lot too; in fact I'm not exaggerating when I say that our contribution to the war is absolutely vital.'

'Yes, I can't believe you knew when you did that Hitler was going to invade Russia.'

'We had to keep quiet about that one, for obvious reasons.' He stopped at the entrance and said, 'By the way, we don't talk shop in the mess. You never know who might be listening, and it's absolutely imperative that ancillary personnel don't get wind of what we're doing. They do like to gossip.'

'Of course.'

'Would you like coffee?' He guided her to a quiet corner.

'Yes, please. That would be lovely.'

The mess waiter answered Alan's gesture with a genteel 'Sir?'

'Good morning, Murchison.'

'Good morning, sir.'

'Do you think you could rustle up coffee for both of us, please?

'Of course, sir. Will the lady be requiring milk?'

'Yes, please,' said Gwen.

'Very good, ma'am.'

Gwen smiled as he left. 'I like the way you did that,' she said.

'What, ordering coffee? It's not difficult once you get the hang of it.'

'I meant the way you spoke to the mess waiter. It annoys me when an officer gives a short, sharp order in the mess without so much as a "please" or "thank you", and I'm sure Murchison appreciates your politeness.'

'Put it down to my humble beginnings as a private soldier,' he said, 'and you're right – it does help to oil the wheels.'

As if to demonstrate the point, Murchison arrived with the coffee and an extra luxury.

'I thought you'd appreciate some biscuits, sir. These were left over from the Colonel's meeting this morning.'

'Thank you, Murchison.'

'Yes,' said Gwen, 'thank you indeed. That was very thoughtful of you.'

'Not at all, ma'am. There's no point in letting them go to waste, is there?'

Alan looked around the mess and counted at least ten officers, all senior to Gwen and him, and none of them appeared to have been given so much as a sponge finger. 'No, Murchison,' he said, 'no point at all.'

Gwen's eyes scanned the room, with its ornate plaster work, high ceiling and crystal chandeliers. 'I haven't known all that many messes,' she said, 'but this one is terribly grand.'

'Yes, Trent Park is rather special, and a touch of luxury always helps when the pressure's on and leave is scarce.'

'Being the new girl,' she said, 'I'm on duty over Christmas.'

'Me too. I imagine you'll be coming to the Christmas Eve dance?'

'It's the first I've heard of it. Isn't it necessary to be invited?'

'No, it's very informal. Of course, you should ideally have an escort.'

'Ah.'

He gave her a playful smile. 'And I'd naturally deem it an honour.'

She returned his smile. 'In that case, how can I refuse?'

⊶⊰⋇⊱⋇⊰⋇⊶

'This is very good idea, said Jake, pouring the last of the wine into Dorothy's glass. 'I am surprised we can get the table at the last moment. There are many people here this evening.' He added with characteristic glibness, 'But none as beautiful as you, darlink, and your gown is very *chic*.'

'Thank you, Jake.' After much deliberation she'd resurrected the dark-green velvet dress, and she was pleased with her decision. 'Most of the girls have used their leave to go home, but the journey takes up so much of the forty-eight hours.' With a conspiratorial but nervous smile she said, 'I'm sure we made the right decision.'

'And so am I.'

'I'd been longing to do something different, a weekend of being spoiled to death, a time to wear decent clothes and eat civilised food. Above all I wanted a bathroom I didn't have to share with half the station. It was all going to be very innocent, you understand, until I met you.'

'But darlink,' he said, reaching across the table to take her hand, 'room in hotel like this is expensive. How you pay for it?'

She laughed. 'Certainly not with a corporal's pay.' She eyed him mischievously. 'Are you familiar with Needham's Pickles?'

'Yes, we have Needham's ketchup in the sergeants' mess.'

'I'm glad to hear it.'

He stared at her incredulously. 'You are Needham's ketchup?'

'It's not just me, but I'm one of the shareholders.'

He seemed to be struggling with the news. Eventually he said, 'But, darlink, you must let me pay for the meal.'

She'd been expecting that. An independent woman was difficult for most men to accept, and Jake was apparently no different in that respect. 'All right,' she said, 'you can pay for the meal. We'll sort it out later.' She placed her free hand on his, feeling more than ever the scarlet woman. 'You mustn't think I do this regularly,' she assured him. 'As a matter of fact I've never done it before.'

His grip tightened on her hand. 'You are the maiden?'

'I'm single, if that's what you mean.'

'No, I try to say....' Clearly his vocabulary failed him.

'You want to know if I'm a virgin? Well, that's debatable because I've done a lot of cycling.' Nerves were making her babble. 'They say that can rob a girl of her credibility,' she ended weakly.

'Cycling? I don't understand this thing.'

'Let's just say I've never been with a man, but I know you'll take that into consideration.'

He motioned to the waiter to bring the bill and gave him the room number. 'Darlink,' he said when the waiter was gone, 'I shall be as gentle as the butterfly.'

'Who could ask for more?' In truth her manner suggested infinitely more self-confidence than she felt. Usually so collected, she was now on unfamiliar ground. Naturally, she understood the mechanics of what was to happen but theory, as always, had its limitations. Unsurely, she accompanied him to the lift, convinced that every eye in the room was on them.

Once in the room they kissed at length and that steadied her nerves. After a while Jake expertly unhooked her dress and ran down the zipper.

'Darlink,' he said, 'I am a thousand miles from home and my country is in the hands of savages, so why am I the happiest man in the world?' He kissed her softly and unhurriedly before going on to keep his promise to be 'as gentle as the butterfly.'

In time to come, Dorothy would find herself in the company of women when, very occasionally, shyly and half in jest, someone would ask her about *her* first time, and she knew she would be able to answer simply, 'It was glorious.'

❦❧

Christmas Eve on the North Sea was comparatively mild. According to the meteorological report an anticyclone had settled over the British Isles, and Jack was grateful for it. Stars shone between the clouds and the moon was reflected a thousand times in the gentle, rippling swell.

He lifted his night-glasses and quartered the horizon, with its seascape of colliers, tramp steamers and coasters. All seemed well. He checked the deck watch. It showed twenty-three fifty-six, just four minutes to Christmas. Owen would be on the bridge soon to relieve him. He'd ordered an extra tot of rum to be issued to the ship's company at midnight, and that would be a jolly affair, but just for a moment Jack allowed himself the luxury of thinking about all the people he would like to be with at that time: his mother and father, Mary and the baby, Dorothy, Kate and Alan. He would never see Maurice again, and that still disturbed him. He wondered how Kate was coping. She sounded brave enough in her letters, but he still wondered.

There was a noise on the ladder and Owen joined him, carrying two glasses, one of which he gave to Jack with a friendly wink. He placed the other on the chart table. 'Back in a jiffy,' he said, disappearing down the ladder.

Turning to the bridge lookouts, Jack said, 'All right, lads, go below and get your tot.'

'Aye aye sir.'

'Thank you, sir.'

'And a happy Christmas.'

The two men returned his greeting.

Jack picked up his glass and sniffed. It was brandy. He stood for a while, inhaling its heady aroma until Owen reappeared with two more glasses.

'The Cox'n and Petty Officer Bryant will be here as soon as they're relieved,' he commented. 'I believe the Cox'n's at the wheel.'

A tinny voice came up the pipe. 'Wheelhouse – bridge.'

Owen leaned over the voice pipe to answer, 'Bridge.'

'Leading Seaman Allen at the wheel, sir. Steady on one-four-five degrees.'

'Very good. Happy Christmas, Allen.'

'Happy Christmas, sir.'

With the Cox'n and Petty Officer Bryant from the engine room now assembled, Owen handed them their drinks.

'A very happy Christmas to you all, gentlemen.'

'And to you, sir.'

'Happy Christmas, sir.'

'Happy Christmas, sir.'

Jack, the Cox'n and Bryant exchanged greetings.

'Peace on earth, goodwill toward men,' said Owen. 'There's no shortage of goodwill around here but peace has some catching up to do.'

'It'll come, sir,' the Cox'n assured him.

As the four men shook hands, it seemed to Jack that, at least for the time being, it promised to be a happy Christmas. They were away from home and in hazardous waters but they were in excellent company, and that was a blessing in itself.

29

'I can't believe the change in you in... how long is it since we met?'

Rachel counted the months. 'It's been more than three months. I believe it was early in May.'

'Just three months.' Kate considered the transformation: the dress, the shoes and the well-cut bob.

'I always did like clothes when I was younger. It just became an awful habit later on, creeping around in whatever was to hand. I suppose I was living down to the image my mother had forced on me.'

'I'm glad you realise that. It's too easy to feel guilty about things that are not our fault.'

Rachel smiled. 'I couldn't see you falling into that trap, Kate.'

'Oh, couldn't you? Well, I did, and for quite a long time.'

'Was it to do with your mother?'

'No, at least I suppose I carried a fair amount of guilt because of her, but it was nothing like I felt after Maurice was killed.'

Clearly it wasn't the answer Rachel expected. 'What on earth,' she asked, 'did you have to feel guilty about?'

'It was about sex,' said Kate, opting for directness, 'or rather, the lack of it.' She smiled at Rachel's reaction.

'I'm sorry. I didn't mean to look shocked. You surprised me, that's all.'

'It's not the kind of thing you expect to hear from a woman of my age, is it?'

'Not as a general rule, but please go on.'

'It's not much of a story really. In fact it was something quite common in those days. You see, like most healthy young men, Maurice had but one thing on his mind, most of the time at least, and I was adamant that it wasn't going to happen. It was so risky in those days, Rachel. There was no pill, and nothing we had available was fool-proof.'

'It would have been an awful risk,' agreed Rachel.

'That's right, but after he was killed, and the shock, the realisation and everything I've told you about began to ebb, I became increasingly conscious that because of my stubbornness he'd gone to his death as celibate as he was born.'

'But who could blame you in the circumstances?'

'Only I could do that,' she agreed. 'It was some time before I began to see it more logically.'

'You weren't very old at the time. You did well to come to terms with it.'

'I'm not so sure, Rachel. The war was great for making us think clearly about the things that mattered and those that didn't.'

Rachel looked thoughtful. 'But importance can be subjective too.'

'I was thinking of accepted values.' She shook her head in confusion. 'At least, I think I was.'

'Do you want to rest?'

'No, Rachel. I'm no better when I'm wide awake and fully charged.'

'I don't want to wear you out.'

'I know and I appreciate your concern, but don't go yet, I mean unless you have to.'

'All right.' Rachel settled once more into her chair.

'What were we talking about?'

'Accepted values. Being able to differentiate between the important and the unimportant.'

'Oh yes, but even then there was a lot of lop-sided thinking. Talking to you about Dorothy the other day reminded me of it, because her mother was the perfect example.' She closed her eyes to remember more clearly.

'Are you sure you don't want to rest?'

'Absolutely. You see, Dorothy wanted to take Jake home for Christmas. After all, the poor man was far from home and all the festivities there, but her mother wouldn't hear of it.'

'Why ever not?'

'Polish servicemen generally had a Don Juan reputation. My mother once told me she thought it was because they came from a cold country and they had to have frequent sex to keep themselves and each other warm. She was as naive as Mrs Needham.'

'Dorothy's mother?'

'Yes. At all events, she didn't want him in the house in case the neighbours saw him and put two and two together. Also, she didn't want him there in case she had to leave the house at some time and the neighbours were proved right.'

'It seems harsh, all the same.'

'Oh well, it was probably better for them as things worked out, because Dorothy booked the hotel again and they stayed there over the Christmas holiday. She said it was much better than being at home and waiting for her mother to go out.' She stopped as one thought prompted another. 'Mind you,' she said, 'it wasn't Dorothy's last brush with racial prejudice.'

30

News in the early part of 1942 was at best lacklustre and often dire, causing off-duty aircrew and ground staff to seek temporary distractions. The most readily available diversion at Market Linfield, as everywhere else, was romance, and cupid's arrow found many a receptive bull's eye.

It was a relatively old story for Dorothy and Jake, who spent every off-station moment they could together. Dorothy, who fancied she was in touch with her emotions, found Jake fascinating, beguiling, entertaining and extremely good in bed. In the absence of previous carnal experience her enlivened senses were sufficient to tell her that. Captivated though she was, however, she was not in love with him. That part of her was reserved, as ever, for a man with special but as yet undefined qualities.

It was impossible for her to gauge Jake's true feelings. She enjoyed his flowery language and protestations of devotion, but she balanced them against the knowledge that at twenty-six he was a man of some experience and that his glibness might easily be the result of considerable practice.

As they lay together in the Imperial Hotel her thoughts were of a simpler kind. She relished the feel of soft, white sheets after the coarse linen she was used to on the station, and that of Jake's warm body next to hers. She nestled closer to him.

'Jake,' she asked, 'how long do you think this war's likely to go on?'

'The end is years away, darlink. Let us say openly, now the Americans are with us and Russia is at war with the Nazis there is possibility to invade Europe, but not yet.' He turned on to his side and kissed her shoulder. 'Darlink, why you wish to talk about the war when we have only this hour made the love?'

'Sorry. Was it a bit soon? I was actually thinking about the things we left behind. I'm sure the day can't come soon enough when you can return to Warsaw.'

'Yes, this is true, but will not happen for a while.'

'Tell me about Warsaw.'

'Okay.' He propped himself up on one elbow and paused, apparently in thought. Then, after kissing each of her breasts slowly and reverently, he began. 'Warsaw is wonderful city. There is much music, opera, ballet and concerts. There are theatres and cinemas as well.'

Dorothy wondered how these admirable but fairly universal facilities made Warsaw so special, but she kept the question to herself.

'Warsaw is wonderful city,' he repeated. 'In fact only one thing is wrong.'

'Go on, I'll buy it.'

'The Jews.'

'What?' She sat upright abruptly, so that he too was surprised.

'What is matter, darlink?'

'I'm amazed you said that.'

'What I am saying to make you angry?' He seemed genuinely at a loss.

'It was what you said about Jews.'

'Of course I say this thing.' He settled back against his pillows to explain. 'Maybe you don't know of them where you live, but let us say openly they are the big nuisance.'

'Jake, that's an appalling thing to say. Have you forgotten that we're at war against Germany because of that kind of hatefulness, the kind, in fact, that made them invade Poland in the first place?'

'I drop the bombs on the German cities because of what they do to Poland, not because of Jews. It goes without saying that they give nothing, but make the profit from Polish people. They are also the most secret of people. Everything they do is secret.' He made it sound like the greatest crime of all.

'Who can blame them for being secretive when there's so much feeling against them? Jake, you really are the limit. Correct me if I'm wrong, but aren't you a staunch Roman Catholic?'

'What is this "staunch"?'

'It means you're devout, you're *keen* on it.' She was too angry to explain further.

'Then, yes, I am keen Roman Catholic.'

'And has it passed your notice that Jesus was a Jew?'

'No.' It seemed he was appalled at the idea. 'He is better than that. He is Lord of Heaven and Earth.'

'Agreed, but he was born in Bethlehem of a Jewish mother, who, let me remind you, has a special place in the Christian faith, and pretty soon after that he was circumcised, a process that's not without religious significance.'

'I have this operation,' he told her with quiet dignity, 'only for the medical reason, not for other reason.'

'I really can't believe any of this.' She slid out of bed and retrieved her dressing gown from its hook. 'Would it surprise you to learn that I'm partly Jewish?'

'No.' Again he was shocked. 'This can't be true.'

'Yes, it damn' well is, and what's more I'm proud of it!' She realised by this time that her voice had risen considerably but she was too angry to worry about anyone in the adjacent rooms. 'My grandmother was Jewish and she married a gentile because she, at least, wasn't eaten up with prejudice like some people!'

'Darlink, please take off the gown and come to bed. This is silly argument. Let us rid off of it.'

'No, I can't.'

'But only one grandmother makes you only the quarter Jewish and that is not so bad thing.'

Dashing away tears of anger with the back of her hand, she said, 'So it's not so bad, eh? Being only one quarter Jewish makes me just about acceptable, I suppose?' Suddenly she could no longer find the words she needed. 'I'm going to have a bath,' she told him, controlling her fury, 'and then I'm going back to the station.'

It would have taken a great deal of effort and willingness to repair their relationship but they were spared the task when Jake's squadron was transferred to a station in Cambridgeshire. Market Linfield was to become a base for the US Army Air Corps. WAAF and other ground staff were posted to various stations, including nearby Humby-on-the-Wold. It was to be Dorothy's home for a little while.

∗※∗※∗

From Alan's point of view the Christmas Eve Dance at Trent Park was entirely successful; he and Gwen had formed an immediate mutual attraction and had met twice outside the Park. Their first excursion was to see Roddy McDowall and Maureen O'Hara in 'How Green Was My Valley', which they both enjoyed very much, and the second time was simply to eat in a restaurant and to enjoy each other's company away from the mess.

On the third occasion, on a twenty-four-hour pass, Gwen made a suggestion.

'I know a decent place where we can eat,' she said, 'and get free accommodation. It's better than paying out lots of money.'

As Alan didn't have lots of money it sounded very promising. They packed their overnight things into the panniers of his Panther and with Gwen in the sidecar they left Trent Park for the short journey to Potters Bar.

Fifteen minutes later they pulled up on her direction outside a small, half-timbered house with an equally small but cheerful garden.

'It's my Aunt's house,' she explained, emerging as elegantly as she could from the sidecar. 'I used to spend half-term holidays here with her when I was at school, but she's gone to stay with a friend in Somerset. Her friend's infirm, so the stay could be a lengthy one.'

Alan blinked. 'When did she go?'

'Two days ago.' She found the key in her bag. 'Jolly handy, isn't it?'

He could only agree. He carried their bags indoors and looked around him at the oak beams, timber-framed walls and wide fireplace with its basket grate. Gwen came behind him with a shopping bag she'd retrieved from the sidecar. Alan peered at it curiously.

'Food,' she told him. 'I paid a visit to the kitchen today and scrounged a few rations for a packed meal.'

'A packed meal?'

'I packed it into the sidecar with me.'

'That's true.'

'And I'm going to cook dinner tonight. As you've probably guessed, this is the decent place I told you about. It was to be a surprise.'

'It's the best kind of surprise,' he assured her, 'a cosy, intimate, tailor-made surprise. It's perfect.' He held his arms wide and wrapped them around her.

'Be careful,' she cautioned. 'I may forget all about cooking.' She returned his kiss nevertheless, until suddenly she shivered. 'The first job,' she told him, 'is to light a fire. We should probably air some sheets. I'll show you where the wood and things are and then you can see to that while I cook.'

<hr/>

Later, after a meal that was more generous that their usual fare they sat together in the firelight.

'We have bacon and scrambled eggs for breakfast,' she told him. 'It's a shame it has to be powdered egg, but fresh eggs there were none.'

'I shan't notice the difference,' he promised.

'One of the WAAF officers who arrived on Wednesday told me about the stuff the Americans have brought over to feed their people: steaks, pork chops, ice cream and all kinds of things we haven't seen since rationing began. It made her green with envy.'

'It's better not to dwell on it.'

They dwelt on it all the same, until Gwen said, 'I'm not terribly keen on that fish that comes from South Africa.'

'Snoek? You're not alone in that, but at least it's not rationed. *Noli equi dentes* and all that.'

'Isn't that "Never look a gift horse in the mouth"? I dropped Latin after School Certificate.'

'Yes, I'm sorry. It's a bad habit.'

She looked up at him speculatively and said, 'You must have been an erudite schoolboy.'

'I was the worst kind of pedant you can imagine. I'm ashamed to recall some of the things I did.'

'Surely not.'

'I was pedantic, self-opinionated, arrogant and superior, at least in my estimation.'

'And they say only women can do more than one thing at a time. What happened to turn you into this man I admire so much?'

'It took the army to make me into something resembling a human being.'

'How did it do that?'

'I'll tell you some time but not just now.'

'Well, good for the army, anyway.'

The log settled in the grate prompting desultory flames and a shower of sparks.

'Are we really going to sleep upstairs,' he asked, 'in the freezing cold?'

'No.' She settled more comfortably against his shoulder. 'Let's stay down here and keep the fire going. You can have the sofa and I'll pull the armchairs together.'

'You're joking.'

'No, it's probably safer and more correct if you go upstairs and leave me down here.'

'Now you really are joking.'

'Yes, I am. I vote we put the chair and sofa cushions on the floor and rough it. What do you say?'

'I've never heard it called that, but yes, it gets my vote too.'

She sat upright to dispense with her collar and unbutton her shirt. 'There's nothing alluring about the ATS uniform,' she said apologetically.

'It can be very alluring in the right circumstances,' he assured her, rising to his feet and beckoning her to follow, 'at such a time as this, for example.' He unfastened her waistband, allowing her skirt to fall to her feet, and then slipped her shirt over her shoulders.

'You've done this before.'

'Once or twice,' he admitted.

'Fair's fair,' she insisted. 'I'm a shirt and a skirt ahead of you. You owe me a shirt and a pair of trousers.'

'Wait a minute.' He unlaced his shoes and cast them aside. She slipped his braces over his shoulders and sent his trousers on their downward journey.

'That was pretty deft,' he said.

'It was my first time with army trousers. I've done Navy blue and Air Force blue, but this is my first khaki assignment.'

He wondered if she was joking about the Navy and the RAF, and decided that she must have been.

She unclipped and peeled off her stockings, explaining that it was a task best undertaken by a woman, stockings being more precious than rubies.

'My turn,' he said, reaching behind her with both hands to unhook her brassiere.

'I bet you can't,' she said.

'I just have.' He draped the garment across the nearest armchair.

'You're ahead of me now,' she complained.

'Hush.' He kissed her softly on the lips.

The firelight cast their shadows against the wall behind them as they continued to undress, until eventually the flickering silhouettes merged into one.

❧❧❧

'I see there are some quite presentable Wrens on the base, sir.' Brian Foster, a lean and hungry young man with a fresh complexion and unbounded enthusiasm was the ship's latest recruit. He'd recently completed officer training at *HMS King Alfred* but, being only twenty, had to be content for the time being with the rank of midshipman. His commission would follow his twenty-first birthday, a milestone he could hardly wait to reach.

'You need to keep your mind on the job,' Jack warned him.

'Carnal preoccupation can be an unhealthy distraction for a young chap at sea.'

'It's good advice,' said Owen, entering the wardroom during the latter part of the conversation. 'Harm can come to a lad when Aphrodite flutters her eyelashes. Never forget that it takes one woman twenty-one years to make a man of her son, and it takes another less than two minutes to make a fool of him.'

'I was only spying out the land, sir.'

'Better leave it 'til you're older,' Owen advised him. 'These women eat young lads like you alive.'

'To turn to a healthier subject if I may, sir,' said Jack, 'I've been looking at some of the duties our new boy might take on, just to give me a breathing space here and there.'

'Good thinking, Number One.' Owen took out his pouch and proceeded to fill his pipe. 'What do you have in mind?'

'To begin with, I wondered if he'd like to take over first-aid.'

'I could certainly do that, sir.' Brian was quick to volunteer. 'I was in St John Ambulance for two years and they made me a medical orderly in the Home Guard.'

'Listen to him,' said Owen. 'The lad has more experience than either of us. If he can hold his tot he may have a future aboard this ship.'

The midshipman frowned uncertainly. 'I rather imagined I'd left rum behind me, sir, when I left the lower deck.'

'Believe me,' said Jack, 'when you're on watch in a force-eight gale and your teeth are chattering like a gossip with the latest scandal you'll be thankful for a tot of Their Lordships' nectar.'

'Well said, Number One.' Satisfied that his pipe was going well, Owen returned his lighter to his hip pocket.

'But sir....' Brian searched desperately for the words to question such a flagrant breach of regulations.

'King's Regulations and Admiralty Instructions are matters for the grown-up navy to worry about,' explained Owen, adding darkly, 'but we, my lad, are pirates. We'd be flying the Jolly Roger had the submarine service not laid their thieving hands on it first.' He blew out a cloud of blue smoke with a flamboyance that might have impressed Blackbeard himself. 'Junior ratings in the respectable navy receive, as you know, a measure of rum to two measures of water daily and at the appointed hour, but we in Coastal Forces deal only in "neaters" and dispense it to officers and men alike when operationally necessary. That way,' he concluded, 'everyone is happy and we continue to scare the wits out of the *Kriegsmarine* with our buccaneering exploits.' He neglected to explain that the regular deficit in the ship's rum issue was always accounted for as 'lost in heavy seas' or 'lost by enemy action,' chilling phrases that impressed the Paymaster's staff and which were never questioned.

'I think also,' said Owen after brief consideration, 'we'll make our new colleague responsible for keeping the confidential books up to date.'

'An excellent suggestion, sir,' said Jack, glad to be rid of a tiresome job.

Owen glanced at the wardroom clock. 'It's time the mail went ashore. Grab a matelot, Number One.'

'I'll do it myself, sir,' offered Jack.

'Good man. I imagine you have an ulterior motive?'

'I just want to spy out the land, sir.'

'In that case,' said Owen, picking up the mailbag and handing it to him, 'spy away.'

'Aye aye, sir.' Jack donned his greatcoat and climbed the short ladder to the upper deck. The temperature had fallen and low clouds threatened snow. He turned up his collar and walked across the dock to the mail office.

As he reached the entrance three Wren ratings came out carrying letters. They saluted him hurriedly and stood aside so that he could enter the office. He decided that one of them could never match Brian's description of 'quite presentable,' another might get somewhere close to it in civilian clothes and with skilful make-up, but the final member of the group looked very promising. Her dark-brown hair was pinned up and concealed beneath her 'pudding basin' hat, and her figure was obscured to some extent by her coat, but Jack was drawn to her clear brown eyes and the friendly smile that was evidently for his benefit.

'Hello,' he said, 'you're new, aren't you?'

'I've been here a year, sir.'

'Of course, I've been spending rather a lot of time at sea. What's your name?' In the corner of his eye he saw the other girls exchange knowing looks before walking away.

'Nine eight—'

'Don't worry about your number, just your name will do.'

She was still smiling, and that was a good sign. 'Irene Stafford, sir.'

'Have you just come off watch?'

'Yes, sir. I'm back on again at oh-eight-hundred tomorrow.'

That was helpful. 'Do you fancy a drink ashore?'

'When, sir?'

'This evening would be good. About seven, at the Grand Hotel?'

'The Grand Hotel, sir? That's very... grand.'

'Not too grand, I hope, but you see I wouldn't dream of taking a respectable girl to one of the low places that sailors frequent.'

'All right, sir, seven o'clock at the Grand.'

'In the lounge.'

'It gets grander by the minute, sir.' She gave him a brilliant smile and lifted her arm in a farewell salute.

'Just one thing.'

'Sir?'

'Let's drop the "sir". If you promise not to laugh I'll tell you my name.'

'I wouldn't dream of laughing.'

'All right, my name's Jack.'

Her expression remained serious. 'It's funny,' she said, but it seems all the men I meet nowadays are called Jack.'

31

'I'm really grateful to you for coming, G-G.'

'I wouldn't have missed it for anything, Luke.' As Kate accepted a kiss from her great-grandson, the tassel of his mortar board fell across her face, lightening, or so she fancied in her irreverent way, the solemnity of the occasion.

'Let's find somewhere for a photograph,' suggested Luke's father, ushering them away from the main crowd of graduates and admiring relations that had recently vacated St Paul's Hall, Huddersfield.

'Luke Featherstone MA,' said Kate, enjoying the novelty. 'Aren't you proud of your son, Tom?'

'Of course I am. I'm just trying to find a space where I can take a photograph.' He'd recently spent a great deal of money on something called an SLR and was eager to take advantage of its complexities. He looked around and found a corner. 'Here we are,' he said. 'Luke, come over here, and Gran, you can stand on his right.'

'You don't want me in the picture,' protested Kate. 'I'm not the one with the degree.'

'I want you in the picture, G-G.' Luke held on to her arm. 'This is a family celebration. It's just a shame Mum's under the weather and I'm between girlfriends. It really is great of you to be here.'

'I'm glad I could step in, Luke, although if you put me any lower down the ladder of importance I'll feel like an imposter.' She actually felt nothing of the kind. The absence of a girlfriend was sheer chance, but Kate was less tolerant of her granddaughter's non-appearance. Rebecca was preoccupied with pre-hysterectomy symptoms and had withdrawn from everyday life, thereby making the whole experience additionally trying for herself and everyone else.

'Come left a bit, Luke. You've got the spire growing out of your right shoulder. That's right. One more.' Tom made an adjustment and took another picture. 'Let's have one of Luke by himself.' He indulged himself with another picture before seizing a passing graduate and persuading her to take a picture of all three of them.

'Have you got enough photos, Dad?' Luke was looking anxiously at his watch. The table's booked for one o'clock and I still have to return these robes.'

'All right, Luke. You take your robes back and I'll stay here with Gran.'

'I think I'll just perch against this wall,' said Kate, whose feet were beginning to ache.

'Are you sure?'

'Yes, Tom, it's an old wives' tale that you can get haemorrhoids from sitting on cold stone.'

'If you say so.'

'Yes, I do.' It was sometimes necessary to be firm with Tom. Luke was infinitely easier, and now she thought of him a question occurred to her. 'I must have asked this before,' she said, 'but you know my memory.' She imagined he did when he wasn't fiddling around with his new camera. 'What was the subject of Luke's thing?'

'Do you mean his dissertation? It was *Churchill: Saviour or Opportunist?* That's with a colon after "Churchill" and a question mark after "Opportunist",' he added helpfully.

'Do you imagine they gave him extra marks for punctuation?'

'It wouldn't surprise me nowadays.' He was a man of learning and therefore unacquainted with levity. 'I can't help wondering,' he said, 'how he managed to get a full-length dissertation out of the subject.'

'Mm. Most of us had no doubts about Churchill at the time. He was inspirational. You know, in nineteen-forty, when we were at rock-bottom and invasion seemed imminent, he made us believe not only in survival but in victory. He had the ability to make a mouse believe it was a lion.'

'He made some bad mistakes, though.'

'I suppose so, but his greatest contribution was his leadership and inspiration. He brought us through some tough times.'

Only two days earlier, when sorting through some old things, she'd been reminded of one particularly awful time, not that there was any shortage of them during the war. The one in question, however, had lingered in Kate's memory, and it had taken place off the Suffolk coast in nineteen-forty-two.

32

'**F**ive bells, sir,' reported the bridge starboard lookout.

'Very good.' Jack continued to quarter the horizon. Five bells of the First Watch meant that it was 2230, and a raid by E boats could be expected at any time.

He was looking forward to leaving the convoy in the Thames Estuary and returning to Lowestoft, especially now that things were progressing so well with Irene. She was fun as well as a treat to behold in civvies. Now he thought of it, she didn't look bad in uniform either, even with the pudding basin hat. Apparently Wrens were going to get new caps similar to those worn by sailors, and that would be a big improvement.

He dismissed the thought and returned his full concentration to the job as Signalman Dryden, or 'Bunts', as all 'bunting tossers' were known, disappeared down the ladder in response to a shout from the W/T office. He emerged within seconds with a message form, which he handed to Jack. It was from Commander-in-Chief, Nore Command and addressed to the Senior Officer and all escorts. It read:

Six-plus E boats sighted 51⁰ 59' N, 1⁰ 56' E. 10ᵗʰ MTB Flotilla engaging. Acknowledge.

'Okay, Bunts, acknowledge.' He waited for Dryden to draft the signal and then signed it for the signalman to take to the W/T office.

He checked the reported position on the chart. It was about five miles to the south of the convoy and as he listened he fancied he heard gunfire in the distance. He called to the bridge port lookout, 'Wells, call the captain.'

'Aye aye, sir.'

Owen came to the bridge as a signal lamp on the destroyer *Savannah* began to blink.

'From Senior Officer, sir,' reported Dryden, receipting the signal. ' "Maintain station for now and take independent action to defend convoy." That's all, sir.'

'Thank you, Bunts.' Owen pressed the button to sound Action Stations and was rewarded to find Brian Foster already on the bridge. 'Good evening, Mid,' he said mildly. 'Stand by for your official induction into E Boat Alley.'

'Oh, jolly good, sir.'

Owen looked at Jack and winced.

'Wheelhouse – Bridge.' It was the Cox'n's voice.

'Bridge.'

'Cox'n taking over at the wheel, sir. Steady on one-five-oh degrees.'

'Very good, Cox'n.'

One by one the guns' crews and depth charge party reported that they were closed up to action stations.

'As there are more than six of the bastards, we have to be thankful for the MTBs,' said Owen. For all his playful talk of piracy, it wasn't the MLs' job to pick fights with E boats, which were faster and more heavily-armed, but to defend the convoy against them when necessary. They were fortunate in having a destroyer as part of the escort, but *HMS Savannah* was one of the oldest in the fleet, the modern destroyers being deployed mainly in the Mediterranean and Atlantic. The other escort, an armed trawler, carried an array of close-range weapons but she was very slow. Much might depend on ML 84.

'Captain, sir.' Brian Foster was at his shoulder.

'Yes, Mid?'

'Radar reports ten-plus contacts at approximately four-and-a-half miles, bearing due south.' He added, 'It's impossible to count them accurately.'

'Thanks, Mid. What can you hear?'

'Gunfire, sir.'

'I can hear engines as well. That's how close the buggers are.

Lookouts, keep a general eye out. I wouldn't put it past one of them to sneak in astern or abeam of us.'

Jack also swept the horizon. He knew how difficult it was to spot a lone E boat, with its long, dark hull and low bow wave.

Brian returned to the bridge. 'As far as we can make out, sir,' he said, 'there are twelve contacts.'

'Thanks, Mid. If the Tenth Flotilla's up to strength it sounds like five MTBs and seven E boats, a fine balance if you count us and *Savannah* as well.'

'Hasn't *Savannah* got twin pom-poms, sir?'

'Yes, my boy, but they're only of any use if she can train them on to a fast-moving target. The old girl's a shade on the creaky side nowadays. She was at Jutland, you know.'

'Gosh,' said the midshipman, 'as old as that.'

'As old as me,' confirmed Owen, 'and older than the First Lieutenant, I believe.'

'That's right, sir,' said Jack, 'but I was at Norway and Dunkirk in an old V-and-W class destroyer and she gave a good account of herself.'

'Quite right, Number One. I was forgetting.'

As the noise increased so did the tension on the bridge. Owen looked around him and noticed that Brian was hatless. He asked, 'Where's your battle bowler, Mid?'

'It's below, sir.'

'Well? Have you got an excuse note from your mother, or what?'

'My mother, sir? No, sir, I just left it in the wardroom.'

'Go and get it before Jerry starts shooting at you. You'll thank me when we've been in action and you still have a head on your shoulders.'

'Aye aye, sir.'

Owen gave Jack a look.

'It's the excitement, sir. He'll be all right.'

'I know, Number One.'

Brian returned via the radar compartment. He was wearing his steel helmet. 'The E boats must be moving this way, sir,' he reported. 'The plot gives the range at about three miles.'

'Stand by, gentlemen,' said Owen. 'Things are about to become unpleasant.'

It was now possible to see tracer criss-crossing in the distance, and one vessel appeared to be on fire.

'It's very low in the water, sir,' announced Jack. 'It could easily be one of theirs.'

'As it hasn't exploded yet it most likely is.' Everyone in Coastal Forces was aware that E boats had diesel engines and were therefore less volatile than their petrol-driven British counterparts. The vulnerability of the latter had been raised in Parliament but the official line was that Coastal Forces were 'expendable.'

Brian emerged from the radar compartment to say, 'There are now ten-plus—'

'We know, Mid. We can see the bastards.' Also the din from their gunfire and their engines was deafening.

The convoy continued with agonising slowness but it would be foolhardy for any of the escorts to leave the convoy and take independent action at that stage.

After a few minutes Jack sighted a white 'V' speeding toward them. 'E boat, sir,' he reported, 'red one-oh.' As it came nearer he could make out the long, grey shape low in the water and at that moment *Savannah* fired a star shell that lit up the seascape like daylight.

'Open fire!'

Jack made his way aft to the waist machine-guns and winced as a line of tracer crossed the ship and a shell exploded against the side of the bridge.

The E boat was too close now for Savannah's main armament but her twin pom-poms were finding their target consistently, so that quite suddenly and with no warning the enemy ship erupted, hurling wreckage over an unbelievable area. Jack watched as the strong south-westerly breeze gradually cleared the smoke, but he knew there could be no survivors. He could only imagine a magazine had been hit or a torpedo detonated.

'Number One!' Brian was calling from the wheelhouse, so he made his way back, holding on to what he could as the ship rolled in the swell.

'Number One, the Captain's been hit!' Owen was on the deck with Brian kneeling beside him.

'Where's he hurt?'

'It's a head injury,' Brian told him, taking a field dressing from his kit, 'shrapnel, I think.'

Jack crouched beside them. He could see that the wound was bleeding freely. 'We'll soon have you fixed up, sir,' he said with what he hoped was encouraging cheerfulness.

'Fiddlesticks, Number One. This is one scrum-half you'll have to play the rest of the match without.' Owen's voice was characteristically calm, as if it were the kind of thing that happened daily. 'Take command.'

The Cox'n's voice came up the voice pipe. 'Wheelhouse – bridge.'

'Bridge,' answered Jack.

'What's happening, sir? Is everyone all right up top?'

'I'm sorry, Cox'n. The Captain's injured.' He added, 'I'll keep you informed.'

'I'm sorry, sir, about the Captain, I mean. Is it serious?'

'It's hard to say. Mr Foster's just taken him down to the wardroom. At least he can walk.'

'Fingers crossed, then, sir.' As always, the Cox'n radiated calm and confidence.

'The Jerries must have gone home, sir,' reported Wells. 'They've had enough.' Certainly there seemed somehow to be fewer ships ahead. Things had become very quiet.

'Keep a sharp look out!' It was no time to relax.

'Aye aye, sir.' A second later Wells shouted, 'E boat bearing red one-five, sir!'

It seemed that one of them had decided to make a lone attack before making for home. Jack's parched mouth became suddenly drier. He trained his glasses on the bearing and saw the E boat, like a glittering fish throwing spray in its wake. 'E boat red one-five. Open fire! Coxswain, starboard fifteen.' That would bring all the ship's guns to bear.

'Starboard fifteen, sir. Fifteen of starboard wheel on, sir.'

'Midships.'

'Midships, sir. Wheel's amidships, sir.'

Now the twin Oerlikons were hammering away at their target. *Savannah* was turning to bring her close-range weapons to bear, but the E boat was too fast. It was going to get through to the convoy.

'Cox'n, port twenty!'

Jack felt the ship shudder as shells tore into its hull. The bridge was hit again and he felt something sharp cut his cheek.

'Port twenty, sir,' replied the Cox'n. 'Twenty of port wheel on, sir.'

'Full ahead both!'

'Both engines full ahead, sir.'

'Clear the focsle!' He was relieved to see the two men on the forward machine guns leave their post and hurry aft.

'Stand by to ram! Wells, warn them below!'

With what seemed like agonising slowness the ship bore down on the speeding E boat. Jack was conscious that his face was stinging as if from a whiplash but he put it from his mind.

Just before the moment of impact he saw the horrified look on the enemy sailors' faces, and then there was a sickening, splintering crash as the ship ground into the E boat, tearing a fatal gash in its side.

'Stop engines. Slow astern both.'

There was a pause, and then the propellers began to turn again, dragging the ship free of its victim's dying grasp.

'Stop both. Lookouts, we're going to pick up survivors. Wells, tell the depth charge crew to lower a scrambling net over the port side.' The E boat was almost submerged.

'Aye aye, sir.' Wells left the bridge, almost colliding with Brian.

'The bows have been shored up, sir and the pumps are holding,' reported Brian, 'as long as we continue slow ahead. We have two dead and five injured, including the Captain.'

'Who are the two dead?'

'Ordinary Seaman Makepeace and Leading Seaman Allen, sir. They're laid out on the after deck. I've sent a man for some blankets to cover them.'

It was cruel that Makepeace had gone. He was barely eighteen, and Allen was as much a key member of the crew as the Cox'n. 'How's the Captain?'

'It's difficult to say, sir. I've stemmed the bleeding but we won't know the extent of the injury until he's been examined by a doctor.' He added, 'He's barely conscious.'

'Thank you, Mid. You've done an excellent job on your first convoy.'

'Thank you, sir.' Brian was looking at him strangely. 'You'd better let me put a dressing on that wound, sir,' he said.

'What wound?'

'Your left cheek, sir. There's blood all over your coat. You must have been hit by shrapnel as well.' He dug into his haversack for a field dressing.

Jack felt his cheek and was surprised to find that his hand was covered in blood.

'I'll have to bandage you up like Marley's ghost, sir.' He passed the bandage under Jack's chin and secured it on the top of his head with a knot, finally replacing his steel helmet.

'Thank you, Mid.' Now Jack thought of it he remembered the stinging sensation in his cheek.

'There are six survivors from the E boat including the captain, sir,' said Wells.'

'Than you, Wells. You'd better join Stevenson below.'

'Aye aye, sir.'

'Signal from Senior Officer, sir,' reported Dryden. ' "Nice tackle".'

'Hell's bells,' said Jack. 'Everyone wants to turn this fight into a rugby match.'

'There's more, sir. "Report damage and casualties." '

'Make to Senior Officer, "Bows damaged but pumps holding so far. Can proceed slow ahead. Two dead, five injured including Captain. Six prisoners. Request early bath." ' He signed the message form, reasonably pleased with his contribution to the rugby dialogue.

Dryden finished sending the signal and waited. The reply came in less than a minute. 'From Senior Officer, sir, "Early bath granted. Proceed Felixstowe. For info, final score: home side 3, Germany 1. Good show and good luck." '

'Bridge – Wheelhouse.'

'Wheelhouse. Cox'n here, sir.'

'Resume one-five-oh degrees. Slow ahead both. We've orders to proceed to Felixstowe, Cox'n.'

'Sir?' Wells was back on the bridge.

'Yes, Wells?'

'The E boat skipper wants a word, sir.'

'Okay, bring him up and then go back and join Stevenson.'

'Aye aye, sir.' Wells descended and reappeared seconds later with a sodden and bedraggled naval officer.

'Good evening, *Herr Leutnant*,' said the German. 'I am *Oberleutnant Zur See* Heinrich Lang.'

'Good evening, *Herr Oberleutnant*. I am Sub-Lieutenant Jack Farthing, First Lieutenant. Our Captain is unfortunately wounded and unable to meet you.' Jack had met many Germans before the war but this was the first time he'd come face to face with the enemy and he was impressed by the officer's civilised manner.

'I am sorry to hear that, *Herr Leutnant*. I have to congratulate you on your quick and decisive action, even though it took the lives of most of my crew.'

'I'm sorry about your men, *Herr Oberleutnant*. I had no choice. My men will find dry clothing for you all and you'll be fed and properly re-clothed when we berth at Felixstowe.'

'I am grateful to you, *Herr Leutnant*.'

Jack bent over the voice pipe and said, 'Cox'n, put another man on the wheel and break out the rum. We'll give our guests a tot as well. After the ducking they've had I daresay they'll be glad of it.' It would also be their last decent drink for some time.

'Aye aye, sir.'

'We'd better not give any to the Captain, sir,' said Brian. 'He may need an operation.'

'Good thinking, Mid. Break it to him gently, will you? Tell him I'll be down to see him soon.' Turning to the German, he said, 'I must ask you to excuse me, *Herr Oberleutnant*. I need to set a course for Felixstowe.' Suddenly he felt weak and light-headed. He picked up the sextant to get an accurate fix before plotting a course, noticing as he did the blood on the sleeve and front of his duffel coat. He'd been unaware of it before, and now fresh drops appeared on the chart in front of him.

As Kate relieved the night staff-nurse she heard the radio in the porters' lodge. Alvar Lidell was reading the 7 o'clock morning news, and she couldn't resist lingering for a moment. He had a lovely way of speaking that was a treat in itself. She heard him say, '....three of our aircraft are missing.' That still evoked awful memories for her but she went on listening.

'Last night our Coastal Forces were in action in the North Sea when E boats attempted to attack one of our convoys. They were intercepted and a fierce fight ensued, during which three enemy vessels were sunk. One of our vessels was lost and there were casualties. Next-of-kin have been informed.

'In the Western Desert....'

At that point Kate stopped listening, because she knew Jack was based at Lowestoft. There was a time when she wasn't jumpy about news announcements, even when Maurice was flying on operations, but his death had changed that. Logically she knew Jack was just one of many based on the east coast, and she told herself it was unlikely he'd been involved in the action, but she couldn't help worrying all the same.

She worried until lunchtime, when she hurried across to the nurses' home to find Jack's parents' telephone number, and then she went straight to the public telephone in the passage. She would miss lunch but that couldn't be helped.

Nervously she pushed two pennies into the slot and dialled the number. After a few rings Mrs Farthing's voice came on the line.

'Cullington one-five-three.'

'Hello, Mrs Farthing. It's Kate Whitehead.'

'Hello, Kate. How are you?'

'I'm fine, thank you, Mrs Farthing. I'm just calling to ask if you've heard from Jack lately.'

'Yes, we had a letter from him last Tuesday.'

'Is that all? No phone calls or anything?'

'No, why do you ask?'

'Oh well, it's probably nothing, just something I heard on the wireless this morning, but if you've heard nothing that means he's okay.'

'Kate,' said Mrs Farthing with deliberate patience, you're not making sense.'

'I'm sorry. There was an incident in the North Sea last night involving coastal forces, but they say next-of-kin have been informed, so that means Jack's all right.'

'I suppose it must. Look, Kate, you've got to calm down. Honestly, I worry about him – I'd be a poor kind of mother if I didn't – but if I took fright at every news announcement I heard I'd be a nervous wreck.'

'I know. I'm sorry. It's ever since Maurice was killed.'

'Don't worry, Kate. I understand, but do try to keep a sense of proportion.'

Kate tried, but she couldn't stop worrying.

That afternoon, as Sister Crowe passed through the ward, she stopped to speak to Kate, who was powdering an elderly man's posterior after washing as a precaution against bedsores.

'Staff-Nurse Whitehead,' she said, 'The national telephone in my office exists for me to communicate with the outside world, not for members of your social circle to contact you or leave messages for you.'

'I'm sorry, Sister, I don't understand.'

'A Mrs Farthing wants you to ring her when you go off duty. Kindly tell her to contact you at the nurses' home in future.'

Kate's pulse quickened. 'Yes, I'm sorry, Sister. Thank you for the message.'

'Hm. Carry on.' Sister continued on her way.

In a voice muffled by the pillow, the patient said, 'It's just as well she was standing up then, Nurse.'

'Why's that, Mr Salter?'

'It made it easier for you to tell her face from my backside.'

'Mr Salter, that's naughty.' It might have been quite funny had Kate been less preoccupied.

'Well, she shouldn't be allowed to speak to you like that. She reckons she's so clever but I know who I'd rather have powdering my cheeks and shoving suppositories up my—'

'That's very loyal of you, Mr Salter. You can turn over and fasten your pyjamas now.' She pulled up the sheet for his privacy.

'You're a nice-looking lass, Nurse,' he said, tying a bow in his pyjama cord.

'Thank you.'

'I expect you have lots of boyfriends.'

'No, I'm too busy looking after naughty old men like you.' If the memory of Maurice was still too fresh for her to talk easily about boyfriends, her current state of anxiety about a close friend made it impossible.

She forced herself to concentrate on her work for the rest of the shift. Then at seven o'clock she handed over to her relief and hurried across to the nurses' home, where she found a probationer making what seemed to be an interminable call to someone called 'Mumsie.' By looking pointedly at her fob watch Kate persuaded her to bring her conversation to its close and, as the discomfited nurse made her retreat, she fumbled for two pennies and dialled the number.

Mr Farthing answered. He sounded surprisingly cheerful as they observed the usual pleasantries.

'Mrs Farthing asked me to give her a ring,' explained Kate.

'All right, love, I'll get her for you.' The phone went down and Kate waited in suspense and confusion until Mrs Farthing came on the line.

'Hello Kate.' She sounded perky as well. Jack *must* be all right.

'Have you heard from Jack, Mrs Farthing?'

'No, but we had a telephone call from somebody called Brian Foster. By the way, do you know what a midshipman is? We're not sure.'

'I'm afraid not.' She wished Mrs Farthing would get on it.

'I think he must be a kind of junior officer on Jack's boat, and he was going on leave today to celebrate his twenty-first birthday, but he called us because Jack couldn't get to a telephone. Jack's been wounded again but he says it's not awful. Apparently he was hit by a splinter, of all things, and he bled rather a lot, which is worrying, but he managed to get his boat to the nearest harbour, so he mustn't have been too badly wounded.'

'So he's all right?' The details were irrelevant for the time being. All that mattered was that Jack was safe.

226

'Yes, it must have been awful out there. The Captain was wounded as well, worse than Jack, and that's why Jack was in charge of getting the boat home.' She added thoughtfully, 'You can hardly credit it, can you? Three years ago he was arranging people's holidays. If it comes to that, it seems only yesterday he was still at school. Mind you, he was always coming home with cuts and bruises even then, and there was one time he broke two fingers playing cricket. He'd put his life in danger rather than miss taking a catch, you know. He's always been daft like that.'

'It's such a relief, Mrs Farthing. I'm really glad he's all right.'

'He'll be coming home on leave soon. If you like, I'll let you know when, and if you can get some time off you can come and see him.'

❧

Owen's head and eye were heavily bandaged but he still managed a lop-sided smile. 'Hello, Jack,' he said. 'It's good to see you up and about.'

'Oh, mine's nothing serious, although it could have been. How about you?'

'I've lost the sight of my left eye,' said Owen matter-of-factly. 'The splinter severed the optic nerve.' He levered himself into a more comfortable position in his chair. 'I have to use my remaining eye to look on the bright side, though, and a black eye patch is going to be very useful when I go back to the schoolroom. It should scare the wits out of the little devils.' He smiled at the thought. 'It's a wonder I didn't think of it earlier.'

'You're looking a long way ahead, aren't you?'

'Not so far ahead, Jack. Let's face facts. They won't let a one-eyed man continue in this job.'

'I'm not so sure. There's a famous precedent.'

Owen shook his head decisively. 'Lord Nelson had connections a village schoolmaster from Caernarvonshire could never aspire to. No, it's back to the schoolroom for me.' He nodded as if confirming it. 'You'll be all right, I imagine, when they take your stitches out?'

Jack nodded. 'They say I'll be left with a scar, but that's all.'

'That'll get you a lot of sympathy after the war, mind. War wounds do that. Our village postman was wounded in the last war and his limp has earned him no end of attention from the opposite sex.' He laughed shortly. 'It would make sense, except he was wounded in the arm. He was always a show-off. He sings all the tenor solos with the choral society.'

Fascinated though he was by Owen's character sketch, Jack had something else on his mind. 'Who's going to write the report, Owen,' he asked, 'you or me?'

'I'll write it up to the point when you took over command. After that it's up to you. It'll be interesting for them, comparing our narrative styles.'

'I'm not interested in style, Owen, but I do want to make sure Brian gets a fair mention.'

'Of course. He did well, didn't he?'

'He was excellent. He was everywhere I couldn't be, tackling jobs where he found them and completely on his own initiative. He even telephoned my parents.'

'He did the same for me. Yes, give him a good write-up. I'll do the same for you. I'll certainly see you're recommended for the DSC.'

It was a surprise for Jack. 'Thank you, Owen,' he said, 'but I'm not sure I deserve anything so grand.'

'That only makes you more deserving.' He seemed to tire of the conversation. 'I'm going to have a little nap now,' he said. 'I tire easily after that bang on the head, but listen, Jack, as you're going home soon. You'll make a good skipper when you get your command, and I wish you well.' He took a sheet of paper from his table and handed it to him. 'Here's my address. Look me up if you ever find yourself in North Wales. You're welcome any time.'

'I will. Thanks for the apprenticeship, Owen.'

'You're welcome. You were a good pupil.' He added, 'For an Englishman, that is.'

The two men shook hands.

33

'I saw him briefly when he came home on leave and that was when I learned the reason he hadn't been able to phone his mother.' Kate stopped, distracted for the moment by Tom, who was looking around the restaurant as if he'd lost something valuable or important.

'Go on, G-G. I'm interested.'

'I'm glad you are, Luke.' Kate glanced at Tom again. His quest appeared to be over, because he was studying the dessert trolley from a considerable distance, seemingly with intense deliberation.

'The wound was a good deal worse than she thought. He'd lost a lot of blood and he was very weak by the time he reached Felixstowe.'

'Was that when they gave him his medal?'

'Yes, he was awarded the Distinguished Service Cross, promoted to lieutenant and given a command of his own.'

'I remember seeing a photo of it, some kind of patrol boat, wasn't it?'

'Yes, a rescue motor launch, a new kind of ship.' She shook her head sadly at Tom, now single-mindedly trying to alert a waitress to his predicament.

'I thought the RAF did air-sea rescue.'

'Yes, but it was a shared job. As I understand it the RAF had small fast boats for high-speed rescues but the Navy's launches were bigger and, although they were slower than the RAF boats, they could operate in rough conditions and stay at sea for days on end. Horses for courses, I suppose.'

'Hooray,' said Tom, 'the sweet trolley's arrived.'

Luke acknowledged his father's pronouncement with a dutiful smile and said, 'I'm glad you could come, G-G. As well as enjoying your company, I've learned a lot from you today.'

'I'm glad I could help, Luke.'

'I don't think I'll bother with the sweet trolley after all,' said Tom after some deliberation. 'I think I'll settle for the cheese board.'

His decision was lost on Kate, whose thoughts were still largely about Jack.

34

'The bitter's off.' The landlord's greeting was brief but not unfriendly. 'I'm waiting for the brewery to deliver. It's the war, you know.'

'More than likely,' agreed Jack. 'How are you fixed for mild?'

'I've got dark mild,' the landlord confirmed. He was a neat man with a well-trimmed moustache and Brilliantined hair.

'I'll settle for a pint of that, then.'

The landlord shook his head apologetically. 'Halves only, I'm afraid, 'til the brewery delivers.' He took a half-pint glass and pulled laboriously on one of the pumps. 'That'll be twopence-ha'penny,' he said, placing the glass of dark-brown liquid in front of Jack.

'Thanks.' Jack handed over a threepenny bit in payment.

'The news from Africa's good, isn't it?'

'Yes, it's well overdue but no less welcome for that.'

'It was high time Rommel was given a taste of his own treatment. He's been asking for it long enough.' He punctuated that judgement by slapping the bar with the palm of his hand and then asked, 'What do think of this Montgomery chap?'

'I really don't know much about him. As a rule I'm not keen on prima donnas, but if he can do the job, fair enough.'

'We don't see many of you blokes nowadays,' said the landlord, giving him his change. 'They seem to stick mainly to the docks nowadays.'

'I'm just having a look around,' explained Jack. 'I've only recently arrived in Immingham and, to be honest, I called in here to get out of the cold.'

'You're from the docks, then?'

'I really can't say. "Careless Talk", you know.'

'Stands to reason,' the landlord insisted. 'You'll be from one of the boats they keep over there.' As there was no one else waiting to be served, he went on. 'It's not like a couple of years ago, when the Navy took over the County Hotel. It was headquarters for some bigwig, although I never heard who he was.'

'Really?'

'Yes, and the sailors used to come here to drink. I expect the County Hotel would be too posh for the likes of them.'

'I expect so.' Jack was in a generous mood.

'Of course, you're an officer and that makes a difference.'

'It's decent of you to say so.'

'Not at all.' The landlord's attention was suddenly diverted as a man walked into the bar wearing a fawn trench coat and brown trilby. His collar was turned up, presumably against the bitter November wind, and Jack would never have recognised the newcomer until the landlord greeted him.

'Hello, Mr Halstead. Where've you been hiding? We haven't seen you for a while.'

'Hello, George. I'm only here for a meeting. I'm based in London now, you know.'

Jack couldn't help listening to the conversation, because he realised he was now looking at his pre-war boss, the branch manager at Farrar's Tours.

Eventually Halstead looked around the bar, saw the blue-uniformed figure by the window and hesitated for a moment.

Jack raised his glass. 'Good afternoon, Mr Halstead.'

'Well, blow me down if it isn't young Farthing.' He pointed to Jack's glass and said, 'Let me get you the other half.'

The landlord left them to catch up on the past three years. A great deal had happened to both of them and Jack learned, among other things, that Halstead was now serving with the National Fire Service in London.

'I was too old for the forces at first,' he explained, 'and it made no difference that I'd served in the last lot. Like everyone else, of course, I'd no way of knowing they'd eventually raise the upper age limit. Anyway, I joined the AFS, as they called it in those days, and they posted me to the London Docks.' He laughed drily. 'Considering the way Goering's been plastering Hull, I'd have been just as useful if I'd stayed put.'

'But what are Farrar's doing now?'

'Troop transport, basically. I got out before they could involve me in that. By the way, you know my wife and I parted company, don't you? It was just before the war.'

'No, I didn't know. I'm sorry.'

'There's no need. It was very unpleasant.' He motioned to the landlord for two more halves.

'I'll get these,' said Jack.

'Good man. Yes, where there's a complete lack of trust there's no relationship and, as far as I'm concerned, no loss.'

'I see.' Jack wondered about the lack of trust. Halstead's philandering ways had provided endless gossip at the Hull branch.

'So I decamped and found a place, a cottage, on this side of the river because I always suspected Hull would attract the attention of the *Luftwaffe*. I keep it going so I've somewhere to come back to.'

'Where is it?'

'It's in Ulceby, about five miles from here.' Suddenly he smiled and said, 'As you're based nearby, you and I could do each other a favour.'

'What do you have in mind?' Jack had never been at ease with Halstead's wink-and-nudge manner.

'I just wondered if you'd keep an eye on the place for me, make sure everything's as it should be and forward any mail that arrives, and that sort of thing. When you're around, that is.'

'I'm afraid I won't be around all that often. Duty calls, you know.'

'When you can, Jack, and I wouldn't expect you to do it for nothing. I mean there's no reason why you shouldn't use the place when I'm away. What do you think? A handy retreat when you have the odd night off? A place where you can entertain when you're not at sea?' He gave a conspiratorial wink which Jack pretended not to notice.

'I'd say that's a fair deal, Mr Halstead.'

'Fine, I'd take you over there now but I'm a bit short of time.'

'That's all right.' Jack looked at his wristwatch. 'I have to get back to the ship soon to meet my new first-lieutenant.'

'Okay, give me your address and I'll send you directions and a spare key.'

⛝⛝⛝⛝⛝

It was to be a day of reunions, as Jack discovered shortly, and the second was particularly welcome. He was in the wardroom when he heard footsteps on the ladder and a figure wrapped in a scarf and greatcoat materialised.

'Sub-Lieutenant Brian Foster, come aboard to join as First Lieutenant, sir.' His words came through a cloud of vapour.

'Well, I never.' Jack shook his hand. 'Welcome aboard, Brian.'

'Weren't you expecting me, sir?'

'No, I was told the First-Lieutenant was coming but they didn't tell me it was you.'

'As we were free at the same time, I suppose they decided to keep us together.'

'I'm glad they did. Come in and have a drink.'

'Thanks.' Brian unbuttoned his greatcoat. 'Something warming, I think.'

'Whisky?'

'That should do the trick, sir.' He sank gratefully on to one of the bunks. 'By the way, sir, thank you for the "mention".'

'You're welcome, Brian. You earned it.'

'And congratulations on your DSC.' Brian was looking at the blue-and-white ribbon on Jack's tunic. 'If I may say so, it was well-deserved.'

'I really don't know about that.' He handed Brian a glass of whisky. 'But thank you for the compliment.'

'Thank you. Have you heard from Owen recently, sir?'

'Yes, I had a letter from him two days ago. He says they're not discharging him after all. They've found him a desk job in Whitehall. Intelligence, I imagine, but he wasn't in a position to say.'

'I can't see him taking kindly to a desk job in any department.'

'Oh, no, Brian, he's raring to go. He says the Admiralty suffers from intellectual constipation and it's long overdue for a dose of Welsh opening medicine. You can almost hear him saying that, can't you?'

'I can.' Brian finished his whisky and put the tumbler down. 'Maybe he's right, sir. Maybe they need that the same way the Eighth Army needed Montgomery.'

'I don't know, Brian. Maybe time will tell. About Owen, I mean. The desert war's beyond me.' He stood up and picked up his cap. 'Let's go and meet the Cox'n.'

'Aye aye, sir.'

'And remember, when we're on the job we're "Sir" and "Number One", but at other times I'm "Jack" and you're "Brian".'

It was a proven formula.

⁕⁕⁕

The only sounds were the soft ticking of the log in the grate and the wind moaning around the chimney tops.

Gwen burrowed deeper under the covers and laid her head cosily against Alan's chest. Feeling him stir, she asked softly, 'Are you awake?'

'Mm, of course.'

'It's a point of etiquette with you, isn't it, not to be the first to drift into the sleep of the just-after?'

'If I can manage it, yes.'

'Even in the ultimate abatement you remain a gentleman.' She kissed his midriff in acknowledgement.

'I'm glad you noticed,' he said, turning on to his side to face her. 'Actually I'm not at all sleepy. I was thinking.'

'Profound or superficial thoughts?'

'Just an idle notion that in the midst of war this place is a haven of peace, at least until I have to get up to put another log on the fire.'

'That's true. Do you imagine we'll ever use the bed upstairs?'

'Not until spring at the earliest.'

'Good.' She snuggled against him more closely. 'I like it down here.'

'We have until sixteen-hundred tomorrow, and then the war requires our attention.'

'Mm, it's happening much too often.'

'It was the war that brought us together. Don't forget that.'

'I haven't, and things are improving, I'm told.'

Kneeling at the hearth, he took a log and placed it on the fire. 'Do you mean El Alamein?' He rejoined her on their makeshift bed. 'Fair enough, it was a big victory, although the word is that the whole thing was planned by General Alexander.'

'Really?'

'Yes, they say Montgomery merely took the credit for it. It certainly sounds like him.'

'What a nerve.'

'But, be that as it may, I think Churchill hit the nail on the head when he said it wasn't the end.'

' "But it is, perhaps," ' she mimicked, ' "the end of the beginning".'

'That's good,' he told her. 'I can almost smell the cigar smoke.'

'But that's not all,' she insisted. 'With the news from the Atlantic and the latest feedback from *Luftwaffe* prisoners, who couldn't be optimistic?'

35

'How was the degree ceremony?' Rachel hung up her coat and followed Kate into the sitting room.

'It was very nice, really. It's good to see the great-grandchildren do well.'

'What did he get?'

'In what sense?'

'What's his degree?'

'Oh, I see. It's an MA by research. The title of his paper is "Churchill: Saviour or Opportunist?" '

Rachel smiled. 'I expect you could set him right about that,' she said.

'Oh, Luke and I are in full agreement about Churchill. Tom was a pain as usual, but that's only to be expected. The main thing was that Luke enjoyed the day.' Then, as one thought gave way to another, she said, 'I was terribly honoured, you know.'

'Oh?'

'Yes, apparently I was standing in for his mother and his girlfriend. He's actually between girlfriends but I suppose the principle's the same.'

Rachel smiled again. 'I imagine it is.'

'And what about you, Rachel? How's your love life progressing?'

'Oh, Kate, you ambushed me with that one.'

'Really? How much warning do you need?'

'You're just very direct.' Her face twitched momentarily.

'There's nothing to be gained by beating about the bush. Have you seen him again?'

Rachel nodded self-consciously. 'Twice.'

'What's his name?'

'David.'

Kate waited for her to go on.

'All right,' said Rachel, 'he's forty-one, he and his wife parted eleven years ago, they were divorced two years later, and there are no children.' Having delivered the information, she placed her hands on her knees with their palms down and awaited Kate's response.

'I'm only taking an interest in your welfare, and it wasn't all that difficult was it?'

'Not really.'

'Good.'

'So I'm going to ask you about your love life, Kate.'

If Kate was surprised she gave no indication of it. 'That ended ten years ago,' she said, 'and it had been very uneventful for some time, as you might expect of two people in their eighties.'

'I mean much earlier. I know you were devastated when you lost Maurice, but there must have been a time when you began putting yourself together.'

Kate thought. Eventually she said, 'It was a long process. I hadn't had much to do with men in Hull. I suppose I was too busy, and it's remarkable how the sound of bombs going off all around you takes the edge off the romantic appetite. At least, that's what people told me. As far as I was concerned, the male world consisted almost entirely of doctors and porters, and that continued to be the case for some time after I was posted.'

'When was that?'

'Oh… I think it was well into nineteen-forty-three, in fact, yes, it was spring. I remember looking through the carriage windows on the way to Dover and seeing blossom on the trees.'

'Very romantic.'

Kate smiled sadly. 'Not for me,' she said. 'At least not for a while.'

'What about the others?'

'Dorothy and the boys? Well, as far as I know they led very normal lives, although Dorothy found time to enjoy herself.'

36

Personnel arrived at RAF Humby-on-the-Wold as others departed. It was the same on most stations, and ground staff generally tried not to dwell on casualties and their replacements, not out of disinterest but rather reluctance to enter the precarious and menacing world inhabited by operational aircrew. The statistics were bleak enough without the complication of names and even friendships to make them distressingly personal.

There were those who took that risk, however, and Sergeant Dorothy Needham was one of them. The object of her interest was Daniel Innes, a sergeant flight engineer from Hawke's Bay in New Zealand. Physically, he was unremarkable. If pressed for a description his fellow crew members might have said that he was a neat, well-groomed man with an immaculate centre parting, slight of build and not exceptionally tall. Some wondered why Dorothy had given him a second glance, but if there was a mystery she was quite unaware of it. He was quiet, unpretentious and an attentive listener, qualities she was quick to appreciate in a world of adrenalin-fuelled egos and high spirits.

They sat together one evening in The Black Horse pub, a favourite with aircrew and ground staff alike because of its proximity to the station.

'Have you heard the latest about the raid on the dams?' Daniel set their drinks down on the table and took his seat.

'They burst two of them, didn't they?'

'They certainly did, and the papers say the flood waters have spread over fifty miles. "Happy Valley" is now one of the wettest places in Europe. I'd like to know how they did it, though. For one thing, the accuracy needed to hit such targets doesn't bear thinking about, and what kind of mine did they use? I've never heard of anything that would breach the wall of a dam.'

'Perhaps it's better not to talk about it here.' As a signaller Dorothy was more security minded than most aircrew and she was wary about discussing operations in a public bar frequented by civilians.

'You're right, Dot. "Careless Talk Costs Lives." It's official, so it must be true.'

'You can depend on it. Let's talk about something else, such as what we're going to do when your tour of ops is up and you get posted. It's just five more ops, isn't it?'

'Stop there.' He held up his hand like a policeman holding up traffic. 'That's something else we don't talk about, and it has nothing to do with security.'

'No?'

'No, just superstition. We don't talk about the end of a tour until it's over.'

'Oh, say no more.' Dorothy knew about aircrew and their foibles. It was a nonsense that had to be respected, if only for their peace of mind. Worrying about superstitions distracted them from the main job, and no one wanted that to happen.

'That just leaves us with gossip,' she said. 'What do you know?'

'Not much,' he admitted, 'except that you've just been recognised.'

'Have I?'

'Some people wait all their lives for that, you know.'

'For what?'

'Recognition. It eludes all but the most fortunate, or self-seeking, I suppose.'

Dorothy turned to see what he was looking at. As she did so he felt a hand on her shoulder and heard a voice from the past.

'Dot, you bugger! I thought it was you!'

'Connie!' They hugged each other until Connie remembered that Dorothy wasn't alone.

'Hey, I'm not playin' gooseberry, am I? Tell us if I am. I'll be seein' you later anyway, when we're on duty together.'

'No, you're not playing gooseberry. This is Daniel. Daniel, meet Connie. We joined and did our basic training together, and I think I'd better explain that in the north of England "bugger" is sometimes a term of endearment. I just thought I'd tell you before you get the wrong idea.'

Daniel shook Connie's hand. 'Take a seat, Connie,' he said. 'I'll get you a drink. What'll you have?'

'Just a half of cider for me, please, Daniel.' She peered at his shoulder flash as he stood up, and said, 'I thought you sounded Australian or something.'

Dorothy winced. 'Duels have been fought for less, Connie.'

'Have I stuck me foot in it, like?'

'New Zealanders don't like to be taken for Australian,' she explained. 'It's like Newcastle and Gateshead.' As an afterthought she added, 'Or Sunderland.'

Connie was immediately contrite. 'I'm sorry, Daniel. I didn't mean to insult you. I was always hopeless at geography, an' they're both a long way off, aren't they?'

Daniel smiled and nodded. 'Don't worry, Connie. You haven't insulted me.'

'Me and me mouth,' said Connie when he'd left for the bar. 'I should have known. We had Rhodesians at my last station and they always took it amiss when somebody called 'em South African.'

'Daniel doesn't take offence easily,' Dorothy assured her.

'Are you keen on him, like?'

'I enjoy his company. He's different from the others.'

'How's that, then?'

'He's considerate and not full of himself.'

Connie was unconvinced. 'Doesn't he keep his brain in his pants like the rest of 'em?'

Dorothy smiled at the thought. 'He's normal, Connie, but he knows there's more to life than that.'

'Lucky old you. As soon as a bloke tells me I've a pretty face I know me face is the last thing on his mind.'

'It's usually the case, isn't it? Anyway, what have you been doing with yourself?'

'I've been at the same station 'til now. I thought I was going to take root there.'

'Where was that?'

'Scampton. You'll have heard all about the dams raid, I suppose? It's put Scampton on the map.'

'I think we all have. Daniel was talking about it earlier and I had to remind him about careless talk.' She thought a timely warning wouldn't go amiss with Connie either.

'I should say so. What about you, though? A sergeant already?'

'Ah well, I had a flying start. I was an instructor at Cranwell, I was posted to Market Linfield and then I came here. I must be fated to see out the war in Lincolnshire.'

'I shouldn't be surprised, bonny lass. There's more air stations here than anywhere else in the country.' She looked over Dorothy's shoulder and said, 'It looks as if the drought's ended.'

'Here we are, girls.' Daniel put their drinks on the table. 'I saw my skipper at the bar so I stayed and had a word with him. I thought you two would have some catching up to do.'

'See what I mean, Connie?' Dorothy inclined her head towards Daniel. 'He's not like the common herd.'

'I should say he's not, and thanks for the drink, Daniel.'

'You're welcome.'

'What I don't understand is why you travelled across the world to be bombed and have to eat wartime rations.'

'Well, things were sort of quiet at home, and the old country needed a helping hand. It seemed only right.'

'Nobly put,' said Dorothy.

'Well, I'm glad my old friend Dot's found herself a gentleman. If you know of any others you'll put a word in for me, won't you. Daniel?'

<hr />

The letter had obviously come from the base, and the envelope was simply addressed to *Lt. J. Farthing, D.S.C., R.N.V.R.*

Jack slit open the envelope and took out a blank message form, which he turned over to find a hand-written note. It read:

Dear Jack,

Would you believe it? We're neighbours again, but not entirely by coincidence. One of the girls at Lowestoft got a draft chit to Immingham at the worst possible time for her as she'd just got engaged to a matelot back there, so I volunteered to go in her place. Apparently air-sea rescue is busier than ever now that the Yanks have joined the party and taken to ditching in the North Sea, so they need extra help.

By the way, congratulations on your D.S.C!

Anyway, if you're still footloose and fancy-free and you'd like us to meet again you know where to find me. I'm on the all-night-on tonight, off tomorrow night, all day on Wednesday and then I'm off Thursday and back on again on Friday. In any case do get in touch.

Love and stuff,
Irene
XXX.

Things were looking up at last. Barring accidents, 97 would be stood down for 24 hours on Thursday, and there was just time to write a quick note and send it ashore with the mail before going out on patrol.

⊕⊷⊰⊱⊸⊕

For the first time in three weeks the signals section at Humby was fully manned. The arrival of Connie and a new girl called Betty Hodgkins had brought R/T up to strength, so Dorothy was able to relax a little.

Being new and very junior, Betty was listening out on 'Darky' Watch, the net that covered a ten-mile radius for aircraft in difficulty or simply needing a bearing. Connie was in charge of R/T generally, a development that appeared to trouble Section Officer Benson.

'Sergeant Needham,' she said quietly, glancing sideways at Connie, 'I do believe we've drawn the short straw.'

'Really, ma'am? What gives you that impression?'

'The new corporal. How on earth is she going to communicate with anyone? Her accent might be intelligible in a Tyne shipyard

243

but the control room of a bomber station is a different matter. Also, how is she going to cope with the new procedure when it comes into force?'

'I know Corporal Sellers, ma'am. She'll be on top of the job.'

'I hope you're right.'

W/T matters claimed Dorothy's attention during the night, but as the aircraft were returning she was able to give the R/T section her full concentration. Before long she heard Connie answer a call from F Fox. To Section Officer Benson's surprise she carried out the exchange clearly and without a hint of dialect. Dorothy allowed herself a sideways glance at the officer and smiled to herself, remembering Connie's talent for mimicry.

Suddenly a call came on the 'Darky' frequency, loud and clearly audible from Betty's headphones. 'Hello Darky, Hello Darky, Hello Darky, this is Inkpen O for Oboe, Inkpen O for Oboe, Inkpen O for Oboe. Are you receiving me? Are you receiving me? Over.'

Betty froze. O for Oboe transmitted again, but it was as if the girl had been struck dumb. Dorothy was about to go to Betty's side but Connie was there before her, switching the loudspeaker on.

'Come on, bonny lass. He's comin' over strength five, so give him "okay".' She placed a hand on Betty's shoulder and it seemed to steady her.

'Inkpen O Oboe, Inkpen O Oboe.' The girl's voice shook but she carried on. 'This is Crayfish, Crayfish. Okay. Standing by. Over.'

'Good girl. Now carry on.' Connie squeezed the girl's shoulder again.

'Crayfish this is O Oboe. My navigator is wounded. I require a course for Middleton. Over.'

Betty picked up the microphone hesitantly. 'Inkpen O Oboe this is Crayfish. Wait one. Out.' One minute was probably all the Control Officer needed, and it was good that Betty had remembered that.

Connie took a sheet of paper from him as he came off the phone, and handed it to Betty. 'Carry on,' she said.

'Inkpen O Oboe this is Crayfish. Fly on three-one-five magnetic for seven-zero miles. I say again: fly on three-one-five magnetic for seven-zero miles. Over.'

'Crayfish this is Inkpen O Oboe. Thank you. Roger. Out.'

'There now.' Connie patted Betty on the back. 'I reckon you'll be all right next time.'

Almost panting with relief, Betty smiled her thanks.

'I don't understand, Sergeant.' Section Officer Benson seemed as disapproving as she was perplexed. 'Why on earth didn't the corporal simply take over from the wretched girl?'

'I imagine she wanted to avoid destroying the girl's self-confidence altogether, ma'am.'

'But all she had to do was to follow the procedure.' She shrugged as if the matter seemed too obvious for words.

'Until a short while ago, ma'am, ACW Hodgkins was working in a shoe factory in Northampton, and I doubt if she'd ever so much as used a telephone before joining the WAAF. She was under pressure for the first time and she froze. Now she's over it I'm sure it won't happen again.'

'Are you really sure?'

'As sure as I can be. Both Corporal Sellers and I have seen it happen.'

'I see. I hadn't thought of that – about not using a phone, I mean.'

'You're not expected to, ma'am.'

'And I consider that remark to be impertinent, Sergeant.' The officer returned, tight-lipped, to her office, and Dorothy imagined she'd not heard the last of the matter.

One by one, the station's aircraft returned until only three were unaccounted for. Thankfully Daniel's was one of the first to land. Then, as aircrew reported to Intelligence for de-briefing, it became known that one had been seen in flames over the target. W/T would continue to keep watch for the remaining two, of whom nothing had been heard since take-off.

The next call, however, came from a Wellington from another station.

'Hello Darky, Hello Darky, Hello Darky, this is Earwig A for Able, Earwig A for Able, Earwig A for Able. Are you receiving me? Are you receiving me? Over.'

Connie was on her feet but Betty answered immediately. 'Hello Earwig A Able, Earwig A Able, this is Crayfish, Crayfish. Okay. Standing by. Over.'

'Crayfish this is Earwig A Able. Mayday, mayday, mayday. I have two wounded on board, my starboard wing is damaged and I'm flying on fresh air. Request permission to land. Emergency routine. Over.'

At the Control Officer's emphatic nod Betty answered, 'Earwig A Able this is Crayfish. My lights are on. You are clear to land. Over.'

At his desk the Control Officer spoke on the telephone. Within seconds an ambulance and fire tenders would be racing to the end of the runway.

'Crayfish this is Earwig A Able. I'm south of you and making my approach. Over.'

'This is Crayfish. Roger, out.' Shaking with relief, Betty put down the microphone.

Connie was first to congratulate her. 'Well done, bonny lass. We'll make an R/T operator of you yet. Now, log all that before you forget.'

Dorothy added her approval. 'Well done, both of you.'

'It's all in a day's work,' Connie told her.

'So it is,' agreed Dorothy, conscious of Section Officer Benson's presence at her side.

As she returned to the job of locating the missing aircraft, she found a weather report on her desk. It seemed that conditions were set to deteriorate for the next few days. It would be a welcome respite for aircrew and it might also create an opportunity for her to spend some time with Daniel.

⊶⊰⊱⊷

Random Harvest was recommended unreservedly, it seemed, by all who'd seen it, but Alan was finding it difficult to concentrate on the film. It looked very much as if Ronald Colman had been kitted out by the US Army and, whilst it was an understandable mistake for a Hollywood wardrobes department to make, Mr Colman himself would have known the difference, having served on the Western Front in the 1914-18 war. Still, there he was, a British officer wearing an American cap and wandering aimlessly through thick fog, having slipped out of a lunatic asylum somewhere in the Midlands. It wasn't a promising start, although

Alan was sure Greer Garson would put that right just as soon as she made her entrance.

In fairness to the wardrobes people, Ronald Colman's cap wasn't Alan's only distraction. He'd been intrigued for much of the day by the transcript of a conversation between a senior German officer and a recently-captured major in the Luftwaffe, in which the latter had referred to the recent raid on the Möhne, Eder and Sorpe dams in the Ruhr Valley. The major claimed to have seen aircraft flying at a very low altitude to release bombs that proceeded to bounce several times along the surface of the water before sinking beside the dam, where they exploded. His companion had laughed and assured him that a spell of abstention from alcohol in a British prison camp would surely cure his problem. Alan, on the other hand, was inclined to be less dismissive. The Air Ministry had asked Trent Park to pay particular attention to references to the dams raid. Transcripts were to be delivered by hand to a named officer in RAF intelligence, but Trent Park personnel were still no wiser about the raid. It was a tantalising mystery.

Greer Garson's exquisite limbs were now in view, possibly for the first time in her film career, as she danced around the stage and delivered a skilful tribute to Sir Harry Lauder. It was during this sequence that Alan's concentration returned.

The film turned out to be as good as its reputation suggested, a fact that Alan mentioned to Gwen as they left the picture house.

'Yes,' she agreed, 'it was very nice.'

'Is that all?' Gwen was as susceptible to a tear-jerker as the next woman but she'd left her seat on this occasion dry-eyed and apparently unmoved.

'I'm afraid I was rather preoccupied.'

'Were you? I was so caught up with my own concerns it never occurred to me that you might have something on your mind. Look, let's have a drink and you can tell me about it.'

'Do you mind if we don't?' She took his arm as they stepped into the black-out. 'Could we just go straight back to our quarters?'

'If that's what you want to do. What's it like in your new quarters?' Gwen had moved fairly recently from the mansion to the recently-completed female staff and officers' quarters.

'Most unpleasant but I'll survive.'

'That's a shame.' He side-stepped to avoid a lamppost. 'I'm sorry,' he said. 'By the end of the war we'll be used to the black-out.'

'That's all right.' She took a breath and said urgently, 'I'll have to tell you this sooner or later. The fact is I'm late.'

He hesitated for a moment, unsure of what she meant, and then cold realisation dawned. 'Significantly late?'

She nodded. 'Two weeks. I'm usually like clockwork.'

'But we've been so careful.'

'Those things aren't infallible.'

'Evidently not. Look, maybe we should have that drink I offered you. It's not the kind of thing we can discuss on a motorbike.'

<hr />

Kate's new place of work was the casualty department of the County Hospital at Buckland, Dover. Like a great many free hospitals it had begun life in the eighteenth century as a workhouse infirmary but much had changed since then and the casualty department was housed in modern buildings with access to underground bunkers. The latter, however, were of limited use, as Sister Newman explained.

'In the Blitz they used to move the patients down to the bunkers,' she explained, 'but the main threat now is from the guns in Sangatte, and there's no warning when a shell comes over. There's just an almighty shriek followed by an explosion.' She added, 'You just have to be fatalistic. Where have you come from, by the way?'

'Hull Royal Infirmary.'

'Oh. Did you get much bombing up there?'

'Yes, Sister, all through the Blitz.' She hoped she didn't sound as indignant as she felt. So far it seemed that people in the south of England thought they had the war to themselves.

'I see. They never told us in the news. It was always "a northern city" or "a coastal town", wasn't it? I suppose they didn't want the Germans to know the results of their efforts.'

She was probably right. Sisters were always right. Staff-nurses, on the other hand, were fallible, and Kate was no exception.

She would have to prove herself in Casualty, a department that presented a number of challenges, and she hadn't long to wait for an opportunity.

The only warning of attack was a screeching roar like the noise of an express train, which continued for several seconds before terminating in a thunderous explosion that shook the hospital building. With no patients currently in Casualty the staff took shelter in the bunkers as more shells screamed over.

'I think they're aiming for the castle again,' said Sister Newman. 'They haven't managed to hit it yet, which is surprising when you consider the size of it. Mind you, they've done enough damage elsewhere.'

Kate nodded. From what little she'd seen, most of the town seemed to be in ruins.

'Are you all right, Staff-Nurse Whitehead?'

'Yes, thank you, Sister.'

'You're a cool one, I must say.'

Kate merely nodded. Shelling was probably worse than bombing because there was so little warning, but once the shells began to fall the experience was much the same. The fear was always there but so was the coping mechanism that had seen her through the Blitz, and it was serving her just as well now.

There were two more explosions and then an unnatural silence until Sister Newman stood up and said, 'It won't be long before we're needed up there. Let's go.'

They made their way to the surface and reached Casualty just as the first of three ambulances drew up outside, and for the next thirty minutes Kate and her team of probationers were kept busy cleaning and dressing minor wounds. The people of Dover had become adept at disappearing into the shelter of the chalk caves. Only a few needed stitching and Kate was beginning to sense a lull when a voice from behind her seized her attention.

'Nurse, this one's lost a lot of blood.' An ambulance woman was drawing her attention to a patient on a stretcher. He looked like a soldier but his uniform was unfamiliar. When Kate looked more closely she deduced that he was American. More importantly, however, his right trouser leg was drenched with blood.

'Don't worry, soldier,' she said. 'We'll have you fixed up in no time.' Leaning towards the doorway that led to the treatment rooms, she spoke quietly to the Casualty Officer. 'Doctor Fuller, we have a patient bleeding heavily. Apparently he's lost a lot already.'

'Right, bring him through.'

Kate motioned to the ambulance women, who carried him into the treatment room, where the doctor was waiting.

'Hello, old chap. Let's have a look at your leg.'

The man merely moaned.

'Another bloody tourniquet,' sighed the doctor, finding a necktie that had been knotted above the wound by some well-meaning person. He waited for Kate to cut it free, and said, 'Cut his trouser leg off as well, Nurse. Then we can see what we're doing.'

'Yes, Doctor.' As she applied her scissors she said, 'I'll have to leave you with one of the second-year nurses, Doctor. I need to be in triage.'

'Very well.'

She inspected the man's dog tag. 'His blood group's O RH positive, Doctor.' She left one of the nurses to assist him while she resumed her place in triage. More casualties were arriving, although none of them was hurt as badly as the soldier.

When she'd seen everyone she took a clipboard and an admission form to the waiting area, where the American casualty's friend was reading an out-of-date magazine for people who kept rabbits and guinea pigs.

'Are you keen on rabbits or just bored?'

He looked up in surprise. 'I guess it's a little of both, ma'am. I kept rabbits when I was a kid, and I'm waiting to hear about my friend. Can you tell me what's happening to him?' His hair and complexion were dark, possibly Mediterranean, although it was hard to say. It was nice, however, to be called "ma'am."

'Yes, he'd lost quite a lot of blood, so he's having a transfusion. We'll have to keep him here for a while.'

'How long?'

'It's hard to say but he'll stay here overnight.'

He nodded. 'I guess I'll have to leave him here, then.'

'Have you got transport?'

'Uh-huh, I left the jeep outside.'

Kate took out her pen and said, 'I have to fill in this form. It's just your friend's details so that we can let your people know where he is and what's happening.'

'I already told them.'

'All right, but we have to do it officially.'

'Okay.' He looked at the form and said, 'That's kinda funny, you saying you had to fill in your form.'

'Why is it funny?'

'Just that we say "fill out", not "fill in", and you asked me if I had transport. We call it "transportation".'

'But the differences are tiny when you consider how far the language has travelled.'

'I guess.' He nodded thoughtfully and then said, 'Okay, what do want to know?'

'First of all, his full name.'

He answered each of her questions. It transpired that they were from the air base near Ashford, about twenty miles away, and that they'd been sightseeing in Dover when the shelling occurred.

'I don't mind telling you, ma'am, it gave me quite a shock. It was the last thing we expected, and I'm ashamed to say I felt kinda shaky, but I had to get Carl to the hospital.' He gave her a shamefaced look and said, 'I was still a little shaky after you took him in.'

'Are you all right now?'

'Yes, thank you, ma'am. I'm fine.'

'Did no one offer you a cup of tea? I'll get one for you now if you like.'

'No, thank you. Don't take this the wrong way, ma'am, but I don't like tea and I'm not keen on the way you British make your coffee either.'

'You wouldn't get coffee here anyway.'

'No?'

'Both tea and coffee are strictly rationed, coffee more than tea.'

'Now you mention it, I've heard about this rationing.'

'Be thankful you've only heard about it.' Then, because he was nice and because it was part of her job anyway, she said, 'Don't worry about getting the shakes. It's quite normal. The first time I was in an air raid I shook like a leaf, and I was treating casualties at the time.'

'When was that?'

'In nineteen-forty.'

'Nineteen-forty? I didn't know they were bombing you then. We called it "The Phoney War".' He made the remark in innocence and it made her smile.

'Believe me,' she said, 'there was nothing phoney about it that night.' She stood up and smoothed down her dress. 'Thank you for your help. There's no point in hanging around now, and we'll be in touch with your people at Ashford if there's any change.'

'Okay. Thank you, ma'am.'

'Not at all. Goodbye.'

She returned to the treatment room, where she found that the soldier's wound had been sutured and dressed and he was currently receiving blood. She checked the needle, the drip chamber and the dressing.

'Well done,' she told the probationer who'd been looking after him. 'Haven't they a bed for him on the ward?'

'Not yet, Staff. They're moving one in for him.'

'Okay. How's he been?'

'He keeps dozing off, Staff.'

'Losing consciousness, Nurse, not "dozing off".'

'Sorry, Staff.'

'That's all right. We all have to learn.' As she spoke, the patient moaned.

'You're all right,' she told him. 'We've stopped the bleeding and we're giving you a transfusion.'

'British blood?' His voice was weak but defiant.

'Yes, we've no American blood left so we're using what we have. It means you'll go home half-British. You never know, you may develop a passion for tea, cricket and understatement.'

'You don't say.' The prospect seemed to cause him some unease.

'Of course not. Blood's the same the world over.'

He seemed satisfied, but then he asked, 'Why am I on my head?'

'You're not on your head. Your feet are elevated to increase the blood flow to your head.'

'Why, for Pete's sake?'

'Because you're in shock, but don't worry, you'll be fine.'

'I can't be in shock.'

'Why not?'

'I'm a guy, for Pete's sake.'

'What you have is haemorrhagic shock caused by loss of blood. You're confusing it with emotional shock.'

'That's okay, then.'

'If you say so, but even heavyweight boxers can suffer emotional shock.'

'You don't say.'

'And so can soldiers.'

'I'm an airman, Nurse, in the United States Army Air Forces.'

'Gosh.'

He eyed her uncertainly. 'Are you wising off at me?'

'I wouldn't dream of it, Corporal.'

'I'm a technician fifth grade. Corporal's the next step up.'

'I beg your pardon. What were you doing when the shelling began?' She already knew the answer but it was a convenient way of changing the subject.

'Just sight-seeing. My buddy and I thought we'd take a look at Dover Castle on account of we don't have castles at home, only they wouldn't let us in.'

'Why not?'

'It's a military base, would you believe? And I thought you guys had moved on from hiding up in castles and fortresses. I hope you're not still using bows and arrows.'

'The castle's there, so they may as well use it.'

'Well it don't impress me.'

'I'm sorry.' More to keep him quiet than for any clinical reason, she slid a thermometer into his mouth and took his pulse. It was stronger and steadier than when he arrived, and his face was a better colour. She was also conscious that now he was recovering from shock his manner was extremely candid to an extent she found quite challenging. In one matter, however, he was prepared to be magnanimous.

'Has any guy ever told you you're pretty?'

'One or two.'

He seemed not to understand. 'Well, was it one or was it two?'

'Several, actually, but I try not to let it go to my head.'

He gave up the struggle with idiomatic English and said, 'You have a neat figure too.' He gave it his overt consideration and ventured, 'Size eight, I guess.'

'No.' Unnerved though she was by his frank appraisal she had to correct him. 'Size ten, actually.'

'Okay, but British size ten is the same as US size eight.'

'Is it? How do you know about dress sizes?'

'Before I enlisted I worked in a clothing factory in Trenton, New Jersey. I only have to look at a dame and I know her size.'

'How unsettling.'

'So, when do you get off duty?'

She'd suspected he was working up to it but the question still took her by surprise. 'That would be telling.'

'So tell me.'

'No. I'm a nurse, you're a patient, and that's how it must stay.'

'So I guess there's a guy in your life.'

For a moment she considered inventing one, but then opted for the truth. 'My fiancée was an airman,' she told him. 'He was killed two years ago.'

'That's too bad.' The news seemed to deter him at first, but then he said, 'But two years is two years, damn it.'

'I know,' she said, concealing her irritation, 'but he was very special.'

<hr/>

'In spite of shortages and all the enemy can throw at us,' said Irene, 'that was a very nice meal. Thank you, Jack.'

'You're very welcome. I'm afraid the wine's a bit second-rate but I suppose we have to be thankful for what we can get.'

'An old school friend of mine is a WAAF, a stewardess, on one of the American air stations and she says there's no shortage of wine in their officers' mess.'

'They make the stuff in America, I believe.'

'Yes, in California.'

'Surely not,' he said. 'You're thinking of syrup of figs.'

'Don't be foul.'

'I can't help it, it's a family failing.' More to escape the subject of scarcity than for any other reason, he asked, 'What kind of thing did you get up to before the war?'

'What do you mean?'

'What interests did you have?'

'I don't know, really.' She wrinkled her nose in thought. 'The usual things, I suppose, shopping, going to the pictures, dancing, shopping....'

'You must have done a lot of shopping. That's twice you've mentioned it.'

'Oh, I did, and I'd do much more if it weren't for rationing and shortages.' She added, 'and the pittance they pay us Wrens.'

'Presumably you're talking about shopping for clothes.'

'What else is there?' It was a guileless question. 'Anyway, what sort of thing did you do?'

'The same as you minus the shopping. Oh, and I also did a lot of cycling.'

'Ugh. That's hard work.'

'It gets easier the more you do, and it's the cheapest way to see beautiful countryside.'

'The country doesn't do a lot for me. I'm more of a city girl, really.'

'The city being London, I suppose?'

'That's right.' Out of uniform and with her dark-brown hair down she was even more appealing than when they first met, and her brown eyes twinkled with fun when she said, 'You know, you look even better with that scar. It makes you look more heroic, if you know what I mean.'

'I wish you hadn't mentioned that. I'm very sensitive about this scar, like Cyrano de Bergerac was about his nose.'

'You're just full of bull, aren't you?'

'You're a hard, cruel girl.' He looked at his watch. 'Twenty minutes to pumpkin time,' he announced sadly. 'It's time to get you back to the wrennery.' He motioned to the elderly waiter for the bill.

They walked back to the docks and as they came to a convenient alley between two rows of houses he drew her aside. Sheltered from public view but aware of how little time they had, they kissed.

As they broke apart and walked on, she said, 'It's a pity there's nowhere private we can go.'

'Actually there is.'

'Oh?'

'I'm looking after a cottage for my ex-boss from before the war. It's not far from here.'

She stopped in her stride. 'And your boss is not around?'

'He's with the Fire Service in London.'

'Why didn't you mention it earlier?'

'Be fair, Irene, this is the first time we've been out together since you came to Immingham. I was going to tell you, but I like to work up to these things gradually and with a measure of finesse.'

Clearly Irene was unimpressed. 'Do I have to remind you,' she demanded, 'that there's a war on?'

'Only very occasionally and when the guns stop firing.'

'Time and tide wait for no man, Jack. Where is this place?'

Dorothy entered the office and saluted the squadron officer.

'At ease, Sergeant Needham. Come in and take a seat.' She pushed a wooden box across the desk towards her. 'Cigarette?'

'Thank you, ma'am.' Dorothy rarely smoked, but just for the novelty she took one and accepted a light. It felt very odd because she'd been expecting at least a harsh reprimand.

'I imagine you know why I've sent for you.'

'I suspect it has something to do with Section Officer Benson, ma'am.'

'That's right. She wanted to have you charged with insolence.' The squadron officer's use of the word 'wanted' was interesting. Presumably the charge wasn't going ahead.

'I can answer Section Officer Benson's accusation, ma'am.'

'Then do so.'

'Miss Benson made scathing remarks about a corporal and

an ACW. The first was based on social prejudice and the other on ignorance of human nature as it exists beyond her experience. The corporal proved her wrong by acquitting herself as the excellent NCO and signaller she is, whereas I simply pointed out a fact of life that had escaped her.'

'But you went too far, Sergeant.'

'Yes, ma'am. I should have made allowances. That is the sergeant's lot as I understand it. I'll naturally apologise to Miss Benson.'

The officer stubbed her cigarette out in an already overflowing ash tray and blew out a long cloud of smoke. 'The easiest course of action for me would be to discipline you for insolence, but I'm reluctant to do that, because in all other respects you do an excellent job.'

'Thank you, ma'am.'

'At the same time, however, I can't have you speaking to my officers the way you spoke to Section Officer Benson.' She lit another cigarette and said, 'Your record shows that you turned down an offer to be considered for officer training. Why was that?'

'I couldn't see the point, ma'am. I know far more about signals than any junior officer, so I think I'm more useful to the service as an NCO.'

'But haven't you considered how much pleasanter life would be as an officer? For one thing you'd have the shared services of a batwoman, and the catering facilities and accommodation are very much better than anything you're used to.'

'My family have always led a comfortable existence, ma'am, and I had a particularly good job before the war. Even so, one of my most enjoyable experiences since enlisting has been that of mucking in with everyone else. I've made friends with girls from every conceivable background and I've benefited from the experience. When this war is over I shall most likely return to my old job and continue to enjoy the services at home of a cook, a maid and a gardener, but I don't think I'll ever regret having served in the ranks, because, when all's said and done, a holiday is only a change from normal routine.'

'I never imagined you would change your mind, Sergeant.' The squadron officer referred to a handwritten note that she took from her 'in' tray. 'That's why I spent some time this morning on the telephone. I've been in communication with Number One Signal School at Cranwell. I see from your record that you've spent some time there already.'

'That's right, ma'am.'

'Well, I've pulled a few strings for you to be posted there as an instructor on the signals course for trainee officers. They'll have completed their initial training in Windermere, and Cranwell will be the next and final stage for them. It'll give you an opportunity to learn something of what these young women are faced with. You'll find out how much they have to learn in the short time they have, and you'll get some idea of how they must feel when they come under the scrutiny of experienced NCOs. If you can show them a little of the understanding you've reserved in the past for girls in the ranks, I think you'll do them and yourself a power of good.'

'Very good, ma'am.'

'Oh, and you'll not be going alone.'

'Ma'am?'

'Corporal Sellers is going with you.'

It occurred to Dorothy that Section Officer Benson must have considerably more influence than the average junior officer, but the squadron officer refused to be drawn on the subject.

'Very convenient.' Irene completed her brief survey and sat by the newly-lit fire. Only two days had elapsed since they'd last seen each other but time and tide or, more accurately, Irene had prompted an early excursion to Ulceby.

The cottage was snug, simply furnished and cosy. Her assessment was a fair one.

'And, as the sun is over the yard arm, a drink is in order.' Jack handed her a glass. 'Have a pink gin.'

'Where on earth did you find gin and bitters?'

'In the wardroom.'

'Won't they miss it?'

'Who? Don't forget I'm the boss. Anyway, I put it on my mess bill.'

'Of course. I'm not used to being in such elevated company.'

'It's all right. There's no need to be shy. Just the usual deference due to a commissioned officer will suffice.'

She grimaced. 'The only thing I have to be shy about is these stockings, the only decent pair I have. Uniform stockings. I ask you.'

'They're no detriment, believe me.'

She shook her head in wonder. 'What is it about men and black stockings?'

'Some would say they're the only good thing to have come out of this war.'

'In that case you'll be able to tell your grandchildren about them. When they ask you about the war you'll be able to say, "Wrens wore black artificial silk stockings and that made the whole thing worthwhile. Oh, and I got a medal as well." ' Then as if the thought had just occurred to her, she asked, 'Why did they give you the DSC, Jack?'

'That's a question you should never ask.'

'But everything that happens out there is a mystery to us. We're cooped up in a boring W/T office while you're at sea searching for adventure and excitement.'

'I didn't go searching for it. I sort of... bumped into it, in a manner of speaking.'

She stood up to face him and said, 'You're not going to tell me, are you?'

'No.'

'In that case,' she said, kissing him provocatively, 'I'll have to wheedle it out of you, like Mata Hari.'

'D' you mean you're going to seduce me?'

'Yes.'

'Okay, but you may have to prompt me from time to time.'

Playfulness gave way to disbelief as she asked, 'You're not a virgin, are you?'

'No, but it's been a long time and I have a terrible memory.'

'Oh, I think you'll remember what to do.'

It seemed that the only time Alan and Gwen could have a private conversation was when they were walking in the grounds of Trent Park. The officers' mess was always busy and privacy was non-existent.

He caught up with her after lunch two days after their cinema outing. She was looking less strained than when he'd left her but she said nothing until they were quite alone. Eventually she told him, 'You can relax. It was a false alarm.'

'You mean you're not...?' He couldn't help looking around him to ensure they were still alone.

'No, as of this morning I'm not.'

'Thank God for that.'

'Amen to that. It was a horrible two weeks.'

'I wonder what made you late. I remember you're saying you were usually so regular.'

'I've been thinking about that and I think it was moving to the new accommodation block that did it.'

Alan struggled with the information but had to ask, 'How was that responsible?'

'It's a curious quirk of nature,' she said, 'that when females live in an enclosed community such as a boarding school, a convent or even a military accommodation block, their cycles become synchronised.'

'Do you mean they all... at the same time?'

She nodded. 'Like a Greek chorus.'

'Good lord.'

'Yes, you'd think women would behave more independently, but it's a proven fact.'

'Well, it's welcome news.'

'Yes, I should have thought of it earlier instead of frightening you to death.'

'You didn't. I was just concerned.'

She smiled. 'You were concerned enough to offer to marry me, and that meant a great deal, believe me.'

'I didn't offer. I said I wanted to, and I still do. The scare simply prompted me to say what I'd wanted to say for some time.' He studied her face in vain. 'Say something,' he urged.

'This place is about as private as Piccadilly Circus,' she said, but her delight was transparent. 'I can't react here. You'll have to take me somewhere special and propose properly.'

'All right.' In his euphoric state he was ready to agree to anything. 'I'll push the boat out.'

'Good for you. And another thing we need to do,' she said, 'is to find out which cinema is showing *Random Harvest*.' She added, 'Now that I can give it my full attention.'

37

Kate put the almost-empty bottle of detergent back on the shelf, making a mental note to put it on her shopping list. And now she thought of it, she dried her hands so that she could add it to the list while it was on her mind. Mental notes might have worked at one time but she no longer trusted them.

She stacked the last cup on the draining rack and poured away the water carefully. It was one of life's unsolved mysteries that there was so often a teaspoon left in the bottom of an apparently empty bowl, but on this occasion there was none, so she picked up a towel and began drying the dishes. The old dishwasher had died a few years earlier, and she had seen no point in replacing it now that she was alone.

As she dried, her mind returned to Alan and Gwen. She'd been thinking of them only that morning, or was it yesterday? It didn't matter. What really mattered was that somehow, by sheer chance, those two had found each other, and what a couple they made. Alan had never been Kate's ideal, even after what Dorothy had called his 'conversion', but she had to admit that he had hidden qualities.

The azure emulsion on the kitchen walls was looking rather tired, but it seemed extravagant to get a painter in to do it. She stopped for a moment, trying to remember what she'd been thinking about before she noticed the emulsion. Alan, yes, and the other boys, Maurice and Jack. They all had special qualities, and Dorothy as well, posted away because she was too critical of the officers. She'd always lived by her own rules, long before

262

it became fashionable for women to assert themselves. Did the war really happen so long ago? She dropped the tea towel in the laundry basket as scraps of memory began to come together.

38

A Halifax of Coastal Command had given the position of the ditched Lancaster. It was thirty-three miles off the Dutch coast, too close to enemy-held territory for anyone's peace of mind, and two hours had elapsed since that sighting. The dinghy could have drifted a considerable distance. Also visibility had deteriorated, making the job as near to impossible as it could get. There was a chance the crew might be picked up by the enemy, but the likelihood was even worse, that they wouldn't be found at all. However, until the signal was received ordering a return to base, RML 97 would continue a box search with lookouts peering ever diligently through the patchy fog and drizzle.

The search went on for almost a further two hours but eventually the bridge port lookout called, 'Distress flare fine on the port quarter!'

Jack turned and saw it before it was obscured by a bank of swirling fog.

'Hard a-port, Cox'n.' A feature of the latest RMLs was the absence of a wheelhouse. Instead the wheel was positioned on the bridge, a development that made communication with the helmsman more immediate.

The Cox'n responded and the ship made a wide turn to approach the source of the flare, which soon turned out to be a dinghy.

'Midships.'

'Wheel's amidships, sir.'

'Dead slow ahead both.'

'Dead slow ahead both. Both engines dead slow ahead, sir.'

Jack counted all seven of the crew in the dinghy. Hopefully no one was wounded.

'Stop both.'

The starboard watch swung out the boom with its scrambling net and two men descended to help the ditched airmen, whose hands and limbs would be too numb with cold for them to help themselves. The encouraging voices of Leading Seaman Barlow and his party would be a welcome sound to the survivors.

Soon everyone was on board, wet and dirty clothing went over the side and the survivors enjoyed the luxury of soap and hot water for the first time in twenty-four hours. Then, with four tucked up in the sick bay and the other three occupying the wardroom bunks, Jack left Brian on the bridge so that he could go down to the wardroom to speak to the captain of the Lancaster, an Aberdonian called Stewart.

'It was a welcome sight all right,' Stewart told Jack, 'your wee boat coming out of the fog. I have to say, though, it took you a while to find us after the Halifax had spotted us.'

'Ah well,' said Jack, overlooking the criticism, 'there'll be another welcome sight along very soon. I've ordered an issue of rum.'

'We could have used some o' that when we came on board.'

'I'm sure you could, but the medical advice is to wait until you're warmed through before we give you spirits. It's to avoid causing shock by sending a rush of cold blood to the heart, apparently.'

'Aye,' said Murchison nodding, 'but as we're nicely warmed now, could ye no flout convention and give me a whisky instead of that awful rum?'

'If that's your preference,' agreed Jack, 'that's what you shall have. Actually, we'll have to requisition more rum after this patrol. We picked up the crew of an American B-Seventeen yesterday, and they carry ten men. That's a lot of rum.'

'Where on earth did you put them?'

'Some here in the wardroom, some in the sick bay and the rest on the messdeck.'

'The what?'

'The men's quarters.' Then, as the Coxswain appeared with a tray of tot glasses, he said, 'Here comes the rum. I'll pour you a scotch.'

'Single malt, is it?'

'No, only blended. There's a limit to what we can offer. I'm continually reminded that there's a war on.'

'Aye well, if ye've nothing better, I daresay it'll go down well enough.'

Jack took his leave and returned to the bridge, having met six very relieved and grateful airmen and an officer for whom, it seemed, life would always be less than perfect.

Even so, he was happy. Very much against the odds Ninety-Seven had made a pick-up and was now returning to base. There was also the prospect of another encounter with Irene.

⊕⊰⋅⊱⊰⋅⊱⊕

'I hope we're going to make a stop soon,' said Connie, looking uncomfortable. 'It's a pity I didn't think about all this bumping and jolting before I had that second mug of tea.'

'Yes, men don't think about that, do they?' She glanced in the direction of the two men in the cab. The journey from Humby to Cranwell had to be made by RAF transport, in this case a three-ton lorry.

'Only when they've been drinking, and then they can't stop often enough.' Her remark triggered grins from the two airmen opposite them, although they made no attempt to communicate with the girls. They were both aircraftmen, lowly beings popularly known as 'erks', and were disinclined to attempt familiarity with a sergeant and a corporal, even when the NCOs in question were female.

'It's a shame about you having to leave Daniel behind,' said Connie, speaking so that only Dorothy could hear her over the growl of the lorry. 'You were quite keen on him, weren't you?'

'I liked him,' admitted Dorothy. 'He was keener than I was.'

'So it wasn't a big romance for you?'

Dorothy shook her head. 'I couldn't see a future for us, and we were going to be separated anyway. He has just two ops to go before he completes his tour. After that they'll post him away.'

'I suppose so.'

They both winced as the vehicle hit a pothole in the road.

'At least they kept us together,' said Dorothy when the going became smoother.

'Why aye, and that came as a surprise. Wouldn't it be nice to have as much influence as Section Officer flaming Benson?'

Dorothy gave a bored sigh. 'I learned yesterday that Daddy is an Air Vice-Marshall,' she said, 'and I imagine whatever his darling girl wants she usually gets.'

'If you ask me she needs a smacked arse.'

Dorothy smiled at the thought. 'I don't think she'll get that.'

'And now we've got the job of training more like her.'

'Let's hope there won't be too many like her. In any case it's going to be part of our job to discourage that sort of attitude.'

'To tame them before they get too big for their boots, like?'

'If we can.' Dorothy considered it for a moment and said with a smile, 'It's quite a responsibility.'

They both dwelt on that for a while, and then Connie said, 'You know, even with the likes of Section Officer Benson around, this job beats anything I did before the war.'

'At work or in your spare time?'

'I didn't have a lot of spare time, and even when I had some I was too hard up to do much with it.'

'That was cruel.'

'You can say that again. What did you do with your spare time, Dot?'

'Oh, the usual things, you know, and I did a lot of cycling with a club. There was a little gang of us, two girls and three boys who used to get together, basically because we were the youngest. The older members kept very much to themselves.'

'What were the other four like?'

'Kate, the other girl is a good friend of mine. She's a nurse, and when she's not patching up casualties she saves the day by delivering impatient babies. I could never do that kind of thing in a million years but Kate thrives on it.'

'She sounds like a canny lass. What about the lads?'

'Maurice was killed in action back in 'forty-one. He was shot down over Germany and it was heart breaking because he was really nice. He was engaged to Kate.'

'Oh, poor lass.'

'Then there's Alan, the clever one, who had a bit of a thing about me for a while. He's in intelligence. The other one, Jack, is in the Navy. I always had a soft spot for him, mainly because we're usually on the same wavelength. He's captain of a rescue motor launch.'

'Is he very posh?'

'Jack?' Dorothy laughed at the idea. 'No, Jack's not at all posh. You'd like him but he's based at Immingham so I'm afraid I can't introduce you.'

'That's a shame.' Connie's attention appeared to be divided between what Dorothy was saying and the fact that the lorry was pulling up outside a café.

'It is. He tells me he's recently taken up with a Wren. He says she's a brazen hussy and she's bound to lead an innocent young chap like him astray, but I've no doubt he'll survive.'

The corporal who had been a passenger in the cab and who was now unfastening the tailboard said, 'We've stopped for a cup o' char and a jimmy riddle, girls. D' you want a hand down?'

'No thanks,' Dorothy told him. 'Just turn your backs while we climb down.'

⊛⊷⊱⊰⊱⊰⊷⊛

Jack and Irene spent a good deal of their time at the cottage in Ulceby until Irene became curiously unavailable on two occasions. It puzzled him for a while, although he had his suspicions, and he was returning one morning from the mail office, when their paths crossed. She saluted him because they were in uniform and under the eyes of authority, and he returned her salute but was surprised by her cautious expression.

'Jack,' she said, 'I've been meaning to speak to you.'

'Well, here I am.' He knew already what she was going to tell him.

She looked uncomfortable and said, 'The thing is, we have to stop seeing each other.'

268

'Okay. May I ask why?'

She hesitated again. 'I'm seeing someone else.'

'Oh well, that's your privilege.' He was disappointed but not particularly surprised, knowing her as he did.

'Don't be awful, Jack. I didn't mean this to happen.'

'I'm not being awful. It was nice knowing you and I wish you luck.' There was little else he could say, and he was about to take his leave of her, but then he asked, 'Is he anyone I know?' It would be too awful if the chap turned out to be one of his colleagues in the flotilla.

'Only slightly.' She hesitated. The question seemed to cause her more embarrassment than ever. Eventually she said, 'He's one of the American airmen you rescued last week.'

The colonel took the glass that was handed to him and inspected its contents. As far as he knew sherry had been unobtainable for quite some time.

'It's the Jerez dry fino, sir,' the mess waiter assured him, 'the last bottle in the cellar.'

'Good work, Murchison.' The colonel turned to the young couple beside him and said, 'Well, Lieutenant Lofthouse and Second Subaltern Davidson, now that you've stood me a glass of sherry you can call yourselves officially engaged. Let me offer you my congratulations.' He shook hands with both of them and they chatted briefly until he was called away to the telephone.

'I never knew,' said Gwen.

'Never knew what?'

'About this tradition of asking for the colonel's blessing.'

'I think it's just something he invented so that he could cadge a drink occasionally. At all events it's a harmless, friendly thing to do.'

'Oh, I couldn't agree more.'

'Speaking of friendly gestures,' he said, taking a letter from his pocket and handing it to her, 'have a look at this. It's from a chap I met early in the war.'

Gwen took the letter, smiling as she read it, and then handed it back. She asked, 'Was "Prof" your nickname in those days?'

'Yes, although not a complimentary one. A university education was quite a handicap in the barrack-room jungle and the other chaps gave me a hard time, but it was basically my fault.'

'That's hard to imagine. You and Harry must have been friendly enough.'

'Eventually. The change came after a lecture, believe it or not, about venereal disease. The medic who gave the lecture treated it rather as a performance, and most of the chaps didn't understand half of it.'

'That's awful, dangerous too.'

'My thought exactly, so I explained it to them and after that they decided I was human after all. Harry and I became pals, we went to France together, served in the same mobile signals unit and we were evacuated together.'

'When you say it quickly like that it doesn't sound too awful, but I'm sure it was.'

'It was worse for Harry because he was seriously injured. They had to take his leg off when we reached Dover.'

'Poor man.'

Alan nodded. 'He has a job in Sheffield now, assembling radio equipment. His old job was painting and decorating, not an ideal trade for a chap with an artificial leg.'

'We have so much to be thankful for.' She pointed to the pocket that contained Harry's letter and said, 'And now we have Harry's blessing as well as well as the Colonel's.' It seemed somehow right.

39

Rachel studied the colour chart. 'I like it too,' she said, 'but I don't like the idea of you working on a step ladder.'

'I'll use a long-handled roller.'

'But you'll still have to do the fiddly bits in the corners and round the light fitting with a brush.'

'They are only little bits.'

'Kate, you're infuriating.'

'I know. When are you going to introduce me to David?'

'You've done it again.'

'Done what again?'

'Wrong-footed me. We were talking about painting your kitchen and suddenly you asked me about David.'

'I've told you before, Rachel, I haven't time at my age to be subtle. Anyway, you were bullying me.'

'I'd hardly call it bullying.'

Kate leaned forward to give Rachel's arm a friendly pat and said, 'Let's talk about something else.'

'All right. What happened to Dorothy after they posted her to… where was it?'

'Cranwell. She went there to train officer cadets and I think she enjoyed it. She always sounded happy enough in her letters.' She paused for a moment, remembering something. 'Apart from one time, I think, late in nineteen-forty-three. It was before Christmas, anyway, and she had some bad news. She wrote to me at the time but apart from offering long-distance sympathy there was nothing I could do. I was stuck in Dover and I hadn't been there long enough to get leave.'

Rachel looked puzzled. 'From things you've told me I've always had the impression that Dorothy was very strong and self-contained.'

'She always seemed so but like anyone else she could hurt inside. It was good that we were all ready correspondents.'

40

Jack was in the wardroom when Brian came down the ladder.
'Good morning, Brian. Good leave?' Foul weather meant that all aircraft were grounded and consequently half the ship's company were currently on leave.

'Excellent, thank you. I called at the mail office on the way here.' He handed two envelopes to Jack. 'One of yours bears a woman's hand.'

'They both do. One's from my mother.' He picked up the other, recognising Dorothy's handwriting, and opened it. He'd had a letter from her within the last two weeks and it seemed odd for her to write again so soon.

'You know too many women, Jack. I'm sure it's not good for you.'

'Knowing them doesn't mean I ever get to see them.' He unfolded Dorothy's letter and began to read, little knowing that the situation was about to change.

Dear Jack,

As we're only about fifty miles apart and there's absolutely nothing happening just now, perhaps we could meet somewhere. If you can get leave or even if you can't, please phone me between 0800 and 1800 on the number below. Ask for the Signal School and sound official.

Lots of love,
Dot XXX

It would be an opportunity to use the Morris van that was

his new toy. He phoned her later that morning after speaking with the Flotilla Leader and the Base Commander and securing a seventy-two-hour pass. She sounded unusually relieved to hear his voice.

'Hello, Jack, you'd no trouble getting through?'

'No, I told them I was phoning from Air-Sea Rescue at Immingham and they put me through straight away. Are you all right? You sound edgy.'

'I'm fine. Well, I'll tell you later. Can you get away? I've got a seventy-two-hour pass from twelve-hundred today.' She was sounding even less like the self-assured Dorothy he knew.

'Yes, there's no problem. Look, if you can get to Lincoln I can pick you up at the bus station. I've got the use of a van.'

'Lovely. How did you manage that?'

'It belongs to a local greengrocer but he hardly uses it. I'll tell you about it later.'

'Okay. By the way, where are we going?'

'I'm looking after a cottage for my ex-boss. It's not far from here and there's easily room for two of us.'

'I should hope so.'

'I mean sleeping accommodation. Two rooms, that is.'

'Oh, Jack.' She laughed and for the first time her tone lightened. 'You're such a gentleman. I'd almost forgotten.'

'I just didn't want you to get the wrong idea.'

'I know.'

'Okay, can you get to the bus station by about two o'clock?'

'Yes, there's a bus at ten-past each hour. I may even be able to cadge a lift.'

'Okay, I'll pick you up there.'

'Lovely. I must go. I have a class in five minutes.'

Dorothy transferred her attention from the passing scenery to Jack. 'You were going to tell me how you came by this van,' she reminded him.

'Yes, it belongs to old Salter, one of the local greengrocers. His son used it before the war. The old man prefers his horse and cart. Cars and vans are noisy, dangerous things, you understand.'

'But doesn't his son mind you using it?'

'He's not around anymore. He was killed at Tobruk.'

'That's awful. I'm surprised his father lets you use the van.'

'Ah well, there's more to it than that. In exchange for petrol coupons I keep him supplied with pipe tobacco and the occasional quarter-flask of whisky. Also, he's working hard at selling me the van. He's a canny old lad.'

'So are you, by the sound of it.'

'Not really, it just seemed too good an opportunity to miss.'

They drove on, arriving at the cottage at a little after four. Jack got out and opened the passenger door for Dorothy.

'It sticks sometimes,' he explained. 'I suppose that happens with disuse.'

'Yes, it's certainly seen better days but it got us here, so never mind.'

'Let me have your grip.'

'Oh, Jack, I can carry this thing. It's not heavy.'

'That doesn't sound like you.' He unlatched the gate and led her to the door. 'By the way,' he said, 'I hope you packed an evening dress for tonight.'

'One for each evening, actually.' She never took him seriously.

'Welcome aboard,' he said, holding the door open for her.

'This is lovely. How old is it?'

'Early nineteenth century, I believe.'

She looked around her appreciatively as she stepped in, and Jack couldn't help recalling some of Irene's more prosaic observations.

'Oh good, there's a fire,' she said, rubbing her cold hands together.

'Yes, I lit it earlier to heat some water.'

'You think of everything.' She put her hand on his arm and said, 'I suppose a bath's out of the question in a cottage like this.'

'Follow me.' He led her to the extension at the back of the house and opened the bathroom door. 'It's cosy,' he said, 'in fact it's tiny but I daresay you'll manage.'

'Oh, I shall.'

'Have a bath by all means but let me boil a kettle first and you can have a cup of tea.'

'Jack,' she said, slipping her arm through his and kissing him on the cheek, 'you're just what the doctor ordered.'

He filled the kettle and placed it on the hob above the hearth. 'Let me take your coat and I'll hang it up.' He helped her out of the heavy RAF greatcoat, wondering how any woman could look so elegant in such a shapeless garment.

'Where am I sleeping?'

'Upstairs. You can't miss it, because it's all there is up there.' He added, 'There's a fire in the bedroom, just a small one but it'll do the job.'

'You're the perfect host.'

⚜

A little later, bathed and changed into a dark-blue dress, she rejoined him.

'Oh my word, Dot, it really is you. I'd been wondering. I kept looking at that character beside me in the greatcoat and thinking she looked a bit like you, but now I'm convinced. You look magnificent.'

'Thank you, even though "magnificent" is a gross exaggeration.'

'You must bear with me if I appear overawed. Where did you find a dress like that in wartime?'

'It's from my pre-war wardrobe. A wool and silk mixture like this is impossible to find nowadays. When we enlisted, we were supposed to send all our civvies home in a parcel and not bring any back when we returned from leave but I cheated.' She wrinkled her nose mischievously. 'I have my own rules,' she said, 'and they don't always coincide with the Air Ministry's.'

'Silk stockings too,' he observed. 'They're a rare luxury.'

'Yes, these were also a peacetime precaution and I've only a few pairs left. To get the new nylon ones it's necessary to be well in with an American.'

He nodded glumly. 'I know someone who's gone down that road.'

'Not that girl you were seeing?'

'Mm, she took up with a chap we picked up from a ditched B-Seventeen.' He added grumpily, 'I should have left the bugger in the North Sea.'

'I'm sorry.' She was shaking gently. 'I shouldn't laugh.'

'You're allowed to.'

'No, I'll change the subject. What are we doing about eating tonight?'

'We'll eat here.'

'Here?' For the first time a look of unease crossed her face. 'I hope you don't think I'm capable of anything as technical as cooking.'

'No, but I am.'

'I didn't know you could cook,' she said, anxiety giving way to relief. 'I mean it's not a man's thing, is it?'

'You should see my knitting and embroidery. I'm thinking of taking up tapestry too.'

'No, really, how did you learn to cook?'

'I taught myself. When I lived in Hull my salary didn't run to full board or a service flat, so I had to fend for myself and I rather enjoyed it.'

'How marvellous, so what are we eating?'

'Seabass with potatoes, carrots, cauliflower and a cheese sauce.'

Her eyes opened wide in astonishment. 'How did you get those things?'

'The vegetables, cheese, milk and things I got from the galley. The fish was fresh out of the sea this morning. One of the minesweepers came in with a huge catch after the accidental detonation of a floating mine. It happens all too often.'

'I miss out on so much.'

'I'm sure you do. I still think you'd have done better in the Wrens.' The mental picture had never left him.

'Oh, I think I've found my true wartime vocation. I just have to be careful not to overstep the mark as I did at my last station.'

'Which mark was that?'

'The diplomatic limit when dealing with officers.' She told him about her experience with Section Officer Benson and the reason for her posting back to Cranwell.

'You're a dyed-in-the-wool sergeant, aren't you? You're

impatient with junior officers who know less than you and at the same time you feel that to take their place would be beneath your dignity.'

'You're almost right. The impatience is pretty well under control now it's my job to guide their footsteps. I have to say, though, most of them are all right.'

'So it's going well?'

'Pretty well.'

He studied her briefly and said, 'Something's troubling you, though.'

'You have a sixth sense, Jack. Come and sit with me.'

He joined her on the sofa and waited.

'I was seeing a chap recently,' she said, 'a flight engineeer, a New Zealander, called Daniel. He was very nice and good company, but he didn't quite light the fire for me. I liked him tremendously but not like that.'

'Did he know that?'

She nodded mutely. 'He was in love with me. It took a while for that to surface but he told me eventually and said he wanted us to get married and live in New Zealand after the war. I had to tell him it was impossible.'

'Better than keeping him dangling, I suppose.'

'He took it badly. Inside, that is. He tried not to show it but I knew how he was feeling.'

In the absence of anything to say, Jack simply nodded. He found it strange to find Dorothy suddenly squeamish about ditching a bloke. It had never worried her much in the past.

'I left for Cranwell and he completed his tour. He was posted to an Operational Training Unit. They do that to rest them after forty ops.'

'That makes sense.'

'And then I heard last week that he'd been killed in a crash.'

That answered Jack's question. He waited for her to go on.

'He'd gone up in a Wimpey—'

'A what?'

'A Wellington bomber. They call it the "Wimpey" after a cartoon character.'

278

'Do they really?'

'Yes, apparently. Anyway, the aileron controls were defective, and the pilot had banked and was making his approach to the runway when the aircraft failed to level out. It hit the ground with one wingtip and crashed, killing the whole crew.'

'Poor devils.' He took her hand and held it. 'But none of this was your fault.'

'You know just what I'm thinking.'

'But why do you feel guilty?'

She shook her head hopelessly. 'I could have tried harder and given it a chance. I might have developed feelings for him.'

'You know it doesn't work like that. In any case he was killed. How would that have worked?'

'Maybe if he'd not been distracted, if he'd been concentrating—'

'Oh Dot, you're not thinking straight. The aircraft was in the pilot's hands. In any case you can't possibly know what was going through his mind at the time. I can tell you from experience that when an emergency occurs you forget all about your personal life and concentrate solely on the job in hand.' He added, 'I speak as one who's been ditched frequently.'

'Really?'

'I am routinely discarded, very much like the contents of a dustbin. At least that's how it feels.'

'No, what you said about concentrating on the emergency.'

'Absolutely. Nothing fixes the mind like the prospect of violent death.' He watched her nod slowly but he knew she wasn't convinced. 'By all means keep talking about it if it helps,' he said, 'but I think you'll see what I mean.'

'It's good just to have a sympathetic ear. My friend Connie's a lovely girl but her idea of listening is to tell me to pull myself together. She comes from a tough background.'

'I haven't been exactly soothing.'

'But you have.' She stroked his hand. 'Kate told me how good you were for her after Maurice was killed, and I can see that now.'

'I do what I can.' He pondered that for a while before looking at the clock and saying, 'I'm afraid you'll have to excuse me while I prepare the vegetables.'

Looking rather more cheerful, she asked, 'Can I help? I know how to peel spuds and carrots.'

'Do you really? No wonder they made you a sergeant.'

⊖⊢⊟⊸∣⊹⊟⊶⊷

As they returned to the sofa after dinner, Dorothy asked, 'Where did you find the wine? It must be almost impossible to get nowadays.'

'The base wardroom steward found it for me.'

'You amaze me. You've stocked up on wine, found food I'd forgotten existed, lit fires and driven to and from Lincoln, and all for my benefit.'

'Well, I had to push the boat out. When did we last see each other? It must have been after I came back from Dunkirk.'

'Yes, three years ago. I hadn't even enlisted, and so much has happened since then.'

'Who else have you seen?'

'Do you mean out of the original gang? I've seen Kate twice and I saw Alan after he returned from France. He'd taken up with a local girl. I forget her name.'

'Iris.'

'That's right. And, of course, I saw Maurice sometimes when he came over from York to see Kate.' She looked down at her lap. 'Poor old Maurice. I do miss him.'

'I think we all do.'

'Yes, he was so genuine, and he was like a little boy who had to be protected, usually from Alan. I was happy to do that.'

'Yes, I remember it.'

'You know, I don't think Kate's recovered yet from losing him.'

'I'm inclined to agree. Alan, by the way, is a changed man.'

'I know. I sense that in his letters.'

'Does he still write to you?'

'Occasionally. You know he's engaged now, don't you? She's in the ATS and her father's something in the diplomatic service.'

'Yes, he told me.'

'One down and three to go,' she said, holding up four fingers and folding her index finger, 'but I'm not ready to settle down yet, and Kate's not at all interested. That only leaves you.'

'Not yet by a long way.'

'No?'

'No, I have to think of my reputation as a Don Juan. Brian, my first-lieutenant, says I know far too many women, although that could be envy on his part. He's very young.' He lifted the bottle. 'More wine?'

'No, thank you. I'm still recovering from the pink gin you gave me before dinner.'

'I could put some coffee on. That came from the base wardroom, by the way.'

'No, let's just sit here. This is the first time I've relaxed for days.' She rested her head on his shoulder and said, 'It really is good to be with you again, especially now.'

'Trust me,' he said, 'when you've thought more clearly about things you'll feel a lot better.' He freed the arm that was trapped between them and slipped it round her shoulders. 'Meanwhile just sit back and go where the current takes you.'

She opened one eye to look up at him. 'That's a new one on me.'

'We sea-dogs have a vocabulary all of our own. There are times when even we don't understand it.'

'Same old Jack,' she observed. 'Whatever you do, don't change.'

'It's unlikely. I've tried to change, but all in vain. My father used to say, "Tha'll never make owt o' thysen if tha stays t' way th' are, Jack." '

'Your father's never spoken like that.'

'I know, but if he did, that's what he'd say.'

'Idiot.' She spoke so softly it sounded like an endearment, an invitation. As she continued to look up at him he lowered his head so that his lips touched hers. She made no hesitation but drew him closer.

After a while she said a little breathlessly, 'I've wondered sometimes what it would be like with you.'

'I'd never have known.'

'Men are slow to read the signs.'

'In that case you should make them less cryptic.'

'Okay, kiss me.'

He obliged, exquisitely conscious of her perfume, her quickened breath and the soft curves beneath the fabric.

After a while she asked, 'Where were you going to sleep?'

'Here on this sofa,' he told her, quietly encouraged by her use of the past tense.

'You can't do that. It must be at least twelve inches shorter than you.'

'There's always the deck.'

She shook her head. 'I wouldn't hear of it.'

'I don't want you to think I'm taking advantage of you in your distressed state.'

'You're doing wonders for my distressed state.'

They left the sofa and climbed the stairs to the bedroom, where the fire was going well. The room was warm and welcoming.

'Will you unhook me?' She turned and held her hair aside so that he could find the hook and zipper. To a man who'd always believed women's clothing to be complex and mysterious the task looked pleasingly straightforward, and he released the hook and lowered the zipper so that she could lift the dress over her head. From that point onward disrobing was relatively simple. The women in Jack's limited experience had been frustratingly independent in that respect but Dorothy was happy to accept his assistance and to lend hers in return, so that the operation was carried out with amicable co-operation.

He held her for a moment, delighting in her nakedness and the satin feel of her skin. One question remained, however, and it seemed only good manners to ask, 'Which side do you prefer?'

'You quaint, old-fashioned thing,' she said, drawing back the covers. 'Let's play it by ear.'

41

'Jack was quite keen on Dorothy.' Kate smiled to herself in recollection. 'I suppose most men of her acquaintance were. She had that effect on them. I think Jack knew her well enough to see the risk, but it still ended before he was ready.'

'Was he terribly hurt?'

'I think he must have been. He was always one to play such things down, but his letters took on a serious note for a while.'

'What about Dorothy? Did she go on leaving a trail of broken hearts behind her?'

'Oddly enough, no, she didn't.' Kate pushed the plunger into the cafetière and poured the coffee. 'Things began to change for her at Cranwell. Life took a completely different turn.' She allowed herself once more to smile at the memory before asking, 'When are you going to bring David along? I'm dying to meet him.'

'I've spoken to him about that,' she said, 'and when I mentioned that you were planning to redecorate your kitchen he suggested doing it for you. He's very good at that sort of thing, and he knows how close we are and how much you've done for me. Also, I really don't like the idea of you going up and down ladders.'

'Good grief. I mean it's a lot to ask of someone I've never met.'

'Well, that's his offer, and anyway, you're not asking.'

'He certainly can't do it for nothing.'

'His terms are that you buy the paint and he'll do the painting. There's no question of payment.'

'Well, that's a very generous offer. I'm truly grateful. Thank you.'

'Good, I'll speak to him. I just don't want you to do anything silly.'

'I'll stay on the floor where it's safe,' promised Kate.

'Quite right.' Apparently satisfied, Rachel returned to their earlier conversation. 'I can't help thinking about poor Jack,' she said. 'I feel I know him so well I can sympathise with him.'

'Oh, Jack came bouncing back. He was never down for long; in fact by the time he was transferred to Dover he was his old self.'

'When was that?'

'It was in the spring of nineteen-forty-four, during the preparations for D Day.'

Rachel looked puzzled. 'I thought he was in air-sea rescue.'

'He was, but business had pretty well fizzled out in the North Sea. According to Jack the *Luftwaffe* was very thin on the ground by that time. He said that raids on German airfields by the allies had reduced them to a spent force.'

42

As they sighted Dover's eastern pier an Aldis lamp flickered its challenge from the signal station.

Jack noted it and said to the signalman on watch, 'Give the reply, Bunts.'

'Aye aye, sir.' He made the response for the day, and it was only when they drew closer Jack saw the signaller was a girl, who waved happily to them as they made for the submarine basin.

'Noted, Number One?'

'Noted, sir. I imagine there'll be no shortage of you-know-what hereabouts.'

'Your ribald utterances offend my sensitivities, Number One. You have to remember I was brought up in a strict, moral northern community.'

'Just as long as you remember that, sir.'

Jack shook his head at the thought of it. 'I try, honestly I do.'

Their conversation was interrupted when Telegraphist Fowler appeared on the bridge.

'From *HMS Wasp*, sir: "Proceed to berth fourteen, bows to seaward." That's all, sir.'

'Thank you, Sparks.' Leaning towards the voice pipe, he ordered, 'Dead Slow ahead both, Cox'n.'

Brian was already searching the berth numbers marked out in white paint against the timbers of the mole. Suddenly he was distracted. 'What have we here?' They were approaching a line of boats, each flying the American flag.

'They're PT boats, patrol torpedo boats, to give them their

Sunday name. They're very good too, based on the original British Power Boat Company design but with Packard engines.'

'Fast, then?'

Jack nodded. 'About the same as our MTBs.'

Brian was inclined to be sceptical. 'Just wait 'til we get a heavy sea,' he said, still scanning the berth numbers.

'Spoken like a true ML officer, Number One. I'm proud of you.'

'Number seventeen, sir.'

'Hard a-port, Coxswain.'

The ship made a leisurely 'U' turn, during which both Brian and Jack spotted their berth, one of five empty ones.

'Stop both, Cox'n. Dead slow astern together.' After ten seconds he gave the order, 'Stop starboard.'

'Starboard engine stopped, sir.'

'Dead slow astern port. Stand by aft. Stand by for'ard.' His last two orders were to the seamen waiting to secure the mooring lines. 'Midships, Cox'n. Stop port.' His order was confirmed. 'Dead slow ahead together.' The ship was almost alongside the mole and no longer making way. 'Stop both.'

'Both engines stopped, sir.'

'Finished with engines. Thank you, Cox'n. Make fast for'ard, make fast aft.'

Impressed, Brian looked fore and aft as the deck parties secured the mooring lines and springs. 'That was a nice piece of reverse parking, if I may say so, sir.'

'Thank you, Number One. It'll be your turn tomorrow.'

⚓

Flight Lieutenant Bill Preston was slim with dark hair and round glasses that set Dorothy in mind at first of a cigarette-card picture of the bandleader Henry Hall. It was a fleeting impression because she had little interest in a man's appearance beyond the basic requisites of good taste and smartness. Uniform gave no clue to Bill's taste in clothes, although Dorothy couldn't imagine him wearing anything awful and, in any case, smartness in uniform was mandatory.

They met one pay parade when, after a brief exchange, he asked, 'Do I detect the merest hint of a Yorkshire accent, Sergeant Needham?'

Wondering the same, Dorothy answered, 'Quite possibly, sir.'

'I thought so. My home's in Knaresborough.'

'Really, sir? I know it quite well. I'm from Cullington.'

The WAAF clerk seated next to him looked bored as she passed Dorothy's pay to him. She was very plain and clearly had little joy in her life.

'Well I never,' he said. 'We're almost neighbours.' He counted her money and handed it to her together with the vital ration coupon for soap.

'Thank you, sir.' She saluted him smartly.

'Not at all. Look, now we've established that we're both from God's Own County, would you care to join me for a drink one evening?'

The clerk raised her eyes in disapproval but Dorothy didn't care. The girl looked as if she could disapprove of St Peter. 'Yes, sir,' she said, 'I'd like that.'

'Good. How does this evening sound?'

'It sounds inviting, sir. I'm free after eighteen-thirty.'

'Excellent. As a nod in the direction of discretion, do you think we could meet at the Fox and Hounds at seven?'

The Fox and Hounds was less popular with RAF personnel than its neighbour and for that reason it afforded the discretion Mr Preston was looking for. He was evidently confident that his clerk would have more interesting things to discuss with her hut mates than the social life of her superior officer.

'I think that might be arranged, sir.'

⊕╫3╫│╫€╫⊛

As he poured tea for the visitor Alan knew he was about to hear the answer to a long-standing mystery. He'd reported another strange conversation to the named officer at the Air Ministry about low-flying aircraft and bombs that bounced quite miraculously on water, and this time his message had prompted the wing commander's hurried visit. Just as expectantly Lieutenant-Colonel Whiteley accepted the cup of tea Alan handed him.

'This whole business,' said the wing commander, 'is tremendously sensitive. You know, of course, that it's about the raid on the Möhne, Eder and Sorpe dams in May 'forty-two. Basically, we've had to keep our ear to the ground to learn what the enemy knows about the actual mechanics of the raid simply because of the threat of them doing the same to us, hence our reliance on you people to keep us informed. You see, the fact is that those stories you've heard about bouncing ordnance are true, and it's been decided in view of what you've heard that we should now let you in on the details, but I must impress upon you that what I'm about to tell you must not be discussed outside this room or with anyone else.' He paused and looked at each of them in turn. They both nodded.

'Very well. Mines were dropped with a degree of back spin so that they bounced over the anti-torpedo nets and along the surface of the water until they reached the dam, when they sank and exploded at a predetermined depth. I imagine you've both skimmed flat pebbles across a pond or lake and made them bounce several times before sinking, and this worked on the exact same principle. In this way the attacking aircraft were able to breach the Möhne and Eder dams and, in doing so, cause devastation. The mines had to be dropped at an exact altitude and range, and training for the operation was particularly intensive, making security all the more difficult. Even the aircrew involved, with the exception of Gibson himself, were kept in the dark for as long as possible.' He gave a half-smile. 'Some day, gentlemen, the full story may become known to all but I doubt if I shall be around when that happens.'

'Astonishing.' Whiteley was the first to speak. 'The pictures in the newspapers told their own story. Devastation was surely the word.'

'It was,' agreed the wing commander. 'The enemy insist that they had everything cleared up after six weeks, and that may well be the case, but at what cost? To do that they had to bring in workers and equipment from goodness knows where, leaving projects half completed and causing problems all over the *Reich*. I don't think we've heard the last of it by any means.'

'I've been wondering,' said Alan, 'if there's been any follow-up to the raid, I mean, to hamper the rebuilding. We certainly haven't heard of anything.'

'No,' said the wing commander. 'As things were, the dams were fiercely defended by anti-aircraft fire and we lost eight of the nineteen aircraft and, of course, fifty-six men. After the raid the Germans strengthened their defences and brought in night-fighters to patrol the area. Further raids would have been suicidal. I think we should be quite satisfied with what Gibson and Six-One-Seven Squadron achieved last May.'

Later, in the mess, Alan found Gwen. She asked, 'Good meeting, darling?'

Still marvelling at what he'd heard that afternoon, Alan said, 'I suppose so. It was basically routine stuff.' Even lovers had to keep secrets from each other, and particularly in wartime.

'You haven't wasted any time, Number One.'

'No, sir.' Brian was unrepentant. 'There she was when I arrived at *HMS Wasp*, waiting for me in the Confidential Books Office, pretty, friendly and available. What else could I do?'

'You could have asked her if she had a friend.'

'Rest assured, sir, I shall. Meanwhile what are you doing tonight?'

'I'm entertaining the United States Navy; at least, three officers thereof. I think it's a crying shame they're not allowed alcohol on board their ships so I'm offering them some of ours. An element of barter will surely take place, hopefully involving food. Otherwise I'm simply welcoming them to dear old Blighty. Hands across the sea, and all that sort of thing.'

The three officers duly arrived, Lieutenants (junior grade) Simcox, Delaney and Emmerson, and Jack took them down to the wardroom to regale them with gin and Scotch, having taken the precaution of procuring a quantity of ice from the base wardroom. According to the steward there Americans never drank anything without a small mountain of the stuff.

Lieutenants Simcox and Emmerson, who wished to be known as Harry and Jeff, seemed very outgoing and friendly whereas Paul Delaney gave the impression of being rather more serious than his brother officers; in fact it soon emerged that he was inclined to take things, and Jack, rather too seriously. This became apparent when Jeff made a remark about the luxury of being able to have a drink on board ship, and Jack offered his sympathy.

'Of course,' he couldn't resist saying, 'you have your forefathers to blame. If they'd stayed with us instead of listening to that Washington chap you wouldn't have had the problem. Now, in this outfit, if we couldn't offer our men their creature comforts there'd be mutiny.'

'In that case,' said Paul, 'maybe your navy has something to learn from ours about discipline.'

'Oh, I don't doubt it for a second, Paul, and we're always ready to learn.'

Harry smiled awkwardly and said, 'You'll have to make allowances, Jack. Paul's still fighting the War of Independence. It's a game that boys in his neighbourhood play.'

'Oh, I don't mind. I'll get some more drinks while you break the news that it's all over. I'll leave it to you to tell him who won.'

Maybe to introduce a friendlier note, Jeff asked, 'Do you play poker, Jack?'

'I did once. I just about got the hang of it, although it was some time ago. We have a pack of cards if you fancy a game.' He opened a drawer and took out a sealed pack. 'Mind you, I have to set a limit on my losses. The Admiralty's not as generous as your people, although I think I can afford to lose ten shillings.'

'Ten shillings?' Paul was aghast. 'That's only about two dollars fifty.'

'Yes, I agree it doesn't sound a lot when you convert it.'

'Okay,' said Jeff, 'we won't relieve you of more than ten shillings.'

'I'm obliged to you, gentlemen.'

Still visibly recovering from his disbelief, Paul asked, 'Do you know the rules of five-card draw poker?'

'Vaguely. Maybe you'd run through them for me?' It seemed that Jack had saddled himself with another stultifying game of cards, but if hospitality meant that and possibly the loss of ten bob his duty as a host would be done.

'Okay. The dealer deals you five cards face down. When you've looked at your cards a betting round begins. If two or more players are left at the end of the first round, each player says how many cards he wants to replace. Are you okay so far?'

'I think so.'

Paul gave his colleagues an eloquent look and went on. 'You get your replacement cards and then there's another betting round, okay?'

'Yes, I'm still with you.'

'When there are just two of you left you have a showdown.'

'I see.'

'Good. How well do you know Dover, by the way?'

'This is my first visit.'

'Mine too, and I'm not planning to return. From what I've seen it's not much more than a bomb site.'

Jack felt obliged to defend the place. Kent was a long way from Yorkshire but it was part of his mother country after all. 'I believe,' he said, 'there was a thriving town here before the enemy began using it for target practice.'

'Yeah, and now there's a castle and nothing else, and what about those famous white cliffs? They're not white at all, they're grey.'

'Oh well, you have to blame the war for that. They just can't get the labour.'

'You mean they actually pay guys to clean them?'

'Yes, well, not guys exactly. They usually dangle boy scouts over the edge on ropes, each with a bucket of lime whitewash and a brush. They do a good job too, but they're all busy nowadays, helping old ladies across the roads in the blackout.' He added, 'And if you're expecting to see bluebirds you're in for another disappointment.'

'Yeah?'

'They were a howler on the part of the chap who wrote the lyrics. They're as rare here as rattlesnakes, coyotes and covered wagons.'

Jeff and Harry exchanged a smile, but Paul shook his head in disbelief. 'Okay,' he said finally, 'you understand how the game's played, so let's get started.

※※※※※

Two hundred miles away Dorothy accepted a glass of cider from Bill, who took the seat opposite her.

'I'm sorry to bring you so far from the station, Dot. It's just not a good idea to be seen by all and sundry.'

'Oh, I appreciate that, and I'm a keen cyclist so it's no hardship.'

'Are you really?'

'Yes, my preference is usually for something more sophisticated than a station boneshaker but needs must when there's distance to be covered.'

'Quite. I'm a member of a cycling club at home, although it seems an age since I last took part in anything.'

'Me too.' She told him about Cullington Cycling Club and they chatted happily about their shared enthusiasm.

Eventually he asked, 'What do you plan to do after the war, Dot?'

'I'd like to stay in retail as a buyer, preferably in women's fashions. It's what I did before the war.' She added, 'It sounds terribly girlish, I know, but there's much more to the job than buying pretty frocks.'

'I'm sure there is. In any case I'd never associate you with anything trivial.'

'But you hardly know me.'

'Some things stand out from the beginning. For instance, I know that you're very able, that you're extremely good at your work at Cranwell and that you have a mind of your own, all very important qualities.'

With an accusing look she said, 'You've been peeping at my records.'

'Not at all. I just made a discreet enquiry. The rest was intuition.'

'I'm flattered, but what about you, Bill? What are you going to do after the big All-Clear?'

'Like you, the same as I did before the war. I was an accountant and I'm happy to return to that, although not necessarily with the same firm. There was a kind of sameness about the work there that I found tedious.'

Dorothy was beginning to warm to him. He was uncomplicated and unassuming, and those qualities alone made him interesting in her eyes. Jack had been fun and he'd given her comfort when she needed it but she'd had to call a halt back in December before he became too involved. At least, she hoped he wasn't too involved. It was impossible to tell with Jack. All that was in the past, however, and it would be interesting to see how things worked out with Bill.

⊷⊷3⊶⊰⊱⊶⊰⊷

Jack's previous luck at the table continued to hold, and Harry and Jeff watched in amusement, having dropped out earlier. Paul, who was determined to win back his losses, if only for the sake of pride, finally showed his hand.

'Two pairs,' he announced confidently.

'Flush.'

'Holy shit.'

'Look, Paul, I feel awful about this, offering you my hospitality and then taking your hard-earned dollars.'

'No, a bet's a bet.'

'I don't want to take all your cash, Paul. Surely we can come to an arrangement.'

Paul frowned at the suggestion. 'What kind of arrangement?'

'Payment in kind, perhaps. Do you, for example, have access to some of those fabled nylon stockings that are the talk of the nation?' Christmas and birthdays meant that presents had to be found whenever the opportunity arose, and stockings would always be well received.

'Sure.'

'Good. Let's make a deal.'

They did, and when the time came for them to leave, Harry and

Jeff thanked Jack for his hospitality. Their losses had been relatively light and the company had been entertaining. Paul joined in with the thanks despite his run of bad luck, and promised to send over the merchandise the next morning. As he was leaving he hesitated and said, 'Just one thing, Jack.'

'Yes?'

'You're mighty keen to get your hands on those stockings, I mean rather than anything else. I have cigarettes, chocolate, gum, soap, all the things you guys are short of over here.'

'Thanks, but I'm only interested in stockings.'

'You sure are. Anyone would think you wear the goddam' things yourself.'

'Hush.' Jack put a cautionary finger to his lips.

Paul's eyes grew wide. 'You mean you *do*?'

'Only on Friday nights,' Jack assured him.

⟡⟡⟡

Kate was on the day shift, so contacting her was easier than Jack had imagined. She was naturally delighted to hear his voice on the phone and agreed readily to cycling down to the submarine basin, where he was waiting to sign her in.

After a chaste and discreet hug because there were ratings present, she began with an apology.

'I'm afraid I had to come in uniform,' she said.

'And you look magnificent.'

'Don't be silly. I couldn't come in civvies because I've no stockings left, only these wretched woollen things.'

'Walk this way and the problem will be solved.'

'What do you mean?'

'You'll see.' He returned a salute from two ratings and led her along the jetty past several vessels, each of which prompted expressions of wonder. Finally they reached RML 97.

She gasped, 'Is this really your boat? It's much bigger than I imagined.'

'This is she,' he confirmed, stepping on to the plank. 'This thing's safe enough, but let me take your bike.'

The quartermaster stood aside to let them on board. 'Good evening, sir. Good evening, Miss. The First Lieutenant's in the wardroom, sir.'

'Good evening, Andrews. Will you look after this bicycle, please?'

'Aye aye, sir.'

'Thank you.'

Turning ceremoniously to Kate, he said, 'Welcome aboard RML Ninety-Seven.'

She looked around her in bewilderment. 'What a lovely boat.'

'Thank you. As she's a hundred and ten feet long she qualifies as a ship rather than a boat, but never mind. Hang on a second.' He leaned over the hatchway and called, 'Below!'

Brian's voice answered, 'Up top!'

'Lady coming down the ladder, Number One.'

'And right welcome she is too, sir.' For the benefit of any ratings in the vicinity he ordered, 'All hands keep clear of the wardroom ladder for the next minute!'

'All right, Kate,' said Jack, 'take your time.'

'Oh, this is easy.' She descended the ladder and stood to one side as Jack came down.

'Brian,' said Jack sweeping the wardroom curtain aside, 'I'd like you to meet Kate Whitehead. Kate, this is Brian Foster, our First Lieutenant.'

'Hello. Aren't you the officer who telephoned Jack's parents when he was wounded?'

'I am,' he said, shaking her hand.

'Thank you for doing that. It was such a relief.'

'It was no trouble at all.'

'This young poodle faker's itching to get away,' said Jack. 'He has a date with a Wren.'

'In that case don't let us keep you.'

'I shan't, and I'm delighted to have met you, Miss Whitehead.' He put his cap on and favoured her with the smartest of salutes before scrambling up the ladder.

'He *was* keen to get away,' observed Kate.

'He's very young.'

'Whereas you're positively ancient.'

'True.' He indicated a bunk. 'Please take a seat and tell me what you'd like to drink.'

'May I have a gin and tonic, please?'

'You may. Would you like ice with it?'

'Ice?'

'Hard, cold stuff that turns into water in warm temperatures.'

'I know that. I just didn't expect to be offered it.'

'I've been keeping a stock since I entertained some American officers here. They take ice by the bucketful with everything.'

'In that case, yes, please.'

He prepared the drinks and put them on the table. 'I have something else for you,' he said, taking two cellophane packets from a drawer.

As Kate took the packets from him her eyes grew wide with delight. 'Stockings,' she breathed.

'Nylon gold,' he confirmed.

'Oh, Jack, thank you. Wherever did you get them?'

'One of the American officers sent them over. We'd had a poker game and I was particularly lucky, so he paid me with those things.'

'What a lovely surprise.' Then she wrinkled her brow. 'I don't remember you having any interest in cards.'

'I haven't, and I don't play if I can avoid it. I've just played poker twice and been lucky each time.'

'I can't help wondering if that famous Farthing inscrutability might have tipped the balance.'

'I'm sure it did but I still don't intend to make a habit of it.'

'Good.' She reached across the table to turn his head a little to the left.

'What are you doing?'

'Looking at your cheek. The wound was always going to leave a scar, but it's healed remarkably well.'

'Of course, I still had the stitches in when we last saw each other. It seems ages ago.'

'Yes, an awful lot's happened since then.' She looked around her in wonder, not for the first time. 'It seems unreal,' she said.

'What does?'

'Jack Farthing from Cullington is now captain of his own boat.'

'Ship.'

'That makes it even more unreal.'

'But things change quickly in wartime, don't they?'

'They certainly do.'

Jack's perception of Kate had changed. She'd always been physically attractive; he could see the appeal she must have had for Maurice, with her lovely chestnut hair and smiling blue eyes but more importantly he'd come to admire her for qualities that had only emerged with the war. In her letters she'd told him about her experiences in a bland, matter-of-fact way, but a little intelligent thought told him a different story.

They chatted for some time, recalling past experiences and acquaintances, and then Jack realised he was staring at her.

'Is something the matter, Jack?'

'Yes,' he said quickly, 'the tide's out.'

'How can you tell when you can't see outside?'

'I mean in your glass. Let me get you another drink.'

She looked down at her glass critically. 'Will you make it a small one? I'm still not much of a drinker.'

'Yes, you don't want to be arrested for being blotto in charge of a bike.' He poured a tiny measure of gin over a quantity of ice and drowned it in tonic. Then he remembered the limes. 'These things are so new to me,' he said, cutting a wedge and dropping it into her glass. 'I clean forgot about them.'

'What are they?'

'Limes. Our nautical forefathers were reputed to drink the juice from them to keep scurvy at bay but I'm just happy to take some with a gin and tonic.'

She took the lime and tasted it. 'Mm, it's a bit like lemon but nicer. I've never even seen one of these before.'

'Neither had I before the Americans came on board. Mind you,' he added, 'if it comes to that I haven't seen a banana since before the war.'

'I can just about remember what a banana looks like.'

'Kate?' He didn't want to talk about bananas.

'What?'

'Can we meet again?'

'Of course we can, now we're neighbours.'

'I just wondered if you were maybe seeing someone.'

'That's very thoughtful of you.' She appeared to consider the question. 'I'm actually seeing two men currently, although "seeing" isn't really the word I should use as one of them is in Italy just now, but I'm sure we can arrange to meet without causing too much upset. Of course we'll have to be discreet.'

'Naturally.'

'I don't know what it is about servicemen but they can be so jealous. Some more than others, I have to say. The Army and Air Force seem forever to be looking over their shoulders.'

'I don't want to rock any boats.' She hadn't mentioned anyone in her letters, and he was quite taken aback by the news that she had two men in tow. It seemed so unlike her.

She held her thoughtful expression a moment longer before her face crumpled and she gave way to laughter. 'Oh, Jack, you really believed me, didn't you? I'm obviously better at it than I thought.'

'You had me fooled all right,' he admitted, also laughing. She'd beaten him at his own game, which possibly showed how susceptible he was.

'There's been no one since Maurice,' she confided. 'I've danced with men at hospital functions and that sort of thing but I've never got involved with any of them.'

'I can understand that. Maurice was special in so many ways.'

She gave a nod of silent agreement. 'I know you and he were good friends,' she said.

'It was difficult not to be friends with someone like Maurice.'

'Funny you should say that.'

'Why?'

'He used to say the same about you. He admired you, you know. You always seemed to him to be very adept, perhaps not clever in the way that Alan was, but quietly capable and very much in charge. That was what he said when I told him you were going to be an officer. He said you were modest as well, and I have to agree with that.'

'Now I'm embarrassed.'

'It's true, though. According to your mum and dad, when you got your medal you treated it as an embarrassing secret.'

It was true. He'd been found out. 'You know,' he said, 'every man in the ship's company deserved it as much as I did.'

'You're just a reluctant hero, Jack.'

It was time for a change of subject. 'I've asked my parents to send my bike down,' he told her. 'We could go off and have a picnic somewhere.'

'It's a lovely thought, but what are we going to do for rations?'

'Oh, don't worry. I'll take care of that.'

'You're full of surprises. I wonder what it'll be next?'

He wondered about that too, but before he could say anything there was a shout from the upper deck.

'*Cave* below!'

Jack smiled at Brian's somewhat clumsy diplomacy. 'Come down and have a drink with us, Number One.' Then it would be time to take Kate back to the main gate.

43

It was a time of expectation, impatience and frustration, and Kate remembered it vividly. It was hard not to, when the skies were filled with aircraft and the roads were crowded with military vehicles moving troops, tanks and supplies to goodness-knew-where. The most telling indication, however, that something huge was about to take place was the transfer to other hospitals of all civilian patients who could be moved. It was no secret that the County Hospital was to be reserved for military patients. Everything else, it seemed, was very secret.

She saw quite a lot of Jack, who complained of the monotony of carrying out air-sea rescue patrols when the allies were flying over France and Germany largely unchallenged by enemy aircraft. He said it was like minding a shop that had no customers.

They made two visits to the cinema, which made exactly two more than Kate had in three years. The first time they saw *The Scarlet Pimpernel* starring Leslie Howard and Merle Oberon; the second time was to see *Ali Baba and the Forty Thieves*. She remembered them vividly and now, seventy-one years later, she could barely recall what she'd seen on TV the previous evening. Memory was a strange thing, especially at the age of ninety-whatever. Her age was something else that frequently slipped her memory.

Another thing she remembered clearly was the way Jack's feelings for her had intensified since that reunion on board his ship. She'd felt very confused at the time, and that had been awful for him. It came to a head when they were enjoying a picnic on Shakespeare Cliff.

44

The sea was a gigantic glittering mirror, and Jack turned away to rest his eyes from the dazzle.

'It was ninety degrees at noon,' he said. 'I checked the thermometer on the bridge before I came ashore. Flaming June begins tomorrow.' He added, 'I thought I'd warn you.'

'Were you surprised, Jack? It's enough for me to know that it's damned hot.'

'Do all nurses swear?'

'Yes, some more than others. They're not all as ladylike as I am.'

'I'm lucky then.' He leaned over her and kissed her to celebrate the fact. 'Have another sandwich.'

'No, thank you. I've no appetite in this weather.' Looking at the sandwich tin, she said, 'I haven't seen an Oxo cube since before the war. Where did you find the tin?'

'In the galley. We get through lots of stock cubes. They make the food edible.'

'Lucky you, and you'd know just how lucky you are if you ever tried hospital food.'

'That's why I bring you up here and spoil you occasionally.' He moved the umbrella a couple of inches to follow the sun.

'I'm glad you brought your brolly, Jack.'

'I never go anywhere without it strapped to my crossbar.'

'That must cause a few problems when you're at sea.'

'When we're at sea,' he told her archly, 'we expect the occasional soaking. It's all part of a rough, tough seafarer's existence.'

They lay side-by-side on the grass for a while, idly aware of the sound of waves breaking below and the scent of samphire, which grew in profusion on the cliff top, and then he propped himself on one elbow and said, 'There's going to be a dance at the base soon. I forget exactly when, but I'll find out. If you can get away would you like to come?'

'Yes, I'd like that. I believe the ballroom in the old hotel is very grand.'

'Very posh indeed. Lots of famous people stayed overnight at the Lord Warden Hotel before sailing, including Charles Dickens, apparently, and by a strange coincidence his great-grandson was skipper of one of the MTBs until fairly recently, but he went on to greater things before I arrived here. I believe they gave him a destroyer.'

'What's an MTB?'

'Sorry, a motor torpedo boat. A fast and flashy toy that's absolutely hopeless in a heavy sea.'

She gave him a suspicious look. 'Wouldn't they let you have one?'

'No, but I don't care now. Speed isn't everything.'

It seemed that the invitation to the dance at *HMS Wasp* was still on her mind, because she asked, 'What's your favourite dance?'

'I like a slow foxtrot. It gives me time to think where to put my feet next. Waltzes need to be slow for me and I'm not at all keen on the quickstep.'

She gave him a sideways look. 'You've danced with me in the past. You did very well, as I recall. You're just being modest again.'

'Modesty comes naturally, Kate. There's more than a little of the Uriah Heap about me.'

'I hope not.'

Changing the subject to one that had been very much on his mind, he asked, 'What are you going to do after the war?'

'Everyone's asking that nowadays.'

'It's important though.'

'Okay, I want to specialise in midwifery.'

'Really?'

'What's wrong with that?'

'Nothing if that's what you want, but the thought of childbirth

302

terrifies the wits out of me.'

'Don't worry, Jack.' She patted his arm soothingly. 'It's most unlikely you'll ever be called upon to give birth.'

'Phew.'

'But it's the most natural thing in the world, and the miracle never wears thin for me.'

'It is miraculous,' he agreed, 'that a microscopic egg can take a direct hit from an even tinier projectile and then launch a fully-formed baby just nine months later.'

'It's not naval warfare, Jack, but I'm glad you can see the wonder of it. Anyway, what about you? What are you going to do?'

'I'll probably go back to Farrar's Tours. That's if they're still in business, and when I last spoke to Mr Halstead they were.' He made a dismissive gesture. 'That's only work, though. Weekends and evenings are important too, and what I really want is to have a boat. I don't mean anything grand, just something with an inboard engine and a modest cabin. Even if all I ever do is fishing trips and taking holidaymakers round the lighthouse, that's what I want, and it'll be quite a luxury being able to do it without having to keep an eye out all the time for E-boats and the like.'

She sat up and smiled down at him. 'You sound like a little boy talking about what he's going to do when he grows up.'

'Yes, well, it's important to me, and there's something else that's very important.' He reached for her hand, unable to postpone the moment any longer. There was something he'd wanted to say for weeks now. 'I want you to be part of it all, Kate. I want that very much.'

She lowered her eyes and for a moment she was silent. Eventually she said, 'Oh, Jack, I'm sorry. It's very difficult for me. It's silly, I know, but....'

Suddenly he felt hollow. 'It's Maurice, isn't it?'

'Partly.'

'What else is it, then?'

'I'm not sure, Jack. I'm very fond of you but I really don't think I could commit myself. I know it sounds ridiculous but I'm very confused just now. It's almost as if I need something or someone to shake me and make me think more clearly, because I really don't understand my own feelings.'

He heard himself say flatly, 'I'm sorry I put you on the spot.'

'I'm the one who needs to be sorry. I feel as if I've led you on. I really didn't mean to.'

'No, you haven't. I was just being over-ambitious.'

'Honestly, you're the last person I'd ever want to hurt, and it would be awful if we couldn't see each other again as friends.'

'I'd rather not think ahead just now, Kate, but don't feel badly about it. I've trodden this path so many times I'm almost immune.'

There was an awkward silence and then she began packing the picnic things away. 'Are you going to have this last sandwich?'

'I don't think so.'

'Aren't you hungry?'

'No, not very.'

⊷⊱⊰⊹⊱⊰⊶

Jack was silently berating himself for being an impulsive fool. If he'd only waited until his relationship with Kate was better established he might have had a chance. As things stood, he'd blown his chances for all time.

He was mercifully distracted by a question from his first-lieutenant.

'When do you think we'll get the midshipman they've been promising us, sir?' Brian had been labouring long and hard on the defects list demanded by the flotilla commander, and was justifiably keen to shed that and several other onerous tasks.

'It's anybody's guess, Number One. Chances are he'll arrive out of the blue, just as you did.'

'Oh, those far-off days of my youth.' Brian was nearing twenty-two and feeling every day of it.

'Let me buy you a drink on the strength of the defects list.'

'Thank you, sir. Gin will be most welcome.' Then, remembering his manners, he asked, 'I trust the afternoon went well, sir?'

'Not especially; in fact not even remotely.'

'Oh, damn. History has a tiresome habit of repeating itself.'

'It does where I'm concerned.'

'Then I'll return the compliment and buy you a drink, sir. I daresay you need it.'

'You're a gentleman, Number One.'

They were drinking in comradely silence when Telegraphist Fowler appeared in the wardroom doorway.

'From *HMS Wasp* to all flotilla commanders and ships under their command, sir: "All shore leave suspended forthwith. Orders to follow." '

'Thank you, Sparks.' If Jack needed a diversion from his misery, this one promised to be on a grand scale. Why else would shore leave be cancelled?

⇔⊷⅊⅊⅊⇔

Kate's only distraction was her work and, with most of the patients now transferred to hospitals further inland, work meant cleaning the hospital in preparation for the expected influx of service casualties. It gave her ample opportunity for reflection.

Whatever Jack said, she knew she'd hurt him, and that mattered very much to her. He was one of her oldest friends, and when she'd needed a friend quite desperately he'd gone to a lot of trouble to be with her, doing everything he could in the short time he had. The memory of it only increased her misery.

'Staff-Nurse Whitehead?' Sister Newman was calling her from the corridor.

'Yes, Sister?'

'What are you doing?'

'I'm cleaning the sluice room, Sister.'

'Can't you get a couple of probationers to do that? You'd be more usefully employed in the minor operations theatre.'

'Yes, Sister.'

Sister Newman stood in the doorway to the sluice room. 'You're very quiet, Staff-Nurse. Is something the matter?'

'No, Sister, I'm a bit preoccupied, that's all.'

'Oh, there's no time for preoccupation when there's a job to be done. Put your shoulder to the wheel, Staff-Nurse. We must be ready.'

'Yes, Sister.' Some things were best kept private anyway.

45

'Excuse me.' Kate attracted the attention of a youthful assistant. She didn't know how young he was, but everyone she looked at was younger than her. 'Will you help me with the name of this paint, please? It sounds silly, I know, but I've been having trouble with small print lately.'

'Let me see.' The young man took the colour chart from her.

'It's this one.' She pointed to the blue rectangle that appealed to her.

'That one's called "Algarve." We've got it in stock. Would you like a sample pot?'

'You know, that sounds like a good idea. I'm going to need a gallon so I need to make sure I've got the right shade.'

'It's the safest way,' he agreed. 'When you do come back for the paint you'll need to park nearby. Five litres of emulsion will be a lot for you to carry.'

Suddenly Kate was embarrassed. 'Oh, how silly of me not to think about that. I don't drive nowadays.'

'That's all right, love. We can deliver it if you like.'

'Oh, can you? That really is a relief.'

'No problem. Have you got a roller and some brushes?'

'Yes, thank you. I've even got a young man to come round and do the job for me.'

The assistant smiled. 'You haven't lost it, then?'

'What on earth do you mean?'

'I mean you can still attract young men.'

Kate returned his smile. 'I haven't been able to do that for a good many years,' she said.

She left the shop and made her way to the bus stop, remembering what the assistant had said. Only that morning she'd been recalling the awful time Jack had left for Normandy just days after she'd disappointed him.

46

After a false start caused by foul weather on the night of the fourth of June, the flotilla was ordered twenty-four hours later into prescribed positions in the Channel, where they witnessed an epic procession of transport aircraft heading towards Normandy. It was an impressive armada requiring a strong air-sea rescue presence but in the event the RMLs were not required. It was still very necessary, however, to keep a look out for E-boats. Most of the *Kriegsmarine* lay beneath the waves or in harbour, bombed and wrecked; E-boats and a depleted force of U-boats were all that was left, but so far nothing had been seen of either menace.

The ships of the flotilla had remained on their various stations until shortly before midnight on the fifth, when the order came to proceed to a position off the designated 'Gold' beach on the Normandy coast. With their shallow draft and well-equipped sick bays the RMLs were now required off-shore to pick up survivors from any vessels sunk or disabled during the assault. For RML 97 it necessitated a journey of more than six hours.

Jack and Brian would both be heavily involved in the action when they reached their destination so instead of standing normal watches they shared the journey, each doing three hours. Brian agreed to stand the first three, leaving Jack to retire to the wardroom, although not for long. He soon found that sleep was impossible, partly due to the natural tension caused by the knowledge that the ship was about to take part in something that was to eclipse all previous invasions and that might hopefully change the course of history. That alone would have kept Jack awake, but another matter was seldom far from his thoughts, and that was Kate. The ship, the lives of its crew and those who might depend on them depended in turn on his concentration and clear thinking. He had to forget her for the time being. He knew well enough that self-recrimination and regret amounted to nothing more than wasted energy; they would solve nothing and make him feel even more miserable, if such a thing were possible, but the niggling continued in spite of his efforts. Impatiently he climbed the ladder to join Brian on the bridge. The First Lieutenant looked at his watch but showed no surprise at seeing him.

'I can't imagine anyone being able to sleep just now, sir,' he said.

'Nor can I,' Number One, but you're welcome to try.' He inclined his head towards the wardroom ladder.

'No, thank you all the same, sir. Let's greet this one together.'

'As we're about to see history made, I think we should.' He welcomed the company, and the conversation over the next few hours kept his mind from straying into the past.

At 0500 he ordered 'Up Spirits' to be piped, and fifteen minutes later, 'Action Stations.' Owen's mantra continued to live on. Jack could still hear him saying, 'Never send honest sailors into action stone-cold sober, Number One. Only the English could be insensitive enough to do that!'

They were still five miles from the beaches at 0545, when they heard the bombardment begin.

'God help anyone on the receiving end of that lot,' said Brian after a while.

'You're talking about the enemy, Number One. God is on our side. It's official.'

'Even so, sir, you can't help but feel sorry for the poor buggers. They climb out of bed expecting bacon and eggs and instead they get a salvo of fifteen-inch shells.'

'Yes, it'll be interesting to see who's opening the bowling for our side.'

In fact, as they passed Sword and Juno Beaches and progressed towards Gold Beach they were able to read the pennant numbers of the battleships *Ramillies* and *Warspite* and the monitor *Roberts* as well as numerous cruisers. As the day went on they also identified the American battleships *Arkansas* and *Nevada*. Considering the weight of the onslaught, Brian had been right to spare a moment's sympathy for those on the other end.

The greater share of their sympathy, however, went to the army personnel waiting to go ashore. The sea state had not been a problem for the MLs, whose crews were used to being at sea, but it was a different matter for soldiers in flat-bottomed landing craft. Most of them would arrive on the beach weakened by seasickness, to be welcomed by machine-gunfire directed at them by an enemy whose only impediment was that he had been taken by surprise. At least that was how it seemed to Jack as he received his orders and took up his station in readiness for being called into action.

⚜

Now promoted to captain, Alan caught up with Gwen at around eleven o'clock and suggested a brief walk.

'Are you going to tell me about your meeting with Colonel Whiteley,' she asked, 'or is it very hush-hush?'

'No, there's nothing sensitive about it.' He led the way out of the officers' mess and they took their familiar route. 'I'm going to France.'

She stopped in mid-step. 'Good lord. Why do you have to go to France?'

'To interrogate prisoners. The theory is that by the time I arrive there a number of senior officers will have been captured.'

'But surely they'll bring them over here, won't they?'

'I imagine so, but Whiteley's plan is for me to get to them before they've had time to recover from the shock of being caught napping. He thinks they're more likely to be indiscreet.'

'When are you leaving?'

'I'm leaving for Portsmouth this afternoon. I'll sail some time tomorrow morning.'

'It's very sudden.'

'Only because, like millions of others, neither of us knew the invasion was planned for today.'

She gave him an impatient look. 'I mean we can't even have a

310

meal or a drink together before you go. We haven't even celebrated your promotion.'

'I'm not going to be away for very long. A few days, I imagine, and I'll be back.'

'Let's hope so.' She stopped and put one hand on his arm. It was as much as she could do in public. 'Do take care, darling.'

⊷⊱✦⊰⊶

'I've seen everything now, Number One. I thought Dunkirk was spectacular until the curtain went up on this lot.' They were watching the landing craft, square and ponderous as they approached the water's edge. Ahead of them armoured vehicles and infantry emerged from the shallows and made their perilous way up a beach already littered with motionless bodies.

'It's no picnic, is it, sir?' Brian evidently found the spectacle equally sobering.

'Not for those poor buggers, certainly.'

'All things considered, though, we seem to have taken Jerry by surprise.' He broke off to watch the bombarding ships. 'Those guns,' he observed, 'must be red hot by now.'

Jack's attention was centred on the awful but compelling sight on the beach. 'I wouldn't swap places with any of those blokes just now,' he said, unable even to guess at the number lying in the sand.

Suddenly Brian said urgently, 'One of the landing craft is hit, sir! An LCT, I think. Four, no, five hundred yards on the starboard bow.'

Jack saw the stricken tank landing craft. 'Full ahead both, Cox'n. Starboard fifteen.'

With what seemed like agonising slowness, the RML bore down on the luckless craft now wallowing drunkenly and listing to port. Men were crowding the side, waving desperately to the RML.

As they closed the sinking craft, Jack ordered, 'Stop starboard. Slow ahead port. Port ten.' He'd intended to go alongside and let the survivors leap aboard but the craft was listing too heavily.

'A wash deck transfer's out of the question, Number One. If the tanks or whatever she's carrying roll over she'll capsize and take us with her.' To the deck party on the starboard side he shouted,

311

'Stand by the boom!' The ship inched forward until the two were almost level. 'Stop port. Scrambling nets out.'

They heard the LCT's loud hailer. 'Ahoy RML Ninety-Seven. All but two of my rafts are wrecked. I have five wounded on board and some of the soldiers can't even swim. They've got life jackets but we can't tow them across in this sea.'

Through his loud hailer Jack asked, 'Can you get the wounded and non-swimmers into the rafts? The others will have to swim for our nets.' It would save valuable time.

'I think so. It'll be a tight fit but it's all we can do.'

Some of the soldiers from the LCT were already in the water, swimming for the RML as the LCT's seamen launched the two Carley rafts and lowered the wounded. It was a delicate job made harder still by the worsening sea state that threatened to whisk the frail life rafts away from the descending casualties. Miraculously, though, the task was carried out successfully so that the non-swimmers could now make their descent.

By the time they were embarked the first of the swimmers was being hauled over the side by members of the RML's crew.

Jack gritted his teeth as a shell screamed closely overhead. Through the loud hailer he asked, 'Are they all away?'

'The last man's away now so I'll join him.'

They watched the LCT's skipper abandon ship and then, as he reached the nearest life raft, grasp the rope lanyard looped around it. Other hands caught the RML's heaving lines and made them fast so that the rafts could be hauled in. Jack watched anxiously, knowing that they were all sitting ducks until they were once more under way. The operation seemed to be taking an age, and the enemy's shellfire was becoming ever more accurate. Shells were falling worryingly close.

One by one the survivors were helped over the side and the wounded taken to the sick bay. Eventually Leading Seaman Barlow was able to report that all survivors were on board.

'Start engines, Cox'n. Half ahead port. Steer hard a-port.'

As the Cox'n repeated his orders there was a noise like a mile of tearing fabric followed by a gigantic water spout close on the port side. At that point Jack blacked out. It must have been only for a moment but when he opened his eyes he saw through a cloud of smoke that the port wing of the bridge had ceased to exist. Still partly stunned, he looked around him and found Brian and the Cox'n prone on the deck. The latter was very obviously dead and where the port bridge lookout had been there was an empty space. His opposite number on the starboard wing stood transfixed as shells continued to scream and fall around the ship, which was now turning, unbidden, to starboard.

Jack hauled himself upright, coughing strenuously. Clutching whatever came to hand, he crossed to the starboard wing and looked aft for a seaman. Through the smoke he saw Leading Seaman Barlow and three others on the after deck, which was littered with debris. The explosion, which must have been from a near miss, had severed the mast and they were hacking it free.

'Leave them to it, Barlow,' called Jack. 'Come up here and take over the wheel.' He knelt beside Brian, who was unconscious and bleeding from a head wound. 'Crawley,' he said to the dazed lookout, 'snap out of it and find a field dressing for the First Lieutenant, quick as you can!'

Like someone waking from a dream, Crawley opened the bridge first aid box and took out a field dressing.

Barlow had taken over at the wheel and was correcting the ship's wandering course. 'The ship's answering the wheel, sir,' he reported.

'Thank you, Barlow. Start engines. Steer due north for now. Full ahead both.'

'Course due north, sir. Both engines full ahead.'

As Crawley knelt to stem the flow of blood from Brian's temple, Jack set about drafting a signal to the hospital ship *Apollo*, so that he could transfer the wounded from the LCT and no doubt some of his crew as well, although in the chaos he had no information yet about casualties. As he did so, other enemy guns were finding their range, and shells were falling ever closer to the ship, which was only just beginning to gather speed.

Dorothy was taking a class through the new R/T procedure. Each trainee sat at a bay with headphones, a microphone and a book of exercises.

'Look this way, everyone, and I'll give you your indefinite callsigns.' Pointing to the nearest cadet and then to each in turn, she began. 'Baker One, Two, Three, Four, Five, Six, Seven, Eight, Nine and Ten. I am Baker Control. Okay, headphones on.' She gave them a few seconds to adjust their phones. 'Right, Exercise One. All Stations, this is Baker Control. Radio check. Over.'

'Baker Control, this is Baker One. Loud and clear. Over.'

'Baker Control, this is Baker Two. Loud and clear. Over.'

There was a pause before Dorothy said, 'Wake up, Baker Three. The world is waiting.'

'Sorry, Sergeant. I've torn a nail.'

'I'm sorry too, Baker Three, but we can't hold up the war while you have a manicure. Raising her voice above the general laughter, she said, 'Baker Three, this is Baker Control. Radio check. Over!'

'Baker Control, this is Baker Three. Loud and clear. Out.... Sorry, Sergeant, I mean "over." '

The exercise continued with only an occasional hitch. Dorothy guided them through the first part of the course, which took almost an hour, and eventually the session ended.

'Right, everyone, tidy up the bays and remove any notes you've made. Then you may dismiss. Miss Clayton, I'd like a word with you.'

The hapless girl stood before Dorothy's desk, nervously gripping her cap.

'The war's far from over yet,' said Dorothy. 'Welcome though this morning's news was, there's still an awful lot to be done and we can't afford to relax.'

'No, Sergeant.'

'Try to imagine a damaged bomber returning from Germany. Its wireless operator calls your station requesting permission to make an emergency landing, but the WAAF operator is unable to reply because she's broken a nail. Imagine you're the Duty Assistant Section Officer. You're not going to be too impressed with the girl, are you?'

The alarm in the trainee's eyes told its own story. 'No, Sergeant.

I really am keen. It's just that I'd caught my thumbnail on the prestle switch and torn it down to the quick.' The tears that were forming in her eyelids had nothing to do with the torn nail.

'Let me see it.' She examined the girl's nail and grimaced. 'Yes you need to have that seen to. I imagine it's quite painful.' She regarded the tearful face for a moment and relented. 'In view of what you've achieved so far, I think your behaviour this morning was exceptional so we'll say no more about it. I just want you to remember that one day the lives of a bomber crew or maybe a fighter squadron could depend on your total concentration. They're not distracted by torn nails and neither should you be.'

'No, Sergeant. Thank you, Sergeant.' The girl was almost panting with relief.

'Just put everything you've got into your training and justify my faith in you.' She gave the girl a reassuring smile. 'We both know you can do it.'

'Yes, Sergeant.'

'All right, you can dismiss.'

The awful thing, she reflected as the girl left the classroom, was that some of those trainees made her feel much older than her twenty-six years. It came of recruiting children to do the work of grown-ups.

She closed the classroom door, raising her spirits with the thought that she would see Bill that evening. She found herself looking forward to their meetings with increasing eagerness, and she knew Bill felt the same.

⊷⊷⊱⊰⊱⊰⊷

There was an unreal atmosphere at the County Hospital, almost an air of detachment, and Kate was relieved to find that she wasn't the only one to have remarked on it. The hospital had been scrubbed from top to bottom in readiness for casualties, a task that had involved the entire nursing staff in a great deal of hard work, but there was still a feeling of being in limbo. There was also time to dwell on other matters.

On the previous day Kate had cycled, almost without thinking, down to the submarine basin, unable to assuage herself of the awful guilt she felt after that last meeting with Jack. Her thoughts were still in turmoil. She knew she wouldn't be allowed in to speak to him, and there was little likelihood that he would want to speak with her. She just had a crazy idea that she wanted to be close enough to him so that she could feel she hadn't entirely abandoned him.

She stopped and dismounted before she reached the gate, hoping to saunter past the basin, hopefully unnoticed, but she'd reckoned without Jolly Jack's natural proclivity for making contact with any available female.

'Looking for somebody, love?' The sentry tipped his steel helmet back a fraction to make eye contact with her. He had an open, friendly face.

'Not really,' she said awkwardly, 'although a friend of mine is captain of one of the RMLs.'

'Is he now? I'm afraid you're out of luck, love.' He jerked his head in the direction of the berths that the RMLs had occupied and said, 'They're all at sea. I can't tell you where, but you'll have heard the news, I reckon, and a wink's as good as a nod, they say.'

It was, but the news wasn't what Kate had wanted to hear. She'd thought of air-sea rescue as taking place in the open sea, but it seemed now that Jack was somehow involved with the invasion. Suddenly her remorse was compounded with fear for his safety.

◈⊷⊰⊹⊱⊷◈

With all the survivors and wounded transferred to *Apollo*, Jack was left with just half of his crew to nurse what was left of RML 97 as far as Portsmouth. Brian was wounded and unconscious aboard the hospital ship, the Cox'n and four of the crew had been killed, and three were seriously injured. The ship's hull had been holed just above the waterline but the damage had been shored up and so far the pumps were holding. If she maintained a speed of no more than ten knots and as long as the sea grew no rougher, she might make it. Jack could only hope. Telegraphist Fowler had rigged a temporary antenna, so they were at least in contact with Portsmouth.

A seaman arrived on the bridge to relieve the weary lookout. The deck watch showed that it was 1154, the end of the forenoon watch. Jack returned his salute and said, 'Relieve Leading Seaman Barlow at the wheel, Tyndall. I can keep an eye on things up here.'

'Aye aye, sir.'

Turning to the lookout, he said, 'Go and get your head down, Rush. I'll send for you if I need you.'

'Thank you, sir.' The seaman headed gratefully for the ladder and then paused to ask. 'Do you reckon she'll make it, sir?'

It seemed a silly question, as everyone would find out the answer sooner or later, but Jack said with as much confidence as he could muster, 'She'll be fine, Rush. I've nursed an ML home through worse than this.' As he spoke the ship ploughed into a towering wave that broke over the bridge, drenching them both.

Rush removed his cap and wiped his face with his sleeve. 'I expect you have, sir.'

At twenty-six Jack was seen by most of his youthful ship's company as an ancient mariner, and if that gave them confidence he was happy enough. 'Off you go, Rush.'

'Aye aye, sir.'

Jack continued his lonely vigil. The weather forecast wasn't at all reassuring. He could only hope and pray that the ship wouldn't founder before she reached Portsmouth.

Less than twenty-four hours later Alan reported to the make-shift intelligence centre in Lion-sur-Mer on Sword Beach. It appeared to have been at one time a seafront café or restaurant but it was now in a parlous state; all its seaward windows had been blown in and a man was hurriedly sweeping away the rubble and general detritus. Unfortunately his efforts were raising clouds of dust, which seemed to defeat the purpose of the task.

'Leave it for now,' Alan told him. 'I'd like to see the first of the prisoners.'

'Very good, sir, I'll tell the corporal.' The man departed, no doubt thankfully as his task had been a hopeless one from the start.

After a minute the corporal entered, came to attention and saluted.

'At ease, Corporal.'

'I wondered if you'd like a cup of tea and a sandwich, sir.'

'Thank you, Corporal, but just a cup of tea would be very welcome.' He was still feeling queasy from the crossing.

'Very good, sir. I'll get that sent in for you and then I'll bring the senior prisoner. He's a lieutenant-colonel called Fürst, sir, and he doesn't speak much English. At least that's what he says.'

'Thank you, Corporal.'

'It's no trouble, sir. Right, I'll get you that tea.'

'Thank you. That's with milk but no sugar.'

'Very good, sir.' As the corporal came to attention the door opened and a small dog pushed its way in. Its breed was obscure, and Alan suspected it might have been the product of a chance liaison. At all events it seemed to know the corporal, because it sat in front of him, apparently in expectation.

'I'm sorry about this, sir,' said the corporal. 'This is Bonzo. We don't know who he belongs to but he won't leave us alone. The lads have been feeding him, you see.'

'In that case you can't blame him for hanging around.'

'No, sir. Come with me, Bonzo.'

The dog waited patiently while the corporal came to attention again and saluted, before following him out of the room.

A few minutes later the corporal reappeared minus the dog but carrying an enamel mug of tea and ushering in a senior officer of the *Wehrmacht*. He consulted a signal form and said, 'This is *Oberstleutnant* Fürst, sir. Sorry if I didn't pronounce it quite right.'

'You're forgiven, Corporal.' He accepted the tea and said, 'Please take a seat, *Herr Oberstleutnant*. I am Captain Alan Lofthouse of the British Army Intelligence Corps.'

The *Oberstleutnant* eyed him coldly and said, '*Ich spreche kein Englisch.*'

'Oh well, let's not worry too much about that.' He took out his cigarette case and offered it to the prisoner, at the same time switching on the recording machine. '*Bitte, nehmen Sie sich eine Zigarette.*'

318

The prisoner viewed the cigarettes in Alan's case as he might regard a casket of gems. Taking one, he said with rather more warmth, '*Vielen dank, Herr Hauptmann.*'

The interview proceeded in German, in a way that Alan found encouraging. Whiteley's idea, like so many of his, had been a good one.

⊕⊢G⊹⊱⊱⊱⊱⊰

'I'm lucky to be alive, Nurse, an' I'd be a fool to say otherwise, but I don't know what I'm going to do with only one leg when this is all over.' The soldier was fretful and anxious, talking compulsively as if to conceal an even greater fear that threatened to overwhelm him, and Kate was careful to be matter-of-fact without sounding too distant.

'Yes, it's bound to take a while for you to adjust, but you'll get help, and there'll be others at the limb centre with the same problem. You'll find lots of support there.' He certainly needed it. The night staff-nurse said he'd had an awful night, and the horrors had stayed with him well into the day. She asked, 'What did you do before the war?'

'I was a window cleaner.' He closed his eyes momentarily and said, 'Don't tell me there's always the Chinese laundry. I've been told that at least a dozen times.'

'I wouldn't dream of it,' she said, returning his notes and charts to the foot of his bed.

'I hate that George Formby,' he said. 'Joking about window cleaners. What a liberty.'

'And Chinese laundrymen.' She smoothed his turned-over sheet and was about to move on when he said, 'You wouldn't believe some of the things I've seen, Nurse.' The words came out in a rush, almost by accident, and it seemed that Kate's impression had been correct. She had plenty to do, of course; hospitals on the south coast were filling up with wounded, Dover was no exception, and she was needed elsewhere, but the man had lost a leg. Such a thing was shock enough but it seemed he was deeply troubled about much more so she let him continue.

319

'I've seen men slaughtered like cattle, shot down as they got to the beach. It was horrible.'

Kate nodded. It was all she could do.

'All that training and waiting, and then to be killed just as they reached dry land....' He shook his head, almost tearful. 'Some of them didn't get that far. I saw men dead in the water, Nurse. I saw landing craft hit by shells. Rescue boats had to take off survivors.' He shook his head again mutely. Eventually he found his voice and said, 'I saw one of the motor boats get shelled.'

Kate felt her blood turn to ice. 'Were they quite big boats,' she asked, 'Navy boats?'

'Yes, Navy boats. There was a few of them there.' He closed his eyes and a tear ran down one cheek. 'It got shot to pieces, Nurse. It was horrible.'

It was happening again, just like a recurring nightmare, except that last time the whole thing had been resolved with a telephone call to Mrs Farthing. There was no question of phoning her this time; Kate had no idea if next of kin had been informed, and she didn't want to alarm Jack's parents unnecessarily.

Guiltily she remembered her duty and forced herself to speak calmly. 'It's all right,' she told the soldier, giving his top sheet a final tuck. 'You're safe now. It's all over.'

❦⊰⊹⊱❦

'Here, Bonzo. Here, boy. Come and get a biscuit.'

At the mention of food the dog came readily to Alan's feet, sat back and lifted his forepaws in supplication.

'The men have taught him to do that, sir,' Corporal Kennet told him. 'Some of 'em haven't the sense they were born with.'

It was certainly a strange outfit. 'So you're the senior NCO, Corporal,' he said, feeding the biscuit to the dog. 'What happened to the others?'

'Well, a unit the size of ours doesn't qualify for a sergeant-major, as you know, sir, and we lost our sergeant before we embarked. He went down with appendicitis, sir.'

'That was unfortunate, but you're coping very well without him.'

'Thank you, sir. I've been coping all my life.'

Alan was faintly curious. 'Go on,' he said.

'Well, sir, I coped without a father after the last war, but then so did a lot of kids, but then I coped when my mother got bored and ran off with the rent man, and then I've been coping with everything the army's thrown at me since the war started, so I reckon I can manage without a sergeant.'

'I'm sure you can.'

There was the sound of footsteps outside, and the unit's officer, a youthful second lieutenant appeared in the doorway.

'We have some more officer prisoners for you, sir,' he reported. '*Waffen SS*, no less.'

'Good, what rank is the most senior?'

'He's a *hauptsturmführer*, sir, the equivalent of a captain, I believe.'

'That's right. I'll see him first.' He handed another biscuit to Bonzo, who took it eagerly. It was good that someone appreciated British Army ration biscuits, although as gourmets went, Bonzo wasn't exactly discerning.

The door opened again, and the second-lieutenant ushered his prisoner into the room.

'*Hauptsturmführer* Fleischer, sir,' he announced.

'Thank you, Lieutenant. Come in and take a seat, *Hauptsturmführer*. Corporal, remain with us, will you?'

'Very good, sir.'

Whether or not the SS officer understood Alan's invitation, he remained standing and gave the Nazi salute. '*Heil Hitler.*'

Alan merely shrugged and took out his cigarette case. 'Would you care for a cigarette?'

'I do not smoke.'

'But you speak English, evidently.' He switched on the recorder.

'Of course.' Fleischer eyed the corporal and Bonzo, seemingly with equal contempt and asked, 'Must I be interrogated in the presence of a mere *Gefreiter* and this animal?'

'Yes.'

'Why is this so?'

'Because I insist on having a live witness in the room and because the dog is welcome company.'

Fleischer nodded slowly, as if processing the information, and said, 'I have shot stray dogs without hesitation.'

'What a good thing it was that we disarmed you.'

'It will not be for long, Captain. Soon you and your American allies will be pushed back into the sea.'

'We shall see. Meanwhile, what was your function as part of the occupying army?'

Fleischer frowned. 'My function?'

'Your responsibility.'

'I see. My responsibility was... *is* to hunt saboteurs, a task to which I intend to return as soon as we have overturned your ridiculous invasion.'

'You speak English remarkably well, *Hauptsturmführer*, although I imagine you hunted French saboteurs.'

Fleischer shrugged. 'French, English…. They are all the same.'

'Did you catch many?'

'Of course.'

'Were they given a fair trial?'

Fleischer smiled for the first time. 'Why should they be given a trial? They were guilty.'

'So what happened to them? Did you have them shot or imprisoned?'

'Some are shot and some are sent to places where they might be useful to the *Reich*.'

'Have you shot any of them?'

'Of course.' Fleischer's expression suggested that the question was quite unnecessary.

'Can you recall any of their names?'

'Yes, but such information will be of no use to you once we have repelled your attempted invasion, and that will be very soon.'

'In that case I'm sure you'll agree that there'll be no harm in naming a few names and incidents. After all, you appear to derive some satisfaction from your work, and I'm sure your victims' families would want to know the truth.'

⌖⟐⌖⟐⌖

For Kate the torture continued to the extent that at one stage she'd been physically sick. Common sense told her that Jack could have survived the invasion and might be patrolling the Channel again, searching for airmen as before. He'd told her there were four boats in the flotilla, and surely they couldn't all have been sunk, so there was hope, but the soldier had painted a picture so awful that she couldn't get it out of her mind. Also the knowledge that she'd hurt Jack very badly made her even more desperately worried. It was completely illogical, she knew, but that was her tormented state of mind as she tended the many wounded brought into Dover by the hospital ships.

After a week she was allowed a half-day off and she and her colleague Beryl Horsfall used it to go into town. They made that decision more to escape from the hospital and the suffering within it than for any practical reason. They had no shopping to do and, in any case, neither had much money, so they found a café in Snargate Street and ordered a pot of tea.

The café was almost empty and, considering her current worries, Kate found it oddly peaceful. Then, as a reminder of her woes, a naval officer walked in with a Wren officer. The man wore three gold rings on his sleeves with white rings between them. She didn't know what that meant, except that he was pretty senior. All the same, he looked rather nice, and so did the Wren officer. They took a table away from the window and gave their order to the waitress.

Kate looked at Beryl, who shrugged and said, 'Why not?' That gave her the courage to speak to them.

'Excuse me,' she said, 'I'm sorry to disturb you. I was wondering if you're from *HMS Wasp*.'

The naval officer smiled and said, 'I'm afraid we can't tell you that.'

'Of course, I should have realised. I'm sorry, it's just that a friend of mine is captain of one of the rescue motor launches and I was told they'd all gone to the invasion beaches. I'm desperate to find out if he's all right.'

The two officers exchanged a look that Kate found far from encouraging, and then the naval officer said, 'I don't know who told you that, but he shouldn't have. Who is your friend, by the way?'

'Lieutenant Farthing. His boat is RML Seventy-Nine.'

Again the two officers glanced briefly at each other, and the naval officer said, 'I have nothing to do with operations, you understand – I'm the Paymaster Commander – so I'm afraid I can't tell you anything. I'm sorry.' He looked genuinely concerned, so Kate believed him.

'There's one thing you could try,' said the Wren officer. 'Has he any family you can contact? They would know if anything had happened to him.'

'Will next-of-kin have been informed yet?'

'I'm sure they will. The landings took place six days ago.'

'Oh, I wondered, you see, with there being so many casualties. Thank you for telling me, and I'm really sorry I've taken up your time.'

'There's no need to apologise.'

'I hope it's good news,' said the Wren officer.

'Thank you. You've both been very kind.'

Now all she had to do was phone Jack's parents.

47

'Phoning them was the most frightening thing I'd ever done. My hands were shaking when I picked up the phone.'

Rachel and David waited for her to continue.

'Jack's father answered the phone. He always did it in a very important, business-like way. "Geoffrey Farthing, electrical contractor." ' Seventy years later she could still mimic his telephone manner. 'He sounded bright and cheerful, though, so I wasn't afraid to ask him about Jack, and I'll never forget his reply. He said, "You've just missed him, love. He went back to his ship this morning." I almost fainted with relief. It seemed he'd been given seventy-two hours' leave. If I'd phoned a day earlier I could have spoken to him.'

'What a rollercoaster ride,' said David. He was a sturdy man of about forty, not particularly tall and with thinning hair, but his most remarkable feature was a gentle face that seemed to invite trust. Kate found him quite engaging, and she suspected Rachel had made a wise choice.

'So what happened next?' Rachel was characteristically eager to hear more.

'I wrote to him asking if we could meet. He was still based at Dover but his boat was such a wreck he'd had to leave it behind in Portsmouth. They gave him a different boat because its captain had been killed. It was an exhilarating time for some,' she said pensively, 'but it was devastating for many.'

48

'I saw American flags when I passed the submarine basin yesterday.'

Jack nodded. 'They'd be the PT boats. I know some of their skippers.' He opened the door of the 'Goat and Grapes' and held it for her.

'Were they the officers you played at poker?'

'That's right.'

Kate smiled at the thought. 'I still can't imagine you doing that.'

'I have hidden depths.' He said it without humour, and she felt more awkward than ever. He'd been polite enough when he collected her from the nurses' home but even then his greeting lacked some of its customary warmth.

He found a table and gestured to her to take a seat. 'What'll you have?' He looked at the bar and grimaced, adding, 'Not that you have a lot of choice.'

'Oh, cider if they have any, please.'

'You may just be lucky.' He joined the group at the bar waiting to be served, leaving Kate to wonder quite how she was going to raise a particularly sensitive topic. The pub was hardly the ideal place for it; it was noisy and filling up rapidly. It was only to be expected at seven-thirty on a Saturday evening, but that was of no comfort.

After a few minutes Jack returned from the bar with a pint of bitter in one hand and a bottle of cider and a tumbler held precariously in the other. Deftly depositing the bottle and glass and then the beer on to the table, he took the seat opposite her and asked somewhat abruptly, 'Why were you so keen for us to meet?'

'Oh, Jack.' She looked down hopelessly at her hands. 'This isn't at all easy, and you're being prickly doesn't help.'

'It seemed a fair question. Last time we met you blew me out of the water, so it should be no surprise that your letter aroused a hint of mystery.' He took her cider and poured it into the tumbler.

'Blowing you out of the water isn't a nice way of putting it.'

'I can't think of a nice way to describe it. I'll admit I was at fault in not fully appreciating your state of mind at the time but, be that as it may, between fending off the attentions of the *Luftwaffe*, the *Kriegsmarine* and the *Wehrmacht* I've been feeling very "prickly", as you put it. You see, despite my brave act on the cliff, your rejection was more than a disappointment.'

'Oh dear.' Her task was becoming increasingly difficult.

'Actually, I haven't been strictly accurate. I saw nothing of their navy or their air force, but their army was nuisance enough.'

'You've had a rotten time, and I haven't helped. I'm truly sorry I hurt you, Jack. Maybe you no longer want us to be friends.'

He appeared to consider the possibility, but only for a few seconds before saying, 'I don't want us to fall out. That would be ridiculous. I just feel that it's a bit soon to be carrying on as if nothing's happened. Maybe later, after some other girl's given me the brush-off and I'm smarting about that, then we may be able to meet on easier terms.'

'You don't have much luck with women, do you?'

'I'd put it more strongly than that. I have no luck with women; in fact I'm thinking of turning homosexual, just for a trial period at first to see if I'm more successful.' He looked up when he heard a woman's voice say something about the crowd at the bar, and her companion said, 'I'll get served all right. Watch me.' The man, a sailor, suddenly recognised Jack and said, 'Begging your pardon, sir. I didn't expect to see you in here.'

'That's all right, Littlewood. Don't let me cramp your style. Show the lady how you get served in a crowded pub.'

'Aye aye, sir.' The sailor pushed his way to the bar, the girl gave Jack a look of bemused embarrassment, and Kate smiled in spite of her distress.

'Only you could have done that, Jack.'

'Done what?'

'Go from being annoyed with me to joking about becoming a… what you said, and then being so pleasant to that sailor, and all without a change of expression.'

'Why shouldn't I be? None of this is his fault, and who says I'm joking about joining the Men Only Club?'

All conversation in the pub was suddenly silenced by a rasping drone that seemed to be coming ever closer. It continued for a few seconds more before stopping abruptly. Someone said urgently, 'Doodlebug!'

Everyone rushed to take what shelter was available and in the absence of anything else Jack pulled Kate unceremoniously beneath their table and crouched over her.

As he did so there was the sound of a gigantic explosion that seemed to be to the north, and the floor shook as if in an earthquake. There was no way they could tell exactly where the bomb had fallen but it could not have been far away, because windows shattered and chunks of plaster fell from the ceiling, one scattering dust and fragments over the table above them.

The landlord called out, 'Is anyone hurt?' Incredibly, no one was, although the majority left the pub at that point, most likely to find out if their homes had been damaged or destroyed. 'All right,' their host announced, 'we'll get the mess cleared up and start serving again as soon as we can.' The bells of the fire engines, ambulances and Heavy Rescue Squads seemed at odds with his sanguine pronouncement but the bar staff nevertheless set about clearing the debris.

Jack slithered out and crouched to help Kate up. She said with great feeling, 'I'm glad you survived, Jack.'

'What, just now?' For some reason he seemed amused.

'I meant the invasion.' She added lamely, 'I've been meaning to tell you.'

'Oh yes, I was lucky, unlike a great many.' He dusted off his uniform without much success and then looked around the room. 'Some of these people seem determined to carry on drinking,' he observed, watching a group of mainly elderly patrons, who were helping with the clean-up. They were clearly in no hurry to leave.

'They've been bombed and shelled since nineteen-forty,' said Kate. 'It takes a lot to daunt them.'

'But you're shaking,' he said, taking her hands and holding them.

'I know. I went right through the Blitz without flinching but it seems to have caught up with me. I hope I'm not becoming bomb-happy.'

'You need to get away from this as soon as you can.' He took out his handkerchief and dusted off her chair. 'But first things first, I'm going to get you a bracer if I can get someone to serve me.' He went to the bar, leaving Kate to reflect on the failure the evening had become. She wasn't really surprised; Jack was hurting and he was also working hard at building a defensive barrier. She was aware of it even if he wasn't, and it was making her task harder than ever.

He returned from the bar with a glass and a jug of water. 'I could only get gin,' he explained, 'and all they have to mix with it is water. They tell me it's because of the war.'

'It's certainly different from the wardroom of your boat,' she said, 'but don't worry. Thank you for this.' She poured water over the gin and sipped her drink. 'It's warming me already.'

'I'm serious about getting away,' he said. 'If you don't you could quite easily end up bomb-happy.'

'But there's so much to be done.'

'And you've done more than most.'

'Mm.' It was true, but that wasn't what she wanted to discuss. 'Jack,' she said, 'could we go outside? I can't concentrate in here.'

'Okay, if you're feeling better I'll walk you back to the nurses' home.'

'All right, I just want to talk.'

When they were outside she took his arm and they walked up the hill. Another ambulance rushed past towards a pillar of smoke to the north, and Jack said, 'I wonder where the bomb actually fell.'

'Please, Jack, it's important that I tell you this,' she said. 'You see, you think I don't care for you, and that's not true. I was terribly mixed up that day on the cliff. I had been for some time, I suppose since Maurice was killed, but one thing is much clearer now.'

'You're not making much sense, Kate.'

'Bear with me.' She patted his arm like a parent encouraging her child to be sensible. 'I told you I was fond of you, and I was, but then something happened that made me realise it was more than that. It was after I'd been told that your flotilla was taking part in the invasion. That was bad enough—'

'Who told you that?'

'I'm not telling you. I don't want to get anyone into trouble, but do let me go on.'

'All right.'

'Then a patient told me about a rescue boat being shelled by the Germans, and I was horrified. It was the same feeling I had when you were wounded on the east coast, only I couldn't phone your mum and dad this time in case they'd heard nothing. I didn't want to frighten them. I was desperately worried until a week had passed and I plucked up the courage to phone them.'

He drew her aside to give way to an elderly man. 'You got it right this time. Two boats were badly hit, and poor old Ninety-Seven came close to being blown apart. Brian was wounded and four of the crew were killed. I had to bring the old girl limping back to Pompey with only half my crew.'

'Back to where?'

'I'm sorry – Portsmouth. But what are you trying to say, Kate? Are you telling me that fearing for my life changed the way you felt about me?' He looked and sounded unconvinced.

'Not so much changed as... well, it made my feelings clearer, I suppose.' She stopped and waited for two women to pass by, and then went on before he could interrupt. 'When I told you I was fond of you it wasn't to fob you off.'

'It felt like it at the time.'

'Well, it wasn't.' For the first time that evening she felt impatient with him. 'If you'll only listen I'll explain, at least as far as I can. You see, it's to do with Maurice but not in the way you might think.' She mustered her patience again. It wasn't his fault that he didn't understand. 'It's true that it's taken a long time for me to summon any interest in another man. An American airman asked me out shortly after I arrived here, and I went cold at the thought of betraying Maurice's memory, because that's how it felt. But I feel now that I'm ready to move on, if only in that one respect.' She patted his arm again to discourage interruption. 'I'm more than fond of you, Jack, much more than that, but I'm afraid I'm not ready to take the plunge, even if you still want me to.' She saw that he was shaking his head minutely, as if in bewilderment. 'I know,' she said, 'I didn't understand it until quite recently, but I've thought and thought about it and I've finally realised that it comes down basically to the fact that I devoted myself completely and without reservation to Maurice, and then in a split second I lost everything. Now do you understand?'

'Yes, I do. It makes sense now, I have to admit, except that this war can't last for ever. For one thing, the enemy no longer has a navy or an air force worth mentioning.'

'But you can't be sure, Jack, and it wouldn't be fair to keep you hanging on 'til the war's over. I've caused you enough hurt and exasperation already. I just wanted you to know the truth.'

'Well, I appreciate that, even if your reasoning's flawed.'

'No one's perfect, Jack.'

'But you want us to meet as friends.'

'If we can.'

He shook his head gravely. 'No can do, I'm afraid.'

'No?' She was disappointed but not surprised. It was a lot to ask of him.

'No, I'm going to woo you. That's the right word, isn't it?'

'In the right century, I suppose it would be. You're an old-fashioned soul, Jack, even in the language you use.' She stopped walking because the hospital gates were now in sight. Once they stepped beyond the bus shelter they would be clearly visible from the nurses' home.

'As you said, no one's perfect, and I don't think much has changed over the centuries in the way lovers have gone about wooing, courting or otherwise pursuing the objects of their amorous intentions. They've simply wasted good wooing time by thinking up new names for it, a pointless exercise if ever there was one.'

'Jack, you're hopeless.' She nevertheless allowed him to draw her into the shelter.

'I'm completely hopeless,' he agreed. 'For one thing, I need help with my foxtrot, and there's a dance at the base on the first of July. You said you'd like to come to the next one.'

'If you want me to come, but I'm not going back on anything I've said.'

'Fair enough. Just come to the dance.'

She felt him draw her inevitably towards him.

'I have to say this is a new activity for me,' he said seriously.

'Wooing?'

'No, necking in a bus shelter.'

'I hope you don't think I make a habit of it.' She might have said more had she been able, but at that point his lips touched hers and further dialogue was impossible.

<hr />

At the house in Potters Bar Alan and Gwen were enjoying their first forty-eight hours together since his return from France.

He poured the last of the wine and said, 'Every now and again I'm surprised by the speed at which things can happen.'

'What's happened, darling?'

'I had a meeting with Colonel Whiteley this afternoon,' he told her. 'It seems the army has plans for me.'

'Do you mean you're being posted?'

'Not for the time being. There's quite a lot I can do for them at Trent Park.'

Visibly reassured, she asked, 'Well, are you going to let the cat out of the bag or go on keeping me in suspense?'

'It's nothing momentous. I was just surprised, as I said, at how quickly the top brass have responded. You see, whilst I was over there I extracted confessions from two *Waffen SS* officers, and that seems to have impressed someone with influence.'

'What kind of confessions?'

'They confessed to murder, although they didn't call it that. The victims were alleged saboteurs who were shot without trial. One confession was ridiculously easy to extract. You wouldn't believe the arrogance of the senior officer. He talked freely because he was convinced the invasion would fail and we'd all be at Hitler's mercy. Incredibly, he could see nothing wrong in what he'd done.'

'That's horrible.'

'The other was just as awful but I had to work hard at getting him to confess, and that's what set the ball rolling back here. Someone's been looking ahead to the day the great All Clear sounds, and the intention is that a great many Nazis are going to be held to account for their crimes.'

'And that's where you come in, as an interrogator?'

'*Investigator* and interrogator,' he said, correcting her with mock dignity.

'That can only mean promotion.'

'So soon after my last one? I doubt it, but the work sounds interesting.'

'It does,' she agreed, 'and I'm glad you've found something that appeals to you.'

'Do I detect a "but" hidden beneath that generous sentiment?'

She smiled guiltily at being caught out. 'You were born to be an interrogator, darling,' she told him. 'You miss absolutely nothing.'

'Maybe.'

'It was mention of the "great All Clear" that made me think. There'll be an awful lot for you to do, and I can't help wondering how long it will be before we can have a normal married life.'

'Who can say? It'll be a combined effort on the part of the allies so it's not bound to be a long job.' It made sense, and Gwen was nodding as well, so to keep the conversation light he said, 'I've been looking ahead too, and I've been wondering if we might have a dog.'

She put on her serious face and said, 'Of course you have, darling. It's the first priority in a successful marriage.'

'No, seriously, I'd rather like us to have one.'

'And what prompted that line of thought?'

'It was Bonzo, a stray dog that attached himself to the intelligence centre. I became rather fond of him.'

'It must have been a whirlwind romance, considering the brief time you were there.'

'He was the kind of dog you take to very quickly. For one thing he was a born survivor. He came through the bombardment and the crossfire, he persuaded the first British soldiers he found to feed him, and that wasn't all. There was a minefield outside the café, and Bonzo used to tear around the place, chasing seagulls and anything else that moved. Time and again we expected him to be blown up but he defied all probability. He was a great character.'

Visibly amused by the story, Gwen said, 'Let's hope he stays lucky.'

'The Sappers cleared the minefield before I came home. He'll be safe enough.'

'Oh good.' After a moment's thought she said, 'All right, let's have a dog.' She nodded, as if confirming her decision, adding almost as an afterthought, 'and children.'

'Of course.' Alan was quick to agree. 'The dog will need someone to play with.'

⊷⊱⊰⊹⊱⊰⊷

Dorothy soon found the ideal lovers' meeting place in 'The Grey Goose,' a seventeenth century, half-timbered inn situated a discreet distance from Cranwell and providing the benefit of overnight accommodation. She and Bill naturally spent their next twenty-four-hour pass there.

As they lay together in the dark Dorothy said, 'The room next door has a four-poster. I thought about it, but I didn't want to overwhelm you with the artificial props and trappings of romance.'

'I'm not easily overwhelmed, Dot.'

'No, I don't think you are. You're a dark horse.'

He slipped out of bed to open the blackout curtains but stopped when his foot encountered one leg of the bed. 'Blast it.'

'What's the matter?'

'I stubbed my toe against something.' He limped on to reach the window, where he drew back the curtains.

'Another casualty of the blackout. Come back to bed, darling – carefully.'

'I'm back,' he said, easing himself beneath the covers, 'and my toe might never be the same again, but never mind that. Just look at the sky.'

334

'I think you'll survive.' With uncharacteristic obedience she turned her head to the window and gave a gasp of delight. The sky was perfectly clear, so that the moon and what seemed to be a million stars of varying brightness were framed in that small rectangle.

'It's not often you see it like that.'

'No,' she agreed, 'it's beautiful.' She gazed a moment longer and said, 'I think that's what the newspapers call a "bombers' moon", although one aircrew member I knew told me they weren't keen on too clear a sky. Apparently they like just a little cloud. It's something to hide behind, I suppose.'

'Yes.' It was as well not to dwell on such matters. Instead he snuggled closer against her and asked, 'Why did you call me a dark horse?'

'What? Oh, that. It's just that accountants are supposed to be cool, unimaginative, calculating people, who'd never dream of doing what we were doing a few minutes ago.'

'If it comes to that, beautiful women are supposed to be vain, spoilt and selfish, and you're none of those things. If you were, we wouldn't be here now.'

She hesitated before asking only half in jest, 'Do you mean my physical charms are lost on you?'

'Not at all. When we first met I saw a very attractive woman with gentle curves and legs that looked promising even with flat, uniform shoes. When you spoke to me I recognised a trace of an accent and I thought it might be fun for us to get to know each other better. When we did, I realised you had qualities that were far more important than your appearance.' With his hand he gently traced a line that ran between her breasts, crossed her waist and continued downward. 'Your looks,' he concluded, having reached the end of his journey, 'are a bonus, like the icing on a pre-war wedding cake.'

49

Rachel finished draping a dust-sheet over the sink and worktops. 'I thought you agreed to sit back and let David do everything,' she said.

'I only carried the paint in for him. It's not all that heavy.'

'Thank you, Kate.' David prised the lid off the can of emulsion paint with a screwdriver and began stirring the paint with a multi-coloured stick that must have served the same purpose on a number of occasions. When he was satisfied with the result he poured some of the paint into a roller tray and carried it up the stepladder.

After watching him for a while, Kate said, 'When I use a roller the paint splatters all over the place. I try to get it all on the wall but it insists on showering everything else.'

'Ah well, the secret is not to roll too quickly.'

'Is that all?'

'Yes, it's as simple as that.'

'You're a marvel, David.'

'I'm glad you think so, because I'll have to switch off this light soon, just for a few minutes.'

'Why on earth do you want to do that?'

'So that I can lower the light fitting and paint behind it.'

'How very professional, but do be careful.'

'David's an electrician,' Rachel reminded her.

'I'm sorry, I forgot.'

David came down the stepladder. Obligingly Kate lifted the can of paint on to the linen-covered worktop.

'Thanks, Kate, but I'll use the roller tray.'

'I'll put some coffee on.' She groped behind a dust sheet for the coffee jar and then yelped when she felt a sharp pain in the back of her hand.

'What's the matter, Kate?' Rachel came to her side.

'My hand, it's very painful.' She tried flexing it but it made no difference.

'Let me see.' David peered at her left hand. 'You must have strained something. I'll be back in a second.'

'Where's he going, Rachel?'

'Out to the car, I think. He has a first-aid kit.'

'It's so painful. I must have done something to it when I picked up the paint.'

'Hold it up, Kate. That's right.'

'It feels as if the tendons are on fire.'

'If it goes on like this we'll have to take you to hospital.'

'I hope not. I hate to be a nuisance.' It seemed to her that David and Rachel had done plenty for her already.

'All right, Kate,' said David, taking a triangular bandage from its packaging, 'let's get this on you. Bring your hand up to your shoulder.'

'You're so kind. I'm an awful nuisance.'

'No, you're not.' He finished folding the sling and tied it off behind her neck. 'That should ease it for now.'

'It's not quite as bad as it was.'

'You still need to see a doctor. Will you find Kate's coat, please, Rachel?'

'I've got it here.' She had evidently anticipated the request and stepped forward to drape the coat over her shoulders.

Kate continued to protest for the first mile or so, but then accepted the situation. After all, Rachel and David both had her welfare at heart and they were equally firm on the subject, so further argument was pointless. Instead, she watched the heavy traffic and disappearing streets, thankful that she'd long since given up driving.

Eventually they reached the hospital and followed the signs for Accident and Emergency, where David dropped them before finding a place in the car park.

'Last time,' said Kate, 'I was brought here in an ambulance.'

'Not all that long ago.'

'No, but in that time I've told you the story of my life.'

'Only the war part,' said Rachel, 'and you haven't reached the end of that.' She guided Kate to reception.

'Take a seat,' the receptionist told her, 'and the triage nurse will see you soon.'

'We came at a good time,' said Rachel, looking round the waiting room and then at her wristwatch. 'Late morning is obviously the time to come. This place is usually packed out.'

'Do you come here often?'

'I've been a few times with my mother.'

'Of course.' Suddenly she was distracted by someone calling her name. She looked around, puzzled.

'It's your turn,' Rachel told her.

'Oh, yes.' She levered herself upright, pushing against the side of the chair with her good hand.

The triage nurse asked, 'Do you need help?'

'No, thank you. I'm all right.' She followed the nurse into her office.

'Is it all right to call you Katherine?'

'Just "Kate" will do.' Then, noticing the words "Triage Nurse" on the desk, she said, 'Believe it or not, I was doing the same job as you seventy years ago.'

'Were you? I'd love to hear about it but I think you should tell me what the trouble is. Let me unfasten that sling for you.'

'The back of my hand was very painful. It's much better now.'

'Most likely because someone's elevated it for you. What were you doing for this to happen?'

'I can only think I did it when I lifted a tin of paint.'

'How big a tin?'

'A gallon, I think.'

'Really? Well, that could easily be the culprit. It looks like tendonitis but we need to be certain.' She handed Kate a card with the number on it. 'Let's put your sling back on and then you can take the card to reception. They'll take your details and then you can go through to Minor Injuries.'

Kate's details were already on the computer from her previous admission, so the process was mercifully brief.

'Go straight down the passage,' said the receptionist, pointing the way, 'go left and left again and that'll take you to Minor Injuries. You're booked in already.'

Rachel took her good arm and said, 'I'll take you.'

'Thank you, Rachel. It's all very bewildering. Not at all what I remember.'

'An awful lot must have changed in seventy years.'

'Yes, that's what people keep telling me.'

'I'm sorry.'

'I didn't mean you, Rachel.'

They turned the corner and Kate saw the sign for Minor Injuries. 'Oh, look,' she said, 'here we are.'

In Minor Injuries Kate answered more questions, was examined and taken to X-Ray. Finally a young man arrived and introduced himself.

'Hello, my name is Tom. I'm one of the Accident and Emergency doctors. There's nothing terribly wrong with your hand. It's over-use, but we can remedy that.'

'What on earth is over-use?'

'It's a misnomer, really. It should be called "*mis*-use" because that's what it is. You've handled something awkwardly and caused the tendons to become inflamed. The treatment is immobilisation. I'll ask the nurse to give you a splint and you'll need to wear it for ten days.' He must have sensed her dismay because he was quick to reassure her. 'You can take it off for washing and when you go to bed.'

'I see. Thank you, Doctor.' Through years of habit and ingrained respect she couldn't bring herself to use his first name.

He smiled indulgently. 'You're welcome, but do go easy with the weight-lifting.'

The nurse came to her with an apologetic half-smile. 'I'm sorry to keep you waiting, Katherine. You have very small hands, and we haven't got a splint small enough. We've had to send over to the Children's Unit for one of theirs. It shouldn't take long.'

'Don't worry.' She was more concerned about Rachel and

David, who'd been hanging around for what seemed ages. 'I'll tell you what, Rachel,' she said. 'You and David go and get a cup of coffee or something. I'll wait here for you.'

'All right.' Rachel stood up and asked, 'Can we get you anything?'

'No, thank you. I'll be all right.'

She wanted a little time alone to think about something Rachel had said earlier, about her not having finished telling her story. The 'war part', as she'd called it, had been a major part of their lives: hers, Alan's, Dorothy's and Jack's and, as for poor Maurice.... Alan had got it completely wrong. What had he said that night at the 'Bay Horse'? It was something about "in a year's time" or something like that. No, it was "a year from now". Yes, 'a year from now.' She could hear him saying it. It was when he was going through that silly, pompous phase before the army and the war made him grow up. He'd said it would all be over within the year. But it wasn't. It went on for six years, during which things happened, some too awful for words, that none of them could have foreseen. Lots and lots of things, and there was one very important event that she had yet to relate to Rachel. She would tell her, but not yet, not before she'd remembered it in detail. It had been such a difficult time, a time for heart-searching as well as clear thinking and decision-making when her mind was a jumble of conflicting thoughts and feelings, and she'd never forgotten how trying it was for poor Jack as well.

⟨⟩⊹⦂⊹⦂⊹⟨⟩

When Jack arrived at the nurses' home she was waiting for him in a purple, flared frock with the bows on the shoulders. It was the first time he'd seen her wearing it and he was gratifyingly impressed.

'You look magnificent,' he said, 'gift-wrapped to perfection.'

'Thank you.' She accepted a kiss on the cheek. 'You look very smart yourself.'

'Thanks, but we have no choice in the matter. Smartness is mandatory.'

He held the door of the taxi for her before joining her inside.

'The Lord Warden, I believe, sir,' said the driver.

340

'Yes, please.' Then, seemingly distracted, he asked Kate, 'What perfume are you wearing?'

'It's *Dans la Nuit* by Worth of Paris,' she told him grandly. 'One of the girls on my landing is very well-connected. She's also generous to her friends.' She looked at him uncertainly and asked, 'Don't you like it?'

'Of course I like it. It's beguiling and hypnotic and alluring and... it could turn an innocent young chap's head, you know.'

'In that case you're safe enough,' she assured him.

Soon they reached the imposing portico of *HMS Wasp*, previously The Lord Warden Hotel, where, according to protocol, Jack introduced Kate to the Captain and his wife before taking her into the ballroom.

She gazed around the room, mesmerised by the crystal chandeliers, marble pillars and elaborate plasterwork.

'This is the most magnificent thing I've ever seen.'

'It's very grand,' he agreed.

The band was coming to the end of 'The Last Time I Saw Paris,' and it seemed to Kate the perfect welcome. The song had for so long been a message of sadness, but recent news from France had changed all that.

'Let's get a drink,' Jack suggested, signalling to a steward. 'Would you like a pink gin?'

'All right, but I'm going to make it last. I mustn't drink too much.'

'You shouldn't, especially when you're wearing that seductive perfume.'

'Don't be silly.' To change the subject she asked, 'What's the band?'

'The Dover Garrison Dance Orchestra. I have to say they're not bad for a bunch of pongoes.'

'What are pongoes?'

'Soldiers.'

'You people have silly names for everything. It's like a foreign language.'

'Don't struggle with it. Let's dance instead.' The band was playing 'A Lovely Way to Spend an Evening.'

'All right.' She let him lead her on to the floor and as they joined the line of dance she said, 'I haven't detected anything wrong with your foxtrot yet.'

'I had to say something to persuade you to come.'

'I'm glad you persuaded me, but why are some of the officers wearing those funny short jackets?'

'The "bum freezers"? That's "mess undress", the service equivalent of the short evening dress jacket. It's something only regular RN officers can afford. They need it, you see, because they go to a lot more of these functions than we temporary gentlemen do.'

'Is that what they call you?'

'That and worse, but I like being a temporary gentleman. It means I have to behave courteously only for the duration of hostilities; I can be a complete cad after the war, whereas the RN types you see around you are saddled with the responsibility throughout their career.'

'You do talk nonsense.'

'Yes, but it's harmless nonsense.'

'I'll grant you that.' He was the most harmless man she knew, despite looking rather grand in his best uniform. Even the scar made him look distinguished in her eyes. Beneath all that, though, he was gentle, kind and, with one recent and allowable exception, good-natured. They were just a few of his qualities that had come to mind in the emotional turmoil of recent days.

The number came to its close and they applauded the band.

Someone nearby said, 'They're not bad, Jack, not bad at all.'

The accent was American. Kate turned to see an officer in a strange uniform. She thought he looked rather handsome.

'Kate,' said Jack, 'allow me to introduce Lieutenant Paul Delaney, skipper of one of the PT boats. He provided the stockings. Paul, meet Kate Whitehead, the love of my life, or she will be if she'll only take pity on me and hoist Flag Charlie.'

'I'm pleased to make your acquaintance, ma'am.' Lt. Delaney offered his hand. 'Jack and I got off to a slow start but I think we understand each other now. He plays a mean game of poker and he did one heck of a job at the Normandy landings.'

'It's "Kate".' She took his hand. 'I'm glad to meet you too, Paul. I must say I never realised Jack had made such an impression.'

'He certainly has. Jack, do you have any objection if I ask Kate for the next dance?'

'Be my guest, Paul, and feel free to carry on saying complimentary things about me. I need the testimonial.'

The number was 'Don't Sit Under the Apple Tree,' and Kate couldn't imagine Jack being at all disappointed at being left out. It wasn't his kind of dance at all. Paul, on the other hand, was enthusiastic and outgoing. As he and Kate took to the floor he said, 'I've learned a lot since I came over here, Kate. Back home we didn't know half of what was happening in Britain. You folks have had a pretty tough time, what with rationing and bombing and all.'

'We got used to it after a while. I've been dodging bombs since nineteen-forty.'

'You don't say.' It was as if she'd claimed to have supernatural powers.

'I'm not the only one,' she assured him, 'just one of many.'

'The newsreels don't tell the whole story.'

He was still impressed when, at the end of the number, he took his leave of her and Jack to rejoin his friends at the far end of the ballroom. 'It's been a pleasure to make your acquaintance, Kate, and to see you again, Jack.' With a discreet smile he added, 'let's hope Flag Charlie puts in an appearance pretty soon.'

'You know,' she said when he was gone, 'we were talking about how things were before the Americans came over, and it made me think for a moment about everything we've experienced. It's no wonder they find it hard to imagine.'

'The homeland bombed and threatened with invasion? It must be impossible for them, even after Pearl Harbour. That must have been terrible enough but at least it happened in mid-Pacific.'

'Mm.' She considered that for a moment, and then said, 'Let's talk about pleasanter things.'

'Let's not even do that. Let's dance instead.' The band was playing 'Moonlight Becomes You.'

'All right. I love this number, and it's much more your kind of thing.'

'Sedate and sophisticated,' he agreed, leading her on to the floor, 'like me.'

'It's a good thing I like you for what you are and not what you claim to be.'

'But at least you like me. That's a start.'

'You know it's much more than that, Jack.' She turned her face momentarily away from his. There were things she had to tell him but she had to choose her time.

After a while she asked, 'What's Flag Charlie? You mentioned it to Paul.'

'It's the International Code flag that stands for "affirmative," a posh way of saying "yes". Why did you want to know?'

'Natural curiosity. I couldn't visit a naval base without picking up a bit of nautical lore.'

'If you're interested, there are twenty-five more letters and ten numerals you could add to your repertoire, and that's not counting the substitute and answer pennants.'

'Maybe not. There must be a name for people who get excited about that kind of thing.'

'I'm sure there is. Let's have a drink and leave them to get on with it.' He winced as the band began 'In the Mood.'

'It's really not your kind of music, is it?'

'I think I'm maybe too old for it.'

'Too old at twenty-six?'

'Most of my crew think I'm in my dotage.' He winced again and said, 'Let's find somewhere cooler and quieter.'

'Where are we going?'

'To the wardroom. Don't worry, it's quite respectable.' He led her down a wide passage until they came to a heavy oak door, which he opened to reveal a large room with two long tables laid presumably for breakfast. Of its inhabitants, however, there was no sign. The room was deserted. 'Everyone's in the ballroom,' he told her, 'jitterbugging, or whatever they call it.'

'You sound more than ever like an old man.'

'War has that effect, you know. It can be quite ageing. You may have to prop me up,' he added, drawing her closer to make her task easier.

'You said this was a respectable place.'

'It was until now,' he confirmed, kissing her lightly.

'You're allowed to hold me,' she told him, 'I'm not fragile.'

He drew her closer and they kissed again deeply. She was strangely conscious of his breath on her cheek and the smooth weave of his uniform. More than anything, however, she was aware of a gratifying sense of culmination. She had agonised long enough.

After a while she said breathlessly, 'All right, you win. This beats jitterbugging any day. I'm glad we sat this one out.'

'So to speak.'

'All right, I suppose we could sit down.' She looked around her for a sofa.

'It's too late for that. The number's over.'

For a while neither spoke; their familiar banter had become a habit but they both knew that for the moment it was time to be serious.

Jack was first to break the silence.

'Kate.'

'Yes?'

'Tell me my wooing hasn't been in vain.'

'Oh, I've been thinking a lot about you and me, Jack.'

'You said you might.' He appeared to be bracing himself, as if the limbo between hope and apprehension was too agonising to bear.

'Well, I have, and I've made my decision.'

<hr/>

From her chair in Minor Injuries Kate heard her name being called. The voice sounded as if it were some distance away. It was saying, 'We've got your splint, Katherine.' There was a pause, and then the voice called her again. 'Katherine?'

With an effort she dragged herself back to the present. As she did so she heard another voice. 'Are you sure she's happy about us using her first name? She's ninety-five, you know. Some old people don't like it.'

A nurse stood in front of her, holding a splint for her hand. 'Mrs Farthing?'

'Yes,' said Kate happily. 'I'm Mrs Farthing.' She smiled at the memory still fresh in her mind. 'It took a while, but it was one of my better decisions.'

THE END

Ray Hobbs is a native of the West Riding of Yorkshire but he now lives in Kent with his wife Sheila and their two dogs. *A Year from Now* is his fourth novel to receive a five-star review from *Readers' Favorite*®

Lightning Source UK Ltd.
Milton Keynes UK
UKOW04f2333051117
312248UK00001B/18/P